EVEN STRANGER

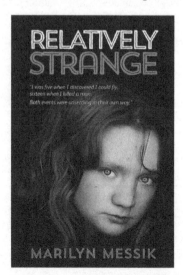

EVEN STRANGER

To Dalia with much love Marilyn Messick xx

MARILYN MESSIK

Matador
9 Priory Business Park,
Wistow Road, Kibworth Beauchamp,
Leicestershire. LE8 0RX
Tel: 0116 279 2299
Email: books@troubador.co.uk
Web: www.troubador.co.uk/matador
Twitter: @matadorbooks

ISBN 978 1785891 960

British Library Cataloguing in Publication Data.
A catalogue record for this book is available from the British Library.

Printed and bound in the UK by TJ International, Padstow, Cornwall
Typeset in 11pt Stempel Garamond by Troubador Publishing Ltd, Leicester, UK

Matador is an imprint of Troubador Publishing Ltd

MIX
Paper from
responsible sources
FSC® C013056

To Sophie, Charlotte, Reuben, Emily and Raphaella –
thank heaven you were all born with a sense of humour!

About the Author

Marilyn was a regular feature and fiction writer for national magazines when her children were small. She set up her first business, selling toys, books and party goods from home, before opening first one shop then another. When she sold both shops she moved into the world of travel, focusing on Bed and Breakfasts and Country Inns in New England, USA. Her advisory, planning and booking service flourished and she concurrently launched a publishing company, producing an annual, full-colour accommodation guide.

In 2007 she set up a copywriting consultancy, to help businesses shape their messages to optimum effect. She's the author of the Little Black Business Book series and the novel Relatively Strange. She's been married to her very patient husband for more years than he deserves and they have two children, five grandchildren and, somewhat to their surprise, several grand-dogs.

www.marilynmessik.com

INTO THE LAKE

*Don't walk before you can run and
don't run before you can fly!*

CHAPTER ONE

There are a lot of things that get easier, as you get older. Flying isn't one of them.

I only got halfway across the lake, before I fell in. As the freezing water closed icily bleak and black over my head, I thought it's a load of hooey, what they say about drowning – you know, your life flashing before you. If, after struggling repeatedly to the surface shrieking, 'Help me for God's sake!' you've time left for a memory lane mooch, you're clearly not trying hard enough to live. I went under again.

"Don't be so dramatic." She muttered in my head. With a mouth full of foully brackish-smelling water, components of which I didn't even want to contemplate, I wasn't in any position to maintain external hollering, mentally I was more than making up for it.

"I'm drowning!"

"You're not drowning." That bloody woman was always so certain of everything, I was tempted to die damply, just to spite her. "It's only deep in the middle," she pointed out. She wasn't wrong, there indeed, if I'd thought to lower my feet from their panic-stricken doggy-paddle, was terra firma. "See?" she said.

I wasn't going to dignify that with an answer. The lake bottom, as it shallowed towards the bank, was thick with silt, a staggering amount of which was accumulating in my soft-soled shoes. It slowed progress no end, as did the lethally concealed clumps of reeds entangling my legs. At least, I hoped they were reeds. For a moment, a vision of palely rotting, white and reaching arms, courtesy of my recent encounter at the hotel, filled my head. That did me no good at all, neither did the November wind, snipping spitefully round me. I was as far from happy, as it's possible for any one person to be.

"What's happened?" Another voice in my head, Glory this time.

"Her own stupid fault," said Rachael Peacock, "Tried to save time going over, not round."

"Hey," I snapped, "Still here! And I thought you were supposed to be helping." They ignored me.

"Glory," said Rachael. "I see her now, get Ed to drive round to meet us, quick as you can."

Had my teeth not been otherwise occupied, chattering, they'd have been grinding. I staggered ungainly from the water – no Aphrodite me – and squelched towards a tall thin form, heading purposefully from the creaking darkness of the trees.

"Not," she said aloud, "Your brightest move, and I thought we said keep it low key. Can you not do anything, without all hell breaking loose? Here get this round you." I reached for the blanket she was holding, but it wasn't my night. From the blackness behind her, a dark shadow had detached itself and was loping towards us at speed. Above the wind, rose the sound of hoarse panting and a shaft of moonlight, struggling against the odds, refracted briefly from a pair of gleaming eyes. Rachael and I reacted swiftly and simultaneously, but there was no time. He hit me with the force of an express train. I went down soundlessly.

"Can't think, for one moment why he's pleased to see you, you smell disgusting. Hamlet, off!" She gave him an authoritative mental tug. He treated my face to a final comprehensive lick from cheek to chin, then reluctantly backed away. Breathing's always easier when a ten stone, Great Dane cross, eases off your chest, though I shivered harder as wind replaced warmth. Rachael Peacock eyed my soaked and spread-eagled form with exasperation and was extending an impatient hand to haul me up, when we were both rocked back by Glory's shock.

"Rachael," she said, "We've just knocked someone down. I think we've killed her."

PART ONE

LEADING UP TO THE LAKE

When people can't believe their eyes – they don't!

CHAPTER TWO

By the time the swinging sixties staggered, slightly shamefaced and flustered, into the minimally staider seventies, I was twenty-two. All around me, mini skirted, Mary Quant-eyed girls were becoming Berketex brides, to the moist-tissued delight of mothers, who'd thought the pill and too many women's libbers, might have put paid to those sort of happy ever afters. My own mother's aspirations were no different. Come to think, neither were mine. After some of the things I'd seen and done, a chartered accountant, a quiet life and a couple of kids seemed mighty attractive.

Naturally, in our close-knit Jewish family, anything involving my mother, involved a lot of other people too. I'd become accustomed to serried ranks of raised eyebrows at family gatherings, accompanied by a chorus of unabashed inquiry into my love life, or lack of. Aunt Edna, my mother's older sister, having seen off her own two girls in a highly satisfactory manner, one to a doctor, the other to a solicitor, viewed me as a further, slightly more challenging hurdle.

"So," she'd pounce, pinching my cheeks absent-mindedly – a little colour never hurt. "I'm still waiting for some exciting news from you." Then she'd turn back to my mother, to bend their formidably combined energies to the locating of yet another young, unfortunate, professional to take me on an excruciatingly awkward date. Throughout their lives, she and my mother tackled all problems jointly. Well, nearly all problems.

I think it dawned on my poor parents only gradually, when blessed by my arrival, that I wasn't quite what you'd call run of the mill, though there was probably nothing they could quite put their finger on, until I was about five. If it was disconcerting to me then, to discover other people couldn't fly, how much more so for my parents to find I could. Heroically pragmatic, under these most trying of circumstances, they were nonetheless in complete accord – whatever the extent of my odd aptitudes, it was, beyond doubt, something best played close to our chests. They shared my strangeness with no-one.

Directed by this decision, life for them, not surprisingly had its ups

7

and downs, with the emergence of each new development taken manfully on the chin. Moving objects, without going to the bother of touching, was, I believe, the next thing that came to light, or maybe it was the fire-starting thing – can't really remember now, which we stumbled across first. Then of course, there was the gradual acknowledgement that I could hear what was going on in other people's heads, accompanied by the equally revelatory realisation for me that everyone else couldn't. I honestly don't know which of us was more disturbed by what.

In my early years, we were just ten years or so post WW2, so maybe my parents had taken on board *Careless Talk Costs Lives* more than they knew, or perhaps it was down to Grandma's influence. My mother's mother trusted no-one, always worked on a strictly need to know basis, and wouldn't, on principal, let her left hand know what her right was up to, even in an emergency. But whatever their reasons, my parents were unwavering in their decision and determination that my upbringing should be as normal as the next person's, even if I wasn't.

Cocooned as I was, not only in the affection of my parents, but in that of our extended, somewhat eccentric family, things jogged along, if not smoothly, certainly not over-dramatically, until I was about twelve. Then I was one of several hundred children selected to participate in a government-funded study which, fuelled by Cold War fears, was actively, albeit covertly, trawling for out of the ordinary abilities like mine. Mercifully, and with help from an unexpected source, I'd emerged unscathed and undiscovered, if not unalarmed. Confirmation though it was, of my long-held conviction that I couldn't possibly be unique, it clearly demonstrated that just because my parents were inclined to the paranoid, didn't mean nobody was after me.

Up till then, what I was hadn't worried me unduly, how could it when I knew no different? But there was no doubt, events had moved into a far darker and altogether stickier area. Things didn't lighten up much when I killed a man. But if you've followed my story, you'll know all about that, and perhaps you feel the same way I did at the time – there was little choice, it was him or us. So, no more to be said.

It was shortly after this, I was around sixteen then, that Glory Isaacs, blind, psychic, chronically short on patience, and last encountered during my unsettling stint at the Newcombe Foundation, stropped back into my life. I owed her, big-time. She came to call in the favour and in an alarmingly short while, my horizons broadened in all sorts of uncomfortable, previously unimaginable ways. They do say, your teen years are tough, and some of them certainly were for me. I couldn't, for one moment, deny the fascination of being for the first time, amongst others like myself. But the rescue of a small boy called Sam, in which I took a highly reluctant leading role, and the appalling price paid for its success, wasn't one I was prepared to pay again. I knew, at that point, with no doubt whatsoever, that normal, or as near as damn it, was going to be the name of the game I played from thereon in.

My parents naturally were delighted at my resolution to put, what they delicately termed 'all that stuff', behind me and to see their lie-low, tell no-one policy paying off. Mind you, had they known even the half of what had gone on during my time with Glory and the Peacock sisters, I suspect defibrillators and CPR might well have been required. But with some rigid self-training and exercising a good deal of restraint – which got easier with time – my life proceeded, for a good long while, along my chosen route. I felt, against the odds, I'd hauled myself on to the normal bandwagon and if I slipped off occasionally, it was simply for my own satisfaction, caused no grief to anyone and didn't detract in the least from my avowed intentions.

By the time I was nineteen I'd acquired shorthand, typing and other equally essential office skills – operating a dolls-eye switchboard and dealing with the diva tendencies of Gestetner duplicating machines. I'd found myself a job I enjoyed and felt I'd got it all satisfactorily sussed. But doesn't smugness always go before a fall? Just as I had things on an even keel, I found myself slap-bang up against something I wanted very much to, but couldn't, run away from.

You probably remember the Lollipop Man? The papers were hysterical about little else at the time and no-one, reading even only some of the details of his vicious attacks, would ever forget. His sixth and last victim – the only one who lived, was Lauretta Sears. She was my friend and work colleague. In her hot, airless, hospital room we spent a lot of time together, she and I. Between us we dredged, from the depths of shock, disbelief and trauma, such an unequivocally clear description, that within a very few weeks they had him behind bars, and the whole sorry, savage saga came to an end. Although for Lauretta, of course, it didn't, it never would.

What happened to Lauretta, ripped a hole in the fabric of a lot of lives, as violence always does. The comfortable routine of our office, offering ad hoc secretarial services and office space, was irretrievably damaged and re-shaped. When the lease on our rambling suite in Hay Hill, off Berkeley Square, came up for renewal, it was no surprise that Colonel and Mrs Hillyer-Bowden called us in to tell us they'd decided not to continue with the business. They planned to retire somewhere warm so they could, as the Colonel put it,

"Piddle about on boats, tackle the odd G and T. Make hay while the sun shines. Because," and he favoured us all with a rueful smile. "You never know, do you, what's going to bite you on the bum, round the next bally corner?" Certainly, it has to be said, when it came to my own onward progress, never a truer word was spoken.

CHAPTER THREE

Back in those days, finding yourself a new job, with shorthand and typing under your belt, wasn't hard. You couldn't walk two paces down London's Oxford, Bond or Regent Streets without tripping over and into an employment agency, each one's window bedecked with coloured cards, shrieking of bigger and better opportunities. Seated across from energetic, enthusiastic women with bulging rolodexes, pregnant with possibilities, you were spoilt for choice; seduced by luncheon vouchers, wooed by three weeks holiday and tantalised by the latest IBM Golf-ball typewriters, self-correcting no less. And if nothing instantly appealed in one agency, there was always the one next door, or indeed the temping option, offering well-paid placements and the comfortable fact that if you didn't like it, you didn't have to stay.

I attended lots of interviews. Interviews were something I was pretty good at, sometimes too good. People are always slightly startled if they ask a question and you give them precisely the answer they already have in their head, so a certain amount of caution is called for. Over the years, because I've had to, I've learnt to effectively shield from the cacophony of thought that always surrounds me. I use a venetian blind concept – stout, sturdily-made, mental slats that can be opened, slitted or sealed, depending on what's called for at any given moment. I'd grown up developing self-protection, so by that stage it was pretty much automatic and instinctive, although it does require a certain amount of concentration. Meeting new people, in new surroundings is still, and always will be, a bit unnerving because you need to keep a wary eye and ear open for what they expect from you. Too little's not good, too much is far worse.

Volume and clarity of thought is like speech – everyone's different and you come across everything from shouters to silents to synaesthetes. Most people adjust their volume, according to circumstance, although that doesn't apply to shouters, who are just plain and painfully loud, wherever they happen to be. To make up for that though, there are lots of others, who're heard only when their thoughts are amplified by emotion, they're far more comfortable to be around. Rarer still, but treasured nonetheless, are those who are pretty much completely silent most of the time, their thinking seems to be (bliss!), completely encompassed and contained. That doesn't mean they can't be read, but you have to reach out and actively do it.

Whilst most people take it in turn to talk, there's no such protocol for thinking, so thoughts and emotions come from every direction at the same time. It's therefore, only common sense to keep my blinds shut most of the time, avoiding overload and migraine and of course, courtesy dictates I no more rummage around in people's heads, than I would in their underwear drawer.

I wondered often as I grew up, and sometimes wonder still, do people I meet suspect there's more to me than meets the eye? I don't think so, why would they, when the truth is so darn peculiar? But there are certainly those, from time to time, who are alerted to me in some way – children more often than adults, because their instincts aren't yet blunted by logic. They sense something. I've seen them react, a shadow of a feeling, a vague looking round for the cause – nothing so formulated as a complete thought, just an awareness of something different, something Strange having crossed their path. It used to disturb me, doesn't really do that anymore, although I don't like to think I make anyone feel uncomfortable.

For a considerable time after my encounter with Glory and the Peacocks, I was on high alert for more people like us, but whilst I sometimes came across those with a touch of Strange, they were mostly unaware of it, just saw themselves as strongly hunch-driven, and after a while I stopped looking. On the whole, by the time I'd reached my early twenties, I'd come comfortably to terms with things, decided precisely who I did and didn't want to be, and felt I had things as satisfactorily under control as anyone in this life can.

CHAPTER FOUR

When I moved on from the Hillyer-Bowden's and Hay Hill, I took a job as secretary to the MD of a fashion store in Regent Street. The carrot there was definitely the staff discount on store purchases, combined with the perfume-laden luxury of the whole place. Sadly, the surroundings turned out to be not so hot, behind the scenes. Once through the Staff Only door, carpeting gave way to concrete, perfumed air to sawdust smells and mirrored walls to white tiled ones. And as it transpired, the MD had a few disconcerting habits, which never came up at interview.

One of his peculiarities was writing out all his letters in longhand, prior to calling me in for dictation. The result, as might have been expected, was such rapid-fire delivery that my shorthand instantly crumpled into incoherence, with me only able to get down an occasional word here and there. This awkward situation was further exacerbated by the high, over-stuffed, gilt-studded leather chair in his office, on which I was expected to perch. At commencement of our daily sessions, I'd launch myself firmly onto the slippery, sloping seat. But as my feet then dangled a good few inches from the floor, it was inevitable, as dictation proceeded, I'd slip slowly southwards, to a deceptively more relaxed position. Struggling to avoid sliding off completely, at the same time as trying to get down even a fraction of what he was saying, wasn't easy.

As if this wasn't tiresome enough, he liked to pace the office briskly as he dictated, slapping his wad of notes on any flat surface along the way. As his office was well-furnished, with a cocktail cabinet as well as a nice wooden filing one, there was a lot of walking and slapping which, after a while became annoying. Every now and then, on his circuit, he'd pause to lean over me, ostensibly to look at my notebook, checking I'd 'Got that last bit down'. I knew he'd even less chance of reading anything back from my shorthand than I did, but the leaning-over began to include an apparently casual, hot hand placement here, there and indeed elsewhere. Luckily, none of these difficulties were insurmountable.

I gave up fairly early on the shorthand, I could be pretty certain of what he wanted to say, and should I forget, he'd invariably toss his used notes in the wastepaper bin, so I simply retrieved them whenever he left the room, and churned out impeccably correct letters. The wandering hands weren't pleasant, but they weren't a problem either. I began to freeze him out, every time a digit so much as veered in my direction. It didn't take him long to cotton on, without understanding in the least why, whenever he came within a certain distance of me, things got very chilly indeed. It certainly put paid to any funny business, but I don't think it nurtured a congenial working relationship. I was only there for three months, all told.

The next step on my career ladder, was as a secretary in the packaging design department of Yardley, the cosmetic and toiletry people in Bond Street. That didn't measure up too well in the longevity stakes either, although I would point out, in my own defence, the fact Rick Medoc, the chap I worked for, ended up in Accident and Emergency, was entirely his own silly fault.

He was pleasant enough when I started, although a bit too full of his own importance for someone who was not that much older than me. I assumed his recent promotion had gone to his head, causing temporary swelling and he'd get less pompous and pernickety as time went on. What I hadn't factored in was an unpleasant bullying streak reserved, almost exclusively it seemed, for a couple of the older women in the office – I don't know, maybe he hated his mother. Whatever his reasons, he rarely missed an opportunity to wrong-foot either one of them. Liz, who acted as liaison between the design department in Bond Street and the Basildon-based manufacturing side of the business, took it very much in her stride. Over a sandwich, one lunchtime, I asked why she put up with it and didn't slap him down. She shrugged a well-padded shoulder, hitched up the thus dislodged bra strap, and chuckled comfortably.

"He's just a kid who hasn't grown into his big boy trousers yet," she said tolerantly. "Needs a good clip round the ear, if you ask me. But, if shouting the odds makes him feel good, no skin off my nose. Seen more like him come and go, than you've had hot dinners, my love!"

Sandy, the other woman, was a different type altogether, and whereas it was water off a duck's back for Liz, Sandy was floundering. She was secretary to the Distribution Manager, had been for about ten years. It was a role involving more logistics, figures and balancing than I could bear to think about. She was a very bright lady indeed and exceptionally good at her job, but even in the few weeks I'd been there, it was all too clear that Rick's continuous fault-finding was undermining her, to a dangerous degree. In truth, an error highlighted by him, often proved to be nothing of the kind, but the more he picked her up on apparent oversights, the more she made.

I was with him in his office one morning, along with a couple of the factory production team, who'd come to discuss the launch of a newly branded range. There was a query on delivery dates for deodorant-stick containers, which were part of the launch. Rick buzzed the intercom for Sandy to come in. As soon as she did, there was a heightening of the atmosphere, she didn't know what he wanted, but was convinced she'd slipped up somewhere. He knew that, and he had an appreciative audience.

I hate bullying, don't you? Whilst firing questions – which he must have known, she hadn't a hope of answering without the relevant information in front of her – he was plunging his middle finger slowly in and out of the hollow plastic container under discussion. He probably thought he was embarrassing her even further, and from the smirk on the faces of the two guys from the factory, they did too. I knew she was in such a fluster, any innuendo was completely passing her by. I did feel though, that what he was doing wasn't nice and indeed, not so much risqué as risky. Plastic can be tricky, especially when heated, which I proceeded to do. The tube obligingly expanded, then contracted as it cooled, wedging itself firmly on his finger. A rigid plastic tube, once wedged, isn't an easy thing to dislodge. It also follows, the more you panic and the harder you tug, the more swollen the finger becomes.

Apparently, after several hours increasingly uncomfortable wait in St Mary's A and E, they were able to cut it off – tube, not finger – although I understood the whole process was quite painful. The abused digit certainly remained heavily bandaged for a good couple of weeks or so. Naturally, word of such an unfortunate incident spreads like a rash, and I believe for quite some time, wherever Rick went, whether in the office or down at the factory, there was much mimed re-enactment and a great deal of merriment at his expense. Still, no more than he deserved.

CHAPTER FIVE

I stayed with Yardley for a year and then felt a change was in order. I'd like to tell you that I subsequently found my calling and everything ran smooth as silk. Unfortunately, it gradually impinged on me that perhaps I wasn't ideally suited to working for anyone for longer than a few months, which was unfortunate, because I definitely needed to earn a living. However, it wasn't in fact until I got to the end of the run in my next job, that things suddenly became a great deal clearer.

I moved from Yardley in Bond Street, to the Reader's Digest in Berkeley Square – I always did like a rarefied atmosphere – where I was offered a job, working in their book publishing department. This time around on the job circuit, I'd been determined not to be seduced by staff discounts, fancy surroundings or free cosmetics. The most important thing, I felt, was to find someone I really liked and could work for with minimal hassle for either of us.

I did the usual interview with Personnel, elegantly elongated, with thick, pale pink lipstick. During our time together she didn't crack a smile – maybe the lipstick was too thick. I explained, despite CV evidence to the contrary, it wasn't that I wasn't prepared to stick at a job, just that as yet, I hadn't quite found my niche. She didn't trouble to hide her assessment that wherever that niche was, it wasn't going to be at Reader's Digest. Nevertheless, she tested my typing and shorthand speeds, sniffed at the results and took me along to see the chap looking for efficient secretarial skills. From the way that tall and elegant handed him my forms, lips pursed, he and I could both tell, she didn't think, with this candidate, they'd struck gold.

I liked him immediately. For a start, his name was John Smith and you don't get much more straightforward than that. Sharp-boned, freckled and sandy-haired, he laughed when he shook my hand and introduced himself, said he felt the least his parents could have done, was opt for a first name which would have made him a little less pedestrian. I guessed it wasn't the first time he'd cracked that joke, it had a well-used air. Personnel said repressively she'd leave us to chat, but warned she'd be back shortly to collect me, would it be possible therefore, for Mr Smith to be brief and to the point? He grinned at me as she left,

"Look," he said, "I'll tell you what I want, you tell me whether you can do it." He slid aside my CV, paper-clipped to Personnel's notes, which I'd no doubt were signed off 'unsuitable', leaned dangerously far back in his office chair and pyramided long, thin fingers under his chin.

"Here's the low-down. We publish books. At the moment we're working on four: English Country Walks; Four Seasons of Cookery; a DIY tome, forget now what we've called that one and the Family Medical Encyclopaedia. Each book's got its own editor and assistant. We've a Design team who turn their creative talents to layout, illustrations and photos and then Marketing gets involved, working on a load of advance promotions, book club deals and the like. When we've all finished doing our stuff and a book is completed, we hand it over to the Sales chappies and plunge headlong into our next effort. We've got Stately Homes and The History of the Automobile in the pipeline. My baby, this time round's the medical one."

I'd tuned out a little while he was talking, what was important to me was not so much what I was hearing, but what was going on underneath. I was pleased I couldn't find any unpleasant under-currents, he seemed to be exactly as he seemed to be, pleasant and straightforward, through and through.

"... so," he continued, "What I'm after's a bit more than the usual secretarial stuff, I need that too, God knows I do." He waved a hand over a desk top which could best be described as a bit of tip, "But frankly, I'm going under with the masses of medical info we've got pouring in – most of which only makes sense if you've had six years in med school. I need someone to use their common sense and write it up so we can make the ruddy book what we're saying it is – a layman's reference." He paused for breath, sat back again in the chair and raised a sandy eyebrow. "Think you'd be any good at converting completely baffling to reasonably understandable?"

"No idea," I said, "But more than happy to give it a go." He nodded his head once,

"I think you'll do nicely, if you fancy, that is?"

"I do actually, but don't you need to know more about me, my work experience?"

"No. Waste of time. Proof of the pudding and all that. Anyway, we take you on for a month's trial, if it doesn't work out, well it doesn't work out, but I like the cut of your jib." There was no double meaning there, he seemed to be dead straight, up and down, inside and out. "I'll tell Evelyn," he unconsciously made a small pursed mouth, "She'll sort out all the details, money, hols and that. Now, when can you get stuck in?"

By the following week I was installed. Personnel, predictably was less than thrilled, she hadn't taken to me, although I wasn't sure she took to anyone that much. Whenever we passed in the corridor, she'd hand me a look which clearly said 'Don't imagine you've got those feet comfortably under the desk for long!' As things turned out, she was more prescient than she knew, but what happened really wasn't my fault – well, not directly anyway.

CHAPTER SIX

I loved that job, and John Smith was exactly that, John Smith, plain and simple, a rare combination of straight talking and straight thinking. He displayed the same gentle humour and courtesy to everyone, from Bertha our constantly martyred tea lady to Basil Hartspring our equally martyred, if somewhat better paid, Managing Director.

The book editors' smaller offices were set around a large, square, main one, where I worked with Diane (Cookery), Fredella (DIY) and Moira (Walks). Diane and Moira were old hands, having already, between them, seen off Castles and Forts and Art and Artists, whereas Fredella and I were mere novices. There were three other editors, two men and a woman, with John in overall charge of the whole department, running it with an easy hand most of the time although he did have, I discovered, an entirely unexpected and very explosive temper. It seemed completely at odds with all else I'd gathered about him, until it became apparent that yelling, extremely comprehensive cursing and the odd coffee mug swept off the desk, were more often than not, caused by intense frustration at something stupid he himself had done.

I worked for John for over a year – which by my standards, qualified as gold watch award time – before things started to unravel. I felt settled at Reader's Digest, relished the work and although rarely meeting a symptom with which I couldn't instantly identify, at the end of the day, hung on firmly to John's oft repeated philosophy, that as there were hundreds of different conditions detailed in our book, it simply wasn't possible for one person to have them all.

For quite a while I knew Tonya, John's wife, only from a desk photo – pretty, thin and pale-faced with a cloud of black curls, posed on a park bench, one arm firmly round their eight year old son, Evan, the other equally firmly round a cream coloured poodle, desperate to jump out of shot. When I did eventually meet her, she'd brought Evan up to buy next term's school uniform and John was going to take them to lunch.

She wasn't in the office for very long and we only exchanged brief pleasantries. She said she was delighted to meet me and I clearly saw, the thing she was most delighted about was I wasn't the scarlet nailed, seductress type, she'd always feared might be hired. I thought I sensed uncomfortable depths of anxiety and insecurity in her, but perhaps I was mistaken and anyway, I shouldn't have been looking. Things weren't helped much by Evan poking his nose where he shouldn't, discovering my stapler and promptly attaching an envelope to his finger. John dealt with the ensuing shrieks from the injured offspring, in his usual efficiently calm way, assuaging bleeding with a plaster, sobs with a promise of chocolate ice-cream and incipient hysteria from Tonya, with a brisk hug. They left fairly swiftly after that, although not before Tonya had made it quite clear that leaving a stapler on an office desk was, in her opinion, just asking for trouble. I didn't feel we'd got off to the best start.

John stopped being his usual, easy self rather gradually, when we all came back to work after the Christmas holidays that year. His endless patience suddenly wasn't quite so endless, his office door, previously always open was now, more often closed and his temper bursts were a little more frequent, although he invariably apologised afterwards as he'd always done.

I was sorry about whatever it was that was going on with him, but I'd learned lessons from the past, what wasn't my business, was best steered clear of. This seemed like a sensible take on things, until one Monday afternoon when I went in with a batch of corrected proofs on bowel problems, and he yelled,

"Get the hell out of here." And threw a typewriter at me.

Had it been one of the electric ones, it would have flown only a short way across the room, being tethered by wire and plug. Instead, it was the small, manual portable he kept for his own notes. He'd thrown it with both hands, so it sailed, unimpeded and at great speed, straight towards my head, before I stopped it in its tracks and sent it crashing to the floor.

For a moment he and I were both frozen, equally horrified. I hadn't been in any danger, but he didn't know that. He sank back down into his seat and buried his head in both hands. After a moment, I bent and picked up the typewriter, absently noting it seemed remarkably undamaged, certainly more than I'd have been had it hit me. I put it back carefully on the desk, picked up John's briefcase from the floor and lifted his coat and scarf from the hook behind the door.

"Come on." I said.

"Where?"

"Preferably somewhere there's nothing heavy to throw." He moaned from between his fingers,

"I am so sorry, I'm so, so sorry. Appalling behaviour, don't know what to say, just lost it. You came in at the wrong moment, wasn't really throwing it at you…" I tutted, this wasn't going to get the baby bathed. I took his arm firmly and pulled him out from behind his desk. I could smell he'd been drinking. I knew there was a bottle of Scotch in the desk drawer for end-of-book celebrations, but I'd never known him touch it at any other time.

The ground outside, in Berkeley Square, was slushy and dangerous with dirty, left-over snow and not a nightingale in sight. Street-lamp and showroom-window lit and shadowed, we shuffled our cautious way to a coffee bar across the road, in Shepherds Market. I held tightly on to his arm, as much for my benefit as his, the pavements were lethal. Seated across from each other in a booth at the back of the room, with coffee ordered, he finally looked up at me.

"Stella," he said. "I've been unbelievably stupid. So bloody, ridiculously, stupid."

"Tell me." I said, although by then I knew. John; sensible, honest, moral John had been to the office Christmas party. Tonya should have been with him, but that morning, Evan had a horribly aching ear, a situation which, by lunch-time had evolved into raging inflammation, high temperature and antibiotics from the GP. John had said not to worry, he really wasn't that bothered about the party. He'd finish off a bit of work, pop his head round the door of the pub for politeness' sake, grab a quick drink, wish everyone merry whatsits and head home.

But by the time he did pop his head round, the party was in full if somewhat awkward swing, the way only office parties can be –

amalgamation of acute reluctance and reluctant enthusiasm. The one polite, quick drink, led to another which led in turn, and in the general spirit of things, to a Hokey Cokey, participation insisted upon by Bert from Accounts, who rather over-relished the role of MC. And so it was that John found himself, and he seemed genuinely bewildered by the turn of events, in a dark nook at the back of the pub, lip to sweaty lip with Fredella (DIY).

I wasn't nearly as surprised as he seemed to be. It was a well-known fact, Fredella had a bit of a crush on John, although I really don't think he'd ever picked up on it. But if it had passed him by before, it certainly wasn't passing him by now. I understood it wasn't much more than a quick and clumsy peck, but it was also now a source of abject guilt and overwhelming mortification – he said, in fifteen years of marriage, nothing, nothing like this had ever happened, he just wasn't like that and he was telling the truth, he wasn't.

I could see things hadn't always been a smooth run for him and Tonya. It was Tonya's chronic insecurity that seemed to have caused most of their problems. From the very early days of their relationship, she'd got it stuck in her head that he was some kind of lascivious, lone wolf, on the prowl for any hapless female who might stumble across his path. I also understood, from what was swirling round in his mind, that these fears had only been exacerbated and exaggerated throughout the years of trying for a family. Evan had only arrived, after a succession of heart-breaking miscarriages, which nearly ripped them apart as a couple. I gathered, although this was really rather more information than I wanted or needed, Evan's birth hadn't been easy, forceps, stitches and all-sorts. Relations, as John termed it, never really got back to normal after that.

But he was a loyal husband and a devoted father, with the conviction that hurdles plague every marriage and were there to be dealt with and overcome. I could also see, that towards the end of last year, things had been easing between them and, for the first time, they'd started tentatively talking about issues instead of turning their back, pretending they couldn't see anything wrong. The stupid incident in the pub had derailed everything. Although Tonya knew nothing about it, John was being eaten up by guilt.

As he nursed his coffee, turning the spoon endlessly between his fingers, apologising over and again for the typewriter and pouring out as much of his story as he wanted me to hear, I saw, aside from his conscience, which was killing him, there was another sizeable practical problem, which wasn't going away. It appeared that what had been a stupid drunken kiss to him, had assumed pulsing Mills and Boon proportions to Fredella.

"Won't leave me alone," he said, his voice cracking, "Keeps leaving notes, I bloody well find them everywhere. In my coat pocket, on my desk, in my case, Christ Almighty, she even found where my car was parked and stuck one under the wiper. She keeps coming into my office, on one pretext or another and saying… things." Even in the dark of the booth I could see him flush.

"Have you told her, there's nothing doing?"

"Course I have," he snapped, "What do you think I am? Sorry, sorry, didn't mean to shout. I said I was tired, bit drunk, should never have happened. Apologised profusely if I misled her in any way. She didn't seem to want to hear. I just don't know which way to turn."

"Maybe best just ignore her, it'll pass." He looked up at me, and smiled, although it was more of a grimace.

"Don't think so. Found this before – hence the typewriter, just lost my temper, could have hurt you, I'm so…"

"Never mind that," I interrupted, putting out my hand. "Show me." He pulled a crumpled envelope from his pocket and slid it across the table. Inside was a flowers and hearts embellished, sweetly scented Waverley notelet, the message hand-written across the right hand side was, 'Always in my heart, until we're together again!'

"See," he said despairingly, "And she's only ruddy well gone and given me a deadline – end of the week. Says I've got to tell Tonya, tell her I'm leaving. If I don't, she will."

"She can't be serious?" I protested, he sighed,

"God, I don't know, seems serious enough to me, doesn't it to you? What in the name of all that's holy am I going to do?"

"Maybe tell Tonya, just get it out in the open, make it clear it was a silly mistake, then you won't have anything hanging over you, nothing you can be threatened with. Tell the truth, explain what happened."

"I can't, you've no idea what it would do to her." And I saw, in that instant, he was absolutely right, saw how emotionally fragile she could be, shared his fears and hers.

"Well, maybe I can talk to her." I said. He reared back in horror, "You can't."

"Not Tonya, Fredella." He shook his head sharply, "Don't be daft, all due respect, but what could you possibly say?"

"Don't know." And indeed I didn't, but someone had to do something. "Maybe I can make her see sense." He shook his head again, but there was a tiny ray of hope. Simply sharing, had released some of the gut-churning tension that was tearing him apart.

CHAPTER SEVEN

"Lunch?" I said to Fredella the following morning. She looked up in surprise. We worked, every day across the large office from each other and had been out a few times with the other girls, but never on our own.

"Today?" she said.

"Why not?"

"OK then."

I turned attention back to the notes I was working on. From force of habit, I always kept my head blinds tight-closed in the office, it was so darn noisy I'd get nothing done if I didn't. It wasn't only the people in my room but the overall, overriding hum from all the surrounding offices, a building chock-a-block full of people focusing on one thing or another, often several anothers, all at once. Because of this, although I worked with a group of individuals, I knew little more about them than they knew about each other and I'd never really wanted to find out more, other than what cropped up in the normal course of conversations.

I did know Fredella was a few years older than me, late-twenties. She was neatly made, but surprisingly ungainly, always knocking things off her desk or someone else's, teased unmercifully for her clumsiness by Diane (Cookery), who had a slightly spiteful edge to her humour and honed it regularly. I knew Fredella had been named after her father and cordially loathed the name. She loathed it even more when others shortened it to Fred, but other than an initial protest, when we'd both first started working there, she quickly saw the uselessness of kicking against office bonhomie, and now nearly everyone used the short form.

She and I hadn't had a great deal to do with each other over the past year, although there was one memorable occasion when we'd both been working late and left the office at the same time, only to get stuck in one of the lifts. There were two of them serving the building, both modern and overhauled regularly but, as John often said, those lifts had old souls, and operated with disturbing jerkiness and a tendency to stop unexpectedly between floors. That time, Fredella and I were the only passengers and when we juddered to a not entirely surprising halt, I pressed and re-pressed the ground floor button in the pointless way you do, before resorting to the red one, which would alert the building caretaker. I knew though, from previous experiences, he never considered a stuck lift any kind of emergency, and would take his own sweet time getting it sorted. When I turned back to Fredella, to share exasperation, she'd gone very pale.

"I only got in because of you." She said.

"Sorry?"

"I usually take the stairs, hate lifts, only got in because you were there."

"Well, not to worry, Mr O'Horgan will be along in a while, he'll give it a kick or whatever he does and get it going, it's always doing this."

"I know it is," she hissed through clenched teeth, "That's why I never use it." I couldn't help but feel I was unfairly shouldering blame for both the lift failure and her presence in it, but she was starting to breathe in a shallow way, a muscle was jerking in her jaw and she was clenching and unclenching her hands in time with her teeth. I tried a couple of light remarks, to take her mind off things, until she told me to shut up. Her face had whitened even more and in the neon light, freckles on her nose and cheeks stood out, lividly discoloured. She had her shoulder-bag clutched defensively across her stomach, and sweat was beading her hair-line. She was also feeling extremely nauseous, I so hoped she wasn't going to throw up. I don't do sick, and certainly not in enclosed spaces.

We waited in increasingly tense silence. In fact Mr O'Horgan, for once, roused himself in a timely fashion and it was probably less than six or seven minutes that we were actually stuck in there, before the wretched thing started up again with a neck-jarring jolt, a moan from Fredella and a sigh of relief from me. When the doors opened on the ground floor, she rushed off without a word. The following day, she came over to my desk, a little shamefaced – she hated small spaces and usually avoided risking the lift she said, she hoped she hadn't shown herself up too terribly.

I'd almost forgotten the incident, although it came back to me when we left for lunch, so I deliberately headed for the stairs. We walked, heads bent against slanting sleet, across to the same coffee bar I'd gone to with John, the night before. I really wasn't sure quite how I was going to approach this, and indeed was worried she might genuinely have some kind of out of control, emotional attachment problem. I knew – we'd just completed the psych section of the book – that odd obsessions could take hold, convincing someone an illogical and skewed view of events was completely genuine. If she was labouring under a misapprehension of affection, I had to tread carefully, and might well be completely out of my depth.

But I was wrong. I was way off the mark. She wasn't in the least little bit deluded, she knew exactly what she was doing and I saw immediately, as we discarded coats and unwound damp scarves, she loved the control, relished the level of power she could have over someone else. I saw clearly, the reason John was so baffled as to how the stupid drunken kiss had happened, was because it wasn't any of his doing, but hers. And this wasn't the first time.

She'd done this to other men before. As we waited for our order and chatted, I understood this was a behaviour pattern started many years ago, with a maths teacher at school, whose career had subsequently and satisfactorily crashed and burned. Meanwhile, she was busy telling me, she and John had a bit of a heated thing going on, but I wasn't to breathe a word to anyone. He was absolutely potty about her, couldn't keep his hands off, if truth be told. It had all been so sudden and unexpected and naturally, not encouraged at all by her in the beginning, married man and all, but it turned out, he was going to leave his wife, who didn't understand him anyway.

She was as animated as I'd ever seen her, repeatedly smoothing the well-behaved fringe of her bobbed hair with her right hand forefinger as she spoke, sparkly-eyed and excitement-flushed. And while I made suitable exclamations of surprise I saw, completely contrary to what I'd imagined, that this was no crush, all that had simply been part of the build-up – she thought of it as laying firm foundations. She really didn't like John in any way whatsoever, thought him too darn nice to be true and mealy mouthed with it, needed taking down a peg or two in her opinion, and who better than her to make him squirm? She knew precisely what she'd done, was doing and planned to do and in her head at one point, as we talked, was the image of a sleek tabby, patting a frantic mouse to and fro between its paws.

She hadn't quite decided yet on her next step, was still deliciously turning over all the options and possibilities. Should she write to Tonya, or should she make an anonymous call? She'd done that before, with explosively spectacular results. On the other hand, she was really relishing seeing him sweat more each day. It was quite a conundrum as to which way to go next and when, but she was having such a good time, she really didn't want to bring it to any sort of conclusion yet. I don't know what we had for lunch that day, didn't taste it much whatever it was. I'd had some unpleasant encounters in my time, one way and another, but the level of pointless personal spite here was quite something. She was a blackmailer, uninterested in money, misery was reward enough and she was milking plenty of that.

On our way back to the office, she linked her arm firmly and companionably into mine and told me what a huge relief it had been, to share with someone who understood the exciting yet tricky position she was in. She said she felt we'd really bonded. I thought I'd sooner rub shoulders with a scorpion, but smiled and nodded. I already had an idea of what I needed to do, after all, I couldn't simply stand by and see this play out, it was just plain wrong.

However, as you may recall, I'd made snap decisions and taken action in the heat of the moment before and whilst there was nothing I truly regretted, some of those actions had caused a certain amount of concerned reflection. No, I needed to think things over properly and make sure there wasn't any other way round this. I duly thought it over as we walked, and there wasn't, so I went ahead. I wasn't sure it would work, but it was certainly worth a hefty try.

CHAPTER EIGHT

Whatever it was I'd eaten for lunch, was still sitting heavily on my stomach when I settled back at my desk. I had some proofs in front of me that needed checking, but I was focused on Fredella across the room. She was working on labels to go on diagrams of U bends, stopcocks and valves, for the Plumbing for the Uninitiated section. Because I'd been with her in the lift, I knew what claustrophobia felt like – clammy, sick panic clamping down, each new breath harsher to draw, conviction the enclosed space was closing in, ever tighter. It wasn't pleasant at all, and I could empathise with sufferers in a way I never had before. I found her thoughts of John immediately, he was very much at the forefront of her mind, and I attached thought to memory. It wasn't something I'd done before and I'm certain I did it rather clumsily, I couldn't even be sure the link I'd made would hold.

Across the office, Fredella rose abruptly to her feet, knocking against her in-tray, which promptly tipped, in the manner of stacked trays everywhere, and shot all its contents to the floor. Fredella didn't seem to notice and nobody else even glanced up – she was always knocking things over and making a clatter. But I saw her face. She looked pretty gob-smacked and not in a good way. I looked down again, away from her, but could feel what was happening. As she was wont to do, she'd just thought again, with pleasure, about John; how dreadful he was looking, how he couldn't meet her eye, how scared he was of what was going to happen next. All of these were feelings which generally warmed her through and through. Not this time though. Panic immediately swept in, fully fledged. Nausea and painful shortness of breath, the sort of thing that only ever happened when she felt trapped, nothing she'd ever experienced before in a large open space like the office. Yet there it was. She sat down again, suddenly. I wondered how long the tie-up of thought to memory would last, and how quickly she'd realise that with one, came the other. She looked up then and caught my eye. I smiled warmly at her. After all, as she'd said, we had bonded.

I went in to see John, a couple of hours later, just before I left for the day. He looked up sharply as I opened the door, on constant alert for unwanted visitors.

"I may have sorted it." I said.

"No! How?"

"We had a bit of a heart to heart and I think she may now be thinking of you in a slightly different way."

"You're kidding me. What did she say? Was she upset?" I considered, I don't believe in lying just for the sake of it.

"Well, she may have been a wee bit put out," I conceded. "But I honestly don't think she's cherishing a broken heart. She's done this sort of thing before you know, gets quite a kick out of it."

"What – to other people? She told you that? Oh God, then why would she stop? What on earth did you say to her? Maybe you've made it even worse?"

"Not worth going over it all. Look, I'm not making any promises but I think, just think mind, she'll probably stop now. Trust me and let's wait and see." I knew he was unconvinced, scared to believe, pessimism warring with hope. But, as it transpired, my previously untried linking skills proved more efficient than I could ever have hoped, evidenced by a definite change in Fredella.

For a couple of weeks John remained, in trepidation, behind closed doors and Fredella spent a great deal of time looking pale, sick and alarmed, arriving late and on a couple of occasions leaving early. Then one day, she didn't turn up for work at all. We were told she'd resigned suddenly, for personal reasons. Not even, said pursed lips Personnel, bothering to work out her official notice.

I hoped she was all right, but reasoned, provided she didn't spend too much time brooding on her thwarted plans for John, she would be. Did I feel guilty? Maybe a little, but there was no question, something had needed doing, John and Tonya were good people and when it came to it, there hadn't seemed to be anyone else available to step up to the plate.

There's a saying, isn't there, 'No good deed goes unpunished', and in the long run, it was my pleasant and comfortable relationship with John that suffered. The fact I knew what had occurred with Fredella was humiliating enough for him, but that I'd been the one to apparently sort it out, having seen him at his lowest, irrevocably changed the dynamic between us, if not from my end, certainly from his.

To complicate things further Tonya, who had known from his behaviour that something was very much up, put two and two together and made five. She convinced herself that John had feelings for me, which he did, although they definitely weren't what she thought. Her acute anxieties, which he had no idea I knew about, together with his own loss of face, combined to make for an increasingly awkward and uncomfortable working atmosphere. I loved the job, and was far from thrilled at the way things were panning out, but the writing was on the wall. I reluctantly had to accept that whatever normal rules I chose to abide by, every now and then, things were bound to happen that took me beyond self-imposed barriers – and there would always be a price to pay.

By the time I'd made up my mind to add Reader's Digest to the list of jobs that hadn't quite worked out, I'd also come to the conclusion that trying to find work that suited me and to which I was suited might, in the long run, be like trying to squeeze a square peg into a round hole – ultimately unproductive and causing a heck of a lot of friction all round.

CHAPTER NINE

It was family stuff that finally focused my attention on what I might do to earn an honest crust. Noisy, good-natured, chaos and confusion was what our extended family get-togethers were all about, but that didn't stop any number of bossy people (of which, amongst the relatives, there was no shortage) trying to organise everyone else. It occurred to me, that what I might actually be rather good at, had probably been staring me in the face for some time, I just hadn't spotted it.

Aunt Kitty was the eldest, most obdurate of my late grandmother's sisters, and the one who lived the longest, with an element of personal triumph as each birthday came and went, subsequent to the demise of her younger siblings. She'd worked into her early eighties, tubing from Hendon Central to a financial institution in the city, where they apparently never dared voice objection to her age which she'd brazenly, over the years, winched ever downward. Rumour had it, she'd gone so far as to change dates on her personnel file, which apparently left managers, probably not yet born when she'd first taken to a typewriter, without an administrative leg to stand on when it came to handing her a P45.

When she eventually did give up, she sometimes chose to play the batty card – vague and increasingly eccentric – although I knew for a fact, she was as razor-sharp as she'd ever been. Always tiny, she got even shorter, thinner and more hawk-nosed as she aged, although she still had more energy than was probably good for any one person. She remained, in solitary matriarchal splendour, in the Georgian Court, mansion block of flats in Hendon, previously shared with Grandma and Aunt Yetta. There was no doubt that whilst she missed the intermittent sparring and armed neutrality of their prickly relationships, the change in circumstance, left her free to indulge her bargain-hunting vices, and she happily hoarded to her heart's content.

The flat was still the main, family social hub, although now gatherings were slightly more irregular and not every week. We were inevitably thinner on top when it came to the older generation but had acquired, in the natural way of things, new in-laws, babies, toddlers and children of assorted sizes, so it remained a noisy crowd to be fed and watered. Kitty still insisted on doing all her own shopping and cooking, as the sisters always had done for these social occasions, although a minor concession to age was made with the acquisition of a red and green tartan, shopping basket on wheels. This was steered round the Hendon shops at speed, with some aggression and scant respect for other people's ankles, especially if they were in her way.

I'd seen her in action, the few times I'd reluctantly accompanied her on shopping trips, during which, it has to be said, we didn't make many friends. We were also not hugely popular in Boots the Chemist, where she became so confused and upset that she completely convinced the sympathetic crowd, gathering round the till, that she'd been short-changed. I'd been choosing some eye-shadow, in another part of the shop, but hastened back when I saw what was occurring. There was no way she was in the least bit confused as to the bill, nor the correct change due. She could tot up a column of figures faster and more accurately than you or I could read them. With apologies, I hauled her away, sharpish, from the flushed assistant. She was singularly unabashed, being of the belief that most shops were out to defraud the poor old pensioner, new-fangled tills were deliberately designed to add to the bafflement and an extra £5 was better in her pocket than theirs. I don't know whether I was more disturbed by her dubious morals, or the fact she'd taken on so many of Grandma's paranoid theories. I made her promise never to do that again and she said she wouldn't – I wasn't convinced.

I chose to take out and air my ideas on my future career direction, at one of these family gatherings. Can't think why, it possibly wasn't the best forum for reasoned discussion, maybe I was reckoning on safety in numbers. I was in the kitchen with my mother and Aunt Edna, who were busy shuttling piled plates of filled bagels, cakes and biscuits to the dining room table under Kitty's eagle-eye, at the same time as filling teapots from the seriously overworked kettle.

"I'm going to set up my own business." I said.

"Don't put those cakes on the table right away, put them on the sideboard first." Said Aunt Edna to my mother, "Everyone should have the bagels first. And look dear, all the cream cheese ones are at the bottom, that's no good, put some at the top, otherwise everyone'll just eat the salmon." She was already busy, following her own instruction.

"What on earth are you talking about? What business?" My mother wiped a cream-cheese smothered finger on her apron.

"Well…" I said.

"Business? What business?" said Aunt Edna, "Stella, dolly, you're talking airy fairy again. Here, take the pot and the milk and here, wrap the dishcloth round the handle, it's hot. No, no, you won't manage the sugar too, you'll drop the lot."

"I'm trying to tell you…" I said.

"What's wrong with the job you've got, you like it don't you, he's a nice chap isn't he?" My mother expertly operated on a Madeira sponge, leaving it fully sliced and fanned on the plate.

"Yes, but…" I started.

"Well there you are then."

"Yes, but…"

"What? What's she doing?" Aunt Kitty paused in the mass bagel buttering, always better to have too many than not enough.

"I'm trying to tell you, if you'll shut up for just one second and listen." I said mildly. Three sets of eyebrows raised, hair-line high, as they all turned to look at me, Aunt Kitty even temporarily suspended the butter-knife action.

"Well?" She said. "Spit it out, these bagels haven't got all day."

"I'm setting up my own agency."

"Agency?" my mother pulled her chin in, her interrogative pose. "What for?"

"Well, anything at all really."

"Sweetheart." Aunt Edna liked to think of herself as the practical one, keeping the rest of us on the straight and narrow. "Girls your age don't set up businesses, girls your age find husbands and have babies."

"What do you mean, anything?" Persisted my mother. "An employment agency?"

"Not exactly," thoughts were, even as we spoke, firming up nicely in my mind. "A help-you-out kind of an agency."

"Like Universal Aunts?" Aunt Kitty, head to one side, bird-like and bright with interest had homed straight in.

"Yes. Yes, that's exactly the sort of thing I'm talking about. I mean, I'm good at organising, getting things done. I'm going to set up this service, for people who need admin and other office stuff done, like we did in Hay Hill. But I'll add in all kinds of practical stuff – errands, pick-ups and collections – that sort of thing. And if it's something I can't do, then I'll find someone who can. It'll be something that can grow in any direction, depending on what people need most of." The concept was taking shape as we spoke, and it felt right and comfortable.

"Sweetie, you know I love you to death, and because I do, I'm allowed to tell you, you're crazier than a cage-full of monkeys." Aunt Edna tended not to be sit-on-the-fence, when it came to an opinion.

"Edna, you can't say that." My mother obviously felt a bit of maternal defence was called for, despite the fact she didn't think her sister was that far out.

"Well, I think it sounds like a blooming good idea. Clever." said Aunt Kitty. I gawped at her, I'd assumed she'd be in the Aunt Edna camp. "Got to be done right, though. Everything thought through, back, front and sideways. Here Rosie, finish these bagels. Edna, you still haven't mixed cream cheese and salmon enough. You, Stella, sit down this minute and write yourself a list. Get what's in your head, on to paper. Going to do it, have to do it properly.

"Fine," said Aunt Edna, redistributing bagels and shaking her head, "Just don't all come crying to me when she's, God forbid, fat, forty and firmly on the shelf."

CHAPTER TEN

John, took the news of my planned departure, with rather less disappointment than I'd have liked, although I wasn't surprised. He desperately needed to close an awkward and embarrassing chapter. He felt he'd let himself down unforgivably, he needed to move on, and there was no way he was going to be able to do that while I was still there. Personnel, also took the news squarely on the chin, and not without a certain degree of smugness. She'd known from the start, I wasn't a stayer.

At the same time as severing those ties, with regret, I was putting into action a host of exciting ideas and plans. It was all rather odd really. I'd always worked within a planned structure – school, college, employment – all places where people told you what to do and where, when and how they wanted you to do it. Setting up a business was a different thing altogether. There was only me to decide which direction to swim in, or indeed, as it transpired, just how deep and far out I was prepared to go.

I had just enough in the bank to put down a deposit on a two-room office, above a travel agent in Brent Street, although I knew, if I got into the second month and hadn't found any paying clients, it would be a short-term rental indeed. My landlord, Martin Meisel, who ran the travel agency was a stooping, anaemic type in his late fifties, carrying the weight of the world on his thin shoulders. He could have been considered a little lacking in the enthusiasm you'd like, from the person planning your holiday fun, but seemed to have a loyal clientele. His wife Hilary, worked with him, and was fractionally more on the jolly side, although possibly only by comparison. They do say, couples grow to look more like each other over the years and certainly, these two could have been brother and sister. I think at some point, someone might have suggested to Martin that he brighten up a bit, but he interpreted that as clothes rather than attitude, and was often to be found in bright red or electric blue trousers, teamed with one of Hilary's knitted jumpers, on which she worked assiduously, when the shop was quiet. She's still the only person I've ever seen who could knit and smoke simultaneously.

I'd received a surprising amount of family support, far more than I'd expected – some welcome, some not so much. My father, who could easily match Martin, gloom for gloom, was acutely pessimistic and convinced this venture stood every chance of falling immediately flat and heavily on its face. He nevertheless, gamely pitched up with a paintbrush, and over the course of a couple of days, the office lightened from dingy brown to a more reassuring magnolia. My mother also insisted on buying and putting up net curtains, which she said, made the place look more homely, undeterred by my pointing out that homely was not the ambience I was aiming for. More usefully, my sister Dawn, who was on the artistic side, sign-painted the upper frosted glass panel of the door, with some pleasingly authoritative black paint and alliteration – SIMPLE SOLUTIONS to PRACTICAL PROBLEMS – which I felt nicely summarised my client offering.

I'd invested in second hand desks, chairs for both office rooms and an impressive filing cabinet. Aunt Edna had donated two electric typewriters from Uncle Monty's offices, a generous gift, of which I'm pretty sure he was completely unaware, and I'd acquired two phones with an officious row of buttons on each, to enable inter-office as well as outside communication.

I was somewhat less gratified by the unexpected appearance, at a very early stage, of Aunt Kitty, who trotted up the two flights of stairs, hauling the ubiquitous wheeled shopping basket, and announced she'd come to sort me out. As the whole ethos of what I was doing, was based on me sorting everyone else out, I wasn't thrilled. Quite apart from which, I was pretty certain that as a vibrant and efficient fledgling business, the last thing I needed was an 83 year old assistant.

"Rubbish." she said, reading my mind as accurately and easily as I'd normally read anyone else's, and looking around the small space for possible trolley storage. "This isn't charity, you know. You pay me what you can afford and I can type, keep the books and answer the phone, just till you get on your feet." I pointed out, as of this moment, I didn't have a book to keep, the phone wasn't exactly ringing off the hook, and this whole exercise was all about me standing on my own two feet. But this was a woman who'd never met opposition she couldn't ride rough-shod over. I was still in mid-remonstration as she was unpacking the trolley, from the depths of which she produced an electric kettle, PG Tips, assorted crockery, milk, Jaffa Cakes and last, but not least, a slightly exhausted looking fern in a pot, which she shook out, dusted down and placed firmly on the window-sill.

"Here, Stella," she said, "Fill the kettle, we'll have a cup of tea and talk things over some more." I grumpily took myself downstairs to the shared kitchen, where Hilary, one bony hip planted on the worktop, was casting on or casting off – as I was never sure what she was knitting, it was difficult to tell.

"See you've got help." She said, "Not quite in the first flush, eh?" I rolled my eyes,

"You wouldn't think someone so small, could steam-roll so effectively." I muttered. Hilary shrugged,

"Makes more sense than having to find a proper wage, at the end of the week." she pointed out, "You don't even know how this whole thing is going to work. Must say, I've got my doubts, honeybun."

"Now, what do you want to call me?" asked Kitty, as I plugged in the kettle and she bustled around with cups. I debated a few choice answers, one of which was a bloody nuisance. She tutted at my silence,

"Well Auntie's not going to work is it? You'd better," she said, tossing aside forty years of happy married life, "Make me, Miss Macnamarra."

"Why on earth… ?"

"Trust me, Miss sounds more secretarial than Mrs and Scottish is always reliable." I wasn't convinced of her logic, but as the main problem wasn't what I flipping well called her, but what I was going to do with her, I didn't waste time debating.

I'd sweated over and eventually finalised, a carefully worded ad to go in the local paper, offering a range of helpful and (hopefully) much-needed, practical services. I'd adopted the royal 'we', and indicated that nothing reasonable was beyond our scope or capabilities, from escorting children and the elderly, to organising house moves, office relocations and travel arrangements, together with a complete range of secretarial and office service options, at our premises or theirs. All of this, caused a deep degree of alarm in the family ranks.

"You can't do that. You don't know who you're going to get answering," worried my mother, "It'll be all sorts, perfect strangers, you won't know anything at all about them."

"Well of course it'll be perfect strangers," I said, "Otherwise, I'd just end up doing jobs for you and Dad wouldn't I?" She reluctantly acknowledged the sense of this, but anxiety was unalloyed. Unexpectedly she said,

"Will you... you know... ?"

"What?"

"Use, you know... " I looked at her in surprise, we so rarely talked about it, we just took what I was, for granted. At home, nobody even noticed any more when something floated gently past their head, because I couldn't be bothered to stand up and get it.

"Use it to check them out, I mean." She continued, "Make sure you don't get involved with anybody who's, you know, odd!"

"What, odder than me, you mean?" I asked. She laughed at that and gave me a hug, "You're not odd, you're special."

But she'd put her finger neatly on something I'd taken for granted, and therefore hadn't thought about too much. I did have a huge advantage, which is why I didn't have too many nerves about my venture, other than worrying whether it could earn me a living. As you'll have gathered by now, I've a healthy respect for my own safety and certainly, even back then, wasn't remotely a risk taker. I suppose I simply always felt pretty secure because of what I could do. So yes, I could take care of myself and no, I absolutely wasn't going to get involved, at any stage, in anything even remotely risky and definitely nothing at all unpleasant. Which only goes to show, prescience wasn't one of my attributes.

CHAPTER ELEVEN

Fortunately for my future profit margins, I wasn't starting off, completely clientless. When the Colonel and Mrs H-B closed down their secretarial agency, we'd stayed in occasional touch, Christmas cards and the like, and they'd sometimes send pictures of them on their boat, raising a jaunty G and T to the camera. I wrote to them, told them what I was planning, and asked if they thought any of their old clients might make use of my new services. They obligingly came up with a list of names and addresses. Picking ones within travelling distance, I wrote and got a definite yes from two and a maybe from a third. One of the yeses was from an old favourite of mine, Professor Lowbell, who not only said he would definitely want secretarial services, but also wondered whether, in due course, I'd be up for taking on some research for his latest book.

I was tickled pink, to acquire my first proper client. I also felt it boded well that it was someone I already knew and liked. In the Hay Hill days, he'd always asked for me to do his work and we'd established a great modus operandi. Professor of English Literature, he was a highly respected expert in his field of obscure folk and fairy tales. His enthralment was with the common threads running throughout all the stories; the same monsters under the bed, the same horrors lurking in the shadows in the corner of the room. These ran consistently down the centuries, woven into different cultures the world over. The psychology of terror, its impact and attraction, for both children and adults alike, endlessly intrigued him. The depth and breadth of his knowledge was impressive and he would have made a superb lecturer, were it not for a stammer that painfully intensified under any kind of stress or excitement. He'd battled it all his life, and there was the huge frustration of a mind, flowing and flooded with ideas and commentary he wasn't able to smoothly share. He had though, over time, evolved a highly effective method of expelling even the most immovably lodged words or phrases, by singing them out in a light tenor.

He was an unusual looking chap, in his early sixties, short and stocky, and bearing an unfortunately strong resemblance to one of his own fairy tale frogs – pouched throat, wide jaw, eyes alarmingly protuberant and an iris so dark, it merged with the pupil, giving him a disconcertingly black and blank stare. When we'd first met, I'm ashamed to admit, I'd thought the emergence of a swift, forked tongue, grabbing a passing fly to pop into his thin, almost lipless mouth, wouldn't have been too much of a surprise. But as I grew to know and like him, any oddity of appearance was completely countered by a sharp sense of humour, sweetness of nature and the infectious, high-pitched, hiccoughing chuckle with which he invariably greeted his own jokes, as well as his speech struggles.

I'd always enjoyed doing his work, and it wasn't hard to get it right, he was highly intelligent, focused and always totally engrossed in whatever we were doing. His mind was more multi-layered and compartmentalised than most, and whilst I wouldn't have dreamt of delving deeply, if I needed information at any particular moment, it was always conveniently floating on the surface. If he got wedged on a word as he dictated, I was always able to supply it as an apparently educated guess and, as we became more comfortable with each other, even sing it out with him, to our mutual amusement.

He lived in Hampstead, in a rambling edifice at the top of a hill. It could so easily have been the setting for any one of his stories and, as my mother pointed out once, when she and I drove past, must be worth a fortune and a half. He'd been brought up there and continued sharing comfortably with his elderly parents until well into his forties before, as he put it, they shuffled off this mortal coil, within a mere two months of each other. I gathered he'd married late in life, and for the last twenty years or so, the house had been occupied by him, his wife Dorothy and, as she was wont to grumble, more books, paper and dust than should be legal.

A woman of few words, Dorothy was built for comfort rather than speed, her fine, chin-length, grey hair fastened back on one side with a slide, from which the odd strand would slip, to trail limply against plump cheeks, untroubled by make-up. She was, she told me on one occasion, and I can't even remember how it came up, a soap and water kind of a girl, splash and a dash had always stood her in good stead. She was also, although I didn't realise it at first, as expert and erudite in her own field as he was in his. She held a doctorate in history, but never used the title. The Professor, rather touchingly, called her Dotty, fondly patting whichever bit of her happened to be nearest at the time. 'Dotty by name and dotty by nature!' he'd say. She seemed to take this in good part although if, as I suspect, he'd been doing it all the years of their marriage, I would have wanted to bash him on the head with the nearest blunt instrument.

Dotty's area of expertise was antique dolls. She once told me, in a brief period of loquacity, as we waited for the Prof to come back from one of his frequent trips to the toilet, that dolls had been around as long as little girls had and were just as important – if not more so! Little girls grew up, dolls didn't and gave us invaluable depths of insight into different cultures, histories, workmanship, techniques and materials. She'd authored a number of books and regularly consulted for museums and auction houses world-wide, as well as being the go-to-guru for serious collectors, seeking provenance and authentication. You'd never, in a million years, guess any of that from meeting her, and I only knew because I'd been curious (nosey?) enough to check her out in the comprehensive reference section at Hendon Library. I knew from what I'd read, she had one of the most impressive collections of antique dolls in private hands. I liked her. She wasn't overly warm, but she was consistently pleasant and courteous, didn't waste breath or time on unnecessary small talk, and had a tightly closed thought pattern, which was just the sort I preferred, so much more restful.

She was certainly no trouble at all, when she accompanied her husband on his visits to our office, as she often did. She'd settle herself amiably while we worked, sometimes sitting in the outer office, at other times with us, producing her own notebook from a tapestry carpet bag, writing with a fountain pen and carefully blowing on the ink to dry it, before any page turning. She illustrated all her notes with excellently-executed sketches from the photos people sent her, preferring to record details that way, because she could then put in her own measurements and notes for future reference. Her drawings were exceptionally good, but when I commented she shook her head, tutting,

"Not my talent you're seeing my dear, but the original doll-maker's, that's what's shining through."

Professor Lowbell and I agreed initially on fortnightly sessions to which he brought all his mail, often hoarding and not even opening it until he was settled opposite me. I pointed out, more than once, there might well be something urgent; he was unperturbed.

"If it's urgent they'll phone." He said comfortably. At these meetings we'd devote about an hour to correspondence. We'd then habitually stop for a cup of tea and cake supplied by Kitty in best Miss McNamarra mode, before going through material to be written up for the next section of the book in progress. If I was pleased to get him on board, he in turn was delighted my new venture was going to provide a much needed service, so much nearer to home. And Kitty loved him to pieces because, not only did he treat her with great gallantry, but more importantly, unfailingly settled his invoice with a cheque at the end of each session.

By the time Simple Solutions had been running for three months, and whilst never one to count chickens prematurely, I felt we were heading in the right direction, although the jury was still out on Kitty. There was no doubt she was efficient – no trace of batty article when she was in the office. I also couldn't help but be grateful she'd taken to handling credit control, with a firmness and vigour I could never in a life-time have mustered. She had a habit of dropping her voice, when on the phone to late-payers, in a way that had more than a touch of the menacing about it. When I remonstrated, she was unrepentant.

"Dolly, you be the nice one they like to deal with, I'll be the not so nice one who makes sure they pay." Whilst there was about her, a distinct whiff of Mafioso, when pressing for payment, on the increasingly frequent occasions that a potential new client made the two-flight trek up to the office, she was charm personified. In fact she had to be restrained from providing a running, coffee and cake buffet – at times our outer office/ waiting room had a rather too convivial feel about it for my liking.

Gratifyingly, within our first three months, we were already finding ourselves busy enough to need additional extra help. I put another ad in the local paper, to say we were looking for a new team member – secretarial skills, clean driving license and three references. I was pleased with the response, although felt most of them could have done without a thorough grilling from my outer office dragon, before meeting me. Our office hierarchy definitely required some clarification.

I interviewed half a dozen women who were eminently qualified, answered all my questions, did great typing tests and produced rave references, but ended up taking on the one I liked best. Brenda Herkomer sailed into the office like a rather stately, square-rigged galleon. She hadn't a single reference to her name because she hadn't, she confessed, touched a typewriter or worked for anyone since God was a boy. She'd been comfortably married, for twenty-five years, to Mr Herkomer, a local bank manager, until one morning he announced, between the cereal and toast, that he was leaving. He'd packed a suitcase, stopped off at the vicarage to pick up the vicar's wife – apparently, singing in the choir hadn't been the only mutually satisfying activity in which they'd been engaged – and vanished. With him disappeared, not only Mrs Vicar but Brenda's comfortable life-style, financial security and house, re-mortgaging being another something he'd neglected to mention.

All of this, she recounted without a trace of self-pity, whilst absent-mindedly tutting over and straightening paperwork on my desk and asking me as many questions as I was asking her. I liked her instantly, and as a bonus, she was the only person who hadn't walked in and thought to herself how young I looked, to be running my own business.

I can't say she immediately hit it off with the other staff member, but then I'm not sure anybody would have done. As it transpired, the settling down period for Kitty and Brenda, took a little longer than I'd imagined and at times, the atmosphere was decidedly chilly, as each tried to out-boss and re-organise the other. I don't think either of them felt they were remotely part of the same team, until a few weeks down the line, when I returned to the office at the end of the day and found them both sitting on a chap who was lying full length on the floor of the travel agency, growling and cursing.

CHAPTER TWELVE

I wasn't in the mood for a drama. I'd been out most of the day, conveying a ten year old, one of our regular charges, from school to the dentist and then home. His mother, Susan McCrae, was a local GP who ran, with total efficiency, a busy practice, an often absent-abroad husband and two other much older children, but fell to pieces when dealing with Devlin. He'd been a late, surprise addition to the family, with an eight-year gap between him and his next oldest sibling. He was, his mother told me, when I first went to see her, a wee bit of a handful. This was something of an understatement, and I could tell at a glance, the butter-wouldn't-melt face, hid a no-holds-barred personality.

The family employed Celine, a French au pair, but as she was inclined to lose what little English she had, when under stress, she probably wasn't the best person to deal with young Devlin, who had an almost forensic interest in seeing just how hysterical he could get her. Celine couldn't drive, so Dr McCrae was delighted to come across the services I offered, especially, she said, because it was so unusual for him to take to someone in the way he'd taken to me. It wasn't, of course, the mutual attraction she fondly assumed, more a sort of armed neutrality. We'd been introduced against a background of Celine's noisy sobs, emanating from the kitchen. I understood she had a thing about spiders and knowing this, Devlin had slipped a fake, rubber one into her coffee a few moments ago, while her back was turned. She'd drained the cup, come face to face and her reaction had been extremely satisfactory, even louder and more panic-stricken than he'd anticipated.

"Devlin," said his mother repressively, once she'd established the facts. "You're a very naughty boy, in a moment, I want you to go right back in there and tell poor Celine how sorry you are." Devlin allowed his lower lip to quiver just a little, and his mother immediately gathered him to her. "Oh, now don't get upset little one. He's such a practical joker," she smiled at me, "Has us in stitches a lot of the time, don't you darling? I expect Celine was just a bit surprised, that's all. You didn't mean to frighten her did you?" I could clearly see his mother couldn't have been more off the mark and decided, if I was to take this job on, boundaries would have to be drawn. Devlin, for his part, was more than thrilled to meet me, another soft touch and further entertainment, he thought. I smiled at him,

"Perhaps Celine doesn't like spiders?" I suggested. He furrowed an angelic brow.

"Didn't know that." He said, giving me the big blue eyes.

"I'm sure you didn't. But we all have things we don't like much, don't we?" Obligingly, into his mind bounded next door's Boxer dog, with its habit of sneaking up unseen to the other side of the fence and barking loudly when Devlin was kicking a football around the garden. The barking was deep, alarming and unexpected, Devlin had been scared rigid, several times now. I tucked that away for future reference, on the basis that the pleasure he took in scaring Celine, was as bad for his moral development as it was for her nerves. I smiled warmly at him again and I think he might just have had a suspicion that I wasn't, as my Aunt Yetta had been wont to say, as green as I was cabbage looking.

The family turned out to be a lucrative and regular source of picking up, dropping and escorting tasks, rarely a week going past without them needing our services, at some stage or another. And to be honest, Devlin never caused me too much trouble; he was a bright child and soon assessed that with me, there were some things that would be tolerated and others, he didn't have a hope in hell of getting away with.

He could be both tiring and tiresome and hence my general rattiness on returning to the office to find the staff busy sitting on a complete stranger. Hilary, it turned out, was also on the floor, in the opposite corner with her head buried in her hands. I shut the door carefully behind me and reversed the shop sign from Open to Closed.

CHAPTER THIRTEEN

"Call 999." instructed Kitty. She was a little breathless, I suppose that was only to be expected, she was sitting on his legs and he was doing his level best to hurl off.

"I'm a bit worried," said Brenda. She was straddling his back in a workmanlike way, "That I might squash him, but I daren't let go." Face-down beneath her, he wriggled and bucked again. She reached up for a glossy cruise brochure on the desk behind her, rolled it and swatted him, none too gently, on the back of the head. "Stay still, you."

"Not the police." Said Hilary, raising her head. "No police." I saw, with shock, there was blood at the side of her mouth, she wiped it with the sleeve of her jumper, the resulting smear made it look far worse.

"It's Martin," she said.

"What's Martin? Did he hit you?" I was completely at sea.

"No, course not." Hilary shook her head, then thought better of it, nursing her sore mouth with a cautious hand. "It's... well, Martin's got a problem."

"What sort of a problem?"

"Rather not say."

"For goodness sake, don't be ridiculous Hilary, what d'you mean, rather not say? Who the heck's this?" I indicated the bloke on the floor. He'd gone worryingly quiet. I hoped Brenda hadn't finished him off. She obviously thought the same, because she shifted a little and he took in a breath and cursed, which was reassuring. "Hilary," I said sharply, "Who the hell is this? What's he doing here? And where is Martin?"

"Travel exhibition."

"And... ?"

"He didn't believe me." She inclined her head towards the supine one.

"And what? He hit you because Martin's out?" I knew people took booking their holiday extremely seriously, but surely not to this extent. Hilary shook her head and again regretted it.

"He wants money, that's why he's here."

"What money?"

"Money Martin owes."

"Who to? What for?"

"Gambling, he gambles, OK? Puts money on horses. Stupid sod, never wins, ever. Got right out of his depth, borrowed a lot and hasn't paid it back yet." Her face was pale and taut.

"And... ?"

"This... person, came to warn him what would happen if he didn't settle. He didn't believe me when I said Martin wasn't here so... " she paused and wiped more blood which had trickled down, "He warned me instead."

"Bastard!" hissed Kitty. "Should be bloody ashamed, hitting a woman like that." I didn't think a lecture on manners was going to make much of difference to the status quo, quite apart from which, I knew the man on the floor was a great deal more dangerously angry than when he'd begun this business call. He bucked his legs viciously, trying to shift Kitty, then yelped and cursed comprehensively as she gave his calf a sharp pinch.

"Listen," she said, "Nothing you've got to say's going to shock me, so you might as well shut up."

I gathered he worked for a small, but highly efficient organisation, lending to those who'd exhausted all the normal channels and were desperate for another, short-term avenue, albeit rather out of the fat and into the fire. These though were lenders who liked loans and accruing interest repaid, and repaid promptly. When this didn't happen, as it so frequently didn't, action was called for and it was best called for from an employee who was highly effective, because he really relished his work. He not only invariably collected the requisite amount, but enjoyed the process as much as the payment. A man happy in his work.

In the normal course of events, a visit would have been made, threats issued and a return appointment arranged to pick up the fruits of the threat. Today hadn't gone quite to plan, and because reputation and status are powerful things to those that have them, this was one deeply unhappy chappie. He'd turned from landing 'a smack or two', on the wife, only to find her shrieks had brought reinforcements from upstairs. He'd seen who it was, and had never been less perturbed in his life. He'd simply carried on doing what he'd come here to do – expanding on what hubby could expect, if payment wasn't pronto.

Concentrating on the task in hand, he was startled to find himself suddenly hit hard on the head with a firmly wielded office stapler which, not unnaturally, caused him to stagger a little. At this point, a chair on wheels had hit him painfully behind both knees causing, him to swiftly assume a sitting position, although by then, the chair had been whisked away, so he landed hard on the floor instead, whereupon two crazy women rolled him over and sat on him. He could, he thought, have thrown the old one off without missing a beat, she was like a bleeding skeleton but the other one, fat cow, had somehow managed to pin both his arms down with her legs, which were on the substantial side.

He couldn't quite believe how he'd wound up like this, and his language was pretty choice, there were certainly a few words I hadn't heard before, although luckily he was a bit short of breath, so really couldn't spit out everything that was going through his head. The problem was, we had ourselves a bit of a rattle-snake situation. The minute they let go, he'd swing round and lash out indiscriminately. I could see he was so lividly humiliated, he couldn't care less who he hurt, as long as it was someone and badly.

Hilary, meanwhile, had hauled herself up unsteadily from the floor and was leaning shakily against a desk.

"Martin's got the money." She said. "What he borrowed and extra, for the interest. I told him." She jerked her head towards the floor. "But he says it's not enough."

"Where is it?" I said.

"What?"

"The money, where is it?"

"Here, it's in the cash box, couldn't risk leaving it with Martin, could I? He'd only bloody gamble it away again, silly fool."

"Right. Give it to me."

"What, now?"

"Yes, now." I snapped. She produced a key from a chain around her neck, the cash box from the drawer and, after a moment or two, a plump wad of notes. I put my hand out and she gave it to me.

"OK," I said. "You, yob on the floor." He grunted. "This is what's going to happen next. I'm not going to call the police, much as I'd like to see you locked up and the key thrown away. I'm going to ask these nice ladies to get off you. You'll then stand up, slowly, with your hands at your side. Understand?" He grunted again and I saw that what he had in mind, in no way included standing still with his hands at his side. I also knew, because he was planning on getting it out at the first opportunity, he had a flick-knife in the back pocket of his jeans. I nodded at Kitty and Brenda, they both looked at me doubtfully – and they didn't know the half of it – I nodded at them again and Brenda climbed off cautiously, and extended a hand to the older woman.

The second Brenda's weight was off his back, he was up, lip curled, fist raised, sending Kitty flying off his legs. Brenda and Hilary both grabbed for her and hauled her in, before he could land a blow and I knocked his legs right out from under him. He hit the ground again, hard. I have to confess, it gave me a bit of a headache, it was a long time since I'd moved anything as heavy, I usually only shifted cups or plates. I shook my head at him,

"I said, not to stand up too fast. Didn't do what you were told, did you?" I was a little alarmed to hear myself sounding just like Kitty, when she was credit-chasing, but maybe a bit of menacing was called for. "Now, let's try it one more time, shall we? Stand up. And don't move too fast, or you'll go over again. It's possible," I added helpfully, "You've got a bit of concussion. Dizzy? Headache?" I went into his head, but with care, the last time I'd attempted this in a difficult situation, the consequences had been rather dire. He sat up, measurably slower this time and immediately clasped hand to forehead and winced, I thought I'd probably done enough.

"Upsadaisy." I said encouragingly, "Slowly now, and keep those arms down, where I can see them." This time he followed instruction, I think his headache was giving him grief. "Now, there's a very unpleasant little knife in your pocket. Take it out," I instructed, "And don't even think of trying anything. Put it down on that desk." He gawped at me, reached into his pocket, extracted the knife and promptly flicked open the blade – honestly some people are just so unreliable. I heated the handle to red-hot, he yelped in agony and threw it down.

The three women, meanwhile, had retreated into Hilary's corner. I noted, Brenda and Kitty had a firm hold of each other, automatically forming a shield for Hilary – a promising sign, I thought, for future working relationships. Standing, our visitor towered over me, overworked biceps straining at a tight leather jacket. He was a bit lop-sided, on account of having to hold his head, where it was thumping unpleasantly, at the same time as flapping his rapidly blistering hand back and forth to try and cool it. He didn't smell too good, inside or out, a combination of leather, sweat, stale cigarettes and rancidly sour, anger and frustrated violence. He didn't know which of us in the room, he wanted to do the most damage to. I felt I needed to bring this to a conclusion, and the sooner the better.

"Right," I said, "Listen up. I'm going to hand you this money. You're going to take it." He shook his head, he really was a tryer.

"It's bloody short. She's not given you enough. Can't go back with just that."

"Oh, I think you can. If it's short, you make up the rest, you're not getting any more here. Bit of a tough guy huh? The one they call, when they want to put the frighteners on? Not going to sound good, if it comes out you were knocked silly by a few women. Don't want that getting around do you, might dry up the hard-man jobs a bit." He opened his mouth to offer me a few suggestions, as to exactly what I could do with myself. But then what I'd said, started to sink in – he wasn't the sharpest knife in the drawer, even if one of the most vicious, but I think he realised, he wasn't coming out of this smelling of roses.

"Take the money and go." I said sharply. "Before I change my mind and send you out with nothing." He put out a hand and snatched the cash.

"Bitch." He spat, with feeling. I turned my back on the others and moved in closer to him, so they couldn't hear.

"I know who you are," I said softly, "And I know who you work for. I can make a whole load of trouble for you, any damn time I choose and, trust me, it'll be trouble that hurts – a lot. I don't want to see your ugly mug within a mile of any of us, ever again. Are we absolutely clear?" He snarled sour breath into my face, and turned away, a touch of bravado returning, as he felt for the door handle.

"I want my knife." He said.

"I want a Rolls Royce," I responded, "We don't all get what we want."

"I'll remember you, you little cow." He said with bitterness.

"And I'll remember you." I said. "If I ever come across you again, headache'll be the least of your worries." And I gave him a thump to the temples, saw him recoil as it registered painfully.

"Out!" I jerked my head. He went, and I locked the door after him.

CHAPTER FOURTEEN

We tidied up the office, not saying much. I think we were all a bit tired by then. An hour or so later, Martin returned from the travel exhibition. He was given a tongue lashing by four angry women, jabbed sharply several times with a handy pair of knitting needles by one of them and was made to promise this would never, ever, happen again. He duly swore, he'd die before crossing the threshold of another betting shop and Brenda, took it upon herself, to assure him firmly, that this most definitely would be the case. I hoped to God he'd learnt his lesson.

Brenda and Kitty, pragmatists both, whilst shaken, viewed the whole thing as a job well done under the circumstances. They retired upstairs, for a recuperative nip from a bottle of sherry I hadn't even known Kitty kept in the filing cabinet. They all thought a bully boy, faced up to and outnumbered, had simply backed down, none of them had the remotest idea of the real depth and danger of what had been going on in the room, which was probably no bad thing.

For a week or two, there was somewhat of a strained atmosphere between us, upstairs and Martin and Hilary downstairs. I know they felt far more had been revealed than they'd have liked, and whilst they were both grateful for our intervention, they'd have preferred us to know a lot less about their personal affairs than we did. But after a while, things, as they usually do, settled down again and they were able to meet the eye of any of us, without looking awkward.

It also helped that we were all pretty busy work-wise, and Martin and I had come to a further mutually agreeable arrangement. With a small additional increase to my rent, he'd let me put up my Simple Solutions office sign, beneath his name, on our joint front door. Hilary was delighted at the thought of making us more permanent. She felt Martin was intimidated by the combined force of Brenda and Kitty, which provided an ongoing insurance against future straying towards the horses, on Martin's part. In this spirit, she'd gone out of her way, to make the new arrangement work well.

Without consulting Martin, who grumbled a fair bit about the cost when everything arrived, she ordered an impressively posh reception counter, with polished wooden frontage, on top of which she installed a small PBX phone system. She also purchased a tastefully, florally decorated, folding wooden screen. About four foot high, and standing behind the newly titled 'Reception Area', this partition meant travel agency customers could be directed into Hilary and Martin's main office, while our clients were graciously shown the stairs.

Hilary's use of her own initiative, had apparently quite gone to her head, and she'd taken on a junior assistant, Melanie, who, once persuaded the permanent chewing gum had to go, was happy to act as receptionist, operate the phones, usher people where they needed to be ushered and let us know when someone was on the way up. All in all, the whole operation was looking and feeling far more professional and a lot less like the hare-brained scheme it had, perhaps, first appeared.

By the time we reached our first business anniversary, which we toasted in with tea and fresh cream pastries, we had quite a respectable showing of clients to our name, and a regular ad appearing in several local papers. All of this, allowed Kitty to relax a little over our monthly takings, although she still insisted on regularly putting what she called, management accounts, on my desk. I could make neither head nor tail of these, relying rather on her facial expression, to judge how well or otherwise we were doing. Of course, it hadn't escaped my notice or hers, that she'd made herself pretty indispensable and we both knew, but didn't discuss, that the 'first going off' had turned into a 'whole lot longer'.

Brenda's office skills, as I'd been confident they would, had bounced back and been dusted off without too much trouble, and whilst I still looked after old favourites like Professor Lowbell, she was starting to acquire a few regular clients of her own. She and I were also still doing the out of office escorting tasks, picking up and taking people everywhere, from doctors to dentists to vets to airports, which left Kitty in sole, smug charge of our expanding administration, and that suited her just fine. She still insisted, that in the office we all stick to her 'professional' name, and whilst I fully appreciated the sense of that, it didn't roll off the tongue and I usually ended up addressing her as 'Ah... Miss Macnamarra' which made me sound a little on the vague side.

There were only the three of us in the office, but we'd accumulated a fair number of differently skilled contacts who could provide all sorts of additional outside services, as and when called upon. We knew where, when, and how, to lay our hands on useful individuals such as piano tuners, reliable decorators and ladies who were dab hands at turning up a hem. We were fierce in our criticism of any of our suppliers who didn't come up to scratch, and were establishing for ourselves, a growing reputation for reliably meeting a whole range of practical needs. One way and another, I felt, things weren't looking too shabby.

I hadn't laid eyes on Glory Isaacs for over six years, when she turned up in the Brent Street office one morning, while I was sorting out job schedules with Kitty and Brenda. I was both surprised and unsurprised. I suppose I'd always known our paths would cross again, although I wasn't thrilled. Glory always came accompanied by some sort of trouble.

CHAPTER FIFTEEN

Now in her early thirties, she looked not a day older than when I'd first spotted her, standing at the top of the staircase at Newcombe, her sightless eyes, sweeping the crowd of children gathered in the hall below. Her fashion taste hadn't changed much either. Today, wide-cut, black silk trousers, shimmered beneath a psychedelically swirled, scarlet and black, knee-length tunic, which left a retinal after-image if you looked too long. Whatever she wore though, never really took your attention from the supple grace of that slim figure, the glossy black, high-piled hair, milk-chocolate skin and the arrogance of a sculpted profile that wouldn't have been out of place on an ancient Egyptian frieze. No, she hadn't changed one jot.

Ed was with her, naturally, he'd driven. If the intervening years hadn't touched her looks, they'd done few favours for his. His six four frame had broadened, emphasising his disproportionately small, hairless head. His nose, broken at some stage in childhood and thereafter left to its own devices, had taken up position to the left of centre, below small, deep-set, light blue eyes. His face, pale as if untouched ever by sunlight was, as always, immobile. He had Moebius Syndrome, a paralysis of the facial muscles. Throughout his life, his tragedy had been he could read, all too clearly, even the unspoken reaction of others. But he wasn't expressionless, not if you looked into those eyes. He ducked his head briefly, in acknowledgement of my smile.

"We need," said Glory, sweeping busily past Brenda, who'd opened the office door to her sharp knock, "Your help with something."

"Sometimes, people say hello, how are you?" I observed mildly. I broke my own rules and reached out, unsurprised to slide off the smooth grey walls in Glory's head, same in Ed's, although in his, there always played a soothing background distraction, today it was something Sinatra. The staff were blinking, I wasn't sure whether at the vividness of Glory's outfit, or at just how much office space Ed took up. I briefly introduced them without further explanation, then nodded towards the inner office. Glory

57

walked ahead of me, her sureness of movement because she was using Ed's sight, and I shut the door on the open mouths of Kitty and Brenda.

Moving behind my desk, which I felt gave at least some illusion of authority, I indicated the couple of visitor chairs. Glory sat swiftly, Ed less so, he was always cautious about the security of furniture he didn't know. She predictably didn't waste time.

"We need your help Stella."

"No."

"You haven't heard what it's about yet."

"Trust me," I said, "The answer's no, whatever it is."

"It's important."

"Glory, you can't swan in again, after all this time, demanding my help. I've got other things going on. Anyway, after we got Sam out, you couldn't get shot of me fast enough, remember?"

"You wanted out."

"That's not the point. Anyway, I've moved on, things have happened."

"Yes, I know." And into my mind she shot, for just a second, a multi-coloured lollipop, "You helped get him, didn't you?" She said softly. I didn't answer. "And I know how much you didn't want to do it." She added. I hated it, that no matter how strong my shielding, she always found her way in.

"You'll know then," I said sharply, "Why I've absolutely no intention of getting involved in anything else like that, ever again."

"This is different."

"Not interested." I said. She continued as if I hadn't spoken,

"Look, I understand how you feel and why." I snorted disbelief,

"You clearly don't, or you'd have left by now."

"Stella, hear her out." Ed spoke so rarely, that when he did, people tended to listen, I raised an eyebrow at him and he looked back impassively.

"We really do need you." She repeated.

"You've said that. Why?" They exchanged a thought, faster than I could catch, and Ed nodded, which I took to mean, cards on the table.

"Look, this isn't anything dangerous," said Glory, "Nothing like last time. It's really more of a…"

"… situation," supplied Ed unexpectedly. He'd turned positively gabby, I chuckled and he shrugged,

"Isn't it?" He said to Glory, who nodded and added,

"It's a question of putting right a few things that aren't." She said.

"So who am I, Batman?" I said, although even as I spoke, I winced. Someone else had said that to me a long time ago, with the same biting sarcasm and I suddenly felt ashamed.

"Coffee?" I said, "Then you can tell me. I'll listen, but don't expect anything more."

In the intervening years, since I'd waved goodbye to them in Oxford, the Peacock sisters had, Glory told me, expanded their practice with considerable success. They offered their combination of educational therapy and counselling, to a wide age range, working as often with colleges and universities as they did with schools, as well as taking GP and Social Services referrals. Their reputation, as skilled and intuitive problem-solvers and solution-providers, for a whole range of learning difficulties and behavioural issues, had grown apace. So much so, that Glory now worked full time with them, getting involved on many of the cases, and restraining, as much as possible, the tendency of Ruth and Rachael never to say no to anyone. Ed provided all the practical assistance and back-up needed. With their assorted skill sets and abilities, the four of them made an unsurprisingly formidable, effective and sought-after team, and Ruth or Rachael were called upon with increasing frequency to appear as expert witnesses in custody and other cases.

"Sounds," I said, "As if you've got it all fairly sussed." Glory nodded,

"We have, more or less. It's frustrating at times and obviously we have to be careful, but we can, and do, make a difference."

"And you're still finding them?"

"Them?"

"Don't play daft. Others, like us,"

"Occasionally; as you know, we're few and far between."

"And when you do?"

"When we do, we help or not, as appropriate. There are still, always

will be, government backed projects on the lookout and we warn, where necessary, and when we think we'll be listened to. As I said, we're careful."
I nodded, what we were was always going to be problematic.

"And you're here now, why?"

"Let me show you, it's quicker." I hesitated, this was a path I hadn't been down for some time, not in fact since I was last with Glory and the Peacocks, and I really didn't want the intimacy of it.

"Oh, for God's sake Stella." Glory tutted – she had the patience levels of Vlad the Impaler – and she stretched across the desk for my reluctant hand. She didn't need to do that, she was perfectly capable of getting into my head, without any contact whatsoever, it just made what she was giving me, even more high definition.

CHAPTER SIXTEEN

Glory was seated, a few rows back from the front, in a room crowded with people, there were very few empty chairs. I knew Ed must be near, because she was using his sight. We were in a modern, hotel conference room. Garishly patterned orange carpet, tall, lavishly curtained windows running down the left side of the room, crimson upholstered, gilt chairs, divided by an aisle, facing a small raised platform with an as yet blank-paged flip-chart on an easel. The crowd surrounding us, were a mixed bag, not instantly categorisable, all ages and types, no obvious correlation. There was a tight, low-level hum of expectation, people talking softly and that distinct, before-the-curtain-goes-up, type of tension.

Then suddenly, the double doors at the rear of the room were thrown open, and a woman, unsmiling, stood framed there for a moment, before striding purposefully down the centre aisle. As she advanced, people craned to look and someone started to clap, so as she reached and stepped smoothly up on to the platform and swung on her heel to face us, it was to a rising round of enthusiastic applause. She wasn't tall, but her presence was such that she took control of the room instantly, raising a manicured hand for silence and looking around slowly, making eye contact with individuals, one after the other.

It was an overlong, albeit extremely effective pause – you could've heard a pin drop. Late thirties or early forties, high back-combed, blonde chignoned hair sprayed fiercely into place above professionally applied make up. She was in spike-thin stilettos and a wasp-waisted, black business suit, with a brief revere of crisp white shirt beneath. She looked like a rule-with-an-iron-rod executive. But when she finally smiled and said how much it meant to her, to be here with everyone today, it was in an unexpectedly high, sweet and breathy voice, with just the faintest trace of a lisp and an American twang. The crowd sighed, in recognition and welcome. I pulled my hand from Glory's,

"Come on," I said, "We haven't got all day, what exactly is this all about?"

"Don't be so impatient." she said, and whilst I was still formulating pot and kettle responses, she regained my hand. I sighed and let her.

The woman gestured to a young assistant, ready and waiting at the side of the platform. Dressed, like her, in black and white – trousers and a crisp shirt, he carried a large, square silver tray and flushed bright red, as he suddenly became centre of attention for a room-full of people. He began to pace slowly up the centre aisle between the chairs, turning at the top, to come back down again. As he passed them, people were reaching out, stretching anxiously over each other, as well as handing items along the line, so in a short space of time, the tray surface was more than full of a variety of small objects. At this point, he turned his back on those still with hands desperately out or up and carried the laden tray back to the front of the room, settling it carefully on a table next to the flip chart.

The woman nodded her thanks, waited till he'd stepped down again, then moved decisively to the flip chart. Taking up a felt-tip, like a teacher introducing herself to the class, she printed in firm capitals MARTHA VEVOVSKY, which elicited another excited burst of applause and she raised her hand for quiet again.

"Now," she said to laughter, "That's for any of you good folk who might not know my proper name." She seated herself on the chair next to the table, crossing shapely legs at the ankle and tucking them neatly to one side.

"My dear friends, shall we take one small, silent moment before we begin?" She bowed her head, as did the majority of the audience.

I knew who she was, she'd filled a whole host of column inches over the last couple of years and I'd also seen her doing the rounds of the talk shows, moving smoothly from Russell Harty to David Frost to Michael Parkinson, always distinctive, immediately recognisable, in her trademark black and white. Early on, a journalist, who'd done an in-depth interview for the Sunday Times Magazine, had coined the name Martha Vee. It had stuck, was certainly the name most people knew her by and was even used,

I now saw, on the cardboard stand loaded with glossy-jacketed books at the side of the platform. Glory squeezed my hand, re-focusing my attention.

Martha Vee raised her head slowly, looking out again over the crowd and, eyes still on them, reached to her right, moving a plump-fingered hand slowly back and forth over the silver tray. Because I was seeing and hearing Glory's memory, I had no real senses of my own, but even just looking at those faces closest to us, knew the atmosphere was palpably tense, as crimson-tipped fingers hovered. She was a showman, I'd give her that. I pulled my hand from Glory's again.

"OK, I know who she is," I said impatiently, "No need for all the dramatics. I know what she does, don't need to see the whole performance. What's all this got to do with me, or you for that matter?" Glory took a sip of, what was now probably lukewarm, coffee.

"She's bad."

"On the contrary," I said, "I think she's very good."

"No," said Glory, "I mean she's doing damage, a lot of damage. And she's enjoying it."

"And again, what's that to do with me. Is she like us?" Glory shook her head,

"No, not really, she's what we call a Tipper."

"Meaning?"

"She can push."

"For goodness sake, Glory," I said, "Hate it when you talk in riddles, just explain in plain English, can't you?"

"She can't read very much and she can't put thoughts into people's head that don't already exist. But she can catch something that's already there and embed it, endorse it, make it infinitely stronger and more powerful." I considered what she'd said, and came back with the logical question.

"Well, can't any of us do that?" Glory nodded,

"Of course we can, but when was the last time you did?"

"Don't think I've ever… " I said, then stopped as a memory came from nowhere – years ago, on holiday, in Bournemouth, walking along the front. My sister and I each had an ice-cream cornet with a flake in, I finished mine first and I wanted another one. "My father said no." I said aloud, then I paused, Glory raised an eyebrow, "And then I changed his mind and he said yes." I finished.

63

"Precisely." She said. "It's about power. I suspect we all do it, from time to time, without even realising it and if it's as harmless as an extra ice-cream, it's probably not so very dreadful and anyway, we don't have time to bat moral issues back and forth, right now. Just stop asking questions and let me finish telling you what we know." I sat back and nodded. Glory continued,

"She's British but spent time in America, in the late fifties, early sixties, hence the accent, which she plays up. In those days she was plain Mary Barns. She originally took herself to LA, to try and break into films, but spent far more time waitressing than auditioning. She was quick enough to realise she wasn't likely to make a fortune, let alone a living. She cut her losses, signed up as a dancer, with one of the last of the vaudeville shows, touring provincial theatres and state fairs. After a few months, she married a chap in the company. He was a moderately successful memory man, so she ditched the dancing shoes and joined him in the act.

Her married name was Vevovsky – bit more exotic than Barnes, and she persuaded the husband to change the act from memory stuff to mind reading. You know the sort of thing, the assistant collects objects from the audience and her blindfolded partner on stage correctly identifies even the most outlandish and unlikely items. They use codes of course, but when it's done well, it can be pretty impressive.

Then they started to re-shape things again, left the touring company and set up on their own. Only this time round, not as mind readers, but mediums – it was, they found, far more lucrative. And they swopped roles, Mary, who you can see, knows how to hold a stage, took the lead and Hank took over the assistant role.

They were pretty successful, even did a couple of TV appearances and were getting a fair bit of publicity. But then there was a scandal. Hank got himself involved with another medium on the circuit, and was planning to leave Mary. The whole thing was, of course, a godsend for the local media, two psychics in a head to head over a man – it was just crying out for Who Saw That Coming? headlines. Things didn't end well."

"What happened?" Against my will, I was drawn in. Glory always did spin a good tale.

"The other woman shot and killed Hank, then she killed herself."

"Ah."

"Indeed." Glory said. "And knowing what we now know, we suspect there was probably more to that than met the eye at the time! Anyway, for a while Mary played betrayed and devastated, and did pretty well, in publicity terms, on the back of it. Then she took the decision that there might well be richer pickings back home. Once here, she kept the Vevovsky, but changed Mary to Martha and began doing the rounds of Psychic Fairs." Glory's opinion of these, was evident in her sniff, "Healing crystals, numerology, tarot cards, pendulums, you know the sort of thing, all used to gull the gullible."

"Oh come on, isn't that a gross generalisation?" I protested. She laughed,

"You know I've never been afraid of a gross generalisation, and cynical's my middle name."

"You can't dismiss it out of hand."

"I don't," she said, "I've seen too much in my time to do that, but I do know what I'm seeing when I look at Martha Vee."

"And I still have no idea where all this is leading." I said.

"Well you would, if you'd just pipe down and listen. Mary, now Martha, has as I said, a small amount of psi ability – although not anywhere near as much as she likes to think she has – but she's built on that, enough to be able to do away with an assistant feeding her codes, because she's also an instinctive and astute interpreter of body language and responses. She's a born, bright, manipulator and over the last few years, she's gathered a sizeable fan base, many of whom follow her faithfully from venue to venue. She's built herself quite a reputation, she's earning a substantial living and she's discovered she can pull a whole lot of strings. She likes pulling strings."

"So do a lot of people," I pointed out, nastily. Glory let this sail over her head and continued,

"For whatever reason, she attracts an inordinate number of younger people, not the usual type who're drawn to this sort of thing, but she's become a bit of a cult figure. You know what it's like, one person gets involved and takes along a friend or two, and then a whole peer group gets drawn in. Since Martha's been on the scene though, we've started seeing some unpleasant patterns – spikes in suicide rates amongst young people – which is how Rachael and Ruth got involved. In many of the instances we've followed up, the original victim attended one or more of Martha's 'meetings'.

"Original victim?"

"Do you know anything about cluster suicides?" She asked, seemingly at a tangent. I shook my head. "Suicides, are notoriously difficult to chart and track, especially as some attempts, even the more serious ones, never get into any of the statistics, might not even get reported in the first place. Nevertheless, it's a fact, that multiple suicide occurrences – clusters – follow a disconcertingly similar pattern with the majority of victims under age 25." She paused, sipped coffee and resumed. "This age group's particularly vulnerable for any number of reasons; exam stress and expectation; bullying; mass hysteria; depression; low self-esteem; guilt for not spotting warning signs in a friend, you name it they're likely to be feeling it." She sighed, "There are any number of reasons and often a combination of several, none of which may have any kind of solid foundation."

"Still don't see." I said,

"We're certain, over the last few years, Martha Vee's been involved indirectly in more than one suicide, and something she does to these kids means they're more than ordinarily 'infectious' when it comes to others following suit. Anyway, we can theorise till the cows come home, theories don't save lives." She looked at me. "But you might be able to."

"No. Why won't you listen? I do not want to get involved."

"Hear me out, Stella. This is serious. She needs a spoke put well and truly in her wheel." As my tone had risen, hers had lowered to even more reasonable, "There's no real risk, not for you. All we want you to do is go along to a meeting."

"Real risk?" I said, "What does real mean? And, what's behind it all? If you're right, why on earth's she doing it?"

"Because she can. And because she enjoys it enormously."

"Oh great, she enjoys it? Well she's a pretty dangerous and unpleasant individual, isn't she? Sorry, I don't want to know, apart from which, what could I possibly do?"

"Frighten her off."

"Frighten her off?" I repeated. Glory sighed,

"Don't do that annoying echo thing again. We need to give her a short, sharp, unpleasant shock, one that just might put her off playing vicious games with people's heads for a while. If you can put the wind up her and save even one individual, hasn't that got to be worth a try?"

"Well, why can't one of you do it?" I asked. Glory shook her head,

"Much better if it's someone who can blend in, look ordinary, vulnerable and, most important, harmless."

"Thanks a bunch."

"At least think about it?"

"Look Glory, I'm sorry about what's going on, she sounds ghastly and I'm truly shocked and sorry if she's hurting people, but I'm not... " Ed interrupted me mid-flow.

"Excuse me Stella." He said politely, "Before you make a final decision, Rachael wanted me to ask you something. She wanted to know if you still have the strap?" I glared at him,

"Bloody hell, Ed!" I exclaimed, he looked back impassively. Yes indeed, I did still have, in a drawer at home, a small package, not looked at or touched for years. The wrapped object, in now, slightly yellowed tissue paper, was a small, broken leather strap such as might fit the thin wrist of a child. It was dark brown, scuffed leather on the outer side, with lighter brown staining on the inside – Sam's blood. It was the only thing I'd retained from the last time I'd become embroiled in a plan of the Peacock's. There were three words on a piece of paper, torn from a notebook and wrapped round the strap – 'Job Well Done' they said. I wondered if that inked message of Rachael's had faded in the intervening years. If the ink had, the memories hadn't. I sighed.

"What you want me to do?" I said.

CHAPTER SEVENTEEN

There was no question, the re-appearance in my life of Ed and Glory and, by default, the Peacock sisters, risked destabilising its smooth, onward progression, on which recently I'd been congratulating myself. I was determined, however, not to let it derail me. My priority was running and growing my business and I decided I'd look at this troublesome, Martha Vee situation, as just another job I was taking on. It wouldn't show up anywhere on Kitty's accounts, but the personal reward would be a comfortable conscience and hopefully, Glory off my back.

Following Ed shooting his mouth off, I'd somewhat ungraciously committed to go along to the next Meet Martha gathering the following Thursday which, it turned out, was at a hotel about ten miles away. I'd grumbled mightily about not being given more notice, ignoring Glory's sarcastic aside that in future, perhaps Martha might like to liaise with me, when setting her dates. Ed was going to pick me up from my office, drive me there and wait to take me home again. In the meantime, I put Martha Vee on the back-burner and re-focused on real life and a Laura Gold run.

Like Devlin and his family, Laura Gold and hers, had become regulars of ours. Her husband, recommended by another client, had made an appointment to come along and meet me at the office, one afternoon. He was looking, he said, for some assistance for his wife who'd recently lost her driving license, due to an unfortunate encounter with two traffic islands and a nearby parked car.

"Medication," he explained, "For migraine, you know, might have made her a little woozy, she's not really too clear exactly how it all happened. Anyway, no point crying over spilt milk, eh? Nobody hurt, just a little shaken and when push comes to shove, a car's only a piece of metal isn't it?

Most of the time I can drive her wherever she needs to go, or our son does, but on the occasions we can't... thought maybe you'd be able to step in, that is the sort of thing you do, right?"

Melvyn Gold had an extremely distinctive voice, toffee mellow and smoothly soothing. It made you feel he could competently deal with anything life might chuck his way although, as subsequently came to light, this was as far from true as it was possible to be. Only in his late fifties and tall, he walked with a one-sided stoop, due to the opposing forces of a chronic back condition and a burgeoning paunch. He bore an air of permanent weariness, and looked as if a good nap and a dust-down wouldn't go amiss, an impression endorsed by repetitive sliding of black-framed, square glasses, up and onto his forehead, so he could massage watery blue eyes with thumb and fourth finger. This was always worrying, because he invariably had a lit cigarette in the same hand. He didn't seem to have done himself any damage to date, but I cringed every time he did it, and was aware, we could be hitting the road to Moorfields Eye Hospital at any time.

Laura Gold wasn't hard to deal with, though she leant towards the unpredictable. An elegant opposite of her husband, she was small, slim and always impeccably dressed. Brenda didn't take to her, 'All fur coat and no knickers, that one.' she said, dismissively. She was a woman on a permanent, unnecessary diet and consequently, anchored to this earth, only by an inordinate amount of chunkily expensive jewellery and a heavy perfume. For the majority of the time she was detached and aloof, perfectly coiffed, blonde-highlighted head slightly angled, as if avoiding a faintly unpleasant odour, beneath her finely arched nostrils. However, under any kind of stress – of which there appeared to be an inordinate amount in her life – she'd delve into her handbag for one of her 'migraine pills'. Whether in fact, they were or weren't anything to do with migraine, I never established, but their effect was disconcertingly swift. She'd defrost faster than our fridge, and was given to reaching for your hand, resting her head heavily on your shoulder and murmuring how very, very fond of you she was. This was awkward at the best of times, more so when driving.

On this particular occasion I was picking her up for a 2.00 Harley Street dentist appointment, waiting for the duration of her treatment, and bringing her home again. Mr Gold, when booking, had asked if I'd be kind enough to make sure I actually took her into the house when I brought her home. She was, he said, a nervous patient, and often had a bad reaction to any sort of medical treatment. This proved something of an understatement.

Our outing was complicated from the off. She tottered down the garden path, fell into the passenger seat, grabbed my hand in a vice-like grip and informed me I was a truly, truly wonderful person and she was beyond grateful, to have me in her life. I sighed, it would appear the pills had come into play early. But a paying client's, a paying client and as she wouldn't let go my hand, we both put the car in gear and headed for Harley Street. She wasn't in a brilliant condition when she went into the surgery. Even less so, when she emerged, some forty minutes later, supported by the dentist and a nurse.

The former, propping her against his side, while the nurse and I wrestled her into her coat, said he was extremely surprised she was having this strong a reaction to what had only been a local anaesthetic. I wasn't. I could see he'd completely missed the moment, whilst his back was turned, when she'd knocked back a helping of migraine pills, swigging them swiftly down with that pink rinsing-out stuff, so conveniently to hand. Could I manage to get her home safely, he asked with some concern, or should we wait until she was more herself? As I wasn't quite sure how many pills, the wretched woman had hoovered up before she left home, let alone whilst in the chair, I'd no conception of when that might be. So I said I was sure we'd be fine. I unwound her arm from round his neck, wound it round mine, and we staggered, in some disarray, down the stone steps, to where I'd mercifully secured a parking spot right outside the consulting rooms.

Thanks to her on-going diet, and my floating her, an inch or so, above the pavement, which I didn't think anyone would notice, I was able to load Laura safely, if unceremoniously into the back seat. This was an operation hindered by having to keep stopping and hugging her back, assuring her she was every bit as important to me, as I was to her. Extracting her at the other end was far simpler, because there weren't other people around and I just floated her gently, giggling – her, not me – up the garden path, securing her with one hand while I found the key in her bag, unlocked the front door and got her inside.

I planted her firmly on a chair in the hall, thinking maybe a coffee might counteract what she'd taken, at which point I could leave with a clear conscience. This was the first time I'd been in the house, I usually just collected or dropped her off. With a quick glance, to make sure she wasn't going to slide off the chair and break her neck, I headed for the kettle, just as a man in a black balaclava, carrying a vicious looking claw-headed hammer, emerged from the living room. Laura looked up and screamed. I reacted instinctively, backing up to hang on to her and knocking him down, he landed heavily, half on his side. The hammer slid, at speed, across the parquet flooring.

"Don't move," I said, as much to Laura as to the chap on the floor, "I'm calling the police." and I reached for the phone on the hall table.

"I wouldn't do that." Disregarding instruction, he was sitting up gingerly, rubbing his arm. He reached up to remove the balaclava and Laura shrieked again,

"Darling?"

"Well, who did you think it was?" He was a little terse.

"You didn't say you were coming over."

"I did. You wanted that picture hanging. I said I'd pop in during the week to do it."

"Well, you gave me the most terrible shock." Laura looked a little shame-faced, as well she might, although she did have a point.

"Mask and hammer." I pointed out, "Not a good look." And because I felt I hadn't got off to a good start, with what now appeared to be the client's nearest and dearest, held out my hand politely. Obviously he'd been brought up well enough to be unable to ignore that, though I was pretty certain he was bearing a grudge.

"Stella." I said. Now, with the mask off, I could see the resemblance, and there was no mistaking the voice that was so much like his father's.

"David. How the hell did you do that?"

"What?"

"Knock me down."

"Judo." I said briefly, "Black belt. Sorry." He gave me a sideways look. I couldn't easily read him. It wasn't a tightness of mind like Dorothy Lowbell's, nor a deliberate blocking, just an introversion of thought. I knew if I went in properly, I'd be able to, but goodness knows, the situation was uncomfortable enough, probably best not to know what he was thinking. Further attack might be the best form of defence. After all, the whole unfortunate incident was his fault.

"Do you normally wear a mask indoors?" I said.

"Only when I'm not expecting visitors." He said, then maybe because he felt that was a little heavy on the sarcasm, added, "Hate getting plaster dust in my mouth and these walls are dreadful." There was a slightly awkward pause before he said,

"Right then. Well, thanks for dealing with things this morning, she hates the dentist." We both looked at Laura, who was still on the chair, but only just.

"Spotted that." I said.

"I'll keep an eye on her now. Do I pay you?"

"No, your father has a monthly account."

"Right." He opened the front door and I beat, what even I had to admit, was a somewhat hasty retreat. Some jobs go well, others with not quite the same smooth professionalism as one might wish.

CHAPTER EIGHTEEN

Ed was as good as his word. When I left the office at 6.00, on that Thursday evening, he was waiting. I'd dressed as Glory suggested, jeans, jumper, flat shoes and a duffel coat. Unobtrusive, she'd said.

I didn't spot him until a horn hooted gently, and he nodded at me, from the driving seat of a black van, high sided and glossy, parked on the opposite side of the road. As I crossed, the nearside back passenger door swung wide. Climbing up and in, not without some effort, it was indeed high. I inhaled that unmistakeably delightful, new vehicle smell. The Peacocks never stinted on expenses, they didn't have to with an income nurtured, in a totally ethical way, Ruth had always assured me, by natural abilities. What she meant was, she spent a fair amount of time in the City, specifically in restaurants and bars, flush with stockbrokers and bankers, where she picked up far more in tips than the waiters ever did. Couldn't that be considered, I'd asked at the time, insider dealing, and therefore illegal? Ruth had frowned crossly and said most certainly not – if people couldn't keep confidential information confidential, then that really wasn't her fault was it?

Glory was in the front passenger seat. I hadn't expected her to be there, neither was I prepared for the sharp, cool peppermint sensation that washed over me as the door swung shut with a well-mannered click. Rachael Peacock swept into my head, as always, without so much as a by-your-leave and tutted.

"Your shielding has become shoddy, Stella." She said aloud, from the seat next to me. Despite myself, I grinned, her approach certainly cut down on time wasted on catch-ups and pleasantries.

"Works well enough for me." I said. "And hello to you too." Rachael, as she so often did, ignored what she didn't think worth answering.

"Right Ed," she said, "Let's go, we'll talk on the way. I don't want her to be late." Ed drew away smoothly from the kerb. Heavy breathing and a van-swaying thump from behind me, indicated the presence of Hamlet, the Peacock's Great Dane cross, a dog whose assistance I'd once had cause to be exceedingly grateful for – though I couldn't see why it was necessary to bring him along on this trip.

"Because he can be a brilliant and highly useful distraction, when we need him to be." Said Rachael. "In any case, he loathes being left for the whole evening." I tightened my jaw. This was taking me back to times past, and not in a good way. I'd forgotten how quickly the wretched woman got under my skin, when she got into my head. I pulled my internal shutters down more tightly. It probably wouldn't keep her out, but might let her know how unwelcome was the intrusion. Should have known better.

"Don't be silly," She said, "We haven't time for shilly-shallying. We need to get on top of this situation as quickly as we can. This woman you're going to see, is not a nice piece of work."

"I still don't know," I said, turning sideways to look at her. "Exactly what it is you want me to do when I get there." Like Glory, Rachael hadn't changed that much in the intervening years. Her uncompromisingly grey hair was maybe worn a little longer than I remembered, but still brushed firmly back from the widow-peaked, high foreheaded angularity of her face, and in the shadows of the car I could see she hadn't swerved far from her usual choice of grey skirt and white shirt.

"There's reason for you not knowing more." She said. I waited, to see if there was going to be further enlightenment, it seemed there wasn't.

"I really could do with a bit more info as to what you want me to do exactly" I said. Glory twisted a little in her seat to face me, large gold hoop earrings glinting, even in the dimness of the van's interior.

"We want her to spot you." She said. "We want you to make yourself a target and make yourself such a tempting one, she won't be able to help fixing on you and in that way, she won't do damage to anyone else."

"Hang on." I wasn't thrilled with the target word. "What happened to the no real risk, you mentioned?"

"There is no real risk, but even if there were, that's why we're here, we'll be near enough to keep track of what's going on. Any trouble, we'll be there to help. But you're perfectly well able to handle things on your own. Right Rachael?"

"Correct."

"You still haven't given me much." I grumbled.

"Deliberately." Rachel said. "Better you form your own impressions, means your reactions will be all the more responsive. We want you to put the wind, well and truly up her, so she'll think twice about doing what she's doing. And remember, if you're taking her attention, she won't be a threat to anyone else." I reflected on this, I wasn't too keen on the threat word either.

"Where's Ruth?" I asked. There was a slight pause, before Rachael said briefly.

"At the Oxford cottage. She's been a bit under the weather." I could see that wasn't the whole story, but not beyond that.

"Is that anything to do with this, with this Martha woman?"

"No, of course not." said Rachael. She was telling the truth, although maybe not all of it. I couldn't help but think, the sooner I got all this over with and could go back to normal, the better. Another thought occurred to me,

"Why does she hold these meetings in hotels?" I asked, "Aren't these sort of things usually done in churches or community halls?"

"Not the way this lady works," said Glory. "She's got herself a successful business that's lucrative and growing. She's achieved that, by making herself different. The venue costs are expensive, but easily covered by ticket takings – it's a numbers game, and she pulls those in consistently. She also sells her books and a lot of other stuff, I told you, she's a great marketer. But the real icing on the cake, is what happens after the public meetings, when people are so impressed, they're clamouring for private readings – that's where she makes the real money. The business side of things is a smoothly run operation. The other stuff we told you about – well, you might call that more of a hobby."

"If all goes well this evening, and you do what we hope you can," said Rachael, "You might not even need to go back."

"Go back? Nobody said anything about going back."

"Well, let's just see how things go, shall we. And for goodness sake, Stella, keep it low-key, the last thing we want is a fuss. We want her scared off, that's all, but we want it done in such a way, that nobody else notices what's happening."

"I think, what you're forgetting." I said, "Is that I'm not sixteen any more. I'll decide what I might do, based on what happens, I won't just go in and follow instructions. Clear?"

"Crystal." Murmured Rachael. I ignored the sarcasm and settled back in my seat, satisfied I'd had my say. I knew, from past experience, there was little point in pushing for more than they were prepared to tell me. Truth be told, as streetlamps flew swiftly past the window, and the van smoothly ate the miles, there was, within it, that blissfully intense silence I remembered so clearly from when I was last with them. Their ultra-efficient blanking of their thoughts, created a comfortable blanket for me too. I liked that. I didn't want them to know how much, but of course, they probably did.

CHAPTER NINETEEN

The sizeable crowd, heading into the hotel for the meeting that evening, was a mixed lot. As Glory had said, a surprising proportion of younger people, but also a lot of professionally suited types, men and women who looked as if they'd headed here, straight from the office. Bridging these two sections were small groups of enthusiastic, carefully-dressed, middle-aged ladies and I was intrigued to see how many of them, fan-like, had adopted the black and white Martha theme. There was an undeniable buzz – excitement, twinned with nervous trepidation, an almost religiously fervent enthusiasm and the stomach-tightening anticipation that goes with any kind of performance.

Ed had navigated slowly up the winding hotel drive, the route minimally lit by intermittent globes, fixed to the trunks of some of the trees along the way. A golf course and wooded areas on either side of the drive were untroubled by our headlights. He hadn't uttered a word, the entire journey, but now muttered, that once past the main hotel entrance, there was an additional service road, utilised by delivery trucks during the day. It ran from the side of the hotel and back down to the main road, winding round a large lake in the grounds. It was along here, he planned to park and wait – the meeting was scheduled to start at 7.30 and finish at 9.00 – before picking me up again. It seemed a bit daft to me, that they'd want to hang around in the van for that long, but if that's what they'd decided, I knew the uselessness of questions.

Meet Martha was impressively and efficiently organised. Prominent, in the middle of the marble-tiled, log-fired foyer of the hotel, was an alarmingly, larger than life, cardboard cut-out of the woman herself. She wore her trademark black and white, plus an enigmatic smile and one cardboard arm was helpfully outstretched, indicating which direction we should take to the meeting.

Planted next to the rather startling, cardboard Martha, and looking almost as smart, although somewhat less welcoming, was a solid, dinner-jacketed individual, nearly as broad as he was tall. He was checking tickets carefully and, despite the outfit, looked slightly intimidating and singularly out of place in the luxurious setting. I assumed he was there to guarantee no unsavoury elements infiltrated. I did my level best to look as non-unsavoury as possible, showed my ticket, was waved forward and followed others along a dark-wood, panelled corridor, politely careful not to tread on each other's heels, as we moved into a comfortably fire-lit, library area.

Here, from behind a table, two flushed-with-importance, middle aged ladies, in black T shirts, white lettered 'Martha Vee Sees!' across their bosoms, were doing brisk business with pre-signed, £20 books from a glossy, rapidly diminishing pile. These were being handed, to over-excited purchasers, in smart black and white canvas bags, emblazoned with yet another Martha picture, the woman was certainly no shrinking violet. I stepped round the book queue to where, at the far end of the library, tea and coffee were being served – unlike the books, these were with Martha's compliments. Out of interest, I tried to do a swift assessment in my head, of the number of people I could see, multiplied by ticket prices, added to book sales, but not being Kitty, failed miserably and gave up. However, I didn't need totals to see it mounting up nicely.

As the now truly hyped and buzzing crowd began to shuffle onwards from the refreshment area, there was another cardboard Martha on standby, rigid arm again, indisputably indicating our route down a further corridor to a sizeable, double-doored conference room. Chairs grouped to the right and left of a central aisle faced a small raised stage with flip-chart and side-table, very much as Glory had shown me previously. To the right of these, was yet another cut-out – she must have gone for a job lot – but there was no denying they were astonishingly effective, a ubiquitous presence, before we'd even clapped eyes on the real thing.

I found myself a chair at the end of a row, not too far from the front. Whilst there were a fair number of others like me, on their own, many people had come in couples or groups and the conversational hum rose busily, fell and surged again, against a background of soft harp music, as seats were found and belongings stowed. Lavishly large, fresh flower displays, were pedestalled at intervals along both sides of the room, the scent heady, heightening as the crowd grew and the temperature rose.

With rows filling up, people were having to look harder for seats. I caught the eye of a frazzled- looking woman, marooned in the centre aisle, she raised her eyebrows and pointed, were the seats next to me taken? I shook my head and smiled, holding up two fingers (in a polite way). She promptly grabbed the hand of the teenager with her, pulling her along and excusing themselves as they edged clumsily past already-seated others. She flopped down heavily with a sigh of relief, giving off a hefty waft of Estee Lauder Youth Dew, which blended, in a slightly sickly way, with the scent of the lilies in a vase on my other side.

"Phew." she said, "Starting to think, we'd have to sit separately. You OK Frank?" She turned to the girl, black-clad, nose-ringed, sulking and determinedly silent, someone who obviously would have preferred to be anywhere in the world but here.

"Your first time at one of these?" inquired new neighbour, battling out of her fur trimmed coat, within the narrow confines of the seating. "Frankie's too." She extracted a tissue from her bag, gave her nose a ladylike swipe and leaning in, confided, "Heck of a job persuading her. Thought it might take her out of herself." On her other side, Frankie rolled her eyes, the way only a teenager can.

"God's sake, give it a rest Mum." She muttered, pulling already over-stretched jumper sleeves, further down over her hands and slumping even lower in her seat – she was going to do her coccyx no good at all.

As lights dimmed, the sense of expectation soared. There was a theatrical pause, before the double doors at the end of the room swung open, and then a communal indrawn breath as the lady herself moved, swift and serious down the centre of the auditorium glancing neither to right nor left, and the applause started. She didn't look up, until she'd climbed the three shallow steps to the stage and was standing above the audience.

Then she raised her head slowly, turning it from one side of the room to the other, meeting the eyes of individuals for a thoughtful second or so, before moving on. She kept this up for just that bit disconcertingly longer, than might have been expected. Then she turned to the flipchart, to do the name introduction thing. She gained the identical laugh. That laugh was key. Once people laugh together, they stop being individuals, strangers and start to become a tribe, for the duration of whatever it is they're involved in. This woman knew what she was doing, when it came to handling an audience.

On this occasion the assistant with the silver tray, was a woman, otherwise the routine was the same, as was the urgency of those desperate to get their objects on board. During the collection, Martha remained standing, silent and serious and such was her presence and hold on the room, everyone waited silently with her. Even when the assistant turned back with a full tray, the sigh of disappointment was politely low key and accepting.

Only then, belatedly, when I was on the spot, did it occur to me that there were a number of other things I really should have insisted on knowing, whether Rachael and Glory wanted to share or not. It was all very well, them wanting my reactions to be natural, but forewarned is forearmed and I really didn't know at all, what to expect from this evening. I reached out cautiously, I knew what was surrounding me would be pretty deafening, and indeed it was. A fully fledged flood of stories, situations, sorrows, angers, hopes and fears. I pulled back.

On stage, Martha was now seated, ankles neatly crossed. In her accented, little-girl voice, she did the 'One small silent moment' request. Everyone stilled and obligingly bowed heads, while I took the opportunity to study her. I didn't want to draw her attention yet, but I immediately identified her mind amongst all the others, she was cloyingly and overwhelmingly pink, the sort of sea-side-rock sweetness that you know, deep down in your soul and beyond a shadow of a doubt, will do you no favours in the long run.

As the moment ended, she breathed slowly out, then deeply in again, before gesturing towards the tray. She was, she said, going to see which best beloved items called to her, but she had one teeny tiny ask. Would the owner of any object she picked, please remain silent and give no sign, until she 'found' them, as distraction could immediately break any chain of communication she might be receiving from the other side. It would also, I thought cynically, create far more of a dramatic impact. The audience nodded as one, with the exception of Frankie, who seemed to have tuned out of proceedings altogether, and was doing severe damage to a cuticle. Her mother nudged me gently in the ribs,

"Amazing isn't she?" she said, I nodded, assuming she meant Martha, not Frankie. On the stage, Martha's hand was hovering. She dipped, touched, moved on, finally picking up an old-fashioned, ornately jewelled, tortoiseshell hair comb, holding it high above her head so all could see. Silent, he may have remained, as requested, but there was no mistaking the sharp mental yell and physical reaction of an older man, flushing with excitement, near the back of the audience, on the opposite side of the room. Martha gave no immediate indication she knew who and where he was, but closed her eyes, tilting her head gently to one side as if listening. As was I. In just a few seconds, I knew more about the comb and the woman who'd used it to hold her thinning hair in place, than I really wanted to. But I was more interested in seeing what Martha knew. She was able to read just enough, to know he was thinking of his wife. But that was all she needed. She opened her eyes, caught and held his and nodded.

"Sir, yes, the gentleman in the brown jacket, red tie. I believe this comb belongs to you now, is that correct?" Less a question than a statement, as another assistant hastened down the aisle, to pass a microphone down the line. Whilst she wasn't able to read a lot, I saw how she was gathering information with every subsequent, brief clever question. It was an exercise in manipulation, simply contrived, disproportionately powerful in result. Within a few moments she'd gained all she needed.

The truth was, this chap hadn't come on any mission of tenderness, but in frustration and fury. When he and his wife divorced, ten years prior to her death, she'd received a far larger settlement than had been expected. He blamed his solicitor, it shouldn't have happened that way, not with the eye-watering fees he'd had to cough up. But before he knew what was what, it was all signed, sealed and remained only to be delivered.

They'd been childless, and they themselves were both only children, so there was no family, other than the odd cousin or two on either side, and they'd never been great ones for socialising and making friends. Thus, they'd both, post-divorce, found themselves far lonelier than either had ever anticipated, possibly just as dissatisfied unmarried as not. Over the years they'd drifted back together again; shared meals out, cinema, she'd even had him over to her small flat for a couple of Christmases. There'd been some talk of them making it official again, and he could have done with that. They still got on each other's nerves, true, but at the end of the day, someone getting on your nerves was better than not talking to another person, from one week to another.

He knew he'd been stupidly spendthrift with his part of the house money, blown most of it in those first heady days. She'd intimated, she'd been exactly the opposite. Saved it, spent carefully, and still had most of it, for a rainy day. And then she upped and had a massive heart attack, always one for the dramatic gesture. He was in her will, but the money wasn't. She had that big, fat, lump sum, put somewhere, he was certain of it, and if ever there was a rainy day it was bloody now, but he'd been through every bit of her paperwork and there wasn't a clue.

"Is there a message?" He wanted to know, and you didn't have to be psychic, to pick up his desperation. "Anything, anything at all, she wants you to tell me?" Martha raised her hand for silence, listened again, nodded once or twice, opened her eyes and smiled warmly at him.

"Indeed, your wife wants you to know, she's at peace now and you're not to worry at all about her, she's in a better and happier place. She wants me to say, although it may not be for a while, she knows you'll be together again." From the apoplectic expression on the face of the bereaved, this looked like it might happen sooner rather than later, but there was little for him to do other than nod. In his agitation, he'd risen, he now sat down again, and found himself patted warmly on the arms by those on either side, thrilled to be so close to one who'd been contacted. 'Wasn't Martha, quite something?' asked a large lady, looming over his shoulder, from the row behind. He nodded, 'Indeed,' he agreed, 'Martha was very definitely something.' Quite what he thought that something was, is really rather unprintable.

CHAPTER TWENTY

Martha Vee continued with the object picking for a while, sometimes hovering over an item for a hope-inducing few seconds, before moving on to pick another instead. There were a lot of indrawn breaths, raised hopes and fears, as she did. I was shocked by the palpable combination of anticipation, apprehension and tension, she was generating. Each item she picked; a plain gold wedding ring; a battered brown wallet; the grubby pink child's glove; a key-ring bearing one sadly solitary key, held a wealth of meaning for the individual who'd placed it. Nobody here was playing, the emotions were deep and heartfelt and, as far as I could tell, there was no evidence of cynicism from anybody – other than me. They were here, because they desperately wanted to believe in what Martha was offering. Unlike Glory, I was perfectly prepared to be convinced, with the proper proof, that there were those whose intentions and even abilities were genuine, but of one thing I was certain – Martha wasn't one of them.

Most of us are dreadful at controlling our physical reactions, be it so little as a shifting in the seat, an indrawn breath, or the involuntary movement of a hand, we can't help but give ourselves away. Every time she held something up, Martha was able to unerringly zone in on the person who'd placed it, because it was impossible for them to remain impassive. Indeed, by repeatedly asking them to do that, she secured, just the opposite, making them excruciatingly aware of the need to not react and therefore, all the more likely to. Of course, in a crowd, reaction from one person, however fractional, cannot help but be felt by those sitting nearest, who in turn respond, often without even realising. The overall effect is like seeing ripples move outward, from a pebble dropped in a pool. It's unmistakeable and from the stage, with its overview of the crowd, it was a doddle. As it was, every new accuracy was greeted with audible gasps from a thrilled audience, she'd had in the palm of her hand from the off. There was no doubt, just how clever was her performance which, as far as everyone was concerned, could have no other possible explanation than the supernatural.

All in all, the Martha and Martha show was a slick, smoothly run, highly professional operation although, as far as I could see, the messages she was giving out were pretty banal. And whilst most recipients (with the exception of the first dissatisfied customer), appeared thrilled right down to their socks, at being told nothing in particular, none of it, so far, seemed to be the type of thing that could cause anybody harm or distress. Quite frankly, if this was how people chose to spend their money, and how she chose to earn hers, I couldn't see it was anything for Rachael and Glory to get their knickers in a twist over and certainly didn't see why they'd had to haul me in. I was getting thoroughly bored, and could feel the creepings of a dull head-thump, starting at my temples and throbbing towards the base of my neck – the inevitable consequence of opening up against such a busy background. What with Youth Dew on one side, the cloyingly sweet lilies on the other and sugary pink, Martha on the stage, it felt like I was sinking into a marshmallow. This whole thing was a fool's errand and I made up my mind that, if fate was kind, and there was an interval, I'd slip out then, head back to the van and let them know exactly what I thought of this whole waste of time. I pulled my attention back to the stage, to see Martha had moved away from the tray. She was standing again now, hands clasped loosely, below her waist.

"My dear, dearest friends," she said. "And I feel I may call you that, because I see so many familiar faces here tonight. I thank you from the bottom of my heart for joining me yet again and for lending me your strength. I want you to know, your contribution to each meeting is unique and entirely precious." Not to mention, I added to myself, extremely lucrative.

"Utilising keepsakes," she continued, "Objects that are, or have been, dear to you and yours, is incredibly powerful and presents me with strong links to spirit, but I do know there are many more of you who have nothing to bring, other than your own emotions. My dears, release those fears and indecisions now and, if I am so directed, I will endeavour to provide you with direction and comfort." The atmosphere in the room had changed subtly again, partly due to some clever, if unobtrusive, stage management. The lights had been taken down and softened to a warmer more intimate tint, whilst the background harp music was gradually turned up a notch or two. It was all very simple, but highly effective – very clever.

Somewhere in the audience, a woman had begun to quietly sob. She was a plant, one of the women who'd been selling books in the foyer, fairly unrecognisable now, with tee shirt replaced by lavender twinset and pearls. Her soft sobbing, on cue, set off several other women in the charged and changed atmosphere. Of course it did. Others laugh, we laugh, others cry and give our own griefs, permission to surface. Martha was speaking again, higher, breathier, more urgent, pacing slowly, first one way then the other, across the small stage, arms outstretched to all of us.

"My friends, what is it that's troubling you, causing you pain? What is it you most fear? What is it that's colouring your life black? How may I and those who work through me, help you? Will you let us in?" The atmosphere intensified and altered yet again, owing nothing this time to cleverly lowered lighting or louder music, it was that word she'd planted – fear. At one end of the scale, it encompassed the universals; health, finance, relationships, the future, but there were a lot of people in that room, sending out far sharper, more specific emotional spikes, painful to hear. Martha was speaking again a sing-song cadence.

"There's a young lady here, whose distress and pain I'm feeling, so strongly." She pointed suddenly, "Yes, you, my dear child." She was indicating a row, about three back from the stage, and an assistant was instantly there with a microphone, passed, hand to hand to a now ashen-faced girl.

The girl was young, nineteen or twenty, clutching a tie-die material shoulder bag defensively in front of her and looking like a rabbit caught in the headlights, as indeed she might, with around 300 people craning to catch sight of her. I could feel what was emanating from her, as could the woman on the stage. I also felt the thump and shock of the sea change in Martha. What she'd been doing, up until this point, was a highly professional job; increasing her income; nurturing her reputation; gaining fans; giving them their money's worth; a demonstration they'd remember, long after the evening ended. Now it felt completely different, much more personal, her full attention was engaged, she was enjoying this far more. Too much more. The girl in the third row had the mic in her hand now, it was mercilessly amplifying and broadcasting the sound of her rapid, hitched breathing. Martha moved to a point on the stage so they were directly opposite each other.

"Take your time honey," she'd dropped her voice to a more normal speaking tone, although her own mic ensured everything she said, reached everyone in the room. "There's not a single one of us here, who isn't with you, we're all giving you our strength and our support in a time of obvious distress. Isn't that right, my friends?" A firm murmur of assent passed through the audience, and someone in another part of the room called out,

"God bless you!" We were all waiting for the girl to speak, but before she could, the woman on the stage had closed her own eyes, swaying a little with fingertips of one hand to her temple, massaging gently.

"It was a watery death, wasn't it?" Martha asked softly. I wouldn't have thought it possible for the girl to turn any paler, but waxen now, she nodded silently, unconsciously moving her own head fractionally, in time with the rhythmic movements of the woman on the stage. "I'm not sure of her name, my dear, there's so much distress and confusion." Martha now had both set of fingers to the sides of her head, "Help me my dear, can you help me?" The girl, fat tears sliding unhindered, licked her lips then leaned them onto the mic.

"Elizabeth… Lizzie, we always called her Lizzie."

"Ah, yes, yes, indeed, that's what she's trying to tell me, she's Lizzie. My dear, your friend Lizzie is here with us." She opened her eyes for a moment to look directly at the girl,

"Your name?"

"Diane."

"Yes, of course, Diane, I wasn't sure whether she was telling me Diane or Diana. My connection isn't strong, there's too much sadness, so much terrible fear. Diane can you help me just a little? What happened to Lizzie? How did she pass?"

"She… she drowned."

"Yes my dear, I know that and I'm seeing blue, a lot of blue water. The sea?" The girl shook her head, the movement magnified and underlined by the brushing of her lips against the microphone.

"It's blue, because she was under the cover." She said. I could see exactly what she meant. A swimming pool in the garden of a family home. Winter. A jaunty, bright blue tarpaulin, wind-rippled, fastened with hooks clipped into concrete-set iron rings, at intervals around the rectangular pool. Lizzie would have had to unfasten at least two of those hooks, to enable her to slip under the cover and lower herself into the painfully freezing water. Once in, she would have had no chance for second thought – numbed by misery and cold, brain blurred by vodka and the unliveable-with despair of a boyfriend's betrayal.

"Diane," Martha was more urgent now, her face flushed, "Lizzie's calling out to you, can you hear her?"

"Yes, well… not sure… maybe."

"Diane, she's telling you she's so very sorry. She wants me to tell you how sorry she is."

"No, no!" Diane, had risen from her chair, "God, no, it's me who's sorry. It's my fault. Don't you understand, I didn't listen to her, didn't believe her. It's me, it was my fault." I could feel the weight of the massive guilt this poor girl was hauling around with her. She hadn't listened. Had been tied up with so many of her own concerns. And Lizzie, a friend yes, but one with so many needs. Always a crisis of one kind or another, that's just how it was with Lizzie, how it'd always been. Best friends through school, less so later on, even though at the same university. It had been both a great revelation and a huge relief for Diane, to discover that not all friends required such hand or head holding. They still saw each other, of course they did, you can't break ties just like that, though they both knew it wasn't quite the same. But Lizzie had told her, had called and told her. Brian had finished with her, started seeing someone else, indeed had been seeing the someone else while she and he were still together, and she just couldn't and wouldn't bear it.

Diane had said all the right things, naturally she had, she was still very fond of Lizzie. So she'd said, far better to find out now rather than later and lots of other fish in the sea and Lizzie deserved far better. But she knew full well, although she hoped Lizzie didn't, she hadn't been really and truly, emotionally engaged. To be brutally honest, she'd heard it all before through the years, all the 'I can't go ons' and the 'Really don't know what I might do nexts'. But then she hadn't even known that Lizzie had gone missing, nobody did, until her parents returned from a cruise. They'd found Lizzie quickly, but by then she'd been in the water, under the blue, for going on two weeks.

Martha had picked up instantly and easily on Diane's intense emotion, had caught brief flashes of the image constantly in her head – white reaching arms, death-dulled gaze, hair swaying with the rhythm of the wind and water. The rest was all pertinently clever questioning and guesswork, information that was just waiting to come flooding out. But that didn't diminish, one jot, the effect this was having on Diane, not to mention everyone else. The atmosphere was electric and I'm sure I wasn't the only one with a shiver up my spine, as the story was drawn out, although my shiver was because I could see what Martha was doing, which the rapt rest couldn't. She was drawing in, all the emotion Diane was giving out – the grief and the almost overwhelming guilt; magnifying it and reflecting it back to her. At the same time, she was smoothly reinforcing what she was doing, with what she was saying.

"Diane, Diane my dearest child, please listen to me. Lizzie wants you to know that she loves you, she always did and your friendship was more important to her than anything." The girl was sobbing deeply now, the mic picking up every wet, ragged breath. Martha continued,

"You mustn't ever, ever blame yourself. She says, it wasn't your fault, of course it wasn't, you must never think that. She loves you and needs you to go on and live your own life, but she says, live for her as well. She says you must relish every single second, just don't ever forget her."

Martha closed her eyes again, and what she did next, rocked me back in my seat. She pushed, and she planted a phrase. It was such a strong push, that it felt physical and I must have jerked and exclaimed, because Youth Dew diverted her attention from what was going on, to touch my arm in concern. She silently pushed a tissue into my hand, from a pack she was holding. I nodded thanks.

What Martha had planted, with surgical precision, directly into the mind of the vulnerable young woman before her, was rock-solid, completely destructive, full of spite and exceedingly simple. She'd re-used the one phrase that had been echoing, guilt-laden, over and again. Endorsed and infinitely strengthened it,

"It was your fault." It was so blatant and so loud in my head, for a moment, I couldn't believe nobody else had reacted, but of course nobody would and they were completely transfixed by the emotion, the drama and the messages coming through from Lizzie on the other side.

Well, I certainly couldn't be doing with this. Enough was more than enough. Rachael and Glory had not been wrong at all. I wasn't worried how people spent their money or their time, if they wanted to jump on the Martha Vee bandwagon and be taken for a ride, jolly good luck to them, if it gave them what they needed. But what I'd just witnessed was pure, unadulterated viciousness, and someone's state of mind wasn't to be played with – although I was prepared to make an exception in this case. I shoved back, fast, hard and harsh,

"Stop. That. Immediately." I bellowed into Martha's head, and saw the shock register. She jerked as if she'd been slapped, which metaphorically, I suppose she had. Her eyes sprang open and she quite forgot all about the swinging, swaying, hand to temple business. She was totally confused, which I found a little surprising; you'd have thought, she more than anyone, would have had an open mind to voices no-one else could hear. She recovered remarkably quickly, as I've said, the woman was a pro. Everyone watching would simply have assumed she was receiving more messages, as indeed she was, just from a different direction.

CHAPTER TWENTY-ONE

Maybe, I should have left it there. I will admit, I have a tendency to over-egg the pudding. But this was a woman deliberately sending an intensely vulnerable, already damaged girl away with a ticking time-bomb in her head, tipping her, in all probability, right over a dangerous edge. And for what? This had nothing whatsoever to do with building a business and earning a living, honest or otherwise. This bit was purely for fun. So, as Martha seemed to have established such a strong line of communication, I saw no reason why that shouldn't continue. Lizzie, poor drowned Lizzie, had more to say.

"How dare you speak in my name?" I thundered in Martha's head, and saw her flinch again. "How dare you use me to hurt her? I know you now, Martha Vee. I know you. And I'll be watching and listening for you." And I transferred, unedited and in full colour, the dreadful floating image from Diane's head directly to Martha's – and not just as a brief flash. Then I remembered Hank, the late lamented husband, whose violent demise by bullet, may or may not have been something to do with Martha's manipulations. I only had to drop his name into her mind, for a very clear image of the dear departed to form – an unappetising, bald, glower of a man. I took that and shot it right back at her and again felt her recoil and her fear.

Right, I thought to myself, with a metaphorical pat on the back. That should have put the wind right up her – gale force! And sure enough, for a long moment, it did. She turned almost as colourless as Diane and then, against all the odds, she hauled herself together.

I'd underestimated her, she may have had only limited abilities, but she was as sharp as a tack and now she was angry. If there's one thing a trickster loathes more than anything, it's being taken for a sucker by someone else. She was truly appalled, not because she really thought a dead girl had turned on her, nor because her ex had returned to snarl – she believed in messages from the other side, about as much as I did – but because the only realistic explanation was that someone in that audience, knew what was going on and was fighting back.

As so often happens, under stressful circumstances, and I make no excuses for myself here, self-preservation and a certain amount of alarm kicked in. And, I thought, maybe now wasn't a bad time for a distraction or two. To one side of the stage, cardboard cut-out Martha, still presided smugly over a glossy pile of books, primed for purchase at the end of the session. I hate to treat books badly, but desperate times – I lifted the top volume off the pile and floated it a little way, before letting it smack hard to the floor. Then another and more. Several people shrieked and clutched each other in fright. The very bottom book in the pile, I reserved for Martha and it whacked her firmly in the chest, before rebounding off to join its fellows on the carpet.

I then briefly levitated cardboard Martha, so for a short while, she hovered fetchingly, above and behind the original, who was temporarily transfixed by all this sudden, unplanned activity. More people were screaming now, and a fair number were hurriedly leaving their seats and trying to scramble over those who hadn't yet. For good measure, I floated the flip chart and easel, danced them around a bit, then up-ended the small table holding the tray, still with all the objects on it. The tray hit the ground first, before the table crashed onto it, causing treasured items to bounce and shoot off in various directions. A tin pig money-box smashed hard into one of the lights lining the side of the stage and the heated glass shattered instantly with a rather alarming flash and a bang.

By this time I wasn't in the least concerned about standing out, because the spikes of emotion – fright, fear and shock – were coming thick and fast from the crowd, the majority of whom were now on their feet, holding on to whoever was nearest. There was a lot of shouting. Youth Dew had grabbed my hand on one side and Frankie's on the other. Frankie, I noted, had abandoned sulkiness and eye-rolling and was veering towards hysterical, though still mouthy,

"Why'd you bring me mum?" She wailed, "Mum, I don't like this. Are you listening? I hate you, I said I didn't wanna come. Why'd you bloody make me?" From the back of the room, the security-sized guy had materialised, and was making his way rapidly towards the stage, along with a couple of assistants. They were just as alarmed as the audience, who still weren't quite sure whether this was all part and parcel of what was supposed to happen. The staff knew it wasn't, and hadn't the faintest idea why or how it was.

Martha meanwhile, was beyond livid, struggling to make herself heard above the escalating racket. She was holding forth on poltergeists and other unquiet spirits and appealing for calm, but nobody was paying much attention. The audience seemed fairly equally divided, the whole thing turning out way too strong for some stomachs, whilst there was an equal number of thrilled-to-bits die-hards, who thought all their Christmases had come at once.

I wasn't sure whether I'd achieved anything near what I'd been sent in to do and indeed, was no longer too clear as to what exactly that had been. But I thought the time might have come, to join those who were gathering belongings and leaving the party. I disentangled myself from the sweaty grasp of Youth Dew, who seemed to have quite forgotten we were holding hands, and moved from my seat. I immediately barged into the over-flowered pedestal, which swayed and toppled dramatically, spraying water and blooms indiscriminately. Still, when it comes to distractions, I'm of the more-the-merrier school of thought, so I didn't let that worry me unduly.

As I followed others, jostling each other up the side of the room, I turned briefly, to look back at the stage and caught Martha's eye. Her fury and confusion washed over me, soured saccharine scented. And in that instant, she recognised me. Well, not me, but what I was. For a moment I felt her trying to push in, before I shut her out. It was unpleasant, like blunt, blind fingers, fumbling over my face. It was the first time I'd experienced anything at all like that and nothing like being read by Glory or the Peacocks. That was quick, honest, incisive and direct, everything this wasn't. I hurriedly continued, excusing my way between those who weren't moving fast enough in front of me.

"Stella, don't go out through the main entrance." Rachael in my head, for once I was delighted to hear from her, although, as usual, where had she been when I could have done with a bit of input and advice? "Carry on, past the bar, beyond reception. There's a side door, not locked, it'll take you out onto the service road. Follow that round the lake, we'll pick you up the other side." As I saw the door ahead of me, I realised I'd left my duffel coat draped over my chair – too bad, wasn't going back for it. Emerging into the chilly night and heading swiftly along the road, as instructed, I could see the lake stretching to one side of me. It seemed an awfully long way, to go all the way round and I did feel, the quicker I got out of there, the better.

"Rachael," I said, "I'm going over, not round, will you help?" It wasn't really that I expected to see the elegantly coiffed and costumed Martha, wearing down her stilettos, belting after me, down the gravelled road, but I hadn't liked the look of that security chap and didn't want to take any chances. I hadn't flown in ages and in fact, as Rachael, who insisted on labelling it levitating, had told me it would, it had become far less easy with the passing of years, something to do with body weight.

So yes, perhaps it was a foolish decision to head over the lake, but we'd all be better off with hindsight, wouldn't we? Slipping my bag strap over my head and shoulder, I checked quickly behind me to make sure no-one else was in sight, but other than the side lights, inadequately lighting the road surface, it was nearly pitch black and I couldn't hear anyone. So I focused on the ground letting me go, felt the familiar release and floated gently upwards, heading out across the lake. As I mentioned earlier, I'd got halfway across before I fell in.

Rachael, tutting in exasperation at my soaked and spread-eagled form was extending an impatient hand to haul me up, when we were both rocked back by Glory's shock.

"Rachael," she said, "We've just knocked someone down. I think we've killed her."

CHAPTER TWENTY-TWO

"Well, you knocked her down extremely thoroughly, but you haven't killed her, there's a mercy!" Rachael pushed away an inquisitive Hamlet, with a firm knee, as she straightened from the girl on the ground. "We really shouldn't move her, until we're sure nothing's broken. On the other hand, we can't stay here. Ed, what do you think?" The girl on the ground was groaning and stirring in the light of the torch Ed was holding. He handed it to Rachael and took her place, kneeling and gently placing his hands, either side of the girl's head. With hands so big, his fingers met in the middle, over her skull, it looked like she'd acquired an odd sort of helmet.

"What's he doing... ?" I asked, shivering, dripping and miserably freezing, from my involuntary dip.

"It felt like we hit her so hard. She just shot out of nowhere and under the wheels." Glory sounded as shaken as I'd ever heard her. "And we were only going slowly."

"Shush, both of you." Said Rachael. "Let him concentrate." I subsided and waited, shooting the question at Glory again. She answered me aloud, speaking softly.

"Sam, showed him how to do some stuff. Ed can't do what Sam does, but he'll be able to tell if anything major's happened, whether we can risk moving her." Ed was already rising,

"Nothing broken, far as I can tell," he said, "She took the main bump on her side and didn't hit her head too hard when she went down, I can't find any bleeding inside. Bruises in the morning though."

"But you can't be sure. We've got to call an ambulance." I said. Rachael shook her head,

"Can't, we'd have to go back into the hotel to do that, not a good idea. Ed, are you pretty sure?" Ed nodded, and just for a minute, let down his barriers, to show us what he'd been working from – it was the same sort of circulating, 3D holographic image I'd seen before in Sam's head. Rachael nodded,

"OK, good enough for me. Get her in the van." As she spoke, she was already opening the back door for Hamlet. Ed bent at the knees and very gently lifted the girl, sliding her carefully onto the back seat. Rachael followed with another blanket, I could only assume she must travel with a stack of them, for unexpected turns of event. She tucked it in as securely as she could, slipping a firm arm round the shoulders of the still dazed girl, to keep her upright.

"Well, don't just stand there gawping," she said to me, "Get in, and try not to make me as wet as you." I wrapped my blanket more firmly round my sodden self, and climbed in next to her, as I did, the soft light of the van's interior, confirmed what I already knew.

The girl had opened her eyes and was trying to work out what the heck had happened. Poor Diane, one way and another, she wasn't having a good day. Guilty, shaken and appalled, she hadn't felt at her best, back at the hotel. The fact she'd subsequently been knocked down, and now found herself surrounded by a rather odd set of people, she'd never clapped eyes on before, wasn't making her feel any better. Still, there's always a bright side, and at least current bewilderment had temporarily over-ridden all the other rotten stuff going round in her head, including the spiteful, festering seed planted by our mutual mate Martha.

"Ed. Go." Said Rachael.

"Where?" he asked, reasonably.

"Just get out of here, then we'll decide, I believe," she said, "We might be getting company." And sure enough, a few seconds later, there were headlights heading in our direction. Ed turned the van, in a slick three-point move that caused me a distinct moment of driving envy, and we headed, sharpish down the service route and from there, onto the main road to blend with a reassuring amount of other traffic.

Our newly acquired passenger was pulling away from Rachael, struggling to sit up and make some kind of sense of everything.

"Stop this car right now." She demanded, her voice rising sharply. "I want to get out. Who are you anyway? What happened? I don't know what's happened. Where are you taking me?" and then, as Hamlet stuck his head enquiringly over the back seat, "Oh my God, what's that?"

"Diane." I reached over and touched her arm. She turned her head sharply towards me, squinting to see my face, in the now dark interior, intermittently lit by the street lights we were passing.

"How do you know my name? I don't know you."

"I was at the meeting."

"I didn't see you."

"There were a lot of people."

"Yeah, yeah there were. Hey, you're soaking wet." Odd, isn't it, how stressed people often fix on the least important things?

"I am," I conceded, "A little damp. I fell in the lake on the way out."

"Oh, for goodness sake, we don't have time for chit chat, do we? Young lady, you left the hotel and ran, hell for leather, straight under our wheels." said Rachael severely. "You could have been very seriously hurt indeed. Only the prompt reactions of my friend here, prevented that."

"I don't remember. I'm sorry, I was… in a bit of a state. Where are you taking me?"

"Well, I think home would be best, don't you?" said Rachael, "Where do you live?" We could all read the jumble in Diane's head and for a moment, none of us, her included, could pin down the information we needed, then she finally dredged it up and gave us a Rickmansworth address.

"Will somebody be there? I don't think you should be on your own." Glory had turned from the front seat.

"It's my Mum's – she'll be there." Diane, I thought, under the circumstances, was holding it all together rather well. For moment there was silence in the van, although not in her head. She was going over, and we all shared, the utter bleakness of despair she'd felt, as she fled the meeting. She knew the hotel, knew the lake was there, had thought – maybe, to ease this pain, it would be better, to be like Lizzie?

"No." said Rachael firmly. Diane didn't question the comment, but relaxed a little against Rachael's arm, which was still around her.

"I feel so tired." She murmured.

"I know," said Rachael gently, "I understand, that tonight's little gathering was more than a bit dramatic? Not what you expected, eh?" Diane nodded slowly, eyelids drooping. "And then you ran into us. Shock can knock you for six, you know." Although there was no perceptible change in her conversational tone, Rachael had taken the girl down to a different level. She was locating the dreadful Lizzie images in Diane's mind. She probably couldn't eliminate them completely, they were very strong, painfully powerful, but she did something that blurred and faded them, making them less of a horror. And then she did exactly what Martha had done earlier. She planted and pushed, tipping the mind-set into another position, although this time, it was an entirely different thought – that in the long run, none of us can ever be entirely responsible for the actions of others. I flashed a query to Glory.

"Will it work?" She answered silently.

"Don't know. It should, but you can never be sure. Rachael's cancelled out what Martha did, but there's not much she can do to change what actually happened. This kid's always going to feel guilt, but maybe now she's got a chance to deal with it in a more rational way – Rachael's done that much. Diane was now slumped heavily against Rachael's shoulder, she didn't stir, when the van drew up and stopped outside a house on the outskirts of Rickmansworth. Rachael shook her gently and she sat up, yawning and embarrassed.

"I'm so sorry, I think…"

"You dropped off. Hardly surprising, you've had quite an evening of it. This is you, isn't it," Rachael nodded towards the house. Diane looked out and nodded, her mind was still swirling, but the hysterical edge had quietened. Now she was just tired, sad and utterly confused. "That your mother?" said Rachel. From the downstairs front room of the house, someone was looking out, no doubt with some alarm, at the large van with blacked out windows, parked outside, engine idling.

"Yeah. I'd better go in, she'll be wondering. Thank you for bringing me home." I saw that she'd rather forgotten who'd knocked her down in the first place. Clever Rachael.

"I'd suggest, straight to bed with a hot drink," said Rachael, "You'll feel better in the morning and you know what?" Diane, halfway out of the van, turned back to look. "In future, my dear, steer well clear of the sort of thing you went to tonight. Do you understand, it will do you no good?" Diane nodded slowly.

"But…" and she looked past Rachael, at me. "You were there too weren't you? What did you think, she's for real isn't she? Martha I mean, she sees things?" I shook my head firmly and smiled at her.

"I'm a bit of a cynic I'm afraid, just went along to see what I thought, because I'd heard a lot about her."

"And?"

97

"She puts on a good show, but then, so do a lot of people. Actually, I didn't take to her, did you? Bit too slick and showman, for my liking." Diane thought about that, and we could already see the erosion of what had happened, as she started to question, remember and misremember what she'd actually seen and heard. She was wondering just how much of it all had been due to her being, as her mother so often put it, 'all over the place'.

A woman, in a pink track suit and slippers, had opened the front door and we could all see and sense her acute relief as Diane climbed out of the van and paused by Glory's passenger window, Ed obligingly pushed a button on his side and glass slid soundlessly down.

"Look, thanks for bringing me back." She said awkwardly to all of us. "Sorry if I seemed a bit rude, I thought… oh, you know, I don't know what I thought. Thank you anyway."

"In future," Rachael said "You watch yourself, young lady, no dashing under the wheels of passing cars." At the same time and silently, she added, "We can never be responsible for other people's choices, understand that." and then aloud again, "Ed, we need to get off now." Ed nodded, let out the brake and we moved away, as Diane turned slowly towards her mother, who was coming down the path to meet her.

Heading back to my office, where my car was parked, we had the usual Peacock, post-mission debrief, which was indeed brief and as frustratingly unsatisfactory as I remembered.

"So, what happened to that subtle, low-key approach we discussed for tonight?" Rachael folded her lips at me.

"Hardly my fault," I protested, "Things just kind of took off."

"As they so often do with you." She commented. I felt this was extremely unfair, and said so, she continued as if I hadn't. "We do though have to put a stop to the vicious little games that woman likes playing. Tonight will have given her pause for thought, she won't know who you were or whether there are others like you. But I'm not sure it's enough. We'll just have to see."

"And if it's not enough?" I asked. She shook her head.

"We'll have to frighten her a bit more."

"How? What'll you do?"

"Nothing you need know about, or be involved in."

"But I am involved."

"You didn't want to be."

"Agreed, but now I am, and I want to stop her as much as you do." I was aware, as so often before with this annoying woman, my tone had skidded from firm to peevish. Glory and Ed in the front seats were silent, they'd sat through a lot of similar spats. Rachael turned to look at me.

"I'm sorry." She said. I was astonished enough, that I completely forgot what I was going to say next. Sorry wasn't a word I'd thought was in her vocabulary. "I'm well aware," she continued, "How you feel about steering clear of all this sort of thing, although, let's be honest, you're not above using what you've got when it suits, are you?" She forestalled me, "I know, I know, that's your affair, none of mine. We all do what we need to get by, with as clear a conscience as we can." She paused before she went on, "Fact is Stella, your heart's in the right place, even if your head often isn't, and you're perfectly capable of making your own decisions, as to what will and what won't work for you. We all of us," a head nod, included Ed and Glory, "Think you've done well, setting up the business the way you have – there's no doubt it's something that suits your talents." She paused. "Whichever of them you choose to use." I opened my mouth, but she held up a hand, "Let me finish. You made a firm decision, back when you got Sam out, and we agreed it was the right one for you."

"So why haul me in again, now?" I grumbled. In the darkness, I couldn't see her expression.

"Perhaps, we wanted to check we had it right." She said. "And I think we did, "You're not really suited to subtle, are you?" The wretched woman wasn't wrong. I could feel the agreement of the other two. In this company, there was no point in trying to put on a face – it was one of the things I both loved and hated – there was no question, honesty was the name of the game. Or was it? There was something she was holding back, I had no idea what, and for a moment I tasted guilt, hers not mine.

"Suppose you're right." I conceded. "As usual." I tacked on, ungraciously.

"Indeed."

The rest of the journey passed mostly in silence, and any probing I did, hit nothing but a blank. Ed drew up, just behind where I'd parked my car.

"Get yourself home and dry quickly, or you'll catch your death." Glory said.

"No, keep it," Rachael said, turning up her nose, as I started to peel off the damp, somewhat smelly blanket. "And do what Glory says. Do you want us to follow you home to make sure you're OK?" I was taken aback, by this sudden maternal turn and shook my head.

"No, I'll be fine..." I paused. "Will you let me know? What happens with Martha?

"Trust me, if anything does, you'll hear."

"Who's Boris?" I asked, it was a name she had in her head.

"My, my," she said, and I'm not sure I wasn't relieved to get the sarcasm back. "You've come on apace haven't you? Never mind about who he is or isn't. Go on now." Halfway out the van, I turned,

"Will you give my love to Ruth and wish her better." For just a second I felt again, Rachael's acute concern about her sister and that coppery guilt tang, then it was gone.

"I will." She said. "Now scat." As I closed the door, they were already moving away.

"Wait." I yelled. The van stopped abruptly, and I ran to the window.

"At least, give me your phone number. I don't even have that. It seems a bit ridiculous."

"Probably right. Here." Rachel scribbled a number quickly on a piece of paper from the pocket of the seat in front of her. "Not," she said, "For casual chit-chat, understand?" I nodded, folding it in my hand. I couldn't think why I'd asked, I certainly couldn't imagine I'd really need it and should I, at any time, feel in need of a bit of chit chat, I was more than certain, Rachael Peacock probably wouldn't be my first choice.

PART TWO

STILL CHASING NORMAL

You can plan as much as you want, but don't count on anything!

CHAPTER TWENTY-THREE

It came as a relief, over the next couple of months, after not exactly covering myself in glory, with the Martha Vee affair, to get back to normal in the office. A place where I felt, even if only nominally, in charge.

The agency was gradually building up a satisfactory head of steam, and Kitty and Brenda seemed to have established, a reasonably workable, modus operandi. There were still aspects, of course, which needed ironing out, one of these being my family members popping in, whenever they were passing, for a cup of tea and an analysis of how everything was going. This was all very nice and sociable, but I felt, in no way contributed to our professional edge. My mother and Aunt Edna, were by far the worst offenders. They'd charmed Martin and Hilary downstairs, and would spend a few moments exchanging news and views with them, before trotting up to the second floor, hallooing cheerfully,

"Only us. Put the kettle on." I felt I had to take a far firmer stance, and this was only underlined when I arrived back at the office one afternoon, a few minutes late for a session with Professor Lowbell. I could hear, as I hurried up the stairs, what sounded like a party in full swing. As indeed it was. Ensconced cosily on our outer office, two-seater sofa, between my mother and Aunt Edna, who luckily were both small statured, was Dorothy Lowbell, whilst her husband was holding forth, from one of the office chairs, wheeled out from behind a desk. Hilary, cigarette in hand, was propped against a filing cabinet, blowing copious smoke and Brenda and Kitty were flitting back and forward, refilling cups and distributing mini Danish pastries from Grodzinksi's, down the road. A convivial cheer greeted me as I opened the door.

"Dearest girl, I was just regaling these delightful ladies," said the Prof waving a gracious arm, "With what it is, you and I are busy working on, when we're behind closed doors – ghosties, ghouls and ghastlies under the bed eh?" And he tacked on, a rather good, Christopher Lee laugh, to general hilarity.

"Now then, Lowbell." It was an idiosyncrasy of Dorothy's that she never called her husband by his first name. "Stella's here now, and you've work to do, before we head upwards and onwards." And she tapped her watch, not an easy move, the three women were wedged pretty firmly on that sofa.

"Dottie, my practical angel and always so right." He smiled widely at her, stuffed the remains of a Danish, saw it down with a gulp of tea and rose to his feet, hitching up his trousers, which had a tendency to head south, when he'd been sitting a while, "Ladies, I must love you and leave you. Thank you for the delicious interlude, both company and refreshments." He picked up his battered briefcase which, he often wryly commented had, like himself, seen better days and, ushering his wife ahead of him, moved into my inner office. I followed, but not before casting an admonitory backward glare at the rest of the room, which I could see, had about as much impact as I'd expected. A far firmer foot, I resolved, would have to be put down. The phone rang, just as I was shutting the door behind us and Brenda's exclamation stopped me.

"Oh God!" she said. "No." She looked across the room at me, hand to mouth, her normally ruddy face, shocked and pale.

"It's Devlin McCrae's brother." She said. "Devlin was knocked down by a car this morning. They've asked if you'll go to the hospital – Stella, it's pretty bad."

The Lowbells insisted on driving me to the Royal Free Hospital, completely overriding my protests, that I was fine to go on my own. They were fully supported in this, by the assembled crowd, who all said I wasn't experienced enough, to drive, having had a bad shock. By the time my mother and Aunt Edna had bundled me back into my coat, which I'd only just taken off, Dorothy had despatched her husband for the car, so we wouldn't have to waste any time. She took a firm grip on my arm, as we headed down the stairs and by the time we got outside, he was at the kerb with the engine running.

He was a surprisingly good driver, don't know what I'd expected, maybe the same stop-start timing as with his speech. But, by dint of taking us smoothly up and down a number of side-roads, we got to the hospital in record time,

"My part of the world you see," he explained, "Been here all my life, know it like the back of my hand." Dorothy wouldn't take no for an answer, when it came to going in with me. And, I have to admit, she was formidably efficient, forging a path to the front desk, sorting out exactly where I needed to go and then shepherding me up to the relevant floor.

To be honest, I'd absolutely no idea why I was there; I was a paid employee, hardly a friend of the family and, given the choice, I'd rather have been anywhere else at all. I was horrified and upset at what had happened to Devlin and, naturally, wished him nothing but well, but I didn't do brilliantly in hospitals. The intensity of emotion, stress and distress seeped through even my vastly improved shielding, and it was red-raw and painful. As a determined Dorothy, still with proprietary grip on my arm, hurried me up and along to the Intensive Care Unit, spikes were needling, viciously sharp, through my defences. I knew that when my own stress levels rose, I was far less able to take care of and protect myself. I took some deep breaths, although they were so laden with that unmistakeable hospitally smell, they didn't help much.

Devlin was in a curtained area, near the nurses' station, briskly indicated by a tall, long-faced sister, who first established, the family had indeed asked me to come. She was sharp and snappy, she hated it when it was a kid, and as she strode swiftly away, I could clearly see, experience told her, this one probably wasn't going to make it. Dorothy Lowbell's hand on my reluctant back, propelled me forward. I turned to thank her and she leaned forward quickly and surprisingly, and kissed me on the cheek,

"Stiff upper, eh, Stella?" She patted my shoulder and stomped off, her rubber soled shoes squeaking protest on the lino floor tiles.

CHAPTER TWENTY-FOUR

The family turned stricken, appalled faces towards me, as I moved reluctantly round the curtain. Susan McCrae was normally a vividly coloured woman – creamy skin, soft brown freckles and flame-bright hair. The freckles now stood out on her face, like numerous, livid little bruises. Russell and Sarah, Devlin's brother and sister were eighteen and twenty respectively, but shock and fear had wiped years off, and they both looked little older than the boy in the bed.

I'd met Philip, the father, only once before, and then only fleetingly. He was something to do with oil – petrol not cooking – flying off to trouble spots worldwide. My brief impression had been then, that he thought rather too much of himself, but like the rest of the family, fear had reduced him. He nodded at me, though I could see he was no wiser than I, as to why on earth I was there and had said so, at length, in a hissed conversation earlier, before Russell had been despatched to call me. Susan stretched out a shaky hand, from her chair at the bedside,

"Stella, thank you so much for coming. As you can see, we're in a bit of trouble here." she swallowed hard, "But Dev's so fond of you. You've been so good for him. You make him laugh. I know you've become close, knew you'd want to be here."

She'd got it completely wrong. Devlin and I got on well, only because he was aware, I was always one step ahead of him. This meant I knew immediately, when into his mind came a fresh ruse, designed to make someone's life a misery, and was swift to ensure it wasn't mine. It had become almost an on-going, unacknowledged game between the two of us. Susan still had her hand out to me, I had no choice, but to move forward and take it, she was ice cold and she pulled me in closer.

"It happened so quickly," she said. "We were crossing, you know, at the end of our road; he was fiddling with one of those wretched sticker packs he loves. I said, put it away, wait till we get home, but he wouldn't listen. As we crossed, he dropped the wretched thing and he pulled away and ran back. I screamed at him, screamed, but... a car..." She swallowed

106

again, her throat so dry, it clicked. "Not her fault, the driver, I mean. Not her fault, Dev leapt out, she couldn't stop, don't think she even saw him."

Devlin looked ridiculously small in the high bed, shrunken and somehow aged. A swathe of curls had been shaved on the right side of his head, and there were black, aggressively open-ended stitches, holding together a zig-zag gash, which crawled a lazy path from his ear, across his head and down to the opposite eyebrow. They stood, harsh and dark against his colourless skin.

"How is he?" I asked, although I already knew.

"Leg broken in two places, a lot of scrapes and a couple of bad cuts, but it's the damage to his brain they're worried about, they can't say when he might wake up." Phillip was pacing. The area was small. He could only take two paces one way, two paces the other.

"Phil," said Susan, "Not when, if."

"You don't know that."

"I'm a doctor," she said quietly, "I know." Around the bed, the sustaining and monitoring machines hummed, puffed and beeped. Fluid leaked drop by drop into his arm, there was a tube taped in place over his mouth, snaking to the respirator, that was doing his breathing for him. To the side of the bed, an electronic line peaked and troughed across a screen. Over his left leg, some kind of protective frame tented the blankets.

"Can you talk to him? Hold his hand and talk to him?" Susan pulled her chair back and someone, Sarah I think, pushed the rim of another one against my knees. I sat automatically. I felt sick. I'd been here before. Not with Devlin, but in another too similar situation, and the last thing I wanted to do was open myself up to it again. As I took the small, nail-gnawed hand, middle finger bracketed by a monitoring clip, in both of mine, I was rocked from all sides by the emotions of those around me, back-grounded by so many others, in this ward and beyond. But in Devlin's head, there was only a deep, dark, bleakly ominous silence. It was nothing I'd come across before, there was no cacophony of sense, feeling or thought, not even an echo. I could feel his heartbeat, steady and strong, a drumbeat in an otherwise silent house, but of Devlin there was no sign. Susan touched my arm,

"Talk to him." She said. "He might be able to hear us." I leaned forward, no idea what to say, but then there was a bustle behind me, as a nurse pulled back the curtain to let through the doctor, bald pate shining under the harsh lights. He had one pair of glasses perched on the dome and another pair, halfway down his nose. He shook hands with Susan, then Phillip, nodding at the rest of us.

"Dr McCrae, so sorry we meet under such circumstances, I'm Mr Naylish, neurosurgeon." He had an accent swiped straight from Dr Finlay's Casebook, oddly but immediately reassuring.

"What can you tell us?" Phillip asked. Sarah and Russell moved closer to each other.

"Mr McCrae, I'm afraid Devlin's showing little sign of any brain activity at the moment." Susan flinched. He continued, "When it comes to the brain though, we're obviously dealing with a vast number of factors, some of them known, others, unfortunately not known. At the minute, there's substantial swelling, either as a result of the blow sustained when the car hit your son, or when he hit the ground. We need that swelling to subside, before we can carry out further tests."

"But you must know, have some idea as to how things might go?" Phillip pressed. Naylish shook his head,

"I'm sorry, every case is unique, different from the one before. What goes on, in a brain with a consciousness disorder, depends completely on the level of that unconsciousness. You should understand, at the minute, all normal activity of Devlin's brain, is dampened down completely."

"Like, asleep?" Sarah said.

"No, I'm afraid not, my dear. When we sleep, our brain's actually quite active, think how quickly we wake when necessary. What we have here, in an injury-induced situation, is quite different. There's almost no brain activity in our boy just now".

"For how long?" said Phillip. Mr Naylish looked at Susan, she nodded almost imperceptibly, she thought it best not coming from her, and he continued,

"Most patients don't remain in a true coma," he paused, "If they don't die of their original injuries, they may move into what we call a vegetative state – again, a different level of unconsciousness. Whilst there then may be minor reaction to stimuli, the individual in question, is entirely unable to interact in any significant way with their environment."

"That's no answer." Phillip said.

"And it's because there isn't one." Naylish touched the other man's shoulder briefly. "We should know more after the next set of tests."

"And in the meantime?" Russell spoke for the first time since I'd got there. It was Susan who answered,

"In the meantime, darling... we pray." She nodded at the consultant. "Thank you." He inclined his head back, he hated dealing with other professionals, illogically it made him even more conscious that he couldn't work any kind of miracles, and he knew at this point, Susan knew that too. In her, hope was already dying.

"Keep talking though," He said, let him hear your voices, talk to him about everyday things. If he's got any favourite music bring it in, play it." He looked at Susan. "As you'll know, there's so much we don't know when it comes to the brain, so anything, anything at all you think might call to him. Nurse, would you mind?" and he nodded to us all, as he left, while the nurse moved to check the monitors and drips. She added to the notes and replaced them tidily in the wooden pocket at the end of the bed, before she too swished through the curtain, letting it fall closed behind her. I was feeling more than acutely uncomfortable, like excess baggage in the room, dazed by the depth of emotion, horrified by what I'd seen, or rather hadn't seen in Devlin's head. It was cowardly, I knew, but I desperately needed to get out of there.

"Look, I'll come again tomorrow, shall I?" I said, and my already stinging conscience had a load of salt rubbed into it, as Susan rose to hug and thank me before I left.

CHAPTER TWENTY-FIVE

I hailed a taxi outside the hospital, to take me back to the office, where I'd left the car and, scrabbling in my bag for money and car keys, realised it was so bulky, because I had a folder full of CV's in there. They were in response to an ad we'd placed, for a printing company client who was recruiting. I'd been through the responses, sorted them and arranged appointments for the following few days. I'd promised the client, we'd deliver all the paperwork directly to their offices, so they'd have it there, when they interviewed. I'd planned to ask Brenda to do it, but what with one thing and another, it had slid completely out of my head. I'd have to do it now. It was just coming up to 6.30, already full dark and bitterly cold, with sleet slanting silver against passing headlights, but their offices weren't that far, and doing something practical and normal was preferable to going home to anxious enquiry.

I wasn't overly thrilled at the sliding-away of the wheels, as sleet thickened to snow, although in compensation, the roads were far emptier than usual. At the forefront of my mind, as I drove, was the total emptiness of Devlin's. Between that and the uncertainty of my connection to the treacherous road surface, I was only peripherally aware of a car behind me, much nearer than it should have been, even in normal driving conditions.

As I reached Stanmore and turned onto Brockley Hill, the car behind me turned too. It was so stupidly close, its headlights kept disappearing from my mirror. I deliberately slowed, I wasn't about to be pushed into going any faster than road conditions and already stretched nerves allowed. Of course, there's nothing a car up your boot hates more than you slowing down. He hit his horn, a long harsh blast, ripping through the dark, and I nearly jumped out of my skin.

There were three of them in the car behind; middle-aged fax-machine salesmen, down to London for some sort of training conference, a boring day of yada, yada, yada, mitigated only slightly by several recent pints in the hotel bar. They were now on their way to a local curry restaurant, highly recommended by the barman – 'Hot enough to blow the back of your sodding heads off.' he'd assured them cheerfully. The driver was unfazed by the weather, and hugely irritated at anyone else who was. 'If there was one thing,' he was saying to his colleagues, 'That really got on his tits, it was little-old-lady-driving, holding up every other bugger.' I hissed in exasperation, stupid man. I slowed down even more, then pulled into the side of the road so they could pass me, go their merry way and leave me to go mine.

But they didn't. They stopped too. I waited a while, but they didn't move off again until I did. And then we were right back to where we'd been before, with them in my boot, so my attention was torn between the road in front and the harassing behind. They were all highly amused, nothing like a bit of road-bullying to entertain. I really didn't need this. I swung abruptly into the side of the road again, forcing him to stand on his brakes, which skidded his car almost full circle. I watched in the mirror, as he flung open the door and got out, his aggressive stride, hindered by snow already settled on the road. His friends were lighting up more cigarettes, sniggering and leaning out to hear all the better. Dean had a right temper on him, and they didn't rate the chances of whoever it was who'd pissed him off. He banged hard on my window with his fist, and I smiled warmly at him – people in a temper don't like being smiled at – and wound it down a little. I don't recall whether 'road rage' was talked about back then, but this was definitely a prime example of someone losing his cool, so I thought, best be cautious.

"Careful," I said, "Awfully slippery, out there." It was probably because he was so busy, calling me some unpleasant names, that it took him a moment to notice his feet were sliding rapidly away beneath him. I landed him hard, on his back, in the slush. I hadn't thought he could get much angrier than he was, but laughter and catcalls from the rest of the party back in his car, together with loss of dignity, not to mention a sore and soggy back, were doing him no good at all.

I thought now might be a good time to take my leave, but really wasn't prepared to put up with any more mucking around. I'm not mechanically minded, although I did recall from films, a rotor arm was often involved, in putting a car out of action. But as I hadn't the remotest idea where one might be kept, nor what it looked like, thought it sensible to stick with something more basic. Cars need wheels, and where you've got wheels, tyres come in handy. I wasn't nearly as good at this as Ed, but I'd seen the big man in action often enough to pick up a few things. I focused on two tyres on the same side of the car. They both burst, almost immediately. There was a chorus of concern from the passengers, as the car developed a pronounced tilt.

"What the... ?" The driver, just upright again and clinging tightly to the roof of my vehicle for balance, was looking over his shoulder, jaw dropped. Not an attractive sight. I wound the window down a fraction more.

"You'll probably need to change those." I pointed out helpfully. And if your back's playing you up, after that fall, you'll find Stanmore Orthopaedic Hospital, just up the road, on the left." I don't think I'd overreacted. But I can't be doing with bullies, who think they've found a soft touch to target. Indeed, I reflected, had I been a little old lady, that horn blast might well have seen me pushing up the daisies sooner rather than later.

I restarted my car, moving forward cautiously, it might add insult to injury if I now ran over him. As I drove away, I could see him in my rear-view mirror, he really was hopping mad, if he wasn't careful, he'd slip over again. I could still feel the unpleasant after-effects of the adrenaline that had shot through me. My heart was pumping double time, blood was tingling as it returned to hands and feet, and my brain continued to fizz from the unpleasant encounter. And I suddenly had a thought.

CHAPTER TWENTY-SIX

I went back to the Royal Free, first thing in the morning, counting on the fact that things were so dire with Devlin, normal visiting hour restrictions wouldn't apply. The same sister I'd seen yesterday was there and she nodded me through. When asked if there was any change, she shook her head briskly and I saw how certain she was, that there wouldn't be.

"'Mum,'" she told me, nodding at the curtained bay, "Is there, been there all night. Dad and the kids have popped home to wash and change. Said they wouldn't be long." When I went in, Susan was awkwardly sleeping, sprawled half in her chair, half on the side of the bed. The machines and screens were untiringly doing their stuff, but other than the slight rise and fall of his chest, the boy in the bed looked lifeless.

I quietly pulled up a chair, opposite his sleeping mother, I didn't want to disturb her. In the cold light of day, my thought of the night before didn't seem to make anywhere near as much sense as it had, newly minted. What if I did more harm than good? I took Devlin's hand. It felt even more inanimate than yesterday, sad and dry, as if life had already leaked away. I moved into the echoing, empty stillness of his head and concentrated. And there, so faint, so far away, I almost didn't hear it, a tiny, fading whisper of Devlin. I knew what I was going to try was risky, but it didn't feel as if he had a great deal left to lose.

I could feel Devlin's regular heartbeat reverberating through me, or maybe it was just mine, syncing with his. I hauled into the forefront of my mind, the memory I'd taken from him when we first met. Back garden; football bouncing on hot, sun-singed grass; lip-puckering tang of cheek-stored Rowntree's fruit gum; insect-buzz; hum of traffic from the road outside. Then... suddenly close, shockingly deep-throated and heart-stoppingly alarming, next door's Boxer, barking long and loud, unsuspected inches away, on the other side of the fence.

Powerful, fear-fuelled adrenaline shocked and shot through us, our hearts pounded painfully, panic swept upwards, icy cold from the base of our skulls, blood rushing to where it was needed, so we could save ourselves. And then electronic alarms were going off, all around us. Shrill, differently toned, designed for urgency and immediate response. Susan woke terrified, as staff surged in. I couldn't let go though. Not now.

Somewhere, deep, deep inside his head, Devlin had shrieked in fright and fear. Way down and far away, but there. They were trying to haul me away from him, ungentle hands on my shoulders, but it was too important to let go, too soon. I had both my hands tight round his upper arms now, leaning right over and into him and I re-ran the memory of the shock, pounding it into his head, frightening him all over again, and then I wrapped my own panic round his, and pulled.

Alarms were klaxoning, discordant, demanding and Devlin was suddenly arching on the bed, thrashing wildly. They thought he was convulsing, he wasn't, he was trying to run away. They were going to sedate him, but that was the last thing they should do. We were choking, both of us, because we wanted to shriek out shock, but had no voice to do it, there was a tube down our throat and our mouth was trapped with tape. And then, swift instruction and action, someone gently withdrawing the tube, all the way up from our throat, we both retched deeply. And then I could let go.

I was yanked to my feet and hustled unceremoniously away. I found myself outside the curtained area, by the nurses' station, with my arms tight round Susan McCrae. We were both shaking a lot.

"What's happening? Oh dear God, what's happening? I thought... but he's not, he's not is he?" Her anguished fingers were digging into me. A nurse hurried from behind the curtain, Susan grabbed her.

"What's happening?"

"Doctor will be out in a moment." Then, empathy overcoming protocol, she patted Susan's arm. "He seems to have woken up, my love." Susan sagged heavily against me, luckily we were near a couple of chairs, because I felt none too steady myself. I put her on one and me on the other. I could still feel the tube sliding up out of my throat, so couldn't say anything, in case I was sick. Susan had gone completely silent now, inside and out – an overload of emotion, blanketing all coherent thought. And then the rest of the family were there, and suddenly I was in the midst of everyone holding on to everyone else, with a lot of sobbing going on. Honestly, I was all in favour of client contact, but this was rather more than I'd ever had in mind. I was thankful, when Mr Naylish emerged from behind the curtain, looking ruffled but pleased, and we all had to break apart to listen.

"Don't know, don't know yet." He said, holding up a hand, to the barrage of questions. "Too soon to tell. We've given him more pain relief for his leg and his throat's a wee bit raw, from the intubation. He's confused, but that's only to be expected. As far as we can tell, just now, he's reacting normally, reflexes doing what we'd want." He looked at me briefly, "Whatever this young lady was saying to him, seems to have done the trick, but, as I say, early days yet, early days. But progress, good progress and far quicker than we might have expected with this sort of injury. Yes, yes, by all means, you can go in now if you want."

I didn't want and made vague noises about not intruding, but got swept in despite that. Hanging back, as the family gathered round the bed, I was unspeakably relieved to see, that in truth, Devlin didn't seem to be in the least bit confused. He was, in fact, already insisting, in a hoarse little voice, getting stronger by the minute, that he wanted some ice-cream, with chocolate sprinkles and he wanted that immediately, if not sooner. That had to be a good sign, didn't it? I breathed out a sigh that came out as a small sob.

It wasn't yet 10.30 in the morning, but what with one thing and another, it had been an active couple of days, and I couldn't wait to take my thumping head out of the hospital. I'd thought, if hearts were shocked to re-start them, it might work the same way with brains. It had been a gamble, with stakes higher than I wanted to think about. Heart said I'd done the right thing, head reiterated the risks, instinct insisted there hadn't been a lot of choice.

In the car, I leant back and closed my eyes, I wasn't feeling too good. I thought it probably best to give the nausea a few minutes to subside, before I attempted to leave, extraction from the Royal Free car park, not being an exercise for the faint-hearted. Someone knocked on my window – that seemed to be happening a lot lately. I jumped, but thought maybe if

I ignored them, they'd think I was sleeping or dead and go away. But they knocked again. I reluctantly opened one eye. An anxious looking chap was peering in.

"You OK?" he mouthed. I smiled and nodded. He made wind down your window motions. God save me from do-gooders. I smiled again, gave him a perky thumbs-up, to show how really fine and dandy I was and put the key in the ignition. He still didn't go away, so I reluctantly opened the window.

"You look awful." He said.

"Thanks."

"I mean, you shouldn't drive."

"No, I'm fine. Really."

"Look, we were going to get a taxi, but let me drive you wherever you need to go, we can get a cab home from there." I looked at him blankly.

"You don't know who I am, do you?" He moved aside slightly and I saw a familiar figure behind him, small and elegant in a tan, cinched at the waist, leather coat. Laura Gold inclined her head a fraction. I could see she was in one of her remote moods, also that her right wrist was in a plaster cast. I instantly understood. My Good Samaritan was acting, not so much out of kindness of the heart, but because I'd proved so useful when it came to his mother, in the recent past. He wasn't too thrilled at the thought of me now driving into a brick wall and upsetting the status quo. He was one of those people I could hardly read, but I got the overall picture.

"Donald?" I said. He shook his head,

"David."

"Right." I said. Laura stepped forward,

"Darling, we really should be going, I'm in quite a lot of pain and if Stella's happy to drive, well…" She shrugged.

"Ma, we can't let her drive off on her own. Look at her." I was starting to get a little ratty, I know I'd had a bit of tense morning, but nobody likes being told they look that bad and I like to think I can take a fair amount of drama, in my stride.

"Get in the car, Ma." God he was bossy. He'd already opened the back door for Laura, shutting it sharply, as she whipped in a length of tan leather and he was now holding my door open, waiting for me to get out and move round to the passenger side. I really didn't have strength or time for an argument, I slid out.

Having got us out from the close confines of the car park, with far less fuss, not to mention damage than I'd have probably managed, we drove for few minutes in silence, which suited me fine. I wasn't in a chit chatty mood. Mercifully, neither was my temporary driver, nor our passenger, who contented herself with the occasional theatrical moan, whenever we hit a bump and jerked the injured limb. After a while, I felt common courtesy, called for a polite query.

"What happened to your wrist, Mrs Gold?"

"She fell. It's broken." David answered briskly for her. Laura didn't add detail, although I clearly saw a chain of events, involving migraine pills, an ill-conceived surge of sentimentality and a sudden urge to get all the family photo albums, down from the loft.

"I'm sorry." I murmured.

"Don't be." He said, "It's hardly your fault. Anyway, anybody daft enough to climb a loft-ladder in stilettos, is asking for trouble. Lucky she didn't break her neck." He was pretty fed up. I could feel the amalgam of irritation, frustration, apprehension and love he had for the woman. Fleetingly, I hoped, if I ever had a son, he'd have as much patience. We went over another road bump and there was a yelp from the back, but he assumed and I knew, it was more pathos than pain, so neither of us paid too much attention. He glanced over at me, critically.

"Looking a bit more human now." He said.

"Thanks."

"Well, you were a very peculiar colour. Were you visiting or… ?" He paused delicately.

"Visiting." I said briefly and then because, under the circumstances, that sounded rather ungracious, I added. "A little boy, we do quite a bit of work for his family, he got knocked down by a car."

"I'm sorry. Will he be OK?"

"I hope so." I said. Rightly or wrongly, this morning's little exercise had been a now or never sort of thing. I'd just have to live with whichever way the results panned out. I briefly felt again, the tube sliding up out of my throat and swallowed hard. David looked apprehensive,

"Not going to throw up are you?"

"No." I said, hoping I could keep my word. Laura Gold from the back, muttered if I did, she'd pass out, she had a phobia! I leaned back in the seat and concentrated on not making things any more complicated than they already were that day. I should have known better. Back at the office, Hilary waylaid me before I even reached the stairs.

"What've you been up to now?" she said.

"Nothing." I said, which wasn't strictly true, but I didn't know what she was talking about, so thought it best to not commit at this stage. "Why?"

"Police," she jerked her head in an upstairs direction. "Waiting for you, in your office." My heart sank, I'd only ever had one brush with the law in the past – and that hadn't gone well.

CHAPTER TWENTY-SEVEN

Kitty and Brenda were at their desks and both nodded towards my office, when I raised my eyebrows.

"Thought it best, to put him in there." said Brenda, "You know, in case anyone else came in. Police here, doesn't look good does it?"

"D'you want me in there with you, funny fellow, don't like the look of him at all?" Kitty, drew herself to her full 4ft 11 inches and looked belligerent.

"Don't be daft. I'll be fine. What did he say?" They both shrugged,

"Nothing much really," said Brenda, and I was pleased to see Kitty getting busy with the kettle, I felt a coffee might be the only thing, right now, that might keep me going. "Just flashed one of those badgy things at us, said he needed to talk to you. We told him, we didn't know when you'd be in. He said he'd wait, because you were on your way." Brenda paused, "Don't know how he knew." I shook my head, but as I hung my coat up, was sorely tempted to put it back on and turn tail.

He unfolded himself from the chair in front of my desk, as I came in, and just seemed to keep on unfolding. He was at least six foot five or six, with a thin, bony frame that seemed totally inadequate to support his height. Receding hair, emphasised the shape and boniness of his skull. He looked as if he was on day release from a medical school lecture room, a jointed example of what the students could expect to be working on in future. He was late fifties or early sixties. From behind round, wire-framed glasses, sharp eyes assessed me and he smiled briefly – I hoped he hadn't caught the skeleton thought. He was totally and unnaturally unreadable. He held out a hand I didn't take.

"I'm Boris." He said.

"Yes, I thought you might be. What do you want?"

"I work with Rachael and Ruth. Rachael told me you wouldn't want to talk."

"Rachael and I don't often agree on things, but this time, she's spot on." He laughed, surprisingly warm and full-throated and his scent washed over me, deep and dark tobacco-scented.

"And are you actually police?" I asked. He shook his head,

"Technically, no. But makes life easier if you show people a badge, lowers so many time-wasting barriers."

"Isn't that illegal?"

"I do work with them, so not totally."

"Right," I said, "Look, let's save ourselves some time here shall we? Whatever you want, the answer's no." I'd seated myself behind my desk, and pulled a pile of files towards me, indicating the time had come to get on with some work. I'd had it up to here with the lot of them, dropping in and disrupting. I just wanted to be left alone to get on with normal.

"You made the right call, this morning," he said, "With Devlin." He'd re-folded and seated himself and wasn't looking like a chap with plans to go anywhere else soon. "No choice really, you had to try and it worked – by the skin of your teeth – but it did work." I glared at him. Now I really was angry. It was one thing Rachael and Glory swanning in and out of my head at will, at least we knew each other, he was a total stranger.

"Sorry," he said, "I wanted your attention." I stood abruptly, knocking over a file which spitefully spat papers all over the floor.

"OK, you've got it." I snapped, "And now I want you to go." If there was a muscle moved, it didn't show. I rarely lost my cool, couldn't afford to. Yes, I got cross and took action, but real anger was rare, it had to be. I could feel it stirring now.

"Please, don't do anything we'll both regret." He said lazily, and for just a moment, I could feel his strength, I also knew mine. I'm not sure whether or not, I'd have tested things, but Kitty, at that moment, opened the door and bustled in with a tray, her anxiety levels running high. They'd heard me shout and shouting at policemen, wasn't at all the sort of thing they thought was a good idea. Kitty put the tray on the desk, tutted over the papers on the floor, caught my eye and swiftly kicked them into a slightly neater pile, before heading out. I sat down, the moment had passed.

"Start again?" He said. I hitched an ungracious shoulder.

"Quicker you say what you came to say, quicker you can go."

"You know about the work Ruth does?" he asked. I nodded, "With children and teens."

"Not that, the missing persons stuff." He said, I shook my head. He reached out a ridiculously long arm for his cup and sipped. "She makes a good cup of coffee, your aunt. You know she's not too good at the moment?"

"Who, Kitty?"

"Ruth."

"Oh right. Yes, Rachael said."

"She's exhausted, but there's something else too, we're not quite sure what, we're sorting it out. The problem is, until she feels better, she's a bit out of action."

"I'm sorry." I said, and indeed I was, it was far easier to be fond of Ruth, than it was to get on with her more acerbic sister. "What's it to do with me though?" The apprehension I'd felt on finding him there, wasn't easing off one little bit.

"I was there, you know, the other week." He said, I didn't like this habit he had, of going off at a conversational tangent, it was disconcerting.

"Where?"

"Martha Vevovsky. Wanted to see what you did."

"What do you mean? Was that some sort of test you were putting me through?"

"More of a two birds with one stone sort of thing." He said reflectively. "Inserting a spoke in her wheel was important – we've done that for a short while I think, though it won't last – but I wanted to see if what the others felt about you, was right." I could feel my irritation surge again.

"And... ?"

"They were." He said. I shifted in my seat and looked pointedly at my watch.

"Give me just five minutes more?" He extracted a white paper bag from his pocket, proffering it to me across the desk. I shook my head and he took out a round sweet and popped it in his mouth. I could smell aniseed – I hate that smell. "What are you hearing now?" He was doing the tangent thing again, I refused to be disconcerted.

"Nothing." I told him. He waited long enough that I felt I had to fill the pause. "Just all the normal stuff. Brenda on the phone, traffic outside, an ambulance siren, just now." He didn't say anything. I sighed, it was that sort of conversation, lots of sighing.

"Try again." He said. I didn't know exactly what he was after, but I knew what he meant. Perhaps the sooner I did what he wanted, the sooner he'd get the hell out. I reluctantly reached out, past his own smooth brown silence and into the office.

Brenda and Kitty in the next room, Brenda, being unctuously polite to one of our stroppier clients, whilst listing in her head, all the things she didn't like about him and what she'd really like to say. Kitty, focused on figures, pleased, but determined not to let me know how much, in case I thought we were home and dry and got too big for my boots. Hilary and Martin downstairs, Martin with clients, Hilary having a crafty fag and blowing the smoke out the kitchen window, because she'd assured Martin she was cutting down.

Further afield; so many streams and different levels of thought, feelings, irritations, anxieties, emotions and all the physical stuff too, headache, back pain, too hot, too cold, too tired. A woman in the supermarket next door, sweaty palmed, did she have enough in her purse to pay for what she had in her basket? The assistant at the till, griping period pains, accompanied by overwhelming relief it had arrived. Someone on their way to the dentist with toothache, already walked past the door three times, scared to go in, too much of an ache not to. A woman and her teenage son, heading into the undertakers down the road, thankful beyond words that the drunken violence would now stop and that through the years, no-one else had ever guessed, how right they'd been, never to have washed their dirty linen in public. New mother, baby in pram, screaming, screaming, how could something so small, stay awake for so long and cry so constantly, without wearing itself into silence. This wasn't what it was supposed to be, God she was frightened, couldn't cope, scared of what she might do to find that silence. Much farther away, someone was muttering paranoia as they walked… I pulled back abruptly, shutting down. He watched me, moving the aniseed ball reflectively from one cheek to the other.

"All that," I said, "Is why I deliberately 'don't hear'."

"All that," he said, "Is why we want you." Curiosity got the better of me.

"Isn't it the same for you?" I asked. He shook his head,

"I have to work at it, look for it. You open up and it floods in. But it's not a mixed bag is it?"

"Mixed bag?" I said and he snorted an aniseed-breath laugh,

"Glory said you'd do that echo thing, can see why it drives her mad. The things you hear, what do they have in common?"

"No idea."

"Of course you do. That's why you don't like it – it's the emotion. You home in on strong emotion." I frowned, but it clicked into place the way accurate statements always do. "Will you go and talk to Ruth?" He asked.

CHAPTER TWENTY-EIGHT

There is absolutely no question, I should have sent Boris off with a flea in his ear, and it was very much against my better judgement, but the following week, when Ruth was back in London, I drove over to see her. It was seven years, since I'd last been at the house in St. John's Wood. Little seemed to have altered, except Ruth.

Ed let me in, inclining his head gently, which was about as effusive as he got and Hamlet appeared from behind him and gamely tried to knock me down. There was the remembered progression along the narrow hallway, before the door opened into the astonishing light of the cluttered living room, which ran the width of the house. It had an almost entire wall of glass doors, overlooking the lushly overgrown garden, and there was a profusion of flourishing indoor plants on every surface, creating an almost seamless blending of outside and in. There were, it seemed, even more books and teetering, slightly dusty, piles of magazines than ever before. The comfort and intrinsic welcome of that room had always lingered in my memory and I was glad to see, I hadn't embroidered it over the years, nothing had changed.

The changes were all in the woman on the sofa. Comfortable plumpness had sunken in on itself, curly brown hair was liberally silver-streaked and the knotted fuchsia scarf, holding it back from her face, was a splash of colour that only underlined her pallor. For a moment, a stranger looked back at me, then she smiled and held out her hands, her unique scent filled my mind and I bent to hug her, long and hard. She felt so much smaller in my arms. Was that because I'd grown or she was diminished?

"A bit of both, I suspect." she laughed, as she hugged me back with surprising force, and the familiar, purple lavender Ruthness of her, surrounded me. She shifted her legs on the sofa, so I could slip in on the end, and we took stock. She was wearing one of her trademark jumpers, bright red with a headache-inducing, angular white pattern woven across the bosom. Her eyes, with their sharp hazel intelligence, so like her sister's, hadn't dulled, they were though, deeply violet under-shadowed. She chuckled again,

"Stella, for goodness sake, don't look so panic stricken, I'm not half as bad as I look, just a bit under the weather."

"What on earth have you been doing to yourself?" I demanded, "What's wrong with you?" She shook her head, absently brushing back a curl that had evaded the scarf, the gesture so familiar, it seemed days not years since we'd been together. Ed was behind her, plumping up the cushions she was leaning against.

"Oh, Ed, stop making like a mother hen." She patted his hand with affection, then flapped a go-away gesture, "Do me a favour, go cluck somewhere else." She turned back to me. "I've probably just overdone things a bit. Sam can't find anything physically wrong." I laughed, couldn't help it. Sam was the little boy we'd rescued from the ministrations of the Newcombe Foundation. He had some highly unusual aptitudes, one of which was an unerring accuracy of diagnosis.

"You still see him?"

"Well, of course, we do."

"He must be what? Twelve – thirteen?" I asked. She smiled, nodding towards a framed picture, fighting for its own bit of space on the windowsill, amongst the greenery. A dark-haired, deep-brown eyed boy with the solemn expression I remembered so well. The chubbiness of childhood was already pulling back, to reveal the shape of the face he would grow into. I opened my mouth, I had a whole host of questions; how was he? Where was he living? Who was he living with? Most importantly, was he well, after all, he hadn't exactly had a brilliant time during his early years. She forestalled me.

"Not now Stella dear, we have other stuff to talk about. What's Boris told you?"

"Not much. And honestly Ruth, I agreed to come today, but I really don't want to get caught up in things again, you know I don't." Under any other circumstances, I'd have given a brief run-down of all the things I'd been doing, why I'd done them, why I didn't want to do them anymore and why I was chasing normal – with increasing determination – because life was complicated enough. It wasn't necessary. She knew and she nodded,

"Sweetheart, you know we'd never force you into anything." I laughed again at that, at the sheer hypocrisy, it wasn't force they'd ever had to use, emotional blackmail being far more effective. She grinned too, sharing the thought and I relaxed a little. Somehow, Ruth reading me, was never as irritating as the others and I appreciated she'd let down her own mental guards, though not completely.

"You and I," she said, "Are alike in certain ways, and it's because of that, we want you to help out again, just until I get back on my feet. I know, I know," she raised a hand as I made to interrupt. "You don't want to, but be a good girl and hear me out. I think we're all agreed, you're not necessarily best suited to nip in and out of anywhere to sort anything quietly." Her grin took any sting out of her words. "This is different, no risks to you, all we want is information, no real involvement. Nothing you could possibly object to." I opened my mouth, to point out their ideas on what I'd object to, almost certainly didn't tie in with mine, but she carried on before I could.

"Look, we don't have too much time, because I get ridiculously tired and then I'm no use to man nor beast. So, quickest way is best?" I nodded, not hiding my reluctance, pointless hiding anything. She extended her hand and I moved closer. As I folded my fingers round hers, she grasped me, her grip tight and firm. For an instant, I flashed back to another time we'd done this and what I'd seen then. I pulled back fractionally. She tightened her hold,

"Don't be silly, this is nothing you can't handle. You're not a child anymore." I wasn't that reassured. Again, I felt there might be sizeable gaps between my assessment and hers of what I could, or indeed wanted to handle.

What she gave me, arrived in my head in an indescribable rush of intensity – images, sounds, smells, tastes, emotions – overwhelming, undiluted and seemingly in no order whatsoever. I jerked back again, but she didn't let go, for someone so apparently enfeebled, she still had a mighty fine grip. Gradually, the swirl swirled more slowly, until it settled in my mind, as if it had been there always.

"Bloody Norah!" I said.

"As you so aptly put it, bloody Norah," she said. "Now do you see? What I do, is such a small part of what needs to be done, but while I can't do it so well, I'm asking you to help." I let go her hand and sat back against the sofa cushions. "Look," she said, "Don't overdramatise and get this out of proportion. It's not something that takes over your life in any way. Sometimes weeks go past and you hear nothing at all."

"And when I do hear?" I asked. She shrugged.

"Then you simply pass it along to Boris, he has contacts he works with – the police and other agencies, although obviously, that's not anything they'd admit to in a million years. They take what you give, deal with it if they can. You've done your part."

"But why you?" I said, "Why me?" She shook her head,

"Just the way we're made my dear, just what we're good at picking up on. It's not half so strong in the others, although I think Sam is already probably a good way there." I opened my mouth to say – well, let Sam do it – then shut it abruptly, even I could see how bad that sounded. Ruth grinned,

"Indeed!"

"But Ruth, it makes no sense." I frowned. "Hundreds of people go missing every year, don't they? It can't be possible to 'hear' everyone who's in trouble." She tutted impatiently.

"Well, of course not, but some people 'shout' louder, it's those people we pick up on." I suddenly spotted the missing piece of the jigsaw which, when I did, slotted into place perfectly with an almost audible click. I sat up straighter and glared at her.

"Wait a minute. We're not talking about people who go missing of their own accord, are we?" I demanded. She adjusted the scarf, tucking another section of stray hair into protective custody and didn't answer immediately. I continued, thinking it through, "You're talking about violence – kidnap, abduction, whatever it's called. Aren't you? That's why the emotion's so intense – it's the level of fear we hear, isn't it?" Her mouth tightened and for a second or so she looked more like Rachael than Rachael.

"Stella dear, don't be more naïve than you have to, of course that's what we're talking about." Dear reader, knowing what you know about me by now, you might well be baffled as to why I didn't leave, there and then, sticking my fingers in my ears and la, la, laaing my way loudly out the door. No, me neither!

"Look," she said, "Don't make more of an issue of this than you have to. This isn't like the Martha Vee intervention, and we only let you get involved in that, because she couldn't really hurt you. All we're asking you to do now, is keep an ear open, understand what you hear, and whatever it is, pass it along. You'll always be two steps removed from any risk or danger. Apart from which, you'll only hear if it's within range."

"In range?"

"Well, you're not going to hear world-wide are you? This isn't magic dear, it's science, it's simply science they don't yet have a name or explanation for. One day they will. Promise me you'll think about it?"

PART THREE

WHAT'S ROUND THE CORNER IS OFTEN A SURPRISE

The curtain between normal and not normal is an exceedingly flimsy divider

PART THREE

WHAT'S ROUND THE CORNER IS OFTEN A SURPRISE

CHAPTER TWENTY-NINE

Other than the reason for which I'd gone there, everything else about my visit to Ruth was delightful. We'd spent a good couple of hours together, sometimes talking, sometimes not. In their odd domestic set up, not one of the three women, Ruth, Rachael nor Glory ever went near the kitchen if they could possibly help it, and certainly not to do any cooking. No, that was Ed's domain and from there, during the course of the afternoon, came sailing, mugs of his deliciously milky coffee and slices of the melt-in-the-mouth lemon drizzle cake he'd just produced. Mugs and plates, landed gently on the table in front of us, complete with spoons for stirring and forks for digging in. It was relaxing, the only place other than my own home, where these sorts of goings on were entirely normal. No wonder, despite everything, I felt so comfortable.

When I eventually did bid Ruth an affectionate goodbye, I hadn't changed my mind-set one jot and I certainly hadn't agreed to do any hard listening, any time soon. She of course knew that, she also knew, devious woman, that once something's in your head, making up your mind not to think about it is a bit like someone telling you to not think of a pink elephant. Go on, tell me that right now, you don't have one extremely solid, pink item, swishing a lazy trunk in your head?

Devlin was out of hospital, but didn't want anything to do with me. I'd called, once I heard he was home, to say I wanted to drop by, with some comics and a couple of the sticker books he loved. Susan answered the door and despite the warmth of her hug and enthusiasm of her welcome, I knew she was mortified. We chatted in the kitchen, with a nervous Celine hovering in the background. I could clearly read that Devlin, incapacitated by his leg in a cast, was several times more problematical than Devlin without his leg in a cast, and the new situation was doing nothing for Celine's nerves. Susan said he'd be so upset to have missed me, but he'd slept terribly last night, his leg was bothering him a lot, he'd fallen asleep after lunch today and she really didn't want to wake him.

He wasn't asleep, he was watching television on the small set they'd moved into his room and he'd been adamant, when she'd said I was popping in. He didn't like me, he said, had never liked me, he didn't want to see me, never wanted to ever, ever see me again and then he'd abruptly stopped shouting and started crying.

All this wasn't as big a surprise to me, as it obviously was to Susan. I suspected Devlin had no real recollection of what I'd done, but somewhere, deep down, was a trace of memory that would forever link me with fright and fear. I didn't blame him in the slightest, under the circumstances, I wouldn't have wanted much to do with me either. I had no regrets though, even as we sipped a cup of tea, and I mentally crossed the McCraes off the ongoing client list. We parted with several more hugs and mutual assurances we'd speak soon, which both of us knew to be a fair old way from the truth.

Poor old Professor Lowbell had been stricken with a bout of the nasty flu that was doing the rounds that winter. He was laid up in bed for nearly two weeks which, Dorothy said, when we spoke on the phone, was unheard of and, she reported, he'd spent most of that time moaning like blue blazes. When he did finally shake off the high fever, it was another week or so before he felt up to doing any work, so things were piling up a bit on the correspondence front.

He finally called to say he was feeling a bit better, but weak as a kitten and would I mind awfully, coming to him for our catch-up session? It was no problem, although I made sure I dressed extra warmly. The Lowbells never seemed to feel the cold in that draughty old house and although there were fiercely efficient-looking, gilded radiators in every room, they fought a losing battle against winds which, at one of the highest points in London, were always spitefully rattling the old-fashioned sash windows in their frames. The greeting, when I got there was warm, even if nothing else was and they wanted to know all about Devlin. I was able to report he was well on the mend and thank them for their help, when I'd needed it.

"Oh, go along now," said Dorothy, "What are friends for?" She was in an unusually jovial mood, which I put down to her husband's recovery. She didn't strike me as being the Florence Nightingale type, and I could well imagine she might have begrudged trudging up and down with hot drinks and sympathy, when she'd rather be doing doll stuff.

The Professor still looked a little peaky, but there was a palpable air of excitement about him. He was delighted to have been invited to be key speaker, at a highly prestigious psychology symposium in Oxford later in the year. They wanted him to talk about the impact and origins of the stories we're all fed during childhood. He was looking, he said, chuckling, for a killer title to knock 'em dead. A great line, on the pre-publicity always helped bump up numbers, and he wanted his talk well attended. We had some fun, batting ideas back and forth, Fairy Tales, Red and Raw; Happy Ever Horrors; Sleep Tight Frights, and finally settled on a working title of Once Upon A Time Terrors, subject to further thoughts occurring. He was concerned about the stammer, but we agreed he might comfortably get round that by pre-warning the audience, they might be in as much for a musical recital as a lecture. That way there'd be no element of surprise or embarrassment in the event of a problem.

Mid-way through the morning, I could see the Prof was flagging a bit. His disproportionately wide-mouthed face, which I always found rather endearing, was paler and more jowly than usual, although his cheeks were hectically flushed and his eyes bright, I hoped his fever wasn't heading back for a repeat performance. I suggested, not just for his benefit, I go and get us a couple of hot teas. I'd already lost feeling in both my feet, my hands were going the same way and I'd developed a nasty headache. I thought if I sat still much longer, movement might no longer be an option. But before I had the chance to shift myself, Dorothy had nudged open the study door with one sturdy, size 8, fur-trimmed slipper.

"Elevenses, for the workers." she announced cheerfully and bore in three steaming mugs of tea on a tray, a welcome sight. We drank in a comfortably companionable silence and I continued sorting through some of the mail he still hadn't got around to, while they quietly debated and chuckled at the various titles we'd come up with for Oxford.

"You OK, Stella?" Professor Lowbell was eyeing me over the half-moon glasses that, oddly enough, made him look more rather than less, frog-faced. "Don't mind my mentioning, but you're looking more than a bit peely-wally." He laughed at my expression, "Scottish nanny," he explained. I nodded absently. He wasn't wrong, over the last half hour or so, although I'd been determinedly trying to ignore it, I'd started feeling not that good at all. From being freezing cold, I'd switched to an uncomfortably hot sweatiness all over. Something wasn't right, and I was pretty sure it was me.

"Look," I said, giving in to it and getting to my feet abruptly and, to my alarm, none too steadily, "I'm really sorry, but I actually don't feel that well at all. Maybe I'm coming down with what you had, there's a lot of it about. Sorry to let you down, would you mind dreadfully if we left it for now and I popped in again, later in the week?" There was instant fluster of consternation and concern, which was the very last thing I wanted. I was feeling pretty rough and suddenly yearned for nothing so much, as to be home in my own bed.

The Lowbells unfortunately, as people do, leapt into immediate emergency medical mode and were having none of it. They said I was in no fit state to drive anywhere at the moment and insisted I put my feet up and had another hot drink. I found myself despite protests, firmly ensconced on the study sofa, draped in a dusty beige blanket while Prof Lowbell patted me ineffectually on the arm and Dorothy bustled off, to return with a steaming mug. She'd opted against tea, she said, and gone for honey and lemon as being more helpful under the circs.

After that, I don't remember anything much at all, until I woke up, to find two very blue, very lifeless eyes in a bone-white face, inches from mine.

CHAPTER THIRTY

I shrieked and threw myself violently backwards, although I think what came out was more of a small mewling sound. I also found I couldn't move very far at all, certainly not as far as I wanted to. It seemed I was lying, in bed, with a sheet and blankets tucked uncomfortably tight around me. I struggled to make some sense of that.

My head felt as if it was expanding and contracting, none too gently, in and out, in and out, it wasn't pleasant. With no small effort, I managed to haul out an arm from the tight-tucked blanket. I thought if I could just stop the inning and outing for a moment, I might be able to think a bit straighter. My arm was encased in pristine white cotton, with a frill at the wrist, it wasn't anything I recognised. I got hand to head and held on for a bit, but it didn't seem to help. I took it away, to reach out slowly – something was wrong with the way my eyes were focusing – and touch my blue-eyed, silent companion. She was as hard, cold and lifeless as she looked. Not quite life-size, but not far off, I expelled a small breath. Nothing to worry about, just a doll. No idea why we were sharing a bed though.

Gradually, and it was like wading through treacle, bits and pieces began to fit together to make some sense. I wasn't well. Everybody said, the wretched flu descended out of nowhere and knocked you for six, although it seemed to have knocked me further than that – and I'd been taken ill at the Lowbell's – God how embarrassing! Still holding my head, because it didn't feel, in any way, securely attached to the rest of me, I risked a look around, although even just moving my eyeballs, hurt more than I'd have thought possible.

The bed, into which I was so firmly tucked, was in an ornately corniced, high ceilinged and elegantly proportioned square room. I could see a mantle-pieced fireplace opposite, with wide, faded tapestries hanging to either side, blowing gently in a slight draught. Turning my head cautiously to one side, there was a door on the far side of the room and on the opposite wall, deep red, full length velvet curtains drawn over the windows. It must have still been daylight, because wintry sunshine was leaking through cracks in the draped material. I had no idea of the time, nor how long I'd been asleep. I lifted my oddly befrilled wrist, but I wasn't wearing my watch and, for the life of me, didn't have the strength, or even the urge, to see if it was nearby.

I felt physically ill and completely mortified that they'd had to look after me. The minimal effort of moving my arm, seemed to have used up any energy reserves I may have had. I felt completely helpless and knew, from the soreness of my eyes when I blinked, I probably had a high temperature. I'd have to get the Lowbells to ring my parents, or perhaps Brenda, certainly someone needed to come and get me, and the sooner the better. I wanted to call out, let them know I was awake, but couldn't seem to manage much more than a pathetically dry croak, I didn't even know where, in that rambling house, they might be. I opened up, to see if I could locate them, but my mind was as fogged and weak as everything else.

"Bit of a pickle, eh?" I muttered under my breath. My companion didn't comment, and I turned my head away, just a doll, but blooming unnerving nevertheless, must be one of Dorothy's prized collection; indeed, maybe this was the doll's bed in the first place and I was the unwelcome addition. I giggled weakly.

Obviously, one of the Lowbells would put in an appearance sooner or later, until they did, there really didn't seem to be much I could do. I tried to take a deep breath, but my chest felt tight and sore and everything, including what I was wearing, seemed to be smelling musty, dusty and dry, or maybe that was the temperature talking. I coughed for a bit and then I suppose I must have drifted off.

I don't know how much later it was, when I woke up again. I'd been dreaming in vivid technicolour, with full sound effects, the way you do when you're feverish. Various fairy tale characters had been trooping through my head, but with rather more blood and gore than one would have liked, and certainly not with any happy ever afterings. I was mildly surprised to find myself propped, a little lop-sidedly, against some stacked pillows. Someone was trying to poke a spoon in my mouth. I opened it to speak, they seized the moment, and I found myself swallowing hot tomato soup, which stung my throat, all the way down. I was having quite a problem with my eyelids, which didn't appear to be operating as normal and certainly not in sync. It seemed a hassle to tackle both of them, so I let the right one stay where it was and concentrated on getting the left open.

"Well, there you are, my dear!" Dorothy Lowbell was seated on the side of the bed, a tassel-shaded, bedside light shining pinkly on her face. "We thought you should get something down you. Lowbell's specially made you up some of his tomato and basil soup." A full spoon advanced purposefully again.

"I'm so sorry," I said, "This is dreadful, I've put you to so much trouble. What's the time? Can you ring Brenda at the office, or I'll give you my home phone number and... "

"I'll do no such thing," she said firmly, "You're in no fit state to go anywhere, young lady." I opened my mouth to say I really would prefer to be at home, and she popped the spoon in swiftly, carefully scooping up a drop or two that didn't quite make it, then dabbing my lips with a stiffly laundered white napkin. It came away looking bloodied.

I had another of the white napkins tucked in under my chin, I could feel it scratchy against my neck. I reached out to read her but couldn't, she was always pretty tightly encompassed and at the moment, my mind felt as wobbly as I did. In fact, I suddenly noticed, the room was circling round me in a slow, stately and thoroughly disconcerting manner. It was making me nauseous, but I did feel, it would be the height of bad manners to throw up the specially made soup. I put a hand out to my right, to rest on the bed and stabilise myself a bit and encountered the rigid arm of my unlikely bed-mate, who I'd completely forgotten was there. I gasped, swallowed soup too quickly and started to choke. Dorothy tutted sympathetically and stood to move me forward a little, so she could pat me firmly on the back.

"Better?" she asked, when I'd regained breath. I nodded then stopped, because that only made the room move faster. I saw, next to me, my inanimate friend was also propped up against her pillows. Gazing sightlessly ahead, she was wearing a high-necked, white cotton, Victorian style nightdress with long sleeves ending in a frill at her wrist. A familiar frill. I looked down and yes, sure enough, we were identically clad. With her hair, a similar shade to mine and our matching outfits, I was starting to feel like two thirds of the Beverley Sisters.

"We thought you'd like some company." Said Dorothy, with satisfaction, and the mattress dipped alarmingly, as she sat down again and smiled happily at me. I nodded my thanks, how thoughtful. Dorothy gently turned my face back towards her, so she could make with the spoon again. But I pulled away.

"Look," I said, as firmly as I could, although I really didn't want to be rude. "This is awfully kind of you, but I should get out of your hair – apart from which, you know what my lot are like, they'll be sending out search parties if I don't turn up soon. If I could just use your phone. I made to climb out of the bed, but she tutted again, pushing my legs firmly back into place.

"Now, Stella, stop that this minute. You're not nearly well enough to go anywhere, you're running a nasty, high temperature. We rang the office earlier, to explain what had happened. They agreed it made sense for you to stay here, at least overnight, and Kitty was phoning home, to let them know. Now, if you've had enough soup, I think you should lie down again. This is a very nasty do, Lowbell was exceedingly poorly with it, so we don't want to take chances. You need lots of rest, plenty of fluids, let it run its course, nothing else to be done, I'm afraid." She whipped out the scratchy napkin, from where it was tucked under my chin, flattened the pillows, and pushed me gently but firmly down again. I didn't put up any resistance because now, not only was the room still turning, but I seemed to be too. It was most unpleasant. She leaned over to switch off the light. The whole thing was all a bit odd and awkward, but the bed was warm and I couldn't keep my eyes open any more.

My dreams were still giving me grief, and when I next surfaced, it was with one of those heart-stopping jerks, that make you feel you've jumped right out of your skin. It was dark in the room, no light now showing around the curtains. It felt like the middle of the night. My mouth was dry, stale and stiff, my lips sore and my nose full of the fusty, musky scent of the room. When I felt a bit more like it, I thought, I'd take myself over and open a window, to get some fresh air blowing in.

I laboriously hoisted myself up on an elbow to see if, by chance, Dorothy had left a glass of water by the bed. Thankfully she had. I drank gratefully, although then realised, I needed the toilet. I couldn't possibly call out and disturb the Lowbells, I'd just have to pull myself together and find the bathroom on my own. Switching on the bedside light I managed, awkwardly, to wriggle out from under the tightly tucked sheets and blankets – the woman certainly knew how to make a bed. After a bit of fumbling with my feet on the floor, I couldn't find any sign of my shoes and couldn't be bothered to look harder. The only good thing at this point seemed to be, I didn't need a dressing gown, I was more than decently covered in the long broderie anglaise effort. Holding it up, tiptoeing across the room and trying not to tread on anything that creaked, I lacked only night cap and candle to be a dead ringer for Wee Willie Winkie.

The bedroom door was stuck. I'd turned the ornate gilt handle carefully and quietly, not wanting any noise, but the door wouldn't budge. OK, this was serious. I really did have to go to the bathroom. I gave up on subtlety. If the doors didn't work, then the Lowbells had only themselves to blame if they were disturbed in the middle of the night. It seemed an age though, before they eventually pitched up.

"Stella, my dear girl, what on earth is the matter?" Dorothy, voluminous in pink flannelette, put both hands out to me, as she opened the door and I stumbled towards her. Behind her, in the darkened hall, a paisley-pyjama clad Professor Lowbell looked equally concerned. By this time though, I was pretty much beyond social embarrassment. She put both her arms round me, shooed the Prof back to wherever their bedroom was, and led me a little way along the uncarpeted corridor. Here, lit by a single bulb at ceiling centre, was a cavernous, arctic-chilled, old fashioned, black and white tiled bathroom with a free-standing, chipped enamel bath tub, but more importantly – a large, wooden-seated toilet. The Lowbells obviously didn't go in a lot for creature comforts, but I was in no position to be picky, I don't think I've been so glad to see anything in my life.

She tactfully waited for me, having cautioned me not to lock the bathroom door – in case I came over dizzy. As she took me back to my bedroom, I was grateful for the solidity of her. My temperature must have been sky high again, because I felt more lightheaded and befogged than ever, each step was a herculean effort and as we moved across the room, one of my legs buckled under me. If she hadn't been holding on, I'd have gone down. I was relieved beyond anything, to climb back into that bed and even the rigorous tucking in seemed more comfort than constriction. I was so out of it by then, I think I might even have murmured a greeting to my friend-in-residence, on the other side of the bed. Dorothy was handing me a couple of pills with a glass of water.

"To bring that temperature down." I obediently swallowed, handing the glass back to her with murmured thanks. "And this," she was pouring thick yellow liquid from a bottle into a teaspoon, "Decongestant, it was what the doctor prescribed for Lowbell, lucky we have some left." I swallowed that too, and suspect I was asleep again before my head hit the pillow.

Coming slowly back to consciousness, goodness only knows how much later, I can't say I was feeling much better. The head inning and outing was still occurring, the room hadn't anchored yet and although the thick velvet curtains were still closed, bright sunlight spiking through, at the sides of the material, was sharp and painful to look at. I turned my head away, the light looked like it was strobing, which only added to the nausea. I wondered when Dorothy would be in with something to eat and drink. I don't think I was hungry, I just wanted to be looked after.

I felt sure there was something I ought to be doing, or at least thinking about doing, but the elaborately carved, floral plaster decorations in one corner of the room, caught my eye and my attention. It was so beautiful, so intricately constructed, I simply wanted to look and look. Deep down, way beyond my current reach, a thought, several thoughts actually, were niggling. I tried to drag my concentration from the gorgeously carved flowers, but couldn't seem to and neither could I pin down my unease. After a moment or two, I gave up. Why bother?

After a while, no idea how long, the door opened and Dorothy bustled in. The sound of the soles of her slippers, squeaking against the wooden floor as she walked, was disproportionately loud in the otherwise silent room, and when she spoke, I winced. My ears seemed to have gone into overdrive. She noticed and lowered her voice,

"And how are we this morning?"

"Not sure about you, but I've certainly had better days!" I muttered, probably a little ungraciously. My tongue didn't feel familiar in any way, it was far too big for my mouth. She chuckled affectionately and lowered a tray to the bedside table. She'd also brought me a fresh nightgown to change into – still the white Victorian look. I started to apologise again, for all the work I was putting them to, but she waved it away with a hand-flap.

"I've told you, no trouble whatsoever and if you feel up to it, you can have a bath later. Let's see how you go on, shall we? Now, I've brought you some fresh-squeezed orange-juice, lots of vitamin C, do you a world of good." She helped me sit up and drink, propping the pillows behind me. I was just about to ask, without sounding rude, if friend in the bed, sweet though she was, could be removed, because she was giving me the heebie-jeebies, when there was a knock on the half open door and Professor Lowbell popped his head comically around.

"Room for a little one?" He enquired, Dorothy waved him in and I smiled at him, at least my brain instructed my mouth to smile, I'm not sure it got through.

"… and a soft boiled egg, lots of goodness in that." Dorothy was spoon-ready again. I hate soft-boiled egg, but didn't have the energy to argue, so let the glutinous stuff slide down without protest. Prof Lowbell meanwhile had made himself comfortable, in the armchair near the fireplace, and was regarding us with a beatific smile.

"Well, this is all very cosy and comfortable isn't it?" He said, although cosy and comfortable were certainly not what I was feeling. "Not often lucky enough to have guests, are we Dottie?"

"Not nearly often enough." She agreed. The juice and egg had revived me a bit. I sat up a little straighter and made an attempt to gather my scattered wits, not to mention my dignity. As I might have mentioned before, I was all in favour of client contact, but that didn't mean I wanted to move in with them.

Reflexively I opened up, I wouldn't normally read them, it wasn't polite, but exceptional circumstances. My mind though, just wasn't doing what it should and I was overwhelmed by a feeling I didn't immediately recognise. I struggled to grasp it, as it slipped down and away into the soft cotton wool that was currently the inside of my head. Just as it disappeared, I realised what it was. I felt powerless. For probably the first time in my life, I didn't have the tools to look after myself. My heart started to pound in time with my head.

"Stella?" Dorothy was holding out two pills again, in the palm of her hand. "For the temperature my dear," she reminded me. "And then two spoons of the medicine."

"No, wait," I shook my head, "I think it might be the medicine that's making me feel worse, too drowsy, I don't want any more." Professor Lowbell chuckled and cleared his throat theatrically, to get my attention, the sound bouncing off the walls of the room.

"No use arguing with Dotty, young lady. Dotty says medicine, medicine it is. She's fierce." I smiled, but shook my head again. They couldn't possibly know, but my reaction to any kind of medication had always been completely disproportionate, it was the reason I hadn't risked so much as an aspirin for years.

"I'd really rather not."

"Open wide now, there's a good girl." He was right, this was a woman who didn't take no for an answer. I didn't seem to have a great deal of choice, nor anywhere near the strength for an argument. I swallowed the damn pills and then she tipped two lots of the thick fluid into my mouth. It trickled, viscous and bitter down my sore throat.

The effect was immediate and I vaguely remembered, last time she'd only given me one spoonful. I wanted to discuss this, but my tongue seemed to be losing the ability to do the sort of thing it usually did, and the light from the now partially drawn-back curtains, was lasering my eyes. I shut them, then with an effort, got them re-opened, it seemed so rude to go to sleep while they were still there.

There was a small, gilt bedecked carriage clock, on a chest of drawers across the room and now it chimed the hour, but my ears had gone funny again – the chimes went right through me and set my teeth on edge. Dorothy was busy flattening out the pillows. She was talking to me, but I couldn't take in what she was saying, I hoped it wasn't important. I would have to try and explain to them about the medicine, as soon as I could, I didn't like the effects and thought it was probably making whatever I had, worse and not better.

CHAPTER THIRTY-ONE

It was the incongruous pop and flash of a camera bulb that woke me next. It was dark again and the bedside light was pinkly on. Friend in the bed, was present and correct and so were the Lowbells, who were sitting on a couple of chairs by the bed, for all the world, as if hospital visiting. I tried to work out whether they'd been there all the time I was sleeping, I sincerely hoped not, that'd be taking hospitality and thoughtfulness a step too far.

Dorothy had a notebook and pen that she put down for a moment as she saw me open my eyes. She stood to re-angle the lampshade, so the light wasn't shining directly on my face. Professor Lowbell was holding an opened lever arch file on his knee, thick with typewritten pages. He bent to put the camera, one of those clever new Polaroid ones, down on the floor beside him. I still couldn't reach out and read either one of them, neither was I able to move anything, I tried gently with the pen and notepad, Dorothy had just laid on the table next to me – nothing, zilch!

"Just a little something to record your progress, Stella m'dear." Prof Lowbell said. I wasn't thrilled, I hate having my photo taken at the best of times and felt this might be an eccentricity too far, on his part. He'd peeled the paper off the photo and was waving it back and forth, to dry it out. I could see the fuzzy, ill-defined image, gradually becoming clearer – which was more than I could say for my head. He was leaning forward now, froggy face concerned. "Now then, how did you sleep?" He was sweating slightly, drops of moisture magnifying enlarged pores on his face. The fire, below the mantelpiece had been lit and was crackling gently. It should have been a comforting sound but oddly enough wasn't – maybe my ears were still playing up.

"Progress?" I said, "I don't seem to be making much, I'm afraid. I'm still feeling rough and I've been having some pretty horrible nightmares." I propped myself up on an elbow and Dorothy reached round to pull the pillows up behind me. She was holding a glass of orange juice to my lips and I sipped gratefully, although it tasted sour, the way everything does when you're ill. "Must be the temperature," I said, "That gives you funny dreams doesn't it?" Professor Lowbell pushed his glasses up his nose with his middle finger, a gesture I'd become so familiar with, over the years, I could almost predict the next time he was going to do it. He leaned back a little in his chair and smiled warmly at me.

"Of course, of course it does. We know our brains are adapting all the time and your's right now is working under the dual stresses of illness and input." Dorothy was solicitously tucking me in again, I must have pulled the sheets and blankets loose around me. I moved away from her hands.

"Input?" I said. He nodded eagerly, opened his mouth, got stuck on what he was trying to say, so sang it.

"Fever, fear and fairy tales." He warbled, spitting the words out like marbles and then, having cleared the blockage, continued, "Fascinating combination – now, look here, my dear, I've been taking the opportunity to do a bit of reading aloud to you, while you were sleeping, some of our stories with which you're familiar. Naturally," he added, "I'm so sorry you've had the misfortune to be struck down with this vicious little bug, sincerely hope it wasn't my good-self who passed it along, but honestly it couldn't have come at a better time, could it?" He leaned forward again, elbows on knees, hands clasped between. "You don't mind, do you? A few days, a few bad dreams, that's all. Nothing too taxing and all in the interests of research? You've always been so interested in my work, haven't you?" He nodded encouragingly and the mattress tipped dangerously again, as Dorothy seated herself on the side.

I shook my head, and then stopped, because it was making me dizzy. As it so happened, I did mind, I minded a lot. This was really silly. Quite frankly, the last thing I had any interest in at the moment, was his work. No wonder I'd been having such awful nightmares, I knew what was in some of those stories and they weren't designed to sweeten anyone's dreams.

"Look." I said, sitting up straighter and concentrating on getting words out coherently. "You've both been very kind, and I truly appreciate the way you've looked after me. But no. If you don't mind, I really don't want to help with any research. Maybe when I'm feeling better, but not now. Now, I really would like to phone home, so they can come and get me, right away." I was just deciding how best to swing my legs past the rather solid obstacle that was Dorothy, when she reached out, put the heel of her hand squarely on my forehead and pushed, hard. I toppled back and my head smacked into the wooden headboard with an audible crack. Dorothy chuckled.

"I don't think so." She said cheerfully.

I've long maintained, the curtain between normal and not normal, is a flimsy divider indeed, but whilst it's always good to have a theory proved, I didn't think this was the time for patting myself on the back. Vision blurred by tears of pain and shock, I gazed at Professor Lowbell and Dorothy and they gazed amiably back.

I think the bang on the head must have knocked into place, some remnants of my common sense. It suddenly seemed clear that, under these oddest of circumstances, the best path to pursue might be a devious one. Accordingly, I burst into tears – it wasn't difficult, I was feeling pretty hard done by and the bash on the head hadn't done my headache any favours.

"I'm sorry," I sobbed, "It's just I'm really not feeling well and would much rather go home, but if you do think I can help you, before I go and if it's important to you, then of course I'll stay a bit longer." It sounded pretty weak, even to me, but to the couple hemming me in, in that overheated room, it appeared to make good sense. They nodded approvingly and Dorothy patted me warmly on the arm.

"Excellent, poppet, that's the ticket." she said, and then turning to the Prof, "Can I show her, can I show her now?" He nodded indulgently. I stared at them. This felt like an optical illusion. Maybe you know the one I was thinking of – the Greek urn which, in an instant, becomes two faces? I'd been seeing two people I knew so well, I could have described their features and funny ways with my eyes closed yet suddenly, my perception, all I thought I knew, had been turned on its head and now, I was looking at a completely different picture.

"Come along then." Dorothy, was helping me out of the bed, holding my arm, walking me across the room. We moved, unsteadily, to one of the floral tapestries framing the fire. Stretching to reach behind it, with a flourish, she pulled a cord attached to runners at the top, and the tapestry folded back on itself. Behind it, five, deep, bevelled glass shelves, were set into the alcove. On each of the shelves were dolls. Dorothy was still holding my arm tightly, above the elbow, and we moved across to the second tapestry, so she could draw that back as well.

On these shelves too, were dolls. Dolls sitting, dolls standing, a couple of babies – blanket cocooned – dolls with beautifully coiffed hair and those with just a few hanks of rotted strands on balded, cracked skulls. There were dolls elaborately costumed and bonneted, others pinkly naked. There were bone-white faced dolls, hectically rouged ones and others with patchily discoloured fabric features. Some were looking boldly at me, others slyly sideways. There were cross-eyed gazes and eyeless faces and the odd smashed nose and badly cracked forehead. The combined impact was more than suffocating. It was as if, revealed, let out from behind the tapestries, they were sucking air from the room. I took a breath – the musty smell was even more in evidence here – and an instinctive step back, but the grip on my arm was painfully firm.

"Well now." said Dorothy, "What do you think Stella? These are my favourite girls, although I do have one or two boys amongst them, but dolls were meant to be girls, don't you agree? I've many more, no room to display them here. All in all, probably one of the finest antique collections you'll find, outside of the museums. Although," she added reflectively, "There are always those special ones you're after, that you haven't yet laid hands on. But there's always time. Precious, aren't they?"

"Now Dotty, my angel, not too much talking." Professor Lowbell was still seated, but had swivelled in his chair to follow our progress. "Stella's looking a little flushed to me, I'm worried her temperature's going up again." Dorothy looked at me assessingly. If anyone was looking flushed, it was her, there was an unflattering, damp sheen of excitement on her chin and forehead and her eyes glittered, I'd no idea she could look so animated.

"Ah, Lowbell, let me just introduce her to Adelaide." She said, "Then it's back to bed for you, young lady." She softly patted my hand, which she'd now tucked firmly into the crook of her arm and led me to one side of the left hand alcove.

Adelaide stood, about eighteen inches tall, reaching out to us with outstretched arms and open hands. She had an oddly shaped head, top-knotted with a faded gold plaited braid, painted deep-brown eyes on a porcelain face and a simpery, sugary smile. Dorothy picked her up, cooing softly as she did. There must have been a key beneath the wide, layered lace skirt, which was probably once red, but was now a darker duller colour altogether. Returned gently to her position on the shelf, Adelaide stared smilingly at us for a moment then, with a deep, rusty sigh, her head began to turn jerkily on her neck, smiling face replaced by a crying face with sorrowfully downturned mouth and artfully painted tears. Her head tilted to one side, as if inviting sympathy and stayed there for a few seconds before, with another whirr and groan, she turned it again. The face she showed us this time was terrified, mouth a howling, horrified 'o' shape and from deep inside her body came a shrill, surprisingly loud and discordant shrieking. Dorothy turned to me, in genuine delight,

"She's an automaton, made in the 1860's. Cloth and papier mâché, apart from her head and hands – they're bisque porcelain. Isn't she wonderful?" I nodded slowly, although wonderful wasn't the first word I'd have gone for. The clockwork cycle had finished with the howling, so it was that face, staring out at us now from the shelf. It wasn't a good look, but I sympathised with how she was feeling.

"Time for your pills I think, and back to bed with you, chop, chop." Dorothy turned me away from the serried ranks of dolls and we walked slowly back. I wasn't sure whether my knees were knocking from flu or fear. I felt totally cut off, because half my senses seemed to have taken a hike and I hadn't a clue whether they were coming back any time soon, if ever. I suddenly didn't want Normal at all. I wanted Strange and all it gave me. Without that, I certainly didn't want to be coping with the couple of raving lunatics, the Lowbells had unexpectedly turned into. It had become increasingly apparent, even in my sadly befuddled state, that they may not have my best interests at heart. For a moment, I thought about taking a leaf out of Adelaide's book and shrieking too.

Dorothy was solicitously and tightly tucking me in again, and the Professor was nodding genially at both of us. She handed me a couple more of the pills, I palmed them, whilst making a show of swallowing and grimacing. The orange juice she handed me to wash them down still tasted bitter, so although I had to have some of it, I took the bare minimum, then waved it away feebly.

"Sore throat." I muttered. We all three smiled at each other. And then we chuckled a little, as I settled beneath the blankets and they both exaggeratedly mimed tip-toeing out of the room. This time, because I was listening for it. I heard the sound of the key turning in the lock. My jaunt to the shelves and back must have tired me out, because, even though I was trying to stay awake and work out some kind of a game plan, I went to sleep and the next time I woke up, it was because of the screaming.

CHAPTER THIRTY-TWO

It was high-pitched and terror-filled. It hurt my head and it hurt my throat, because, it turned out it was me doing the screaming, as I struggled to find my way out of yet another nightmare. The Lowbells were back at the side of the bed. I wondered whether they'd really gone at all, or had they simply tip-toed out then tip-toed back in again.

"Stella, calm down, calm down my dear. Take a deep breath. What is it that frightened you?" Professor Lowbell was leaning over, shaking my arm. He was too close, I caught a whiff of stale coffee on his breath.

"Don't remember," I said, "Gone now."

"Try." He said.

"I'm sorry? I don't…" He interrupted.

"Stella, please, I must ask you to try and be more helpful, it's important. What were you dreaming about? Was it the story I read you earlier? Was it something you remembered from the story that made you scream?"

"Or," I hadn't noticed Dorothy, moving to the other side of the bed. "Was it Letitia?" I must have looked blank, because she inclined her head slowly towards the large doll in the bed. "Look," said Dorothy, "Look at Letitia." I turned slowly, couldn't seem to help myself. Bed friend was lying flat on her pillows as was I, and as I turned my head towards her, she slowly turned hers towards me. As she opened her mouth to speak. I think I was probably screaming again.

Another flash and pop of the ruddy camera, again pulled me back to my senses, although certainly not all the way. I decided, if he didn't stop taking photos of me when I was asleep, I was going to take his precious Polaroid and ram it somewhere the sun didn't shine.

I also decided I wasn't going to take the risk of turning my head to look at the lovely Letitia again. Truth to tell, I was no longer entirely sure exactly what I had or hadn't seen. Maybe it was fever-induced over-imagination, possibly something to do with whatever they'd been pumping me full of, it could even be some kind of post hypnotic suggestion. Of course, the other explanation might be, I'd just gone completely round the bend. Whatever, I had wit enough remaining to tell me, the time had come to take stock, and quickly.

First and foremost, I needed to stop all the panicking and screaming, that was doing nobody any good. Secondly, I needed to make sure I stopped taking any more of what was being dished out and thirdly and finally, I needed to bring this unfortunate little episode to a close. Having assembled a 'to do' list, I immediately felt a little better, there's nothing like an agenda to get your mind in order.

My next thought though was a rather obvious and uncomfortable one and maybe should have been at the top of the list – where could things go from here? The Lowbells had crossed a line, we could hardly pretend they hadn't. How could this conceivably have a neat and happy ending? Through slitted eyelids, I looked over at the two people I knew so well, yet didn't know at all. They were again, planted on chairs by the side of the bed. They seemed perfectly relaxed and at ease and both smiled at me. I smiled co-operatively and sleepily back, the dopier they thought I was, the better for all of us.

The curtains were open, although dusk was drawing in again. I'd absolutely no idea how long I'd been there, maybe two days, possibly three? I'd spent so much time sleeping off whatever bug I'd had in the first place, added to which were the drugs, I was certain they'd been giving me, for all I knew it could have been a lot longer.

The tapestries at the end of the room had been left drawn back, so there were eyes of every colour, shape and texture on me. It was whilst contemplating those unsettling gazes, that another, belated and even more obvious thought sidled into my confused and aching head. Where the heck was everybody? Whilst my family might have accepted I was staying over at the Lowbells' for a night or even two, they surely would have noticed if I'd disappeared for longer – it didn't make any kind of sense. Unless, the Lowbells hadn't in fact let them know where I was. But surely, in that case, there'd have been an indignant crowd, headed up by my parents, not to mention Kitty, Brenda and a fair section of North West London constabulary, banging on the door to find out where I'd got to. And what about Glory and the Peacocks – always there when I didn't want them, where were they now, when I did?

"Now then, what's going on in that busy little head of yours, Stella?" The Professor queried reproachfully. He had his lever arch file open again on his knees and was leaning forward. I didn't think it was politic to let him know, so shook it slightly, smiled vaguely and shut my eyes to do some more thinking.

"Sleeping Beauty." He said, for a moment I thought he was being personal, then realised he was referring to his notes. He shook my arm slightly, "Stay awake now, my dear, I want to try reading to you while you're awake. And then, when you drop off again, I'm going to leave you with a notebook, so you can note down what you remember from your dreams. Can you do that for me?" I nodded slowly. I wasn't happy. I knew what was coming, we'd worked on a number of different texts and editions of the story, tracing it back to its 14th century roots, which were as dark and tangled as those of most of the classic fairy tales. As soon as he started reading from his notes, I recognised his own translation, from Italian, of Basile's, Sun, Moon and Talia. Published around the 1600s, it was a jolly little fable, not holding back on anything including rape, incest and a touch of cannibalism – even Disney couldn't have done much with this version.

I'd unfortunately, come to know the story well, so was able to tune out, whilst still appearing to listen. The familiar tone of Professor Lowbell's light voice reading, was almost relaxing – if you weren't actually listening to the words. I also realised, that whilst I still felt far from well, my head was clearing, the light wasn't hurting my eyes in the same way and sound levels seemed to be returning to where they should be. All in all, if you ignored a few things, like the dolls, the drugging, the locked door, what he was reading and the occasional photographs he was taking of my expressions as I slept – it was all quite cosy.

It must have been around about that time that I first heard a whisper. So faint was it and so full was my head of other stuff, that for a while, it didn't register, so I ignored it. Then it got a little louder, at which point I deliberately ignored it. I didn't know what drugs I might still have in my system, but I wasn't taking chances. If it was Letitia or Adelaide trying to get through to me, I wasn't taking calls. And then, the all-encompassing, musty dank scent of the room, to which I'd grown accustomed, was suddenly drenched and drowned by purple-deep lavender. I sucked in my breath sharply and the Lowbells both looked up.

"That bit…" I said, with no idea where we were in the tale, but confident we'd never be far from a gasp-eliciting section, "… always gets me." Professor Lowbell nodded approvingly and turned his eyes back to the page.

"Ruth?" I said silently. Nothing. I tried again, still nothing and then, when I was about to blame imagination and wishful thinking, she was there, in my head.

"Stella? Thank God. At last. Are you all right? Where are you?" I gave a little sob out loud. Couldn't help myself.

"Sorry." I said to Professor Lowbell, who'd looked up again, sharply.

"This is really most interesting Stella." He said, "You're familiar with this text, yet your reactions are almost as if hearing it for the first time. Significant I think. Dotty, make a note, will you?"

"Done." She jotted, put the notebook back on the table and then patted my arm. "I think my dear we're feeling a teeny bit perkier today, than of late, what do you say? Time for some more medicine soon though, don't want that pesky temperature shooting up again." I nodded and let my eyelids droop.

"I'm actually pretty tired." I said and yawned. "I'll just shut my eyes for a bit first, if you don't mind." After a moment or two, I felt her breath, unpleasantly hot on my cheek, as she leaned heavily over me.

"Hmm, gone again." She murmured to him. "Maybe only one spoonful on the next dose? What do you think, Lowbell?" I could hear him shift in his chair and re-adjust the folder on his knee.

"No, the higher dose is good. More time we have with her asleep, the more access to her sub-conscious. I'm truly intrigued, Dottie, her reactions aren't always as I'd expect." I turned in the bed, onto my side, away from them, concentrating on breathing evenly. Right now I'd been thrown a lifeline, I needed to grab that with both hands.

"Stella, can you hear me?" I wanted to shriek back at Ruth, that of course I could bloody well hear her, but struggle as I might, I couldn't get a thought out there. I couldn't make her hear me again, I felt switched off at source, like an unplugged hoover. The frustration was unbearable. I wanted to cry, scream, shout and bang my head against the pillow. Amidst all the angst though, I was thankful to the core that even if it was a one-way conversation, something at least must be coming back to me, it wasn't gone for good.

"Stella, hang on. The others are with me now – Sam's here too, we couldn't reach you properly before, there's something wrong, blocked." For a second or so, I could feel them all behind her; Glory, Ed and Rachael, before they were over-ridden by the unmistakeable, soft buttery chocolate strength, that was Sam. The intervening years, had in no way faded my memories, and for a second or two, I instinctively tried to protect myself, both from him and the fear I'd experienced then. But as he moved through my mind, I could feel him scanning, assessing, re-adjusting and I reckoned things couldn't get much worse, I might as well let him see what he could do.

There was a sharp, painful, internal tug in my head, that vanished almost as I felt it. And suddenly I was flooded. Cascades of sound, sensation, and thought – loud, loud, loud. I yelped, then remembered where I was and turned it into a snorey kind of a snort. My head felt wide open and – like a library in an earthquake – everything inside had fallen off the shelves, to make a terribly mixed mess on the floor, no sense, no order. I could feel the others, holding back until I'd gained some control and organised everything as best I could.

I knew I wasn't back to normal, there were things missing that shouldn't have been. I could read both Lowbells now, loud and clear and, like the fairy tales, they didn't make for pleasant reading. I'd have to focus on that shortly. But I still couldn't, for the life of me, move anything, I had my back turned to the notebook and pen on my bedside table, but knew they were obstinately static.

"Wait!" Well, no mistaking who'd appointed herself spokeswoman, although I appreciated the fact they weren't all talking at once. Rachael cut through to the nub. "Sam's done what he can. You've been pretty ill with this virus, but you've also got high levels of sedative and hallucinogenic in your system, he can't work out how you're still conscious. Mind you," A swift thought, directed at the others as much as me, "He may not appreciate how bloody minded you are! Anyway, don't worry, you'll get everything back, this is probably only temporary, but listen, don't let them give you anything else. Can you hear me? Can you answer? Do you understand?

"Of course I understand." I snapped back at her. "Not stupid, just in a bit of a sticky situation here."

"Stella, the situation is serious."

"Well, I know that. I am the one stuck in a locked room, with a lorry-load of dolls, drugged up to the eyeballs – me, not the dolls – and two lunatics taking happy snappy, shots." Glory broke in.

"Shut up a minute Stella, do you know where you are?"

"Well of course I do – in Hampstead, at the Lowbell's house, they're clients... "

"No you're not."

"Yes I am."

"No, you're not." It was all starting to sound a bit pantomime and I wanted to laugh, but maybe that was just the sheer relief of being in contact again.

"The police searched the house, top to bottom." Glory said. That stopped me in my tracks.

"Well I must be here, where else could I be?" I paused, "Anyway if Ruth found me, you know where I am."

"She found you, because she heard you, but that doesn't mean you've popped up with an address and postcode." Rachael put in – always with the sarcasm.

"When? When did they search the house?" I asked.

"Last week." said Glory.

"Last week?" I was having trouble keeping up the regular breathing thing. "How long... ?"

"Eight days, you've been missing for eight days."

"Didn't know if you were dead or alive, till just now." Rachael grumbled, although behind the gruffness I caught acute anxiety, I was touched, but immediately thought of what my family must be going through.

"You have to let them know I'm OK... promise me... right away."

"Of course," Glory said. "But listen Stella, we may not have much time. You're not the first."

"Not the first what?"

"Victim." Said Rachael.

CHAPTER THIRTY-THREE

"You know," Sam cut in, "I think she is, where she thinks she is. When Boris went in with the police, he wouldn't have heard her, if she wasn't conscious."

"But they searched the whole house, didn't find anything." Said Glory.

"If she was hidden, they wouldn't have done." Sam, adept as ever, at pointing out the blindingly obvious. But I now had a rather more urgent query.

"What do you mean, victim? Are you saying they've done this before?" There was a muttered confab at the other end, before Glory said,

"We think so."

"And?"

"And what?" she said. I tutted internally, this was no time to dance around an issue.

"What happened to the others?"

"We don't think it ended well." Said Rachael. "But not to worry, Ruth and Sam both agree you're still in Hampstead, we've got it all in hand. Trust me." And of course I did. She might be the most infuriating woman on the planet, but if she said it was in hand, it was in hand. "And Stella," She added. "Try not to do anything at all until we get there, am I clear?"

"Well, I can't do a lot of anything at the moment, can I?" I huffed, "So no need to worry."

"I mean it." She said, and then they were all gone. I felt bereft.

However, I felt more myself at that point, than at any time over the last few (eight?) days, and vastly relieved to have confirmation on the drugging front. No wonder I hadn't known which way was up. It was also a far better scenario than thinking I'd gone ga-ga. Whatever Sam had shifted in my head had been at least part-way effective, and if the Lowbells still thought they could do what they liked with me, they had another think coming – the cavalry was on its way and I was starting to see light at the end of the tunnel.

Dorothy was shaking my arm gently and I turned over and 'woke' reluctantly, flinching as my leg inadvertently touched Letitia's.

"Come on sleepy head, time for your medicine." There were pills again on her outstretched palm and from the corner of my eye, I spotted Professor Lowbell standing by with the bottle of thick yellow stuff and a spoon, nurse's little helper, ready for action. I shook my head firmly as I sat up.

"I'm sorry, but I'm feeling awfully sick, I absolutely couldn't swallow anything right now."

"Nonsense," she said firmly. "These will make you feel heaps better." I shook my head again, more slowly this time. I'd scanned her briefly earlier, when Sam had done whatever it was he did, but hadn't really taken in too much. Now I did, and perhaps wished I hadn't. Behind the so familiar, comfortably plump, erudite, Dorothy mask, was something else altogether. The depth and breadth of that was overwhelming and as her scent washed over me, musky and musty, the taste and smell of fabrics and clay rotted with time, I retched, couldn't help it.

"Dear, oh dear," she said, "Now, that's not good is it? Poor you." Let's leave the pills for the moment then. Lowbell, hand me that bottle please, the medicine will sort your tummy." I wasn't about to point out, that up till now, it had been a decongestant, and I certainly wasn't going to take any, but she had other ideas. Actually, that wasn't strictly true, her mind wasn't similar to anything I'd come across before, it was full of images, rather than any kind of linear logical thought.

"No," I said, "I really can't."

"Oh, I think you can." And before I could move away, she'd placed her thumb and index finger, hard and lengthways against my upper and lower lips, forced my mouth open and tossed in a fully loaded spoonful. "Lowbell." She said, and the Professor who, even in these last crazy days had always treated me with almost courtly courtesy, now obediently reached forward and roughly massaged my throat – just the way my father did when medicating the cat. It was equally effective, I swallowed, impossible not to. And before I could catch my breath, they'd whacked in another dose. Oh this wasn't good, this was very definitely not going to plan.

I don't know whether what they'd just forced into me was different or stronger than before, the effect was certainly immediate. Or maybe it was me that was different this time round? Whatever Sam had done, he'd brought me a long way back to normal – my normal. So when the drugs took me wherever they wanted, a whole load of other stuff came too.

All the previous nightmares of the last few days had arrived when I was asleep – not great – but at least in the realms of the expected. This time I didn't sleep, but the nightmares swept in anyway. Snow White, clutching her bleeding heart in her hand; her stepmother, in red-hot, iron shoes, dancing on in torment till she died; Cinderella's sisters, with bloodied stumps where they'd sliced off a toe to fit into the glass slipper; Kay, from The Snow Queen, shards of ice embedded agonisingly in eye and heart. All in all there was a lot of unpleasant stuff going on in my head.

And then there were the dolls, so many dolls and multiplying. Dolls on the shelves on the walls of the room, now moving round again, a sickening, slow-motion, up and down carousel. More dolls in the head of Dorothy, uncountable images. Bright eyed and sightless; torsos with no limbs, limbs with no bodies; detached heads with gold curls, matted locks tied with pristine ribbon; ripped fabric faces and faces with no features. All carrying their own history, of hands that had played with them; loved them; feared them; cried over them; punished them; lost them; found them; left them to rot.

I could feel myself sinking, going down, overwhelmed. But buried below the vertigo and loss of reality, there was one small, cold part of me that understood, that wasn't lost, that knew exactly what they were doing. I was a lab rat. They hadn't planned to take me, it was too risky, I was too close, but when I was taken ill and virtually collapsed on them, the opportunity was simply too good to miss. They hadn't had something to play with, for a good long time. They wanted to use me, to observe and learn and, to all intents and purposes, I'd dropped into their laps. In one part of the circling, see-sawing room, Professor Lowbell had his camera ready. His wife had her notebook open and was busy jotting. They were both leaning forward, hungrily watching.

CHAPTER THIRTY-FOUR

The drugs had opened me up even more, to what I'd been swamped with, for days now, both awake and asleep. Stories and dolls, sensory overload. No wonder, as Kitty would have said, I couldn't tell my arse from my elbow. It had been going on the whole time I was there, but the effect on me now, with some of my senses regained, was intensely magnified. Of course, they couldn't have known that. Nor could they have anticipated that small, cold core that remained me, in the middle of the mayhem. I was angry. I was very angry and I had complete faith in young Sam. If he said all my abilities would come back, then come back they would – and what better time to see if he was right.

I thought I might start with Letitia, who'd been getting on my wick, for some time now. I focused and threw her out of bed. I was a little clumsy, getting back into the swing of things, and might have misjudged distances slightly. She rocketed out of there, like she'd been shot from a cannon, smashing into the bedside light on her side, and bringing it crashing down with her. Well that was a result – it may have lacked finesse, but I suddenly felt a whole lot better.

The Lowbells exchanged meaningful looks.

"Dear me," said Dorothy, pen poised over notebook, "Now, why did you push poor Letitia like that Stella, don't you like her?"

"I do not like her." I enunciated carefully. Whilst I may have been thinking more clearly, I was still having a bit of a problem speaking, my tongue was still playing up.

"Why don't you like her, Stella? Is it because she looks like you? Does that make you feel unhappy? Do you feel threatened?" Dorothy was leaning forward eagerly, eyes raking my expression. A fresh waft of her washed over me and in her excitement, the images in her mind were swirling. For a moment, in her head, I saw another woman in my bed, fair hair restrained by a green Alice band. Alongside her, lounged a Letitia-sized doll, also blonde haired and green Alice banded. This woman was 'one of the others'. Another lab rat they'd had chasing round their maze.

I opened my mouth then remembered the tongue, and also that actions so often speak louder than words.

From the top shelf, on the wall opposite, I slowly toppled one of the dolls, a rouged item with a perky feathered bonnet and a small basket over her arm. She fell, hit the parquet flooring and bounced slightly. Dorothy tutted and rose to go and restore her to the shelf.

"That's the tube," Professor Lowbell told me, "Runs right under us, pretty deep, but every now and then, we get the odd rumble and vibration." I didn't bother answering, I felt he and I had passed the casual chat stage. As Dorothy reached up carefully, to put perky bonnet and basket, back in place, I swept the rest of the shelf. Half a dozen or so small bodies promptly hurtled down, onto her unprotected head. I wasn't sorry, in fact quite pleased, that a couple of the china ones looked heavy. She uttered a cross between a yell and a yelp, tottered to one side, and there was a loud crack, as she inadvertently stood on and broke someone's face.

"What the devil... ?" The Professor had risen to his feet.

Perhaps, I should have stopped then. I should have quietly celebrated getting back to normal and just stopped. I should have contemplated all the consequences of taking it further, I should have listened to Rachael. But you know me!

I was, in fact, somewhat surprised, at the depth of the pent up fury and frustration I was feeling. It was only a matter of a few days, since I'd been mortified at putting my good clients, the Lowbells, to any trouble and been pathetically grateful for their kind care and attention. It's amazing how quickly attitudes can change, isn't it? I sat up straighter in the bed, and even though my head was still spinning, swiftly cleared the top shelf of the second alcove and continued moving downwards, in an orderly fashion.

Then I wound Adelaide up – I reckoned she had something to contribute, even if it might be a bit repetitive. Dorothy, silly woman, wasn't moving out of the way, instead she was hot-footing it, back and forwards, trying to catch as many of the falling dolls as she could. Her arms were full. She lacked only a couple of cauliflowers, to be a successful Crackerjack contestant. She was making low, guttural sounds of distress. I probably should have felt bad about that. I didn't. Neither did I feel particularly regretful about the several feather-stuffed dolls I'd destroyed, showering their fillings all over the place. By that stage, young Adelaide was in full flow, doing her thing. Smiley face; sigh; turn; crying face; head tilt; sigh; turn; horror face – and shriek! All in all, it was rather noisy, and getting messier by the minute, with doll bodies, piling up left right and centre.

My arm was suddenly gripped painfully above the elbow, beautifully manicured nails – he always took great pride in his hands – digging viciously into my flesh. Lowbell's contorted features, not so froggy-friendly now, were inches from mine.

"What are you?" he hissed, spittle dampening my face. He was breathing heavily through his mouth, and in his excitement, licking his lips. For just a second or so, it seemed the tongue emerging might be endless and forked, I held my breath, waiting for it to flick, it didn't, of course. He hadn't released his hold, and the contact, though it was hurting me, gave greater access. I regretted that immediately. Unlike his wife, his mind was set out as logically and cogently as his notes and academic arguments. Compartmentalised, filed, memories available and accessible. I'd always known his speciality was the study of the fear factor, only now, in this minute, did I appreciate this was no dry academic interest – it was feverishly lustful, coldly cruel and very personal. And no, I wasn't the first of their guests, not by a long chalk. The other women were all appallingly easy to see. Each of them appeared to have her own file in his head, neatly numbered, fully notated. Every twitch, every reaction, every step on the downward spiral of drug-induced fear. These memories never left him, why would they, they fed and swelled his obsession.

His scent, damp and tainted, mushroomy and foetid, was magnified by his excitement. He was clever and, unlike so many other people I'd come up against, he was open not closed-minded. He didn't try and rationalise what he was seeing, what I was doing. He'd always known, gut-deep, that in all the handed down tales, in their consistency, there had to be more than a grain of truth, otherwise they wouldn't have survived, intact through the years. Seers, witches, label them what you will, there'd always been those who defied the norm, he'd just never expected to stumble across one. He didn't know any more, than what he was seeing, but what he was seeing, was proof enough. He couldn't believe, in all the time he'd known me, he hadn't spotted something, and he couldn't believe his luck now. He was going to keep me going, so much longer than all the others. He was going to do whatever he needed, to take me apart, like one of Dorothy's dolls, so he could learn exactly what made me tick.

It had taken only a few seconds for me to read him and him to assess me, but by this time, my arm was hurting badly. I didn't touch him, but I loosened his grip and moved free, he looked down at his hand in delight, although I must have hurt him, I hadn't been gentle. If a grin could be said to split a face, then that's how his was looking, right now. He was beside himself, with anticipation of what the future held. At the same time, he understood he needed me incapacitated, needed to knock me out, at least until he'd thought through tactics.

He raised his fist, I yanked his feet from under him. He hit the floor hard, his glasses skidding and ending up under the bedside table. He eased himself up on one elbow and winced. I think I may have broken something. He was winded, but still grinning happily. He was utterly fascinated, and thinking rapidly. He didn't know the extent of what I could do, although he'd seen me anticipate the punch. I watched him run through the options open to him, at the same time as running through my own. If it was a Catch 22 situation for him, it was for me too. I had no idea how long it might be before help arrived and, idiot that I was, I'd shown my hand far too soon.

"Dorothy." He called. She was still over on the other side of the room, on her hands and knees, cooing softly to the dolls, trying to put together those which were broken, reinstate them on the shelves. She was so distraught and engrossed, she hadn't really noticed what was going on down our end. "Dorothy," he snapped, "Put down those damned toys and get over here. Now!" In the pause, Adelaide, sighed, turned and showed us her crying face, at the same time as Dorothy showed us hers.

She made a cumbersome rise to her feet, regained her balance and advanced slowly across the room. A couple of feathers, caught in her iron-grey hair, added an incongruously festive feel. Her eyes were glittering feverishly and her mind was flickering and cutting in and out, like a TV with poor reception. She'd no idea quite what was going on, nor how it was being done, but she certainly knew who was behind it and she quickened her step.

Distracted as I was, by the level of her rage, I didn't notice the Professor get to his feet. As she approached, he abruptly shoved her hard, from one side and she fell heavily across me in the bed. Pinned down by a woman of

Dorothy's bulk, was pinned down indeed. He swung swiftly on his heel, making for the chest of drawers, in the far corner of the room. I understood, there was a box in there with a hypodermic and a vial of something – I didn't think it would be a vitamin supplement.

Meanwhile, the woman on top of me, had both hands round my throat and was throttling me with a surprising amount of strength and an intense expression of concentration, she was, it seemed, a woman with a mission.

"Bitch," she said. "Bloody little bitch." Fumbling in the drawer, the Professor looked up briefly,

"Stop that Dotty." He said. "I want to keep her." Unfortunately, Dorothy had moved way beyond the taking notice of anyone, stage. I'd attacked and hurt what she held most dear and, like the china faces of many of the dolls, she'd cracked, from side to side. As she methodically cut off my circulation, and everything began to acquire a strong black outline, I saw that any remnant of restraint had fled and the swirling, hideous images in her head, were what insanity looks like.

I could feel myself falling, ever more rapidly, into the dark. Reluctantly, I ventured into the midst of the swirling, because there weren't a lot of choices on the table. I searched, found, twisted and that dreadful, agonising pressure on my throat eased, as she collapsed across me, deeply unconscious and breathing noisily through her nose.

But not out of the woods yet. I was still completely anchored to the bed and the Prof was now trotting across with a loaded hypo. If there's anything I hate, it's needles – so I snapped this one off immediately. I'd have to remember to pick it up off the floor later, not the sort of thing to leave lying around. I don't know which was worse, Dorothy's swirling madness or Lowbell's icy, clear logic which, despite the circumstances, was operating with greater clarity than ever. I reached out to him, before he reached me, found the right place inside his brain, knocked him out and he keeled over. I was relieved to see he was still breathing. Bad things happen to good people and not often enough, bad things happen to bad people, but I'd played judge, jury and executioner once before, I didn't want to do it again.

I think I might have passed out, round about then – there was no getting away from it, it had been an action, not to mention drug-packed, few hours.

CHAPTER THIRTY-FIVE

I don't know how long I was out for, but when I did re-join the world of the living, I was relieved to find Dorothy had been removed – the woman weighed a ton. There was a chap, peering at me from close quarters, too close. I'd no idea who he was, but I wasn't pleased. I didn't think I was looking my best and my last close encounter, hadn't exactly been a load of laughs.

"She's awake." He said, over his shoulder, to someone I couldn't see. I tried to sit up against the pillows, but he pushed me gently back down again, "Stay there for a moment, you're bleeding." He handed me a clean white hanky and directed my hand to my nose, which instantly turned the white cotton, an alarming shade of scarlet.

"I think," I said nasally, "Dorothy might have bashed her head against it. Hope it's not broken."

"Out the way young man." A familiar bossiness,

"Rachael?" I reached out my other hand, with an indescribable sense of relief and possibly, a bit of a sob. She took it, held it for a moment, gave it a brief squeeze and passed it back.

"Didn't I," she said repressively, "Tell you not to do anything until we got here? Why can't you, for once in your life, listen?"

"Steady on." Said the hanky chap from behind her, sounding like something out of a 1950s film.

"Well, you rather took your time turning up." I said grumpily, "Things got a bit heated." and then remembering, "Oh God, the Lowbells," I gestured vaguely and flashed a thought, "I haven't killed them have I?" She snorted,

"No, just unconscious. But we don't have much time."

"Time?" I still felt a bit woozy.

"The police are on their way." Said Boris, his unmistakeably elongated form, appearing behind her shoulder.

"Police?" I said.

"Stella," Rachael said patiently, and aloud for emphasis. "You disappeared for eight days, you've headlined the news every night and you're on the front page of every newspaper – of course, Police. Now, before they turn up, we need to get your story straight."

"Hang on, just one minute." The chap, who now I came to think of it, did look a little familiar, but I couldn't quite pinpoint, was there again, he was starting to compete with Rachael, in the interfering stakes.

"We've got to call an ambulance, right away," he said. "She's in shock, I think she's been drugged or something and she's bleeding and look at her throat." Actually, I thought, if my throat looked as rough on the outside as it felt on the inside, it was probably not a pretty sight. "Then there's these two." He gestured behind him, presumably at the recumbent Lowbells. As he moved, there was a crunching sound from some of the debris on the floor. "It's a crime scene, isn't it, we shouldn't be touching anything."

"Who is he?" Rachael asked silently, with irritation. I made an effort to haul aside the mind fog, focused on him and suddenly it came to me.

"David Gold. Son of a client."

"Well, what on earth's he doing here?"

"No idea. I thought he came in with you. And where are the others?"

"Back at home. Not sensible to come in mob handed, too many people to explain away and Ed and Glory don't exactly blend into the background, do they?" I chuckled weakly. It seemed, the end of the nightmare might be in sight. All I ached to do now, was get home. I couldn't begin to imagine what it must all have been like for my family. I turned swiftly back to Rachael, but she was ahead of me,

"Don't be silly, don't think we'd leave them hanging, do you? They know you're OK." Boris meanwhile, inclined his head towards David and summarised what he'd read, swiftly and silently.

"He came round here to check on you, the day you went missing. Apparently, you were due to collect his mother that afternoon, and didn't turn up. He called the office to find out where you were. They told him you were working at the Lowbells. He had to pass here on his way home. Saw your car parked down the road and stopped to make sure you were OK. But when he knocked on the door, they insisted you'd never arrived. He thought that was odd, so didn't mention the car. When he drove past again, the following day, your car was gone and you were already hitting the headlines. He called the police to tell them about the car, but by then, they'd been all over the house and hadn't found any trace. Apparently he's a journalist, has a nose for a story, didn't like what the Lowbells told him and he's been keeping an eye on the house ever since – saw us turn up just now and tagged along." I interrupted him,

"How come you didn't find me, if I was here all the time?" Boris, shook his head,

"This whole corridor of rooms, is parallel to the main upstairs hall, but the door to it is cleverly concealed behind wood panelling. If you didn't know it was there, you wouldn't know it was there! We only got to you this time, because we could hear you so loudly."

"But how're you going to explain all that?" I asked. Boris shrugged,

"We were driving past, saw the front door open. I'd been here with the police, when the house was searched originally, was suspicious something was wrong. We just walked in, the place seemed deserted, we heard a noise, came upstairs, the door to these rooms was open and…"

"Doesn't that sound really odd?" I interrupted, Boris looked around wryly,

"Stella, this whole situation is really odd." David was looking from one to other of us expectantly, his head swivelling, like a less rusty Adelaide. None of us had said a word and he was waiting for someone, anyone, to respond to what he'd last said, although I really couldn't remember what that was exactly. To be honest, I didn't have anything left, I leaned back against the pillows, closed my eyes and left everyone else to sort themselves out.

By the time I was ready to contribute intelligently again, I was in the back of an ambulance, on its way to the Royal Free, where I couldn't help but feel, I was spending an inordinate amount of time. There was a jolly young WPC with me, who seemed to expect a descent into hysteria at any second. She didn't let go of my hand the whole way, holding it in both of hers and murmuring,

"There, there, my dear, you're all right now. We've got you, we've got you." All of which was a little disconcerting, but appreciated nevertheless. It was only a short journey, but long enough to let me reflect a little and worry a lot. I knew I was odd, but was I even odder than I should be? What kind of a person went through the experience I'd just had, and didn't have hysterics? Maybe I needed to work on that. Mind you, when we reached the hospital, the family were there in force and it would be fair to say, there was no shortage in the hysteria department, even if it wasn't mine.

The hospital insisted on keeping me overnight, because they weren't thrilled at what they found in my bloodstream. They were though, highly intrigued, and a whole host of students were brought in, to gather round the bed and have a look at me.

"What she's been given," said one of the consultant haematologists, gesturing with his stethoscope and scant regard for my sensibilities, "Would have knocked out an elephant. Should have finished her off completely. We've found barbiturates and benzodiazepines. There's also some LSD, and what the lab say is some kind of mushroom extract. One hell of a lot of heavy-duty stuff, if it's all still showing up now. She'll have spent this past week, alternating between spaced out and spark out. To be honest, at best, I'd have expected her to be dribbling in a corner by now, but she appears to be responding more or less normally. I think, oddly enough, she's going to be OK." And having scared the wits out of me, he beckoned his flock and they all white-coated it, out the door.

I was reflecting on his bedside manner or lack of, when my jolly young WPC, whose name was Stephanie, pitched up again. This time with a Detective Sergeant Mousegood, as miserable as she was cheerful. DS Mousegood, and rarely was a name so apt, had a thatch of thinning, dull, fair hair, a stinking cold and a small pointed nose, red raw from a lot of handkerchief action. He needed, he said, to take a statement. He clearly wasn't having a good day, and as he eyed me morosely over his notepad, he didn't think it was getting any better. Apparently, he'd been there, when the house was originally searched and I hadn't come to light. I gathered, my subsequent resurfacing, hadn't gone down too well with his Inspector.

During our hasty session, prior to the police piling in, Rachael and Boris had insisted the safest course of action was to stick to the truth as far as possible – it was always easiest to remember and where the truth wasn't advisable, I should lean heavily, on drug-induced amnesia. Accordingly, as

DS Mousegood sneezed, sniffed, wiped and noted, I recounted the whole sorry tale which, even to me, sounded far-fetched, featuring as it did, the rapid transformation of the Lowbells from esteemed clients to caring hosts to homicidal maniacs.

I went over everything, in as much detail as I could, and by the time we were getting near the end, when things became complicated, found it easy to explain I was so doped up with what they'd given me, that I had only the vaguest recollection of anything at all. I did though remember, there was an awful lot of noise and shouting, things smashing and crashing all around me. I thought, perhaps the Lowbells, who'd already proved themselves more than a little unreliable, may have got into an argument that turned violent.

As DS Mousegood moved, painstakingly, over the pages of my statement. I was chilled to the bone to see, based on evidence found at the house, colleagues and a forensic team were currently excavating the extensive back garden. I thought of the fair-haired girl, with her bright green Alice band and I abruptly stopped reading him. I didn't want to know what, if anything they'd found. I think, deep down, I already knew. There were things I'd seen, during those last desperate moments with the Lowbells, I very much wished I could un-see. I shuddered deeply and Stephanie, who'd appropriated my hand again at the beginning of the interview and held on throughout, patted it. Whilst I'd had to resist the urge to shake her off initially, I was now warmed by the normal human contact, I smiled gratefully at her and she gave me a thumbs up.

In the end, despite my protests, they kept me in for three, very long days, during which time, I'm sure I didn't get as much rest as I should have done. There was a constant stream of family visitors as well as several more police incursions. They wanted to check on different points in my statement and ask further questions about my previous history with, and knowledge of, the Lowbells. They were, as well they might be, mighty puzzled as to how Boris had finally been able to find me, and by the who and why of Rachael and David. I followed instruction, and as soon as questions veered in a direction that was difficult, would shut my eyes and murmur weakly, 'I'm so very sorry, it's all such a blur and when I try and think about it, I just can't remember the order in which things happened, I'm sorry – maybe it's the drugs?'

Every single person I saw, other than my parents, was keen for me to seek some kind of counselling therapy. They said, long-term effects were only to be expected, from an experience such as mine, and it was only common sense to 'talk it all through', get it out of my system. Far better do that, they said, and avoid storing up trouble for the future. My parents, on the other hand, maintained their long-held view that 'talking anything through' with anybody, was the very last thing, under any circumstances, I should ever do and I couldn't help but agree.

CHAPTER THIRTY-SIX

They say, don't they, there's no such thing as bad publicity and, much to my astonishment, this indeed proved to be the case. The papers, radio and television had all been full of me. Me missing, me found and then all the subsequent horrors that came to light after that. And while all this was going on, our client list at Simple Solutions grew exponentially. I personally, felt quite strongly, that getting held in a house for over a week, by a couple of not so sane citizens, didn't go a long way to endorse my skills as an intelligent and reliable organiser, but I wasn't going to argue the toss.

Kitty and Brenda, much to my relief, were meshing a great deal more smoothly nowadays and I gathered, during my absence, Brenda, as worried as the rest of them, had become almost an honorary family member. She'd joined anxiety ridden vigils at the house most days, staying late into the night, providing numerous cups of tea and making and removing endless plates of uneaten sandwiches – a sure sign of how dire, everyone was feeling. I think what hit everyone so hard, alongside the fact that for a good few days, they weren't sure whether I was alive or dead, was the betrayal. The undeniable fact, that the Lowbells had been such delightful company and so much a part of the business family. As Kitty was heard to mutter, with disgust, on numerous occasions,

"If someone's a murderous bugger, they should bloody well act like it." Which summed it up succinctly. Because murderous indeed, they were.

Horrifically, at one point, it seemed that excavation of their large, beautifully kept garden and the dreadful secrets it concealed, would go on indefinitely. The soil reluctantly yielded up, body after body from beneath meticulously maintained (and flourishing) rosebushes. There were eight in all. Eight young women, all in their early twenties, all in various stages of decomposition, all found buried beneath a large, near life-size doll. The disappearances, unsolved missing person cases, dated back as far as twenty years, to the 1950s. It was therefore almost certain, at least one of those girls lost her life, around the same time I started mine. It was, I felt, a dreadful symmetry.

The papers and TV were busting a gut with ghastly detail and speculation, for what seemed like an age, and it got to the stage where I stopped both reading and listening. Boris, whose exact working relationship with the police, I'd never quite established, phoned every few days, for the first couple of weeks, with additional information that hadn't necessarily been made public. I asked him to stop. I didn't want to know any more than I already did, because that was far too much. The reality, that this dual existence of theirs – admired, respected and well-liked academics, with serial kidnapping and killing as a side line – had gone on for twenty years or so, beggared belief. I couldn't reconcile what I now knew with what I thought I'd known. There was also the dreadful, corrosive fact, if someone like me hadn't been able to spot what was under my nose, what hope for anyone else?

As further details of the case emerged, with more and more grieving families receiving confirmation of grim news, they'd been waiting for and dreading, the Lowbells were moved from guarded hospital rooms to Broadmoor in Berkshire for assessment. Neither of them had come round, for a number of days, and when they did, neither it seemed, was particularly compos mentis. In fact, Boris reported, they both seemed as far removed from that, as they could possibly be.

There was time and effort being put in, from a whole range of psychiatric and criminal behavioural experts, to establish whether this was a genuine condition or a ploy. But as time went on, and both of them continued in this same state, it in itself, became a further source of speculation. What was it that had created this identical condition, and simultaneously? The theory gaining most credence, was they'd been doing a certain amount of ill-judged indulging in some of the drugs they'd used on me, although by the time this was put forward, it was too late to test blood for confirmation. Boris's sources seemed to think it was pure chance they'd taken me. Prior to that, all their victims had gone missing from widely differing locations, they'd been careful, through the years, never to prey too close to home. The same sources, thought it increasingly likely, they'd be found unfit to stand trial, in which case, and in due course, a trial of the facts would be set up, with long-term hospital orders, the most likely outcome.

It's never been easy for me to measure myself against normality, I'm on a different kind of scale altogether. Because of this, because I can so easily read the way normal people think and react, I'm well aware there are times I should feel more regret or guilt than I do. I was acutely conscious that the current condition of the Lowbells which was, after all, down to me, should have made me feel far worse than it did. I veered between anger that they wouldn't stand in the dock, to face the ravaged families of their victims and, if I'm honest – and I always have been with myself, and with you – regretting that I hadn't knocked them out of existence completely. On the other hand, maybe they were already being punished far more effectively. It's not for me to say.

What I did know, beyond a shadow of a doubt, was I wanted to put all of this behind me and get back to normal as soon as possible; running my business and attempting to kick-start my social life – which always suffers, when you get kidnapped and have to spend an inordinate amount of time with statement-taking police. It was Kitty, who took matters into her own hands and issued firm instruction to David Gold, to ask me out – at least that's what he said.

He had indeed been ubiquitous for quite a while now, and whilst in all honesty, he'd been more of a hindrance than a help at the Hampstead house, I couldn't help but be grateful, he'd chosen to keep an eye open. I thought that showed a dedication above and beyond, although there was the possibility that as a journalist, he was just after a good story and wasn't a knight in shining armour at all. Do I sound cynical? Are you surprised?

After the whole Lowbell debacle, I'd braced myself for some awkward questions from David, but not too many were forthcoming, he seemed to accept the explanations of Rachael and Boris at face value and I stuck firmly to the 'really can't remember what happened' line, whenever anything came up that I didn't want to get into. Indeed, once the Lowbells imbibing drugs theory was floated, it tied things up quite neatly and, after a while, I felt I could relax a little.

A big plus for me, where David was concerned, was that he was an opaque thinker. One of those people whose brains don't seem to operate on images and emotions, but in an almost linear pattern of words. People like that are difficult, although not impossible, to read. The huge benefit is they're so much quieter to spend time with.

On our first date, we went to see A Touch of Class, featuring Glenda Jackson and George Segal, an unlikely partnering if ever there was one, but then probably no more so than mine and David's. It was a pleasant evening, we said we'd do it again and, much to my surprise and the smug delight of Kitty, it seemed in a short time, without either of us doing that much about it, we were 'going out'. My family were pleased, his mother less so. This complicated matters, because I was still carrying out my professional role for the family and whilst Laura was never rude to me, she was clearly of the opinion, he could do a lot better. Actually, the more I got to know him, the more I tended to agree with her. However, all of these were the sort of issues I felt came under the heading of normal, and that in itself was a great pleasure.

For the time being, I'd decided to stick to my tried and tested policy of not sharing details of my peculiarities. Naturally, I'm all in favour of honesty and being straight-forward, and all that, but didn't think, at this early stage, it was relevant. After all, we might only go out for a few weeks, then the whole thing might die a death in which case, discretion could prove to have been the best way to go. He was nice enough, but I can't say I was as rapturous as the rest of the clan. If things progressed any further, then of course I'd tell him, I'd just have to find the right time and place. In the meantime, I very much hoped he couldn't see, as I could, my mother and Aunt Edna exchange tight little smiles of complicity, whenever they saw him, at the same time as mentally measuring him up for a morning suit.

As things gradually settled down, I was delighted to realise, I hadn't heard anything in the last few weeks from anybody I didn't want to hear from – specifically the Peacocks or Glory. I was also doing my very best to put right out of my head, the conversation I'd had with Ruth. The people Ruth heard and those she wanted me to listen out for, were those who were transmitting on a high emotional level, even if they had no idea they were doing it. They were screaming for help, deeply in trouble and full of fear, I knew what that felt like. I'd just been there. That didn't mean I wanted to go there again, even if only by proxy. 'All we're asking you to do,' she'd said, 'Is keep a listening ear open.' And I'd thought to myself as she said it, NO. No way, this is so not for me.

Unfortunately, as I've mentioned before, once something's in your head, not thinking about it is tough, like with that ruddy pink elephant. Even with my shutters tightly closed, every now and then something flashed through and caught my attention and I couldn't help but hear. So far, every time it had happened and I had listened, I'd heard nothing further. I suspected, when I did hear something worth shouting about, there'd be no doubt about it.

PART THREE

LISTENING

Damn pink elephants

CHAPTER THIRTY-SEVEN

The dreams, at first unremarkable, slunk into my mind so insidiously, that other than a vague unease sometimes on waking – and not even every morning, just now and then – I didn't really consciously register them. Or maybe I just didn't want to. I certainly didn't want my carefully nurtured bubble of normality to burst, at a time when things were going really well.

So, I ignored them for as long as I could, until I couldn't ignore them anymore and then, against my better judgement and with great reluctance, I phoned the Peacocks – perhaps I do have more of a conscience than I think? Rachael didn't waste time on pleasantries and ignored my enquiry after Ruth's health, she assumed correctly, I hadn't phoned for purely social reasons. I explained, I hadn't actually heard anything in the way I'd expected, but had been having some oddly worrying dreams. They were deep, dark, highly unpleasant and worst of all, I knew they weren't mine.

"Right," said Rachael, "I want you to talk to Boris. Where are you now?"

"At the office, but I just want you to pass this along to him."

"Don't be silly, Stella," she said firmly. "You haven't given me enough. You need to talk to him, he'll have questions."

"Well I can't talk to him now." I said. "I've got a client coming in."

"Cancel. Boris will be there in about half an hour."

"Rachael, firstly, as you know, I don't want to get involved any further than just passing stuff on, and secondly, I can't just cancel at the drop of a hat."

"Well, good thing we didn't take that attitude, when it came to getting you out of that mess in Hampstead."

"That's not the point."

"It's precisely the point."

"Well, maybe you're right, but…" I might just as well not have spoken, for all the notice she took.

"Go and wait outside, he'll pick you up and while you're waiting, jot down anything and everything you can remember, it's all important. Be ready."

"I really… " I said, but by then I was talking to the dialling tone.

Boris arrived about twenty minutes later, just as I was huffing out of our office front door. He hooted. I hate it when people hoot, it immediately makes me feel I'm doing something wrong, even when I'm not driving. He was in a green Mini, which looked ridiculous, I couldn't imagine how he'd managed to fold himself in, and his head was rubbing the roof. He made a 'get in' gesture,

"Talk to me." he said, extracting an aniseed ball, one-handed, from a bag he'd leaned over to get from the glove compartment. He proffered the bag. I shook my head, "Tell me what happened."

"Hang on a moment, where're we going?" I protested. We'd pulled away at speed, he was a skilful driver, I could tell, nevertheless I reached for the strap over the window and held on.

"To talk to someone," he said, round the aniseed ball.

"Where and who?"

"Tell me what you heard. What you're hearing?"

"You answer me first and then I'll tell you." I said, folding my arms. He grunted,

"You really are most annoying. We're going to the police – satisfied? Now, can you do me a favour and get things straight in your head, so you don't waffle and waste time when we get there." I bit back a retort and did what he asked. It wasn't an impressive assembly of facts and the more I tried to home in on them, the more ephemeral seemed the dreams and the darkness they'd imparted. Maybe I was simply imagining things. I was seriously regretting my phone call.

We drove for fifteen minutes or so, before parking outside an insalubrious looking café with thoroughly steamed-up windows, set on a parade of mainly vacant shops, liberally plastered with peeling bill-posters-will-be-prosecuted notices. I think we were somewhere in Camden Town, but had rather lost my bearings. Boris extracted himself, not easily, from the car and when I didn't budge, came round to my side to open my door.

"Not a police station." I pointed out.

"This is unofficial," he was moving me swiftly inside. "Thought you understood that."

"Actually," I said sharply. "I'm not understanding a whole lot, right now." The café was as uninspiring inside as out, with a few customers, nursing thick white cups and an overall smell of extremely burnt something or other. We made our way through to the back of the shop and Boris indicated a corner table, where a man was already seated. He didn't look up as we joined him, but pulled a piece off the mangled doughnut, plated in front of him, and chewed slowly.

"So?" he said. He was of generous build, sitting sideways on his chair, presumably because the belly, straining hard against its shirt constraints, would place him too far from the food. His rather high, light voice was at odds with his size. I could feel the hostility rolling off him, along with a strong scent of Brut aftershave which was fighting a losing battle with old cigarettes.

"Where's the other one then?" he said, looking me up and down. I opened my mouth, this wasn't someone I'd taken to, but Boris shot me a shut-up,

"Ruth's not around at the moment but she works with Stella," he said, "Stella, this is Detective Inspector Arthur Cornwall. With the Metropolitan Police."

"Here against his bleedin' better judgement." muttered the DI, heaving a meaty buttock to one side, to produce a crushed pack of Rothmans from a released pocket. He tapped one out, lit up with one of the new Bic lighters and coughed long and heartily. Boris politely waited until he'd cleared his lungs, then continued.

"Stella, DI Cornwall deals with missing persons. Cornwall, Stella was the young lady involved in the Hampstead case. Your chaps got to her just in time."

"Blimey, never realised she was one of your lot." Said Cornwall. "Didn't keep her out of trouble, did it? Thought she'd have seen it coming, wouldn't you? Right, haven't got all day, she got something for me or not?" He was talking to Boris, as if I wasn't there, then was momentarily distracted as his cigarette slipped through his fingers and into his lap. He jumped up, swearing and brushing himself down, there was a small, round, burn hole in the thigh of his trousers. Lucky he was plain clothes, I thought, uniforms were probably more expensive to replace. Boris, amused despite himself, administered a silent rebuke which I chose to ignore. Cornwall sat down again, reached for the pack, thought better of it and looked directly at me for the first time.

"Well?" he said.

"Well what? Considering nobody's really told me anything, I'm working a bit in the dark here." I glanced down at the notebook I'd taken out of my pocket. It held the pathetic few lines I'd jotted down, none of which made much sense, even to me. "All I've got are a few vague impressions."

"That's bleedin' promising," he was heavy on the sarcasm. "Spit it out then." I gave him a look, but then thought, what did I have to lose? I suspected (not to mention hoped), that both Ruth and Boris were mistaken about me, I certainly wasn't convinced I'd have anything worth contributing, however worthy the cause.

"It's not so much that I heard anything." I said. "I've been having dreams. I know it sounds peculiar, but I don't think they're mine."

"Why?" Boris prompted.

"They're dark," I said with distaste, I didn't want to go into details. "With such a lot of anger and violence." I shut my eyes to better concentrate, "It's fierce. There's anger, frustration and…" I paused to put my finger on it, "… and injustice, a tremendous sense of injustice and feeling hard-done-by. Huge chip on the shoulder. But this isn't what you told me to listen out for. This isn't a victim. It's completely the opposite. What I think I'm getting is the person who's doing the frightening or at least, if he – it's definitely a man – hasn't done it yet, he wants to do it. I don't know for sure whether he's actually started yet, but he will."

And then Boris was in my head with me, magnifying and intensifying what I was remembering. For a moment I resisted, but realising what he was doing, went with it. As I did, he flashed through some swift questions to which, oddly, I found I had answers. In a very short time, he had all I had to give and I opened my eyes to the murky glare of the DI, staring expectantly at the two of us sitting opposite. He didn't know quite what had just gone on, but was as fascinated as he was repelled. I could feel that repulsion and in it the fear, the natural fear of anything that's 'other'. It was a quite a while since I'd put myself in a position to feel any kind of prejudice from outside, it wasn't pleasant.

"She's right." Said Boris. "She's picked up on something, but not a victim. She's picking up on a perpetrator." Cornwall, leaned forward, I hoped those shirt buttons were going to hold or someone was going to lose an eye.

"Well, it's what he's frigging well planning, that I need to know, isn't it?" He wafted, what felt like a chimney-full of stale smoke, over me. I coughed pointedly. "You've given me sod all, young woman, we don't even know if he's done anything we can nick him for yet. All you've told me, is he's pissed off and angry well – newsflash – that applies to most everybody I see every day."

"Hang on," I was liking this man less and less by the minute. "I've told you what I know. There isn't any more. End of story. Sorry if it's no use. And it's my time I've wasted, as much as yours."

"No, wait." Boris said quietly. "I think we've probably got something here, from what I saw, this is someone who's a serious risk. If nothing else, you've got a connection with him, we can build on that."

"I don't think so." I said. I knew I shouldn't have made that phone-call.

"What's that smell?" Boris was sifting through what he'd taken from me. For a second, I thought he meant the well-burnt aroma of whatever had been left too long under the café grill, then realised what he was talking about. I pulled back the memory. I didn't recognise it at first, then came the sharp image of my father decorating my office, brushes left overnight in an empty paint tin to soak. It was turpentine. Boris nodded slowly in agreement,

"Some kind of painter?" He said.

"Artist?" Cornwall's tone clearly indicated, artists weren't much further up the popularity pole than crazy psychics.

"Not sure," I said slowly, "Maybe a decorator?" Boris queried me silently, but whilst I didn't know why, I knew that made more sense to me. Boris nodded, if that's what I felt, he trusted me. Cornwall was hauling himself to his feet, not a swift operation, didn't they have fitness tests in the Met?

"Not much to frigging go on, is it?" he muttered ungraciously, shrugging into a well-worn mac that had seen better days, a good while back. He looked me up and down again and lifted one bushy eyebrow at Boris.

"You sure she's the real deal? We got a darn sight more from the other one, where's she anyway?"

"Not well." Said Boris briefly. Cornwall sniffed,

"I'll keep ears and eyes open, see if this fits anything we've had in and you, Missy," he nodded at me. I glared back, I did not like the Missy. "Do the same. Anything else, doesn't matter whether you think it's important or not – get back to him." He jerked a thumb at Boris, "He'll tell me. He extracted, not without difficulty, a crumpled pound note from his trouser pocket, put it under the plate with the half demolished doughnut and left, weaving a lumbering path through the tables.

The drive back to my office was far shorter than my list of questions, so we didn't waste time talking. I learned that the association with the fragrant Cornwall, had begun a couple of years earlier, when Ruth called about a missing child, following an appeal on Police Five. She'd heard something, she was certain she had some information that could help. She was fobbed off politely. As Cornwall later put it, with his habitual charm, after an appeal, along with the might or might not be genuinely helpfuls, they always got their share of raving loonies and Ruth had known full well, it was into that file her name went.

So she got Boris to call again, with the same information, based on the annoying, but indisputable truth, a man was far more likely to be listened to. And indeed, it so happened that a young, on-the-ball constable realised this caller knew rather more about the case, than he should and didn't sound like an out and out crazy. Boris was duly passed on up the line and, as luck would have it, although Cornwall had mixed feelings about just how lucky it was, it had landed in his lap. A little like his lit cigarette.

Cornwall, was not a man with a mind open to a wide range of possibilities, but he wasn't a fool either. More importantly, he was conscientious and, appearances to the contrary, a stickler for detail. Whilst in his raving loonies file, there was an assortment of those claiming all sorts and yada, yada, yada – they didn't usually come up with the number of precise details, Boris was able to supply. Cornwall reluctantly agreed to a meeting, although was less than chuffed when Boris turned up with Ruth. She'd dressed down for the occasion, in a more subdued than usual outfit, but still looked, to Cornwall's apprehensive eye, the epitome of eccentric.

Their meeting was in the same café we'd just left, chosen by Cornwall on the basis they were unlikely to be seen, because nobody in their right mind would want to go there. After all, as he pointed out on more than one occasion, if anyone ever found out who he was talking to and why, he'd be a bleeding laughing stock and his career screwed from here till kingdom come. But if he wasn't a snappy dresser, he was a scrupulous officer. He couldn't un-hear what they had to say and once heard, his conscience wouldn't let him not follow up, if only to prove, once and for all, he was dealing with a couple of nut-jobs.

That first lot of detailed information Ruth had picked up on, led directly to a six year old girl being located and rescued – traumatised but unhurt. It also resulted in the arrest, trial and long-term imprisonment of a man who'd done this before and would have continued doing it in an escalating cycle.

Over the subsequent period, there were more than a dozen occasions, when Boris called again. By then, he had Cornwall's direct line and had worked on a number of different cases, in a vaguely unspecified, civilian consultancy role. Cornwall disliked his connection with Boris and even more so with Ruth. He was deeply uneasy about the whole bally business. However he was, above all, a pragmatist, and there could be no denying, there were bastards behind bars today, who might not have been, if it hadn't been for these two. So far, by the skin of his teeth, he'd managed to get away in reports with '… based on information supplied by an anonymous informant'. Additionally, and even he had to concede this, it hadn't done his career any harm at all, in fact, quite the opposite – so far!

"But why me, why now?" I said aloud, "Why haven't I picked up on this sort of thing before?" Boris paused, as he parked, back where we'd started.

"Probably because we, first me, then Ruth, put it into your head. No," he stopped my protest, "Nothing underhand, we simply, opened your mind to the possibility." He smiled gently. "You could say, we planted the elephant. Now, contact us if you hear anything else," he raised his hand against my reaction, "It's quite likely you won't, that this'll be the end of it, it won't go any further."

CHAPTER THIRTY-EIGHT

I could only hope Boris was right. In the meantime, the business was doing well and, within the last month, I'd agreed with Martin that I'd take on some extra office space which, up till now, he'd been using as a storage room for brochures and stationery. He wasn't keen at first, not that he was ever keen on anything at first. He said, they couldn't possibly manage without that room, until Hilary roundly told him not to be such an idiot, or she'd offer him an alternative location to stick his brochures. She'd had a soft spot for me, ever since the dubious debt collector, and I'd gone even further up in her estimation, by emerging alive from the Lowbell debacle, unlike so many others.

With the extra space, into which, by dint of some sweaty but clever manoeuvring, we'd managed to shoe-horn a couple more desks and two chairs, I'd been able to take on a couple more staff. They were working, God help 'em, under the joint supervision of Kitty and Brenda, who both subscribed to the iron fist in the iron glove school of management, and ran a tight ship.

Ruby had run her own successful florist's business for many years, giving up, reluctantly, when the rent on her small shop rose, as she put it, beyond the ridiculous. She herself was always as impeccably arranged, as I imagined her flowers must have been. She wore her pewter hair, cut close to her shapely head and alternated between two smart, black, business suits, both of which she'd gone straight out and bought for herself, the day she decided to give up the shop. It was, she said, a proper treat, to be able to dress up properly, after so many years of being leaf-strewn and soggy. Her other post-shop indulgence was her nails, which she grew to luxurious lengths and took to be twice-weekly, manicured and scarletted.

At the same time, I'd taken on Trudie. A mother of five, all of them, she told me with grin, of what could only be relief, now off her hands. Quiet and calm – with five kids she'd probably had to cultivate that – she was given to wearing long, peasant style skirts which were always tripping her on the stairs. She also had a collection of exceptionally long, dangly earrings which she loved, but had never been able to wear, through the years of small grabby fingers. Completely unassuming, like Brenda before her, she hadn't worked for years, not since the children started arriving. But, sitting across from her, when she came in to see me, I saw how very bright she was, how frustrated that intelligence had been and what potential there was now, to give all those ideas, free rein. I didn't hesitate to offer her the job, although Kitty and Brenda didn't see eye to eye with me at all and both told me sniffily, on several different occasions, she wouldn't last, mark their words.

My social life, for once, was as perky as my professional one, which again came as quite a surprise to me. David and I were still going out and had settled easily into a relationship that, apart from the normal ups and downs of two people, getting to know each other, felt pretty comfortable. As time went on, I was increasingly aware, I needed to address a few things and bring him up to speed, but as I've said, it's not always easy to find the right moment, so that was still in the pending file.

I was delighted, there seemed to be such demand, for the ever-increasing range of services the agency offered, although that did mean we sometimes veered in directions, I hadn't imagined we'd go – which was how Katerina came into the picture. She was a somewhat bolshie, Borzoi bitch; deep cream with extravagantly lush, chocolatey markings. She was more elegant than any dog has a right to be and, it has to be said, leaned heavily towards the neurotic. She belonged to an equally highly strung, elderly and eccentric client, Doreen Healing, known in our office as Baby Jane as in, Whatever Happened To.

Doreen, who was convinced the sun was not her friend, never left the house without an over-sized sun-hat, wrap-around sunglasses and quantities of sky-high factor sunscreen, which gave, what could be seen of her face, a startlingly whiteish hue. A retired girls' school headmistress, her bungalow and pocket-sized garden were now strangled, smothered and encroached upon by the rumble and dust of the North Circular, and neighboured by compulsorily purchased, boarded up, empty properties. She though maintained, she was going nowhere, and had launched successive appeals to delay the process. Her desk and dining table, groaned under the weight of years of cranky, council correspondence and letters from solicitors, whilst the floor was carpeted with carefully sectioned and paper-clipped press cuttings, of successful and not so successful situations, similar to her own. She and Katarina, who was surprisingly graceful for such a large dog, wove cautious paths through the chaos.

Every wall of the bungalow, was full of framed photos of her with pupils and staff through the years. She spoke often of how touched she was, so many of them stayed in contact. Every bit of their gossip and news, she said, kept her young, making her feel she was still an important part of their lives. The constant contact I knew, was purely in her head, but it was what kept her going. She'd originally approached us, because she needed to take Katerina to the vet, and had convinced herself, any male taxi driver was more likely than not, to rob, rape and murder her on the way. She felt being driven by a woman, might pose less of a risk. I sent Brenda the first time, as being the epitome of solid and trustworthy and, following this initial experiment, from which both owner and pet emerged unscathed, Doreen became a regular. She used us, whenever she needed to go anywhere that wasn't within walking distance. She also regularly booked us to go in and work with her, every couple of weeks, for an hour or so, on her ongoing and invariably contentious correspondence.

Shamefully, when she didn't call to book her usual slot one week, we just assumed she didn't have any work to catch up on. When we didn't hear anything, the following week, I popped round to check on her. I knew what I was going to find, as soon as I rang the doorbell, because I could hear Katerina crying.

Doreen had died peacefully in her sleep, but that didn't assuage the guilt felt for not checking sooner. When asked if I knew anyone who'd look after the dog, I simply couldn't do anything else but take her home, despite the fact I felt she'd always looked down her long, aristocratic nose at me, to find me wanting in every possible way. My parents weren't delighted at this new addition to the household, and the new addition to the household, wasn't over the moon either. But Doreen's only relative was a nephew who, on being contacted, had immediately made clear his only interest, in an aunt he hadn't seen since he was a child, was whether there was anything of value in it for him. I didn't think a nervy, tall and willowy canine qualified.

I wouldn't say Katerina became fond of me, but she did seem to view me as a constant, in a scarily changing world and would pant and cry softly, when I wasn't around. Because of this, I often took her with me to the office, where she'd sashay up the stairs and sigh heavily, before settling herself, elegantly regal in a basket we'd placed for her, in the corner of my room. I thought she added a touch of class to the place, although she did tend to jump convulsively, every time the phone rang, which it did – a lot. David complained that she didn't like him, but I said I didn't think she liked anybody very much, so he really shouldn't feel bad.

Despite the fact that all was going well, I wasn't feeling that good. I was constantly and completely exhausted. I hadn't slept properly for I don't know how long. The wretched dreams that were plaguing me, were coming almost nightly now, and they were unspeakably unpleasant.

It's one thing having your own nightmares, we all have to take responsibility for those, but being invaded by someone else's, is more than anyone should have to put up with. It did seem though, that once that first connection had been made, it had only grown stronger and no matter how tightly I pulled down my usually effective shutters, alien emotions were getting through, sicker, stronger and more frequently.

I was, as I'd said I would, dutifully reporting what I remembered of the dreams to Boris, which was all fine and dandy, but I was starting to feel like a dead letter drop, and as I told him often, it wasn't him who was getting increasingly sleep-deprived and desperate. It also wasn't as if the information I was giving him, was specific enough for anyone to act on. As Boris agreed, the police generally couldn't arrest someone for having unpleasantly violent dreams. Said individual, he pointed out, had to commit some kind of offence and offensiveness didn't count. It was a long game, he said, sometimes the sort of thing I was passing on, came to something, sometimes it didn't.

CHAPTER THIRTY-NINE

I think it was probably about five or six weeks later that I finally reached the end of my tether, as I once again jerked fearfully awake, legs tangled uncomfortably in the sheets. Kat leapt up from the floor – my mother had fought a brief, unsuccessful battle over that, giving in gracelessly after a couple of nights of crying from the kitchen – so there were two of us quivering.

As my heart thumped and sweat dried uncomfortably on my skin, I struggled to recapture what it was I'd seen, even as it began to slip away from me. My mouth felt dry and gravelly, and I honestly didn't think I had much hope of getting back to sleep for a bit. I dragged myself downstairs, for a recuperative cup of tea, Kat padding nervously behind me. I stubbed my toe painfully on a chair, as I made my way across the kitchen, cursed in a thoroughly unladylike manner and, waiting for the kettle to boil, came to a decision.

Enough was enough. My instruction from Boris had been unequivocal. Keep a record of everything I could remember, under no circumstances engage in any way, simply pass any detail along to him and he'd pass it along to Cornwall, to see if it linked with any current case. That was it. That was all. That was as much as we could do. I was simply a receiver, nothing more, nothing less.

Well screw that for a lark. I'd had a basinful of ill-defined, murky, muddy dreams which now, when they came, drenched my sleeping mind with an overwhelmingly unpleasant, feral scent. Reluctant as I was to stick my neck out, or my nose in, I needed to track down this connection and sever it in some way. If I didn't do that and soon, I'd be packing my bags for the funny farm and a comfortably padded cell. As you know well by now, I'm nothing if not risk averse – but I reasoned, if I took action, I could probably sort out this whole stupid, mess myself, whilst still keeping a reasonable distance and without taking chances. And even if I did, at any point, need to get up close and personal, I was more than well equipped to take care of myself. After all, I managed perfectly well on my own, most of the time. I toyed briefly with the idea of letting Boris know what I planned, but dismissed that immediately. I knew what he'd say and I didn't want to listen.

Simply having made the decision to initiate immediate action, made me feel a lot better, although I was, at first, at a bit of loss as to what exactly to initiate. I did know though, that instead of shutting out as much as I could, I needed to change the habits of a lifetime and open up, but to do that, I had to be somewhere I could focus quietly, without interruption and this was more easily envisaged than achieved. The office was always a mad house and even closeted in my inner sanctum, I never knew when the door would burst open, with a query or a client. Home was little better. The solution seemed to be the car.

So, parked near Golders Hill Park, mid-day sun on the windscreen, children's voices rising and falling in a nearby playground, and Kat's even breathing and occasional snore from the back seat, I tuned in. I first opened up a little and then a lot, letting my mind range further and further. A load of stuff hit hard, swirling round and through me, a cacophony of sound, thought, motion and emotion. I jerked back with the impact, my head smacked painfully onto the head-rest and Kat whined softly. I hurriedly slammed the shutters down again. Obviously this search and locate business wasn't going to work well that way – impossible to deal with such an overload of input, looking for the single one that resonated, it was like burrowing for a needle in several hundred haystacks. I re-grouped.

This time round, I focused on the second-hand dreams I'd been experiencing and, most importantly the mind behind them. It wasn't a pleasant thing to do, feverishly angry as they were. I'd always wanted them out of my head, not further in. It was, however, an interesting exercise. I was convinced I'd given Boris all I could, when it came to information, but as it turned out, there were things I'd missed. And, after a while, in the increasing heat of the car, I came to reluctantly understood, this connection I'd never wanted, between me and the other, was strong enough to have created something almost tangible. In my head, was the concept of two cans, linked over a distance by a piece of string, and I nodded slowly, yes, that was it, much as I might dislike the idea, there was an energy line connecting us. I just had to follow the string.

I wound the window down further, to try and get some air in, although the Indian summer heat, was as thick and cloying outside, as it was in. I started the car, with no clear idea where I was headed, I had to trust my instinct and as I drove, I could feel my mind was acting like a kind of Geiger counter, the closer I was getting, to the source of what I was after, the stronger the reaction I was feeling.

I won't lie to you. There was an incredibly strong urge to stop the car, shut off the Geiger counter and make for home. Indeed, I did slow down and almost pulled over to turn around, but having taken it this far and established just how strong the wretched link was, I'd have been letting myself down by giving up. There was a possibility, of course, this whole dream business might end as suddenly and unexpectedly as it arrived, but what if it didn't? I'd carry on sharing nightmares that were nothing to do with me. We all have our own demons, who needs anyone else's? I had to dig deeper.

Just under forty minutes, took me to a leafy, residential area, not far past St. Albans. It was somewhere I'd never been before, but I pulled up, with complete certainty, just down the road from a large, set-back from the street, detached house, fronted by a well-mown lawn and shut off behind tall, ornately scrolled, wrought iron gates. He was in there.

CHAPTER FORTY

I'd imagined there'd be far more clarity in his waking mind, than in the confusion of the dreams I'd been getting. But this didn't seem to be true at all. His thoughts were repetitively obsessive, circulating hectically in his mind and intensified by the level of concentration on the intricacy of what he was doing.

He was painting, directly on to a cream-coloured wall and what he'd created, was amazing. A detailed depiction, some five foot high, three foot wide. White-framed, French windows, opening up on to a lushly planted garden, multi-hued and dappled in afternoon sunlight. His garden was divided by a slim, crazy-paved path, winding lazily between lawns and borders and through a rose-smothered, wicker arch to a small working fountain. The colours were glorious, detail and perspective perfect. It was a trompe l'oeil – to deceive the eye. I'd seen them before, usually in alcoves in Italian restaurants, but nothing so impeccably executed as this. He was kneeling at an awkward angle, I could feel the crick in his back. He was working on the bottom left of the painting, maybe signing it.

He looked up and around for a moment, arching as he stretched, taking in the wide, marble-floored, square hall, warmed with scattered rugs. The several glass-paned doors, around the hall, were flooding it with natural daylight and a light-wood, balustraded staircase, rose from one side, to the upper floor. It was a lovely, luxurious space, but didn't feel in any way like a showcase, just very lived-in. Differently coloured, variously sized, well-used wellingtons were piled under a coat rack, adjacent to the front door. A couple of dog leads hung nearby and there were muddy paw-prints, leading to a door at the end of the hall which was half open. A tall, circular oak table at the hall's centre, midway between front door and stairs, held key-rings, letters and the kind of leaflets that always rain through the letterbox. They shared the table-top with a red-rose packed vase. The flowers had been stuck in haphazardly, but nevertheless blazed a welcome. On the dustsheet, spread below the painting to prevent any mess hitting the floor, there was a radio playing softly.

A dungareed woman, mid-forties, thick dark blonde hair swinging to her shoulders, emerged from the half-open kitchen door, wiping one floury hand on an apron and balancing a mug and plate of biscuits in the other. Through her eyes, I saw a neatly made young man. Not tall, thin and wiry, jockey-build. Young, younger than I'd somehow expected, maybe late twenties, early thirties, with a pleasant, blunt featured, square-jawed face, faintly laced with scars of previously aggressive acne. Already thinning, light brown hair was brushed forward and sideways, over a disproportionately high forehead, which would only get higher with the years if that hair continued to beat a retreat. He jumped courteously to his feet as the woman appeared, to thank her and take drink and plate. She handed them over, her eyes on the painting as she stepped back again, to better take the whole thing in. She laughed in delight, swinging round to him and putting both hands on his arm, in her enthusiasm.

"Jamie, you are pure magic. I don't know what to say, it's better than wonderful." She had a strong, vowels clipped and angled, South African accent. He ducked his head modestly.

"Gideon won't be back until next week," she said, "But I'm so dying for him to see it. We never, ever dreamt it would look this fabulous. You're brilliant, I hope you know that?"

"Honestly it's not hard, not when you know how to go about it, Mrs de Freyt," He said quietly "And I enjoy doing these very much." He was soft voiced, well spoken.

"Well, you've certainly gone way, way, way beyond my expectations. I'm so delighted we found you. You'll do Isabelle's one next, won't you? She's been driving me crazy, she can't wait." He nodded,

"Should be ready to start that for her tomorrow, I'm very nearly done with this, just a few finishing touches."

"Well, Jamie Richman," she said, "If you weren't so damn painty right now, I'd give you the biggest hug you've ever had in your whole life!" He grinned back at her,

"If I wasn't so damn painty, I might like that." They both laughed, comfortably. She was thinking, what a sweet boy, so well mannered. Shy and a bit gauche, but a pleasure to have someone like that in the house – and what a talent. How lucky was she, to have followed up his ad? He was thinking, he'd like to take her artfully highlighted head and smash it hard and repeatedly against the wall he was working on. He could anticipate the impact, the crack of bone, the blood and the satisfying weight of her body as he let her slowly slide down the wall, to the floor – smug, patronising cow!

In the car, outside the house, I shivered deeply, despite the heat. I was no stranger to what went on in the minds of people, a great deal of which was unbelievable, unpleasant and unexpected. I'd spent a lifetime, taking it in and shutting it out, and there wasn't a lot that could shock me. But I was disturbed by the depths of his anger, his aching for violence and his anticipation. People fantasise all the time and human nature being what it is, sex and violence are an ongoing theme. Few take it further than that. But something felt different and alarming here. The contrast between what was in his head and the complete ignorance of the woman, delighted to have him in her home, was awful.

I'd been getting a taste of his mind for a good few months now and hadn't found it pleasant. I had hoped though, the violence in the nightmares was just the normal voiding of frustration and other stuff that accumulates during the day, a shucking off of the inhibitions that bind and control us. Now I wasn't so sure I had it right, I suspected the anger and inherent violence was a constant. I'd located him to find a way of severing the wretched connection, even though not altogether clear how I was going to do that. But now, I didn't know whether I should even try. I certainly wanted to, it was just my conscience was prickling, in uncomfortably familiar fashion.

Kat had been patient all this while and she rarely barked, but now she gave one of her small whuffling noises, like someone clearing their throat, which was her way of reminding me she was still there. I put on her lead, which embarrassed me considerably, whenever we went out. It was black, pink and diamond studded, and I don't think she liked it much either. But Doreen had chosen and loved it, and I hadn't been able to bring myself to throw it out and replace, with something less statement-making. We strolled up one side of the residential road and back down the other. Each one of the houses was individual and completely different from its neighbour, but I wasn't in any mood to appreciate architecture, and Kat was equally preoccupied with her own business.

On our way back to the car, we passed a couple of schoolgirls, twelve or thirteen years old, struggling under the weight of disproportionately large school bags that looked to weigh a ton. They were giggling together, busily unfolding the waists of their uniform skirts, lowering them back to semi-respectable length, before getting home. They stopped to admire and pet Kat, as did most people. Kat tolerated this with her usual, slightly bored air of a star dealing with the public, before one of the girls said goodbye and pressed the key pad next to the black wrought iron gates, which swung open to let her in and closed smoothly behind her, leaving the other girl to continue further down the road. I understood this was the Isabelle, who was going to be blessed with a piece of painted art on her own wall.

CHAPTER FORTY-ONE

Back in the car, I put the key firmly in the ignition and turned it. Then I turned it, equally firmly, back again. Up till now, I'd only dipped a metaphorical toe in the water, but if I was going to try and extricate myself from this mess, that was giving me nothing but aggro, I really did need to find out more, and then make some decisions. I took a deep breath and dived in.

Usually, when in you go deep into somebody's head, it's pretty overwhelming, but you do get an immediate sense of the whole person, who and what they are. Jamie was more complicated to make out. I could see his night-time horrors were an extension of all that plagued him during the day. It was this part of his mind that was doing the rat-in-a-maze racing, bouncing wildly and repeatedly off envisioned acts of violence. There was another part of his mind that was more self-contained and focused on putting the finishing touches to the painting. But the level of his concentration on that, was only intensifying the frantic skittering of the other. You didn't have to know about dance, to recognise what Fred Astaire could do and you didn't have to know about art, to recognise Jamie's exceptional talent. You also didn't have to be a psychiatrist, to know there was something very wrong indeed here.

I could see what it was he'd been working on, at the base of the picture, partially and cleverly hidden in one of the painted, reflective glass panes, of the French window. It wasn't his signature, it was two eyes. That was how he authenticated his work, a symbol, instead of the more usual signature. The eyes, with a few clever strokes, had been finalised to near photographic realism, and whilst they blended easily into the painting, once you'd spotted them, their gaze seemed to follow and it was difficult to look away.

He was tidying up, getting ready to finish for the day, sorting the brushes, dipping them in turps, the smell strong, cleaning them gently and thoroughly with a soft cloth. But he'd stopped looking at and thinking about what he was doing, his focus had changed. He was watching Isabelle head up the stairs. Boris had pointed out to me, more than once, under our

196

present justice system, you can't arrest someone for what they're thinking. As far as I was concerned, that was a major flaw, at least it was, if you were hearing and seeing what I was.

What was happening now, his obsession with Isabelle, had happened before. Had, in fact, happened several times before, with other girls, and had brought him a load of trouble. He wanted, needed, to watch and listen, hear and understand, learn and comprehend. What harm was there in that? It didn't hurt anyone, did it? But whereas he'd only always wanted to watch before, now he wasn't sure that would be enough.

As I went in deeper I saw – as far back as we could remember, we'd been on the side-lines, just missing the point, not getting the joke; whole worlds of communication, flying high over our head even whilst we were reaching up to try and understand. Parents; older brother and younger sister; school mates; teachers; art-college peers then employers and work colleagues, all of them, singing from a song sheet, we didn't seem to have, and however we tried to catch the tunes, the notes just kept slipping through our fingers. We tried, we tried so hard, but with this sort of thing, you can try and try and try again, but you can't pretend.

People know. They know that you laugh a few seconds behind everyone else, that the art of irony escapes you, that the unspoken which is heard and comprehended so crystal clearly by everyone else, isn't seen or understood by you. They know you're different. What they probably don't know, can't know, is how badly that hurts. How every slight isn't just a one-off, but a continuation of others. How every time we laugh late, we know they've already moved on and left us behind. We have no control over any of these things, so we're forced to find areas where we do have control. First flowers; then insects; small birds; mice; a hedgehog; two kittens. Studying them, understanding how they're made, how they function, able to destroy them, when we've learned all we can and they're no longer any use to us.

And if there's no easy understanding and communication with the rest of the world, there's even less with the voices in our own head, Voices; calling, crying, chuckling, muttering and whispering. All during the day, every hour through the night. We've learned, when we concentrate and focus on the intricacies of the paintings, the voices soften. But of course, they can't disappear, won't disappear, because they're not outside, they're inside, they are, each and every one, a part of us a very wrong, very terrible part of us.

No, Isabelle isn't the first and she won't be the last. Like the others before her, she is special, although she doesn't truly know it yet. But we're patient, we have time to let her know, although obviously not endless time. But we're satisfied with what we've done at this point. We've sorted the watching. We have eyes now, here in this house. But we dislike it when other people divert attention from where it should be, people like the de Freyt woman, with her endless gushing. The anger and violence, we feel towards her is shocking, even to us, but it's understandable, forgivable, because people like her screw things up, get in our way, up our nose. We have pride though in our self-taught, self-control. The violence is the one thing we do have control over. We decide if, when, where or how. Oh yes, we can hold our head high on that one.

As I yanked myself violently back and away from the darkness I was being drawn down into, there was a sudden hot and heavy breathing, in my left ear. I shrieked in fright, lurched sideways, hit the car door painfully with my shoulder and Kat leapt backwards, quivering and whimpering. Honestly, the two of us were going to have to get our nerves a bit more in hand. I reached back, a little shakily, to pat her and hoped she wasn't too traumatised. This was the first time she'd ever made any kind of move towards me and I suspected, it might be something she wouldn't risk again. I felt rather sick, it hadn't been a pleasant incursion by any means and I wished I'd just turned that key in the ignition and driven off, five minutes earlier. I decided I didn't want to find out too much more about Jamie, in truth, I'd have preferred to have known a whole lot less.

I don't remember much about driving myself back home, but obviously I did, because that's where I ended up. Whilst Jamie didn't know yet what his next move might be, I was prepared to lay bets, it wasn't going to be anything good. I thought he might be on a one-way and escalating path, but my conscience, or maybe it was my vanity, wouldn't let me comfortably wash my hands of the whole thing. Surely, anyone who could produce art like he did, was worth trying to help, and to be honest, if I didn't start getting some uninterrupted, dreamless sleep soon, he wasn't going to be the only one going round the bend.

I thought I'd go back one more time, see if there was any conceivable way I could sort him out. If I drew a blank, I'd pass it all straight along to Boris and the police, maybe they could keep him under observation and there must be some kind of protocol for cases like this.

CHAPTER FORTY-TWO

I went back, a couple of days later. This time in the morning. I parked where I had before, and hoped nobody would think I was casing the joint. In the back seat, Kat whined, maybe she recognised where we were and didn't think it was a sensible move either. This time he was working upstairs, in what I guessed, from the god-awful mess, to be Isabelle's room. He was creating, with swift, sure, broad strokes – nothing like the delicacy he'd used downstairs – a startling mural of a rock group, in full flow. It was nowhere near finished, but even so; colour, movement and energy leapt off the wall and hit you in the heart. You could feel the thumping of the amplifiers in your ears and chest. This time, he'd painted the eyes first. From down in the corner, at the left hand side of the wall, they were watching.

The hamster wheel in his head was turning, ever faster now. Round and round, went his thinking. He was finally in the room he wanted to be in and breathing deeply as he worked, inhaling the underlying scent of shampoo, perfume and colouring crayons, the mixed messages of a girl her age. Even in the last two days, I could see his mind-set had changed alarmingly. In his head was a disturbing mix of detailed thinking and feverish imaginings, but what was fantasy and what was forward planning? He was still angry, backgrounded by the habitual feeling of being hard-done-by, always the victim. I could see what had caused this latest melt-down, he was compulsively playing and replaying the scene.

Isabelle wasn't in school, some kind of free day for some reason, he didn't know what, didn't care, the important thing was, she was sitting close to him, watching him work and they were chatting. She was asking all sorts of questions, how he did this, why he did that. She was at ease with him, liked him, wanted to know what he had to tell her, find out how he got started, because she thought he was brilliant and she wanted to study art too. All was well and good, until that cow interfered. She'd stuck her head round the door with a smile and chivvied Isabelle firmly away,

"Darling, I'm sure Jamie can't concentrate with you waffling on at him."

She'd said. He'd of course protested, said he was enjoying talking and this way, Isabelle could make sure he was doing the wall exactly as she wanted. But the cow wasn't brooking any argument. He couldn't see, but I could, a mother's first instinct, wouldn't be to leave a thirteen year old, with a man she hardly knew, however impeccable his manners and irreproachable his behaviour. No, Isabelle could pop up from time to time to watch progress, but she had homework to do, which could be just as easily done at the kitchen table. As he'd watched them leave the room, raising his hand in a friendly, mock salute to Mrs de Freyt, he'd been imagining, just how much less she might have to say, with his two hands tight round her throat and her eyes bulging out of her head.

Of course we can all think things – there's probably not one of us who hasn't, on occasion, felt the urge to blip someone else over the head with a blunt instrument – we don't though usually carry it through. However, for this young man it was so close, he could feel his fingers twitching in happy anticipation. If ever a woman needed teaching a lesson, he thought, getting to his feet, it was this one and now was as good a time as any.

Well I couldn't just sit there, in the car outside the house, while things went violently pear-shaped inside. So I upended one of his open paint pots. It turned out to be dark brown and instantly spread a thick chocolatey layer over the dustsheet, on which it had been sitting. That distracted him. He thought he'd kicked it himself and was cursing as he crouched to stop the flow, mop up and check nothing was seeping through to the carpet below. By the time he'd sorted out the mess and restored things to the rigidly ordered, which is how he liked to work, he was angrier with himself than with her, which was a relief. It could only be a temporary reprieve though, it was no resolution.

And then something rather dreadful happened. He suddenly stopped what he was doing, because he heard and sensed me. He knew I was there, sitting outside. For a moment, things stood very still and then, in one instant, his whole world turned on its axis and I saw, what I'd been too blind or stupid to spot earlier. He was Strange.

He was still all the unpleasant things he'd been before, but in that second, and oh, so belatedly, he and I both realised, the voices in his head weren't, never had been, a part of all that was wrong with him, they'd just never been recognised for the reality they were.

How could I not have seen it? Ruth's words of a few years ago, came back to me with complete clarity. 'There are those of us,' she'd said, 'And we're in the minority, who understand ourselves, if not from the very beginning, soon after. The adjustments we put in place, to fit in with the rest of the world, make us the lucky ones. There are others who don't or can't understand what they are. Some end up in psychiatric wards. Others are diagnosed and treated for schizophrenia or the like and a lifetime is spent, struggling to medicate out the voices. Many more find their own way of blotting out, with drink or drugs, what they can't take in.' And as her words ran through my mind, they did through his too and shock, recognition and realisation, literally felled him. He sank slowly to his knees and I thought absently, his jeans wouldn't recover from that brown paint. He caught my thought and smiled too. And then all the anger, blazing in intensity, came flooding back and he came after me.

CHAPTER FORTY-THREE

I took off like a bat out of hell, pulling away from the kerb outside the de Freyt house with a skidding of tyres, and Kat was unceremoniously hurled off the back seat, hitting the floor with a solid thump. She was thoroughly put out, Borzois tend to be on the sensitive side and have long memories, I knew she wouldn't forget this in a hurry. She whuffled extreme displeasure and, probably wisely, decided to stay where she was in the well of the car, in anticipation of further irresponsible driving.

She wasn't the only one, put out. I was berating myself for not recognising him immediately for what he was. I was also acutely uneasy, because I didn't know what it was, that had suddenly changed things for him, was it just my proximity? Was it something to do with the link between us, which now, more than ever, I needed gone. I had no idea of what he might do next, didn't know how much he understood and what the shock might do to an already teetering mind. And on the tail of all those unpleasant thoughts came another, equally unsettling. I had no idea what he could do in terms of other abilities he may have, although perhaps he didn't either yet. Was that any comfort?

It seemed like a good idea, to call in reinforcements, sooner rather than later. I didn't even want to wait until I got back to the office. I found a phone box and luckily it was in full working order, something rarer than hen's teeth these days. I had the number Boris had given me and mercifully, the right change, although I had to empty the contents of my bag to find it. Having overcome all those hurdles, to my huge frustration, the phone rang and rang at his end. I was unreasonably cross, I hate it when people aren't there when you want them. I waited to see if he had an answerphone but the ringing continued, unattended to by man or machine. I pushed the button, got my coins back and looked at the other number I kept on the same piece of paper. It was Glory who answered. I didn't waste time, I didn't know how much more change I could dig up.

"It's me," I said, "I seem to have got myself into a situation. Don't know what's best to do. I need help."

"That makes a change!"

"Glory, I mean it."

"Out with it then." She was physically too far away for me to flash everything over, so I had to talk, which was frustrating. I was aware, Rachael and Ruth were there with her and thus, would hear everything instantly. As I talked, I was fumbling for more coins to feed the phone, but that still wouldn't give me all the time in the world, I concentrated on coherence.

"Right," she said as I wound down. "We know where he is now. Go home, there's nothing more you can do for the moment."

"But, listen, I'm worried about that woman and the child, I tried to get hold of Boris, but he's not there, should I just phone the police?" There was a brief pause at the other end then Rachael, who'd obviously lost patience with getting things second-hand, came on.

"Absolutely not the police. Do you understand? Someone could get seriously hurt."

"I know that, Rachael, that's what I'm worried about."

"We don't know what this Jamie of yours might do next. He's a dangerous loose cannon and the police aren't equipped to deal with that. Leave it with us, we'll handle it."

"But…" I started,

"No buts, Stella. You've got yourself involved in this, you've come to us for help. Now do what I tell you. Understand?" I bit my lip, I couldn't help thinking, with a certain amount of peeve, if I hadn't had those damn conversations with Boris and Ruth, I might have not been listening out in the first place, might not have heard Jamie, might not be where I was now – so it wasn't entirely my fault. But I knew my change would run out, long before I did, when it came to voicing my opinion and if I'm honest, the thought of passing all this unpleasantness over to someone who knew what they were doing, seemed a far more desirable solution. So I said, yes I understood and goodbye.

CHAPTER FORTY-FOUR

Solutions, which seem to be ideal at the time, as often as not, turn out to be anything but. At least this one let me drive back at a more sedate pace, with a mind temporarily eased, and any residual guilt feelings pushed firmly below the surface, often the best place for them. Despite all that had gone on and the fact I felt plumb tuckered out, it was only just coming up to midday and I honestly didn't think I could justify skiving off and heading for home, when we were so busy, so I made tracks for the office.

Hilary and Martin both had clients seated in front of their desks, and there were lots of glossy brochures being bandied about – I was glad they were busy, more bookings always alleviated Martin's gloom, if only fractionally. They both raised an absent hand in greeting, as Kat and I passed by and headed on up the stairs, towards the satisfactory sound of more than one typewriter being bashed enthusiastically.

As I opened our office door, Kitty and Brenda both hailed me cheerfully and brought me up to date with what I needed to know, although I was grateful they were both handling a great number of things, completely capably, on their own. I was also delighted, that despite the odd heated debate that still occurred now and then, over some disputed decision or other, they now got on well most of the time, with nothing uniting them quite so much, as keeping Ruby and Trudie in their place.

Once in my office, Kat settled in her corner, with a martyred sigh – she did martyred, almost as well as the rest of my family. I got my head down, to deal with the weeks-worth of bits and pieces that always accumulate when you're out of the office, for even half a day. I didn't want to spend any more time at all, thinking about my morning. I'd finally done the sensible thing, I just couldn't quite shift an underlying unease. Into my mind, there kept sliding, the eyes on the wall. So well-hidden, so realistic, so unnervingly watchful. I hoped the de Freyts hadn't, and wouldn't ever, spot what was peering out at them from their paintings.

I spent the rest of the day doing that thing – you know, where you sit at your desk and shift papers from one place to another, without achieving a lot, answer the phone, then can't remember what was said, and look at a number of things that need decisions, without deciding anything. At around 4.45 I'd had enough. There had to be some benefits of being the boss. I took myself and Kat out of there, for a long brisk walk. Unfortunately, she was as lazy as I was, and whilst the spirit was willing, the flesh was weak and we both decided, at a shamefully early stage, we'd had enough fresh air. We set off back to the car to head home.

As we walked towards it, I could see there was something on the windscreen. Squinting, I thought it didn't look like a parking ticket, several of which, to my annoyance, I'd accrued recently. As we got nearer, it became clear, it wasn't anything like a parking ticket. It was a very plump, stone dead, blackbird, small, dulled black eyes, gazing vacantly skyward. Kat and I both recoiled, and I did what any self-respecting, emancipated young woman would. I shrieked loudly and ran into the travel agency, to get a man to deal with it.

Martin, obviously feeling much the same as me, when it came to dead birds, faltered a moment, but felt he couldn't show himself up in front of clients. Stopping only to collect a black rubbish sack and purloin Hilary's Marigolds from the kitchen, he strode manfully outside, while I paced up and down the street, muttering 'Eeugh, eugh' to myself and looking the other way. Post removal, Hilary trotted out with a bucket of disinfectant, which she sloshed liberally over the car.

"There you go sweetie," she said. "Right as rain now. Just unlucky it landed on your car. Mind you, better there than on your head!" I was still 'eughing' a few more times at the thought of that when Martin, having disposed of black plastic bag and Marigolds in a rubbish bin along the street, commented, in the authoritative tones of a man who's just coped with a crisis,

"It'd wedged itself, right and tight, probably died trying to get away."

"Get away?"

"Its wing was properly caught up, stuck right under your windscreen wiper." He grimaced, "No idea how it did that, had a job getting it out. Maybe it died of fright, being trapped." I thought about the dead black eyes, and then I thought about Jamie. But that wasn't possible. He'd never even seen me, couldn't possibly have the faintest idea who or where I was.

And then I remembered, how easy it had been for me to track him down. Could he possibly have it in him, to do the same? Oh, that wouldn't be good, that wouldn't be good at all. I shivered,

"Goose walk over your grave?" asked Hilary. I smiled at her,

"No, take no notice of me. Thank you both so much, I can't tell you how grateful I am. Don't know what I'd have done if you hadn't been there. Sorry to have made such a fuss, I have a bit of a thing about birds – dead or alive."

"No problem," said Martin, "Lucky I was here. It wasn't very pleasant."

"No," I said, "Not very pleasant at all."

CHAPTER FORTY-FIVE

What with one thing and another, I completely forgot I was supposed to be seeing David that night, so when he arrived, we were both surprised – me to find him on the doorstep and him to find me not ready. Luckily, our relationship had progressed far enough for recriminations to be exchanged freely, on the subject of some people's unreliability and other people's lack of a reminder phone-call. Once we'd got all that under our belts, I got changed quickly, and he took me to one of our favourite Italian restaurants.

We were greeted extravagantly, the manager kissed my hand, solicitously ushered us to a table for two, in the corner, and presented the menu, which was one of those that can take you a couple of weeks to peruse. Our table was romantically lit by the stuttering flame of a candle in a Chianti bottle, white wax dripping onto the already encrusted glass. I'm not very good with candle flame, something about the way it makes your eye focus on the flicker, always makes me feel funny – I know, call me precious, but there you are, I moved it surreptitiously along to the corner of the table, out of my line of sight.

As the waiter flapped around, planting the napkin in my lap – don't you always find, you've moved your hand at the wrong moment, so it looks as if you're trying to make life difficult for them – I noticed, behind David's back, a window-sized niche in the wall, with a trompe l'oeil scene of Italian countryside. It wasn't that well done, certainly not compared to the work I'd seen at the de Freyt's house. It was just bold, colourful and atmospheric, but it immediately put me in mind of that morning and I couldn't help but look, and keep looking for the eyes. Of course there weren't any, but I've lived long enough with all the oddities that make me what I am, to know, odd or not, my instincts are to be trusted. If I feel uneasy, there's usually a reason, which will rear its ugly head sooner or later. There's no doubt I was feeling twitchy that evening and it was probably all of this, going round in my head, that made David ask, slightly querulously, if I was listening to him at all. I nodded absentmindedly, and squeezed his hand, which was holding mine across the table.

"Well?" he said.

"Well what?"

"For goodness sake Stella, did you not hear what I just said?" I pulled my attention back with a guilty jerk and saw, on the table, a small red box. Simultaneously, I realised, hovering out of sight, round a corner of the room, were three well-primed waiters, with champagne in a bucket, hand-held sparklers and a song on their lips.

"Good Lord!" I said.

"Aren't you going to even look at it?" David nudged the box encouragingly towards me, and I appreciated that here was a man who was rapidly reconsidering his whole strategy and forward planning. It crossed his mind, fleetingly, whether he could possibly simply snatch up the box, laugh and yell 'April Fool!' despite the fact it was October. I grinned at that, it was rare I caught his thoughts because I never looked or listened and usually he was exceptionally closed, but he did have a great sense of humour.

"Well?" he said again. This was awful, I didn't know what to say. My feelings for him weren't in question. Most of the time I'm quite a solitary person, I like my own company and time to debrief in peace and quiet, without constant sensory bombardment. David was the first person I'd ever met, other than the Peacock gang, whose company was just as comfortable as being on my own. That wasn't to be sneezed at.

The problem was, honesty is high on my list of important things, and whilst I certainly felt our developing relationship deserved it, over the last year, an occasion just didn't seem to have arisen, that felt like quite the right time to mention what I thought I should. Somehow the conversation never seemed to veer in the right direction to outline, even one or two of my peculiarities, and I had thought it best to do it on a step by step basis, rather than hitting him with the whole package all at once. Isn't it though, a fact of life, that the longer an issue remains undiscussed, the more complicated it becomes, not only to bring it up, but to explain why it's been kept under wraps for so long. And then suddenly, there you are – up a creek without a paddle, or in this case, in an Italian restaurant at an emotional crossroads.

Whilst I was mulling, things seemed to gain their own momentum. I'd picked up the little red box, because it seemed horribly rude not to, and opened it on an antique ring, a turquoise set with little diamonds.

Unfortunately, the waiters, who'd obviously been champing at the bit and keeping an eagle eye on proceedings, took this as a sign to go, go, go! They hurtled enthusiastically round the corner, champagne and sparklers held high, whilst they let loose with a full throated rendition of O Sole Mio, the other diners started 'aaaahing' and clapping and David slipped the ring on my finger and told me how happy I'd made him. Well, you can see the awkwardness of the situation can't you?

The rest of the evening passed in a bit of a blur, mainly due to the fact that what with everything, I forgot my strict, no alcohol rule and took several reviving swigs of champagne, which promptly went straight to my already, sadly confused head. I'm pretty certain we had a lovely meal, and I seem to remember we discussed all sorts of important things, although not the most important thing. When we left, there was another round of applause, cheers and good wishes and lots of people I didn't know, kissed me and shook David's hand.

When we got back to my house, I stopped regretting the champagne and started feeling grateful that I wasn't completely compos mentis. Not only were my parents waiting for us – David had formally spoken to my father, before we left – Kitty had also been summoned, along with Brenda who, somewhere along the line, had been adopted as nearest and dearest. Auntie Edna and Uncle Monty were there too – they'd brought balloons – and, weirdest of all, Laura and Melvyn Gold.

There was much laughter, noise and excitement – from my parents, who'd had doubts as to whether they'd ever see this day, from Auntie Edna who was convinced they wouldn't, and from Kitty who was hitting the advocaat hard. Melvyn Gold was very sweet, gave me a warm hug and said he was delighted, he honestly couldn't imagine anything more wonderful, than having me as a daughter-in-law. Laura Gold, on the other hand, seemed to be in a similar state of shock to me, so much so, I don't think she'd even had time to knock back a migraine pill. She kissed the air near both my cheeks, said she was very pleased and then wrapped her arms round David and sobbed a lot – I don't think it was with joy.

My ring was exclaimed over, and then everyone started discussing dates. Dates for an engagement party, dates for the wedding and – this was Auntie Edna – dates to start looking for dresses, and how many bridesmaids was

I thinking of? This was all moving way too fast for me and my conscience, but I wasn't sure how to stop the runaway train and get off.

I sat down on the sofa and absently quaffed a glass of advocaat, that had been left unattended – what the hell! And after a while, Kat came over and lay down near me, putting her head on my foot, which for her, was a gesture of wild and abandoned affection. David came over too, sat next to me and we smiled at each other. I didn't even want to know what he was thinking, but hoped to goodness, he wasn't feeling half as perturbed as me. In the opposite corner of the room, Laura had taken some action on the pill front and now had both my mother and Auntie Edna in a firm embrace and was earnestly assuring them, she felt like the third sister they'd never had.

Champagne and advocaat was probably not a happy mix, it certainly didn't feel like it when I eventually got to bed. Or maybe it was just that this was probably the only time I'd headed under the duvet, somewhat the worse for drink. But these were, I reassured myself, exceptional circumstances. I fell swiftly into a deep, dreamless sleep and didn't wake up until I felt someone choking the life out of me. I think that must have been around 3.30 a.m.

CHAPTER FORTY-SIX

I was getting a bit tired of being throttled, it wasn't that long since Dorothy Lowbell had also had a good go, and although those bruises had faded, the memories hadn't. My eyes shot open and my back arched painfully, as I noisily tried to pull in some air through my constricted windpipe. Kat had started up from the floor and was whining. There wasn't anyone else there with me, in the room, but neither was there any doubt about what was happening. I knew instantly who was doing it. I also knew, that when I had a moment or two to think about it, I'd be astonished he'd so quickly discovered what he could do. Right now I had a more pressing matter to deal with.

I broke his hold sharply and felt his surprise and anger. He'd only been able to get to me so easily because I was sleeping, and it wasn't a normal sleep – blame the drink. I'd left myself wide open, how stupid. He'd thought I was a soft touch. He hadn't planned to hurt me too badly, just scare the wits out of me. I wasn't sure why he was so angry. I assumed, it wasn't so much because I'd inadvertently shown him what he was, but because no-one had done it sooner. I sat up gingerly, rubbing my neck, which was throbbing painfully, there would be bruises in the morning. I called Kat over from the corner to which she'd retreated, but she refused to budge. I didn't have the patience for coaxing, so went into her head where, as so often, she was trembling as much inside as out. I soothed her quickly, in the way I'd found that worked, and after a short while, she ventured cautiously back to her usual position by my bed. She wasn't happy. Mind you, neither was I. My fear had become fact. He'd found me just as easily as I'd found him.

The thought of him out there, knowing where I was and watching and waiting until I was at my weakest, was unnerving. I put both hands to my forehead, I don't know, maybe I thought with a quick massage I could clear it quicker, I had to get myself together, to make sure he couldn't get to me again. I was surprised to find a ring on my finger, goodness, I'd completely forgotten about the engagement, that didn't bode well. Once I was sure I was shielded, I settled back down to sleep and hoped I wasn't going to be sharing any of his nightmares tonight. I'd already decided, the best course of action was to pass this latest happening on to Rachael and then, as she'd said, stay well out of it.

It turned out, Jamie had been a lot closer physically, last night, than I'd thought, because when I went out to the car in the morning, the window had been smashed and on the passenger seat, amidst all the glass was another dead bird – a pigeon this time. Kat and I did the shrieking and recoiling, before I pulled myself together. This was all extremely unpleasant and the mind-set behind it, worrying, if childish, but it wasn't as if I didn't know who was doing it and help was at hand, in the form of team Peacock. It did also occur to me, if Jamie's focus was on me, someone well able to take care of herself, then hopefully it wouldn't be on Isabelle.

I steeled myself to do the black bag and Marigolds thing, although I had no intention of touching the bird. I lifted it off the seat, its head hanging limp and unnatural from its neck, and floated it gently into the bag I was holding open, before knotting the top, disposing of it in the dustbin and brushing out as much of the glass as I could. I'd have to call one of those mobile services to come and fix it during the day. With the wind blowing briskly in through the broken window, making a real mess of both my hair and Kat's, I set off for the office, where Martin and Hilary waylaid me with a freshly-purchased bouquet of flowers, a box of chocolates, kisses and congratulations. Hilary was positively bouncing and Martin was as animated as I'd seen him. They both assured me, David was a lovely boy and Hilary winked, said she'd known from the start that something was in the air. I felt, with all my advantages, I should also have sussed the something in the air, before it hit me in the head. I then might have made more of a determined effort to appraise David, of exactly what he was getting into, presenting him with a chance to graciously extricate himself and run shrieking into the distance, before it was too late.

Excitement hadn't abated upstairs either. I staggered up, balancing flowers, chocolates and briefcase, to find Kitty had already been down the road, to Grodzinksi's, for a selection of celebratory pastries for us to have with our coffee. It did cross my mind, if I carried on knocking back chocolate and cake at the rate I was going, Aunt Edna was going to have work cut out, finding a dress into which I'd fit and it was going to take an awful lot of bridesmaids, to roll me down that aisle. Together with Brenda, Ruby and Trudie, Kitty wanted full details of the proposal, which was awkward – I didn't like to say, it had all happened while I wasn't paying much attention. I retreated to the relative peace of the inner office and extricated from my bag, the piece of paper with Rachael's number. It was getting decidedly crumpled, I probably ought, but was oddly reluctant, to officially enter it in my address book. I brought her up to date.

"Hmm." She said. "Right."

"So, what should I do?"

"I told you, nothing. We'll take care of it."

"When?"

"We're working on it now. Don't worry, I'm sure we can get him sorted out."

"That's all very well, but in the meantime, I'm the one coping with dead birds all over the place and him trying to strangle me."

"You're all right aren't you? Not actually hurt in any way?" she asked.

"Well, yes, I'm OK. Bit shaken up."

"Good."

"Good?"

"The more shaken up, the less likely to go getting yourself in any deeper." She said. "Anything else?"

"What about the girl, Isabelle?" I said.

"I told you, it's in hand. Don't worry." And she hung up. It was not, I felt, a particularly satisfactory conversation. Still, nothing much more I could do at the moment, I just had to sit back and hope whatever action they took, and I had no idea what that might be, would indeed sort things.

It was a fairly normal, busy morning in the office, with a couple of inquiries from what could turn out to be new clients, so I didn't have time to brood on the Jamie situation, until about 12.00 o'clock, when both Brenda and Kitty came into my office. They weren't on their own. Jamie was with them. He had his arm crushingly tight round Kitty's middle, almost lifting her off the floor, holding her effortlessly. He had a Stanley knife at her throat.

CHAPTER FORTY-SEVEN

"Hello." He said pleasantly. I didn't respond. I was considering my options, of which there didn't seem to be too many.

"Stella?" Brenda wasn't sounding anywhere near, as cool and calm as usual. Kitty didn't say anything, probably best, under the circumstances. The blade, set in an incongruously cheerful red handle, looked brand shiny new and lethal. It had already scratched the thin skin at her throat, and it hurt me to see a fine string of blood there.

He seemed to have got over his anger of yesterday and last night. He was now, by far the happiest he could remember being for a long, long while and yes, at the same time, perfectly relaxed and at ease with himself and the world. He was relishing the feel of skinny helplessness and panic-beating heart under his arm. He knew he could snap this one, as easily as a twig. One squeeze and a twist, just like the birds and, no doubt, a hell of a lot more satisfactory. He was reflecting, he probably hadn't even needed to bring the blade, but then he always had one on him for work, and everyone understands a knife. It certainly added to the dramatic tension, of which, in the room, there was a fair amount. He liked that. The revelation of what he was, had changed everything for him – his whole world was different, as was his place in it. He knew now that what he'd been hearing and seeing in his head, all his life, wasn't craziness at all. He wasn't a madman, he was in fact, something very special indeed and right now, he was feeling good. Oh yes, this was definitely a chap who'd come into his own.

"What do you want?" I said. I stayed sitting and still. I didn't think I could risk interfering with that vicious blade or with his mind-set. He'd recognise immediately what I was doing, and could probably react, before I had time to stop him. I didn't believe he had any idea of the full extent of what I could do, but the other side of the coin might be that he'd find out, he could do it too.

"Why don't you tell me, what I want?" he grinned happily. His voice was as beautifully modulated, as I remembered from before. It would normally be a pleasure to listen to, his tone was casually conversational, low-toned and polite. "You can do that, right? You can tell me, in fact, you can probably tell me before I even know – right, am I right?" He raised an eyebrow, and I could feel him trying to get into my head. He'd got in before, when I was parked outside the de Freyt's, but that was when I didn't know. Now I did, and I'd shut him out, so he wasn't getting anything other than frustrated. I could still read him though, and whilst his obsessive pattern of thinking was still there, it had slowed considerably, because he was so much more relaxed, so sure of himself.

I rose slowly from my seat, keeping my hands well within his sight – I knew, at any moment, Trudie, Ruby, Hilary or Martin could come swanning in, and goodness knows how much more, that might complicate an already tricky situation. I was also coming to terms with the unpalatable fact that whilst I was, as always, confident of being able to take care of myself, dealing with a very real threat to someone else, was altogether a different and more awkward can of worms.

"You want me to come with you?" I stated. He nodded cheerfully and chuckled.

"Spot on. Give the girl a prize."

"Look," I said, "You don't have to do this. You've got more talent in your little finger than others have got in their whole body – don't throw it away, playing gangster – where's that going to get you?"

"What do you know about it?"

"I've seen the wonderful work you've done. Don't waste everything by being stupid now." I'd hit him where it hurt, he snarled at me,

"Shut up, you know nothing about me."

"OK. OK." I held up my hands, "I'll come with you, if you want. We'll go somewhere and we can talk. But there's no need for threats and it's just going to be me, this lady stays here." He threw back his head and laughed, in genuine amusement. With the movement, Kitty was rocked from side to side and a fresh cut appeared on her neck. She grimaced. She was scared stiff, but she was a game old bat, and hadn't taken anything lying down for years. She'd had about enough of this little so-and-so, manhandling her and I saw one sturdily shod foot extend, ready to whack back and crack him soundly on the shin.

"No!" I hissed. She looked startled and I shook my head firmly. I understood his mood could swing from mild to murderous in a second. He thought I was talking to him.

"I'm afraid you're in no position to say no. Sorry 'bout that." he said, "She's coming with us, insurance, you understand. Yes, indeed, no arguing." He giggled. I stared at him expressionlessly, weighing up the pros and cons of knocking him out, but with that knife against her throat, I didn't think I could risk it.

"All right," I said, "You don't leave me much choice. He nodded, he knew it could only have gone one way.

"And, no police." He said, turning and swinging Kitty in front of him, to face Brenda, "Do you understand? If you so much as think of calling the police, after we've gone, and they come after me, old skinny-ribs here, gets it in the neck, no hanging around, no second chances. Do I make myself clear?" Brenda glanced at me, her normally ruddy complexion a sick shade of greeny-yellow. She was a tough cookie too, but was now as scared as she'd ever been. And I was about to make it worse.

I'd never actually done this before – deliberately planted a thought, but now seemed as good a time as any to start, even if it was unpleasantly reminiscent of Martha Vee. As Brenda looked directly at me, I shot something loudly into her head.

"Phone Boris." I told her. She jerked in shock, her eyes widening. I hadn't thought she could turn much paler, but she did. I hoped she wasn't going to do anything silly, like passing out, we wanted no sudden moves that might startle him. "No police." I told her silently. "Just Boris. Understand?" She didn't waste time trying to work out the how or why, of what had just happened. She fractionally inclined her head and I could see, she knew precisely where she'd filed the card Boris had handed her the first time he'd graced us with his presence. I was infinitely grateful, there's nothing like a sensible woman in a crisis, and this was one extremely sensible woman. I turned to pick up my briefcase that doubled as handbag, from the floor but he shook his head,

"You won't need that." He said, I wasn't going to argue. I moved slowly out from behind the desk, sticking with the no sudden moves rule. As I did, Kat, who'd been quietly curled in her corner, knowing full well that what was going on, didn't constitute a normal working day, moved too. She unfolded herself to her full impressive height and moved up next to me.

"What's that?" he said, taking a smart step back, dragging Kitty with him.

"Kat." I said shortly. I was wondering whether there was anything else vital, I should leave with Brenda.

"Don't get clever with me?" He snapped.

"For goodness sake," I said, "That's her name."

"Well she's not coming." He said. I nodded and tried to push her over towards Brenda, so she could grab her collar. Kat, unfortunately wasn't having any of that, and trying to shift a Borzoi that doesn't want to be shifted, is no easy task. She was now standing completely in front of me, leaning back against my legs, so I couldn't move any further forward. I don't think it was affection, as I've said, I hadn't done anything to make her think especially fondly of me, but for some reason, in her head, I'd become her certainty in an increasingly unpredictable and worrying world.

"Come on. Stop pissing about." He snapped. I could see his good humour dispersing, he was as aware as I was, someone could come in at any moment and change the whole dynamic. I beckoned Brenda over and, with a cautious glance at Jamie, she moved to take hold of the dog, and then Kat did something she'd never done before. She raised her shapely, aristocratic head skywards and she began to howl. For a moment, we were all stunned into silence and, as if encouraged by the reaction, she intensified the sound. It was atavistic, acutely alarming and very loud indeed.

"Shut her up, shut the bloody animal up, now." Jamie was shouting, trying to make himself heard above the high pitched ululation. It was hard to believe just one animal could make so much racket, she never even normally barked. Jamie was shaking Kitty from side to side, in his agitation. "D'you hear me, shut her up, or I bloody will." And he would, he was quite ready and willing to lash out with that knife. I bent swiftly and held Kat's muzzle firmly with my two hands. She shook her head a little, to dislodge me, but I didn't let go, as I soothed her. I had no real idea what was going on in her head and didn't have the time to find out, I took a rough guess.

"She won't leave me." I said. "You'll have to take her too, otherwise she'll just make more and more noise and people will be in any minute, to see what's going on."

"Shit. Come on then, quickly." He turned on his heel, lifting Kitty bodily off the floor as he did, to move her along with him. I held my breath, hoping she wouldn't do anything stupid, but I couldn't see she had anything in mind. "You, get in front," he instructed me. "So I can see what you're doing, and no funny business, mind. And you," he turned briefly back to Brenda, "Remember what I said. One whisper to the police and you won't see this one again." He'd regained his equilibrium and was back to his soft-spoken self. I don't know what I found more alarming, the lightening swift mood switch to threatening, or the threats, issued so politely.

We trooped down the stairs, in a formation I felt should have shrieked, 'Help, two women and a dog being taken against their will!' but apparently didn't. He'd taken his arm from around Kitty's waist and the knife from her neck, but had her elbow in an iron grip and the blade in her back. To the outside eye, it appeared, there was nothing to cause comment, which was confirmed by both Martin and Hilary looking up briefly, smiling and carrying on with what they were doing, as we went past.

CHAPTER FORTY-EIGHT

He had his work van, parked on the street outside. It had a cheery, bold-painted logotype and message on the side – Jamie Richman, Artist, Bringing the Outside Inside. Call Me! I could only see the near-side of the van, but that in itself was quite something. Below the text and phone number, the panel had been cunningly painted to offer the illusion of a side door rolled back, allowing you to see the inside of the vehicle, which was packed to bursting, with colourfully blooming flowering plants and greenery. It was a glorious and clever creation and I imagined, brought him in a lot of business, it couldn't fail. It was certainly attracting attention, laughter and admiration even now, and he was smiling and modestly accepting compliments and interest from passers-by, as he shepherded Kitty, Kat and I towards the van's rear door.

Kitty glanced at me, she was thinking this might be our last chance, should she scream? I shook my head swiftly. If she did, it might indeed turn out to be the last chance – he was utterly swept away and swollen up with his own derring-do, and reality for him, at the moment, was about as illusory as the side of the van. The blade in the small of her back and the sense of power he was experiencing, felt great, better than great. At this point, he still had his feet planted firmly enough on the ground, to know what was sensible and what would hurtle him into something completely different – but it was a tenuous planting. I didn't think she should give him any excuse to give in to temptation and learn how it would feel, to plunge that knife in.

When he opened the rear door of the van and moved aside for us to get in, it was, naturally, a disappointment. No luscious collection of flowers and plants, just a bench seat, along one side and the rest of the space taken up with tools of the trade. He indicated, with a jerk of the head that we should climb in.

"Don't be ridiculous," I said, "You can't expect us to travel in there. Wherever we're going, you won't get us there in one piece. Look at her," I gestured at Kitty, who swiftly adopted a little-old-lady-on-her-last-legs look, I don't think she had to try that hard. "There's plenty of room in the front." I said, "We'll go in there, or we won't go at all." At the same time, I flashed the thought that it made more sense for him to keep us close, so he could keep an eye on us. He took that on board, I don't think he even realised it came from me.

"The dog goes in the back though." He said. Kat looked up at him, slowly planted her rear end on the road surface, and raised her long neck. She couldn't have made it any clearer, this was one bitch that wasn't going in the back of any van. She opened her mouth to howl and he could obviously see potential, passer-by attention being attracted, that wasn't the sort of attention he was looking for at all. With an effort, he restrained himself from giving her the kick he wanted to,

"OK. Her too." he snarled. As we moved to the front of the vehicle, I glanced up. Brenda was watching anxiously from the office window. I inclined my head briefly towards the van and she nodded. Wherever he planned to take us, our transport was hard to miss and Brenda would give a good description.

The front seat was also a bench arrangement, so there was plenty of room for Kitty and me alongside Jamie. He wanted her next to him, and before we set off, he showed us both the knife again, as if it might, in the interval, have slipped our minds. I understood from him that she was dispensable, I wasn't, he had a whole load of questions for me. Kat followed me up nimbly into the van and lay down across my feet, heavy and warm. Before she put her head down on her paws, she bestowed on me, what can only be described as a resigned, what've-you-got-us-into-now look.

As we drove, mercifully, the tension ratcheted down a degree or two, as he gradually regained the feeling of being in charge. Kitty was quiet, which wasn't something I was used to, but then we'd never been in quite this sort of situation before. I found her hand, next to me on the seat and gave it a little squeeze, she squeezed back, lifting one eyebrow slightly. It was a look, as eloquent in its way as Kat's and, I was afraid, expressing very much the same thing.

Her thinking was surprisingly serene, she seemed to have cleared her mind of all the sorts of things I'd thought would be haring round in there, not least, were we going to get out of this in one piece. Instead, she was mentally browsing, what she called her 'bargains' cupboard. She was an inveterate shopper and, for reasons unknown, her vice was linen – bed or table, she was a sucker for either. In the hall cupboard, at the Georgian Court flat, always ready to do a cellophaned slither onto the heads of the unwary, was a formidable and pristine stock, accumulated over the years. The family always joked, she could open and run a substantial group of hotels, for several years, without needing to make a single fresh purchase.

"It's daft, I don't even know your name." I'd been deep in thought – mine and Kitty's, so when he spoke, I jumped a little.

"Stella." I said.

"Right, and I'm…"

"Jamie. I know." I could feel his intense, aching curiosity, he had more questions than he knew what to do with, but all he was getting from me was a smooth, featureless, nothing. I could understand his frustration, I'd been there with Rachael and the others, when they didn't choose to let me in.

There was, in his head, quite a lot I didn't understand and I got the feeling, he understood it as little as I did. I could feel the rapid changes in his mood, the swift swings. It was to do with control, being in charge, on top, the one calling the shots and he hated it when he wasn't. I needed to be aware of that and manage it better. The key to keeping him sweet, was to not score in any way. His unquestionable artistic talent had never been valued by the people he valued – family. From childhood, he'd been made to feel lacking, a bit of a disappointment, odd, so by the time the talent was praised, it was by the wrong people, those whose opinion he didn't value at all. But there were other things in his mind, a very much darker side, he both revelled in and shied away from. And deeper still, was something else, something obstinately hidden from me. I wanted to probe further but was cautious, I didn't think it sensible for him to suspect how much I could find out.

"Where are we going?" I asked. He chuckled,

"Don't you know?" I did know, but only in a limited way and it wasn't making much sense. I could see a log-cabin, two storey, chalet-style building, with overhanging roof and shallow steps to a wrap-around veranda. It was almost completely surrounded by trees, but there was no indication of location, he wasn't thinking of that – he knew the route so well, he didn't have to.

"No," I said, "No idea."

"Well, it'll be a nice surprise for you when we get there, won't it?" His feelings towards me were ambivalent, he wasn't quite sure what he was dealing with, nor the extent of what I could or couldn't do, but he desperately wanted to find out more, because of all the implications it had for him.

For my part, I'd been intent on ensuring he kept his cool and didn't hurt Kitty, which was why I'd wanted to get us out of the office, away from the possibility of intervention, precipitating violence. But perhaps I hadn't thought things through enough – that wouldn't be a first for me. What indeed did he want with us, and hadn't he put himself in a similar situation to my erstwhile pals, the Lowbells? Once you've kidnapped someone or in this case, two someone's, it's not easy to pass it off as an unfortunate oversight. How could this whole situation come to any kind of a comfortable conclusion? I shifted in my seat. Maybe I should act now. He'd put the knife on the dashboard in front of him, within his easy reach. I knew I could easily knock him out, but probably not a sensible move, while we were still driving. Additionally, I couldn't be sure he'd go under as swiftly as a normal person, he might have time to grab the knife and do damage, before he did.

Alternatively, I could, I supposed, jam the accelerator down, forcing him to brake hard and stop, but then what? I surreptitiously felt with my left hand, for the door handle. It was within easy reach and I could feel it wasn't locked. But even if I was able to get Kitty and Kat out quickly enough, what chance would we stand in a chase? After all the trouble he'd gone to, to get us, I couldn't see him just waving us off, as we belted away into the distance, that's always supposing Kitty was up to any belting. I could always start a fire in the engine, but the same issues applied, once I'd done that, what would be my next step?

No, choices were definitely coming in on the limited side. I'd just have to try some mental yelling and hope one of the others would pick up. I recalled Rachael's sarcastic comment, when I'd asked how they'd tracked me down at the Lowbells, something about not popping up with an address and postcode, but I also knew that like it or not, the links were strong between us – Ruth, Rachael, Glory and Ed – and Sam, I mustn't forget Sam, possibly the most powerful of all of us. I had to give it a go, but needed to be careful how I opened up, I couldn't risk giving Jamie any access to my mind, nor any indication of what I was doing. What I sent out had to be something no-one else would recognise or understand. I knew immediately what I could use and why – Sam's strap. If anything had resonance, that did.

I brought it into my mind, wrapped in its yellowed tissue paper, slowly unwrapping it, bringing back the feelings it evoked. After a moment, it lay there, complete in my mind, dark brown leather, still fastened at the buckle, with the jagged tear, further along, where Ruth had ripped it in anger, taking care not to further injure the thin wrist within. When it was solid in my mind, I threw both the image and the emotion that went with it, out there, as hard and loudly as I could.

Jamie heard, I couldn't avoid that, I saw him start convulsively, and stare over at me. I didn't stop doing what I was doing for a full minute, and only then did I appear to become aware of his gaze.

"Sorry," I said, "You picked that up?" he nodded. It was all still so new to him. Not the picking up, he'd been doing that all his life, but the revelation it wasn't him, all the hazy, crazy, constant stuff it wasn't him, it was coming from outside.

"I saw a strap." He said, "A broken strap. That right? That's what I saw?" I nodded slowly and laughed sheepishly,

"I didn't realise. I must have been dozing off." I said, "It's something I sometimes see when I'm falling asleep. It was an illustration, from a children's book, years ago. I don't know why it's stuck, It gave me nightmares at the time and it's been giving me nightmares ever since." I shrugged. "Didn't mean to impose it on you. Sorry." Kitty was watching me, she wasn't unduly suspicious, just a bit puzzled, there was a section of conversation she thought she'd missed, but her hearing wasn't what it was and, as she was reasoning to herself, not much about today had made much bloody sense so far, no reason why it'd suddenly start doing so now.

"Not much longer," he said. I'd no idea where we were and because I'd been so preoccupied, wasn't even sure how long we'd been driving. I did know I was hungry and thirsty, could do with a loo and all in all was pretty fed up. I was also worried sick about Kitty. She was no spring chicken and however I was feeling, she must be feeling worse. I must have been more tired than I thought, because for a moment my guard dropped and he picked up on what I was thinking, I'd have to be more careful in future. He answered me aloud,

"We'll be there soon and then you can relax." Which as it turned out, wasn't strictly true. In fact, it was going to be a while before relaxing came back into the picture. Probably the first intimation of that, was the screaming coming from the chalet in the woods, when we drew up outside.

CHAPTER FORTY-NINE

We'd turned off the main road, a while back and headed down country lane after country lane, shadowed with overgrowing trees and with greedy hedges grabbing and scratching the van on either side. We seemed to be entirely alone on these roads, probably a good thing, goodness only knows what would have happened had someone been coming the other way. After about ten minutes, we took what looked, and certainly felt, like an unpaved farm track, which several times lifted us off our seats and jerked Kat right off the floor. She hated physical knocks, Borzois are especially sensitive to physical pain and Kat proved the rule, crying softly each time, until Jamie snapped,

"Can't you shut her up?" I could see, Kat and he hadn't instantly struck up any kind of a rapport, luckily, before she could alienate him further, we turned through a couple of opened low wooden gates. They were set in a white picket fence, which looked decidedly out of place, here in the middle of nowhere and which stretched as far as I could see in either direction, before being swallowed up by the trees. There were a couple of notices on the gates one, coyly curlicued and enthusiastic, welcomed guests to 'The Chalets in the Woods', hoped they'd love, love, love their stay and return soon, soon, soon! The other, pinned directly below it, wasn't half so friendly, being in shouty capitals, firmly stating 'PRIVATE PROPERTY' and warning 'TRESPASSERS WILL ALWAYS BE PROSECUTED!' Talk about mixed messages.

Jamie knew exactly where he was going, following a roadway that had at one stage been asphalted, but now boasted some fairly hefty potholes, which he swerved neatly to avoid. As we drove, I could see smaller lanes winding off into wooded areas where, in clearings, were set chalet-style, log-constructed houses, some bungalow-like on one level, others taller with two floors. Most of them looked in need of some TLC.

I understood, we were in the middle of what had once been a flourishing business venture, a shining dream that hadn't panned out, but gone down the pan. It had bankrupted Jamie's father, cost him his health, his marriage and eventually his life, when he succumbed to a stress-induced heart attack. Jamie had spent much of his late childhood and teenage years here and, as with so much else, his feelings about the place were sharply divided. It held some of his happiest memories as well as some of the most depressing.

It was still where he felt most at home, although he certainly had no right to be here anymore, his father had been as bad at choosing legal and business advisers, as he had about every other vital decision. The estate was the subject of interminable legal arguments, with knots of complexity over original ownership, still being untangled. Until they were, the development lay untouched and gradually deteriorating.

The house, in front of which we finally drew up, was one of the larger ones and in contrast to the others, immaculately maintained, with sparkling white-painted sills and shutters. Both the logs, that comprised its walls, and the planking of the veranda, appeared freshly varnished. It looked oddly and pristinely Alpine, lacking only Julie Andrews, being jolly in a dirndl. I sensed Jamie's pride of possession. He officially lived in a rented room not that far away, but he'd been using this as well, for the several years since his father's death, with nobody ever seeming to notice. When he turned off the engine, just for a moment, apart from the ticking as it cooled down, the full silence of the place hit us. It was the sort of quiet, where the absence of noise is in itself a pressure on the ears. And then, the screaming started.

"Blimey," Kitty was scared, but blowed if she was going to show it. "Somebody's not happy to be here." She said. Jamie shook his head, regretfully,

"Stupid," he said, "I told her there was no-one for miles around. No-one would hear." Kitty, smiled grimly,

"Well, you were way out there, weren't you? We're hearing, aren't we? We're hearing, loud and clear." I could see she was getting over her initial shock, which was a good thing, although meant a lot of her natural stroppiness was re-surfacing, which might not be ideal – I could see his see-saw temper was rapidly on the rise again.

"We getting out, or are we just going to sit here?" I asked. He nodded, he'd picked up the Stanley knife from the dashboard and waved it under, and dangerously close to, Kitty's nose.

"No funny business, understand?" He said.

"Funny business? Do I look like Coco the Clown?" she grumbled "And watch where you're putting that knife, that's how accidents happen."

"Trust me," he muttered, "Anything happens, it'll be no accident." She ignored him and I reached back to help her down from the van, although with Kat sticking as close as she could to my legs, any kind of movement was tricky. Jamie had taken the car keys and attached them to a keyring on his belt. We walked up the few stairs to the front door, which had a new, shiny, no-nonsense lock. He noticed me looking and smiled smugly. I thought how swiftly Ed would deal with a lock like that, and smiled back. He utilised another key from his keyring, and we all moved forward.

It might have been all Sound of Music outside, inside was something else altogether and I think Kitty and I might both have reeled back a little. Kat whined softly, taking her reaction from ours. The front door opened into a surprisingly spacious, rectangular living area, with a galley kitchen leading off at right angles. Comfortably furnished, it had a grey tweed, two seater sofa and a matching armchair on either side of a small chimney breast and alcove. Within the alcove, was a wood-burning stove, in which flames were still glowing. So far, so ordinary. The walls were something else altogether.

Despite the log construction, the interior was fully plastered, broken up only by a window each side of the front door, so there was a lot of wall-space. From every inch of that space, floor to ceiling, meticulously executed and vividly coloured, leered violence and pain.

His eye for perspective hadn't let him down in any way, and you couldn't help but admire the depth and dimension of everything he'd done. There was study after study, sometimes the same thing over and over, from different angles, a single throttling hand round a throat, a stabbing knife re-entering a bloodied chest, an eviscerated fox, a screaming child, a fleeing woman, a burning man. And everywhere, eyes – old, young, manic, absent, calculating, terrified – watching.

He was watching us too, both elated and ashamed at what we were seeing. These were his nightmares, they'd come to him, day and night, all his life, from the sewers of other people's minds. He'd never had a chance of protecting himself, because he hadn't for one moment, known them for what they were. And the dreadful truth was, they chimed with something already in him, even as he tried to pretend they didn't. The violence in his head was constantly at war with the creativity, but the overall effect of what he'd painted here, maybe an attempt at some sort of exorcism, was unspeakable – death, despair and depravity in unflinching, near photographic detail.

Equally unsettling, was the girl, lying awkwardly half on and half off the sofa, hands and feet securely bound with multiple layers of duct tape, face dirty and tear-streaked. She didn't remember me from our brief encounter outside her house, but she did remember Kat and her eyes widened, as she tried to put everything together and make sense of what was going on. I wished her luck with that.

CHAPTER FIFTY

In those first few seconds, as we entered the room and saw Isabelle, I realised I didn't have a choice, I had to act now, before things escalated beyond the rather desperate point they'd already reached. I needed to knock him out immediately, and get us all the hell out of there. I went into his head with intent and as I did, he hit me twice. First he smashed the full weight of the back of his right hand against my right cheekbone and then, equally painfully, he bashed me mentally. It was a double whammy and I hit the floor without a sound, Kitty and Isabelle both screamed and Kat gave a rare bark.

"I said, don't try anything, didn't I?" he muttered. He'd mashed my cheek hard against my teeth and my mouth filled instantly with blood, hot and coppery. For a moment, I couldn't understand what had happened – not the back-hander – that was clear enough, it was the mental blow that shocked me. I replayed it in my mind and understood that what he'd done had been purely reflexive. He'd felt me come in and had instantly blocked and deflected. He was quick, strong, and all the more dangerous, because he had no idea what he was doing. He had no concept of what I could do to him or he to me. He'd reacted purely instinctively and seemed as surprised as I was, by that.

Kitty didn't hang about, she surged forward, brought her right knee up sharply, you had to admire the flexibility at that age, and kicked him where she knew it would have most effect.

"Taste of your own medicine, you little bugger." She said. It was his turn to go down, although he made a lot more noise than I had. He was doing a fair old bit of rolling around and clasping the injured area. Things were rapidly sliding from pretty dreadful to a lot worse and, as it was getting a bit crowded on the floor, I felt I ought to make the effort to get up. I was reading him loud and clear, what with the pain, the anger and the humiliation, he was broadcasting for Britain and I could see that sane, softly spoken, 'Bringing the Outdoors In.' Artist, Jamie, was all too swiftly morphing into not-so-sane-at-all Jamie. My decision to take things into my own hands had back-fired, a bit of organisational flair and re-grouping was called for. If I didn't try to attack him again, I wouldn't set off his highly developed defence mechanism, which I sensed could be lethal. So, change of tack.

I reached down, caught him by the arm and hauled him roughly upright, I floated him a bit but he was too far gone to notice. I dumped him unceremoniously into the armchair. Then I picked up the knife, dropped when Kitty took his mind off things, and swiftly cut the tape round Isabelle's hands and feet. I didn't need the knife to do it, but didn't want him to know that. She sat back with a sob.

"Those," I said to him firmly "Were ridiculously tight, what the hell were you playing at, you could have given her gangrene." I wasn't too sure of the medical accuracy, but felt the admonitory tone was right. "Kitty," I said, "This is Isabelle. Isabelle, I'm Stella and this is Kitty." Everyone nodded at each other politely, good manners are never out of place.

"You were there, weren't you?" Isabelle said, "Outside my house, the other day, I recognise the dog. But… " I nodded and interrupted her, no time for updating at this point.

"I'm assuming there's a bathroom here?" I said firmly. We all looked at Jamie who nodded, he didn't seem to have much breath for anything else, Kitty obviously packed quite a kick. He jerked his head towards a door, leading off the living room. "Kitty," I said "Why don't you and Isabelle go and have a wash, get freshened up a bit?"

I looked around, if you ignored the walls, and trust me, they took some ignoring, the place had a well-used feel. I understood this had been the house Jamie's family used as a holiday home, when the whole estate was still a going concern. "I assume there's a medicine cabinet in there," I continued, "Maybe you'll find something to clean up those cuts?" We looked at Jamie again, and he nodded reluctantly. "And then," I added, "Perhaps the two of you could take a look in the kitchen, see if there's any chance of us getting a cup of tea and a sandwich of some sort?"

"Hang on. What the hell d'you think you're doing?" Jamie was regaining breath and belligerence. "This is my… . "

"What?" I interrupted, sharply, "Your house, your party, your clever kidnap scheme?" It might not have been the best approach to take, but if any of us were going to get out of this crazy situation intact, it was going to be by not giving into the crazy. I was aware of what a risk it was, challenging him, probably more aware than he was, of what a hair trigger he was on, but time wasn't on our side.

I gently shoved Kitty and Isabelle in the direction of the bathroom and ignored him, while I took myself into the kitchen, located a glass on the draining board and took my time, rinsing out my battered mouth. When I'd done that, I returned to the sofa and the offensive.

"Look," I said, "I've no idea how all this is going to pan out." I wasn't surprised to see, he hadn't either. What he'd had in mind, hadn't really gone much beyond the thought of taking Isabelle and interrogating me. "But, for starters," I pointed out, "You don't need to tie anyone up again, do you? That's really stupid, where on earth did you think she was going to go? We're miles from anywhere." He shrugged moodily,

"Better safe than sorry and that old bitch didn't have to kick me." He said. "Bloody lethal she is. Anyone needs tying up and tying down, it's her."

"Oh don't be daft, and mind your manners." I said, "She's eighty-three years old, she couldn't have done that much damage and she only kicked you, because you hit me."

"Only hit you, because you tried to do something to me." He sulked. I nodded agreement,

"I did and I won't do it again." He nodded slowly, didn't totally believe me – as indeed, he shouldn't. I could feel him trying everything he could, to crawl into my head, force his way in, it wasn't pleasant and luckily he didn't really know what he was doing. But I honestly still thought, at that point, I could handle him.

CHAPTER FIFTY-ONE

Kat had stayed near the front door. With people falling down all over the place, she'd obviously thought it best to keep well clear, but now she moved forward a little into the room and diverted Jamie's attention from me for a moment. He curled his lip,

"Hate dogs," he muttered.

"That's OK," I said, "She's not that keen on people." I called her over and she folded herself down by my feet. He was indeed nervous around her and she certainly didn't trust him. Every few minutes, she emitted the very softest of growls, they couldn't really even be heard, I only knew, because she was leaning against me and I could feel the vibrations.

"You're not struck on birds either, are you?" I said. "What was all that nasty, dead bird, business?

"Letting you know, I knew who you were and where I could find you. It was a message."

"Great, thanks a bunch. For future reference, a note or a phone call – just as good." I was finding it increasingly and disconcertingly difficult, to keep my eyes away from the walls. Anywhere my glance landed, was more disturbing than the last thing I'd looked at. I could feel the effect, the surroundings of his own making were having on Jamie. They were pushing him further and further into a place I'd rather he didn't go.

"Are there lights in here?" I asked, getting up hurriedly. Dusk was fast descending and if the room was creepy in the day, I didn't even want to think how it might feel at any other time. He nodded towards a switch on the wall.

"They never got around to disconnecting the power, for some reason," he said, "Still on in most of the properties, gas too in some of them."

Kitty and Isabelle had come back in and, following my instruction, quietly headed for the kitchen, Isabelle casting an apprehensive glance at Jamie as she passed. She was more or less in a state of shock, which was just as well, it was probably only that, holding her together at the moment, poor kid. When she'd seen his unmistakeable van draw up outside school and he'd waved at her, she'd happily gone over. She'd no reason to disbelieve him when he said, her mother had asked him to give her a lift home. In any case, the rule was don't talk to strangers, which he wasn't, so she knew she wasn't doing anything silly. That was, until he'd stopped the van, to turn and slap a white towel over her face. There was something chemical-smelling on the towel and he'd held her, with unsuspected strength, until she passed out.

When she'd come round, retching and sobbing, she was tied up on the sofa and well down the road to hysteria. And that was before she'd even had a chance to take in what was painted on the walls around her. But she wasn't a stupid girl by any means and knew, hyperventilating never got anybody anywhere, so she'd pulled herself together. She'd had a fair amount of time to think about how all this might end and had come to some grim conclusions. Since our arrival, she'd been even more confused and she hadn't got any real information out of Kitty, who didn't know much more than she did. In fact, having witnessed Kitty's somewhat alarming kick-boxing performance, Isabelle wasn't sure whether us being there made things better or worse, although she was grateful for the company. She still thought the outlook was bleak, the only difference being it was now bleaker for more of us. She was terrified of it getting dark again. It took me a moment to sort out her thoughts on that, but when I did, it made sense. At night he was crazy Jamie – of course he was. It was at night he was picking up the worst of everything – nightmares, fantasies, other people's inhibitions loosened by drink or sleep and feeding his own. Night-time and madness, it was the stuff his paintings were made of.

By the time Kitty and Isabelle had emerged from the kitchen, with mugs of tea on a tray and a plateful of cheese sandwiches – which I suspected were more down to Kitty than Isabelle – I'd made a quick trip to the bathroom myself. Here, a trawl through the medicine cabinet, revealed a nearly full bottle of sleeping pills. I wasn't sure I could risk using them, I didn't think they'd knock him out quickly enough, but you never know when something might come in handy, so I decanted a fair few and tucked them in a pocket, for possible future dispensation.

It was an awkward, understandably constrained group that sat down to partake of refreshments. Isabelle, Kitty and I together on the sofa, Kat at our feet and Jamie in the armchair. The dull light thrown off by a single table lamp and a small, central pendant, was doing nothing to improve the oppressiveness of the room. I'd found the right side of my face had swollen up in a most unflattering manner, and wasn't working as normal, so I had to take little hamster bites and chew on the other side.

Whilst I still felt confident I could sort this out, one way or another, it would be nice to know that Rachael, Ruth or one of the others had heard, and reinforcements of some kind were on the way. I thought this might be a good time to revisit the strap which sat, still intact in my head. I put some power behind it and threw it out again. Jamie looked up at me suspiciously and I feigned a yawn.

The scenario, he'd rather naively visualised, was he and Isabelle spending some quality time together, without her ruddy mother sticking her nose in. He'd assumed Isabelle liked him and would be much more amenable to this, than she turned out to be. He'd also thought he and I would have a huge amount to talk about, he hadn't counted on me having an aggressive octogenarian in tow. The bottom line was, he hadn't had a minute with Isabelle when she wasn't screaming, and hadn't got a scrap of the information he wanted out of me. His mood was darkening dangerously, but then, I suppose, none of us was particularly cheerful.

What puzzled me was his lack of forethought. True, he'd warned Brenda not to call the police, but it couldn't have slipped his mind, that he'd abducted a thirteen year old, in broad daylight, in a van that couldn't be more distinctive and traceable. The whole thing showed a distinct lack of not just planning but self-preservation. I was about to bring up the subject of how we might best move things on from here, when reinforcement did, in fact turn up. It was also, around about then, I realised it wasn't Jamie we needed to fear at all.

CHAPTER FIFTY-TWO

I felt the change happening in him, before I saw it. I looked up swiftly and something else looked out at me through his eyes. And then he launched himself up and out of his chair and started stabbing Kitty, with a viciously, long-bladed kitchen knife. One part of me registered coldly, that the only chance he'd had, to take that from the kitchen was when I was in the bathroom. I really should have paid more attention.

The attack was so quick, Kitty didn't have the chance to make a sound. I lashed out at him, full power, no careful checking where I was going. He was knocked right off his feet and landed heavily on his back, on the other side of the room. I heard something crack when he hit the floor, maybe it was a rib, but that wouldn't incapacitate him enough. By rights he should have been unconscious, if not worse, but in a flash he'd turned over on to all-fours and was crawling swiftly, spider-fashion, back towards us. He still had the knife. I set fire to the handle and the wood flamed instantly. He hissed in pain, but didn't let go and there was a dreadful smell of burning flesh.

Ridiculously, Kitty and I were still sitting, side by side on the sofa, although she'd slumped against me. She had a long, ugly, slash bleeding down one side of her face and there was a lot of blood coming from somewhere else. It was warm as it pumped over me. I moved in front of her, letting her fall to her side behind me. Jamie pushed himself upright and, as he raised the knife, lips snarled back over his teeth, I understood what I was dealing with. I let loose with everything I had. This time I took just that fraction of a second longer, to direct it more specifically, but in that second he continued his downward slash, and I felt the long blade of the knife as it sank deep into my side. It was as agonising when he yanked it out, as when it went in and I shrieked.

He pulled me off the sofa, threw me onto to the floor, and turned, knife raised to go for Kitty again and after that, I presumed Isabelle. There was a solid, sludgy green, Venetian glass vase on the floor, in the chimney breast alcove. I sent it rocketing across the room, hard into his head. It didn't smash, but hit with a sickening thump that rocked him back on his heels. It could have killed him. It didn't. It didn't stop him either. Of course it didn't, because he wasn't on his own. He was no longer, just Jamie, he was being worked from outside and I could feel the power and malign intent of the intelligence that was doing it, adding its own psychic strength, with great glee, to Jamie's. As he shook his head from side to side, to clear it from the blow. I hauled myself back up on to the sofa. That grey tweed was certainly going to need replacing, because now, it wasn't just Kitty bleeding all over it.

For one brief moment, when one of the house's front windows exploded inward, shattering glass everywhere, I felt a huge surge of relief. Then a familiar figure catapulted through and my heart sank again. I wasn't sure how on earth he'd tracked us down, what he'd expected to find, nor what he thought he could do about it. I don't even think I was pleased to see him. A fiancé is all well and good at the right time and place, this was neither.

We didn't have time for a catch-up. I don't even know whether he had a plan, to follow on from his SAS style entrance, but in the event, he had no chance to go ahead with anything. His eyes widened briefly at the scene that greeted him – by this time it must have been looking like a trailer for the Texas Chainsaw Massacre – and then Jamie picked up the vase, from where it had hit the floor next to him and, holding it one-handed by the neck, moved the few paces over to David, and whacked him round the head with it. David went down. My heart turned over, which I put down to the very stressful situation, and for a moment I wasn't sure whether he was breathing, I went swiftly into his head and heaved a sigh of relief, he was knocked out and therefore not thinking anything much, but he definitely wasn't dead.

For a moment or two, Jamie stood over David, swaying slightly back and forward on the balls of his feet, looking like a zombie, George Romero would have been proud to call his own. I could see there was frighteningly less of Jamie in there, than at any time since this latest little incident had kicked off, and I didn't think that was good news. While he was swaying, it gave me a moment's pause to reassess the whole situation and the possibilities open to us – they weren't looking too promising.

David was out, both for the count and the foreseeable future and Kitty was losing more blood than I could ever have imagined, she'd had in her in the first place. Isabelle had flung herself off the sofa, screaming, and, if she'd possessed any common sense, would have run into the bathroom and locked herself in. In fact, she'd lodged herself, in a pathetic huddle with Kat, in the corner of the living room. There was also something really peculiar about my breathing, every time I did it, there were sharp, stabbing pains in my chest and shoulder, I hoped I wasn't having a heart attack, there wasn't time for that.

Jamie, done with the swaying, bent and picked up the kitchen knife, which he'd dropped in favour of the vase. It was now looking a bit hard done by, with its badly burnt handle and blood stains – certainly, no longer up to John Lewis standards. He began to move, slowly and purposefully towards the girl and the dog. Kat immediately sprang forward, growling and snarling, a sound so alien, that even she looked startled. She planted herself, four-square, stiff legged between Jamie and Isabelle, head lowered, hackles raised. Jamie didn't hesitate, but neither did she. He brought the knife down to plunge into her back and she leapt adroitly to one side, sank her teeth deep into his calf, clamped shut and held on. He screamed in pain, twisting and turning to try and get her off, at the same time, trying to keep her still, long enough for the knife to do its work.

I couldn't get into his head at all, any more. Whatever was working him was strong, it had blocked me completely. Jamie raised his arm high, to again try and slash Kat, still hanging on to his leg and I broke it – his arm, not the leg – Kat seemed to be doing enough damage on her own with that. His scream rose in pitch and, thankfully, he dropped the knife. I sailed it over to me swiftly and shoved it under the sofa with my foot, probably something which, in the interests of health and safety, I should have done a lot sooner.

I was aware something was very wrong with me, the whole ghastly scene was starting to fade in and out in a most peculiar fashion and I knew, if for one second, I let down my mental guard, whatever it was that had

Jamie, would have me too and there'd be no going back from that. Isabelle was still cowering in her corner and Jamie was now using his unbroken arm and fist as a club, hitting Kat heavily and repeatedly on the head. She was holding on, but I didn't know for how much longer and once he'd done for her, Isabelle would be next in line.

"Isabelle." I said, "Get over here, behind me, now." She shook her head, whimpering softly, a sound I was more used to hearing from Kat.

"Can't." she said. And I could see she was right, she wasn't able to move, was frozen there, couldn't have moved to save her own life – which was precisely what she had to do. Jamie and Kat were still struggling, but it couldn't go on much longer. Whatever was driving Jamie, wasn't prepared to be beaten, it was having too good a time. I closed my eyes, took a deep breath, which hurt like hell, opened my mind and yanked Isabelle out of her corner. I wasn't operating at 100% and hadn't lifted anything so heavy for ages, so I rather misjudged and she flew over my head, shrieking, and landed behind the sofa, with a thump.

"Stay down there." I hissed at her, with what little breath I had left. I coughed and felt blood come coppery again into my mouth. The next thing I had to do was get David out of the way, he was still lying in the middle of the room and Kat and Jamie, in their desperate dance, were treading on him, left right and centre. I took a shallower breath this time, which wasn't so bad and again risked opening my mind to move him. I simply couldn't do it, seemed to have run out of fuel.

Well, if I couldn't do it my normal way, I'd just have to do it the way normal people would. I nipped in, avoiding the man and the dog, bent, grabbed both his arms and heaved with all my strength. I wasn't able to shift his six foot weight at all, but as I tried, at the risk of a double hernia, he turned his head to one side and groaned. That was promising. I slapped his face sharply a few times.

"David, David, can you hear me?" He didn't respond, so I slapped him again, this was no time to worry about hard feelings, "You've got to move, d'you hear me?"

"My head." He muttered. "God, it hurts."

"Yes I know," I snapped. I realised I wasn't coming across very Florence Nightingale, but there wasn't time. I nudged him hard with my knee, "You've got to get up." He did his best and once he started moving,

I was able to float him a bit too and between us, we got him upright. I wedged my shoulder firmly under his arm and we staggered unevenly, the short distance across the room, where I pushed him down onto the sofa next to Kitty. She didn't seem to be bleeding from her middle, quite as much. I didn't know whether that was a good sign or a bad, but she was deeply unconscious. I swallowed the overriding fear, which wasn't going to do any of us any good, at least now, I had most of my lot in one place.

Stepping in front of the other two, I turned to face Jamie, or whatever he was now. For a brief moment I touched, what it was that was driving him. In those seconds of contact and within that other mind, I saw the level and mix of cold violence and pleasure and in the midst of all that chaos, glimpsed something else that was almost as horrifying – I put that away to think about later.

Kat, brave girl, had finally released his leg and was now leaping up at him, instinctively seeking his weakest point, trying to pull down his broken, damaged arm, so he was forced to keep moving it, which was causing him considerable pain – good! He drew his unwounded leg back, to kick her, and I instantly knocked the other leg from beneath him. This naturally, left him nothing to stand on, and he fell heavily. I called Kat over. She came like a shot. She, like me, really didn't really feel she was cut out for this sort of thing.

For one quiet moment, Jamie lay where he'd crashed, and I held my breath but then, almost unbelievably, he again staggered to his feet. He stared at me with eyes that were frighteningly empty, the lights were on but there was no-one home, or at least, whoever was home, wasn't the rightful occupant. And I still couldn't get in there, to shut him off.

His leg was badly bitten, blood was oozing thickly through the rips in his jeans, and his right arm was hanging useless and awkward at his side, the hand black and painfully blistered, where the handle of the knife had flamed. He had a nasty-looking swelling on his temple, purpling, where the vase had made hefty contact. None of this, apparently, was enough to slow him down. I sighed, which hurt. I needed to formulate a new plan but, truth to tell, what with everything fading in and out the way it was, I wasn't planning too clearly. The pain in my chest was making me ever more nauseous and I had the unpleasant feeling, I might pass out sooner rather than later.

"No, you don't. Not now!" Crisp, fresh, peppermint, swept into my head, the effect, like smelling salts, jerking me back to full consciousness.

"Rachael. Thank God. Where are you?"

"Two minutes away. Hang on. Keep him busy." I would have laughed, had I not known how much it would hurt.

"Oh, right – what do you suggest? A jigsaw? Or maybe we can see if there's anything on the radio? He wants to kill us all. He's changed, he's..."

"Yes, we know all that. Not to worry, we're here now." And I felt them all flood in, the familiar scents and sensations twining and blending in my mind – Rachael, Ed, Glory, Ruth and Sam.

"About bloody time." I muttered to myself and then to them. "Kitty's been stabbed and she's lost so much blood, I don't know..." I became aware I was swaying, much as Jamie had earlier and also that he was now lumbering towards us again, moving with an odd, alien, clumsy gait. This time he didn't have the knife, but his intentions were no less murderous.

David had pulled himself unsteadily to his feet and moved to stand next to me. He was stunned, every which way and wasn't quite sure whether he was awake or still unconscious and hallucinating. He'd just had his first glimpses of the ghastly décor, which hadn't done him any good at all and now there was a horrific, injured apparition making his determined way towards us. As Jamie launched himself, with a high-pitched yell, something insanely between a giggle and a shriek, David moved forward to try and punch him in the face. But I had the others in my head now and we lifted Jamie up; for a moment we held him, struggling helplessly in mid-air, then flung him hard, back across the room. He crashed amidst the shards of glass, spread all over the floor, from David's earlier entry. And then, the front door shot inwards, and only an amalgam of relief, responsibility and reluctance to show myself up, kept me conscious. I did though, back up and sit down heavily on the sofa.

"My," said Rachael, surveying the painted walls, the wreckage, the injured and the blood that seemed to be everywhere. "We have been busy."

CHAPTER FIFTY-THREE

On the other side of the room, Jamie was yet again struggling to his feet –
you just can't keep a good man down – but Ed and Glory had it in hand. I
felt the full, bruising force of their combined power, as did Jamie. His eyes
promptly rolled right up in his head, until only the whites were visible. He
hit the ground, for the umpteenth time that day, but this time, it looked like
he might be staying there a while. Ed issued a swift command to Hamlet
who, needless to say, was part of the party. Hamlet diverted direction briefly,
to greet me, brushing affectionately against my leg and nearly knocking me
over, before moving on, to arrange himself firmly in front of Jamie.

"Bloody hell," muttered David, more to himself than anyone else, "I'm
in an episode of Scooby Doo." I thought it best not to comment, although I
could see where he was coming from. Ruth, Rachael and Sam had gathered
round Kitty.

"Her heart's stopped." Sam said. He had, naturally, grown a fair bit, in
the seven or so years, since I'd last seen him, but I remembered his absolute
confidence in what he knew and I moaned, whether just in my head or
aloud, I don't know.

"She's dead?"

"I didn't say that. All of you. Here. Quick." He had one hand firmly on
Kitty's chest and the other hand out to whoever got there first. I grabbed it.
Glory and Ed moved equally swiftly, Glory reaching for my other hand,
her touch reassuringly familiar, her body pressing close. Ed had one hand
on Glory's shoulder, the other, a welcome weight, on mine. Ruth and
Rachael had arms around each other and Sam.

We all knew what Sam needed, although probably only Ed understood
the mechanics of a defibrillator. This wasn't the first time we'd joined, at a
time and place when the stakes were shockingly high. The power, heightened
by emotion and multiplied by our contact, was there immediately. Sam,
adding his unique strength and innate knowledge, channelled it through
his hand, firing everything we had, into Kitty. We all felt the shock go
through us too, and it rocked us on our feet, but no-one let go. Her body
arched high on the sofa, then flopped limply back down.

"Again," said Sam calmly. And with that second shock-wave and violent convulsion, we felt the lurch, then the slow, sure beat as her heart, once again, took up the rhythm it had maintained for so many years. I didn't have to put my question, Sam responded anyway,

"She's lost a lot of blood, we'll have to strap her up quickly now, but everything's in working order. She's a tough lady."

"Brain damage?" I was scared to ask, I knew that would be worse than death for her.

"No." He said, and so certain was he, that I was too. I was still clinging to his hand and let go slowly. Sam and I hadn't got off to a very good start – he'd tried to kill me – but you can't really hold that against someone can you? He was taller than me now, somewhere still between boy and man, but not yet that far away from the brown-eyed, traumatised six year old I'd first met. We'd been holding hands tightly back then as well, as the two of us and Hamlet, by the skin of our teeth, made it out of the Newcombe Foundation, physically unscathed if not emotionally unscarred.

"Now you, Stella." Sam was brisk. "We don't have much time." He indicated my blood-soaked jumper, which I lifted gingerly, so he could see the damage. David, who'd been moved out the way politely by Ed, when we gathered round Kitty, had stayed exactly where he was put. Transfixed, would probably be a fair description of what he was at that point. Amongst other things, and perhaps because it seemed the simplest thing to start with, he was trying to work out why Rachael, who he'd last seen at the Lowbells, was here now too, but he swore loudly and started forward, as he saw the mess my side was in.

"Stella, Oh God, I didn't realise. What happened?" Now the immediate emergency was over, I had to admit I was feeling pretty ropey, especially as the blood, dried on my ribs, had clotted and scabbed and was now painfully pulled away, with the jumper. The sharp stabbing pains were back, with every breath. I hoped David wasn't going to ask too many questions, I didn't think I had the oomph for explanations, even if I'd actually known where exactly to start.

"And what the hell do you think you're doing?" David, once he'd started moving and talking again, couldn't seem to stop. Sam had his hands a few inches away from and over my wound. In his mind's eye was a rotating 3D image of my insides, which would show him with absolute certainty, where and how I was injured, but David was roughly trying to pull him away. Rachael turned from Kitty,

"Idiot. Stop that. Leave him!" She hadn't raised her voice, she never needed to, it lashed and David swung to face her,

"Are you crazy?" he snapped back, "He's just a kid, he can't…"

"Don't be more of a fool than you have to." She said. I was interested to see, they'd reached a stage of mutual antipathy, far faster than I'd have anticipated. "Haven't you just seen, what he can do?" David reluctantly took his hands from Sam's shoulders, but didn't step back far. He had any number of questions, none of which were putting themselves in any sort of sensible order, nor doing much for his thumping headache.

"Stella," said Sam, "When he stabbed you, he punctured one of your lungs. The pain was because air collected in your chest cavity – which is not at all where it's supposed to be!"

"That's not a joke is it?" I asked, "I hope not, it's going to hurt too much to laugh." He grinned briefly and for a moment, looked like any other teenager. I took an experimental and trepidatious breath,

"Feeling a lot better." I said. "What'd you do?"

"Fixed the puncture."

"Makes me sound like a tyre." I grumbled.

"You'll need to go to hospital, just to make sure it's OK. I haven't got anything here to dress the wound, it's pretty deep, but if you like, I can anaesthetize it a bit.

"Why didn't you say that in the first place?" I protested. He again held his hand over my side.

"Needed to track down the cause and make sure nothing else was damaged. Shut up a minute and watch, it'll work better, if you keep it up yourself." And he flashed what he was going to do, so I could do it too – he was visualising a sort of cooling, cotton-wool construction, which he mentally laid gently over the pain. I copied him with my own construct and the relief was instant.

"Bloody hell, Sam," I exclaimed, "Why didn't I know how to do that, it's brilliant. Thanks."

"I hope," said Sam "You won't have too much cause to use it in the future." He paused, "Although, you do seem to get yourself into some situations, don't you?"

"Don't you start," I said." He winked at me, a brief movement, and I winked back – I couldn't believe he'd remembered. I'd taught him to do that, when we'd last said goodbye.

"I'm assuming," said David, from behind Sam, "That sooner or later, somebody, anybody, is going to tell me what the hell's going on here? And…" he said to Rachel, "Why are you always around when there's trouble?"

"I might," she said, "Ask the same of you, but we haven't time now, Boris is nearly here."

"Who's Boris?" said David.

"Where's he been?" I asked at the same time, cautiously lowering my jumper in anticipation of losing the pain patch we'd just applied, but I found, with just a little mental effort, it was holding perfectly.

"Leading the police on a wild goose chase, to give us a bit more time." Said Rachael.

"For what?" David was still struggling.

"To get things sorted here." Ruth spoke up, for the first time since they'd got here. She was as concerned about David, as she was about everything else, it was a good thing someone was looking out for him. It was my first chance to take a good look at her, and I didn't like what I saw. She seemed to have lost even more weight and her face was dreadfully pale.

"My dear," she said to David, "I know nothing about this makes any sense, but I promise, you'll have it all explained – just not now. At this point, we have to get some stories straight." Poor David, he couldn't work out whether he'd actually seen what he thought he'd seen us do, or whether he was simply suffering from concussion, but he acceded politely, if reluctantly to Ruth – as most people usually did.

"OK, OK," he said, holding his hands up and outwards, an 'I'm out of it', sort of a gesture. "Do what you need to do. Questions and answers afterwards."

Ruth and Rachael had covered Kitty with a blanket someone must have brought from a bedroom, and Glory had wrapped a now-shivering, still shocked and wordless Isabelle, in her own coat which she'd slipped off. It was a multi-coloured, studded and fringed leather item which, I hoped wouldn't make Isabelle feel any more alarmed than she already was. Ed was swiftly checking Kat over and in answer to my unvoiced question, nodded his head, gave me a thumbs-up and flashed that she was fine and physically uninjured, although I didn't hold out the same hope for her psychological stability.

CHAPTER FIFTY-FOUR

With my pain eased off, I felt more able to cope, although how we were going to explain all this, when the police pitched up, I had no idea. I turned to Rachael.

"What'll happen to Jamie?"

"I think," said Rachael, "You'll find it's already happened." She was right. I went into Jamie's head and it was hollow, completely empty, reminiscent of Devlin's. But I'd got Devlin back. Glory shook her head,

"This is different. Right Sam?" she looked over at him and he nodded,

"He's completely brain dead, burnt out. Whatever had hold of him, forced him way beyond what his brain or body could take, he didn't stand a chance."

"There is nothing at all we can do for him now, poor boy." Ruth, when she chose, was as pragmatic as her sister, although we could all feel her pain for the life lost in such a way. "Ed, dear," she turned to him, "It's freezing in here, can we get some heat going?" She was right, the stove had long ago burnt out, it was bitterly cold and I was shivering, as was Kat, still pressed close to my leg, whilst Isabelle on the armchair was juddering like a bus on standby. It wasn't surprising, David had decimated one of the windows and Ed had done the same to the door. Ed, who was next to the stove, opened it and put in some logs from the pile in the alcove. They caught quickly and gave off a welcome warmth of light, although whether they made a great deal of difference to the temperature, I'm not sure.

"Ed," said Glory, "The door?" Ed looked, nodded, glanced quickly at David and then obviously deciding time, not discretion, was of the essence, right now, floated it and its hinges back into place, sending the screws from where they were scattered on the floor, back to where they should be and they screwed themselves swiftly in, one after the other.

"Won't hold up brilliantly," he said, "But the police will probably break it down again anyway, so nobody's likely to notice."

"Hang on a minute," I said aloud, there was something else I couldn't keep to myself, although they probably knew anyway. What I'd glimpsed, what had so horrified me, because I couldn't work out the connection – didn't know whether it was in Jamie's mind or the mind of the other – was an unmistakeable image of Ruth. I showed them what I'd seen and Rachael's lips tightened,

"We know. No time to go into it now, but what did this to Jamie is like…" she flashed a vampire image to me. I looked at her blankly then, in one appalled instant, understood. Glory added,

"The mind that did this, flourishes and feeds off others."

"Others?" I said, "You mean others like us, don't you?" and things clicked into place, "Ruth, you?" She nodded grimly,

"Indeed and isn't it a nuisance? It did damage, before we understood, now we do, we can stop it." Her statement was firm, her conviction less so and I caught the concern of the others.

"No time to discuss now, anyway." said Rachael. I nodded and put it away to think about later. "Right," she said to David, "We're leaving, you need to come too." He shook his head.

"I'm staying with Stella." He said firmly. She tutted.

"Well, I must say, you're a good match, you're as awkward as she is. Have it your own way." She turned back to me. I was thinking of what I should or could have done better to help Jamie, Rachael said silently,

"Nothing you could have done differently Stella, too late, he'd been too infiltrated and damaged. Ruth?" She turned to her sister for confirmation of her assessment. Ruth nodded,

"You know she's right my dear, you were here, saw what happened, how he was. He had to be stopped, but by the time we did that, it wasn't him anymore, it was purely the 'other'." Her mouth tightened,

"But, he was so clever, so talented, look at this." I waved my hand and despite the awfulness of every single subject, there was no doubting the consummate artistry behind them.

"What a wicked waste!" I said aloud. David was looking from one to the other of us. He instinctively understood what he was seeing and hearing as well as all the things he wasn't, he just wasn't ready to accept it yet. Rachael continued speaking,

"Right, Stella and you too, um… David? Listen, this is what the police will know and what will be borne out by Isabelle and her mother; Jamie was working at Isabelle's house; wanted to spend time with her; knew he couldn't possibly under normal circumstances; so he abducted her. He was obviously mentally disturbed and cherishing deeply worrying fantasies," she indicated the painted walls, which not so much spoke as screamed for themselves. "He was a highly unstable young man; immature, isolated and obsessed and then he turned violent. We have to work you into this though Stella, there has to be an understandable reason he took you. When did he first see you?"

"He didn't, he'd never seen me before he took me." For the sake of speed, I flashed the rest through to them, "I told you, I must have just somehow picked up on him – when I was doing what Ruth asked, you know, 'listening'." I grimaced at Ruth, who pretended not to notice. "Isabelle saw me outside her house but Jamie didn't, he just sensed me there, recognised me for what I was and tracked me back." I started to tell them about the birds, but Rachael waved that away as irrelevant.

"No, not good enough." She muttered aloud. "This needs to make sense to the police, he had to have seen you and known who you were. Why on earth, otherwise, would he have kidnapped you alongside the girl?"

"How about," said David mildly, picking up on the fraction of conversation he'd heard. "Stella interviewed him at the agency? A client wanted a painting, someone passed along his details and she needed to meet him before recommending him on." We all turned to look at him, he shrugged, "I'm a journalist, stories are my business." Ruth nodded, absent-mindedly patting him on the arm.

"Yes, good, that makes enough sense." She said, "After all it isn't for us to explain his motives or the way his mind was working – they'll have to fill in their own gaps. Stella, all you know is how you left it with him, after you'd met him. You told him you'd get back to him in due course, but then he turned up again out of the blue, and took you and Kitty."

"OK. And then?" I asked.

"Stick to the truth as far as you can, always best." Instructed Rachael, "He brought you here. His mood was already swinging dangerously from normal to not and then everything escalated out of control, he suddenly turned violent, attacked all of you with the knife. You defended yourself as best you could. Kitty and you were both injured, there was a struggle you may have hit him with the vase, you really can't remember. You were very frightened – shocked and confused is always a good bet when you don't have a straight answer. And then this young man arrived." She turned abruptly to David, "If you insist on staying, you're going to have to explain how you found out where they were being held."

"Well, unlike anyone else here it seems," David grinned briefly, "I can simply tell the truth. Brenda at the office, got the van's registration number, I used an under the counter contact (can't reveal sources, journalist privilege) who got me a name and address. But that was just a rented single room, not ideal for keeping prisoners. I did a quick bit of microfiching – old newspaper files, to find out anything I could about his past. There was a lot of stuff on this place, his father's business going down, ongoing legal disputes and unresolved ownership etc. Reckoned, if I was going to kidnap someone, this is the sort of spot I'd want to hide out – it just felt right." He stopped, but he was in the right place for people sympathetic to hunch-followers. Rachael, Ruth and Glory had a swift silent exchange but couldn't find any holes.

"It'll do." Glory said aloud and then listening, "They're nearly here, we have to go. Sam?" Sam looked up, he'd been sitting with Kitty, constantly checking her. Glory nodded over at Isabelle.

"Right," he said and then he looked over at David and flashed to me "Him too?" I hesitated, it was tempting, but,

"No," I said. "Not him, he's my problem." Sam nodded and he and Glory went and sat, one on either side, of the armchair in which Isabelle was huddled. Glory spoke to her softly, while Sam smoothed away some of her memories.

"What're they doing?" David looked at me.

"Making sure she won't remember having seen them."

"Well, of course they are," he said dryly. "Why wouldn't I have known that?"

PART FOUR

LOOSE ENDS

This isn't magic, it's science, it's simply science for which they don't yet have an explanation.

CHAPTER FIFTY-FIVE

"So," said David, as he drove us home, taking things nice and slow – neither of us felt we needed any more excitement at this point. "Probably just a couple of things we need to chat about?" He raised an interrogative eyebrow, and instantly regretted it. At some stage in the proceedings, he'd sustained a nasty gash, from his hairline downwards. It had been dressed and taped, giving him a bit of a pirate look – although I wasn't sure this was the best time for any parrot jokes.

Both of us had been kept in hospital overnight, for observation. David didn't appear to be suffering too many ill effects from the blow to his head, apart from a stonking headache, which they said was only to be expected. My knife-punctured lung, seemed to have healed itself, which according to the young, fraught but very thorough A&E doctor, sometimes happens in these cases. I was lucky, he said, that no more damage was done. I didn't feel that lucky, every time I shut my eyes, I could feel the knife going all the way in and pulling all the way out again. Most unpleasant. I was however pleased, that being out of the area, we hadn't wound up at the Royal Free again, I didn't want a reputation for being habitually battered and bruised – not good for business.

"I expected that you might have some questions." I said.

"Just the odd one or two." He acceded.

"OK," I said. "We'll talk."

The others had departed the chalet, almost as swiftly, albeit a little less hectically than they'd arrived. They left us with a still unconscious Kitty, a shell-shocked Isabelle and a traumatised Kat, although she perked up considerably, once she'd seen the back of Hamlet.

They also left us with a lifeless kidnapper. He wasn't dead because he still had a pulse, David had gingerly felt for and found it. On the other hand, Jamie had very definitely left the building. What was on the floor was an empty shell that just happened to still be breathing. I have to admit to a certain amount of selfish concern as to where that left me, in regard to how he'd got that way. But there wasn't too much contemplation time because, in a highly dramatic surge of sirens, sweeping headlights and a megaphone, the police and Boris arrived. I decided, best to follow Rachael's rules, stick to the truth as far as possible and hope it carried me through – it certainly wasn't going to be a stretch to do frightened, shocked and confused.

Ed had been correct about the front door, it got knocked right down again. Presumably, the police contingent had taken one look through the window, seen the state of us and wasted no time with the megaphone. What with them and the ambulances, which started to arrive shortly after, disgorging lots of paramedics, it got pretty crowded again. I'm not sure, back in the '70s, that they were that hot on keeping crime scenes untainted, we weren't blessed then with regular episodes of CSI, so none of us were as well versed as we are now, in the finer points of forensic technology. Certainly, at that point, the world and its brother seemed to be tramping every which way, in big boots. I still had no real grasp of Boris's exact status here, but as no-one batted an eyelid at him, and at his height, he was pretty hard to miss, I presumed he had official clearance.

I was more surprised to see my old friend DI Cornwall, who was looking, although I wouldn't have thought it possible, even more fed up than last time we'd met. He didn't seem thrilled to see me either, but his immediate attention, like everyone else's who came in, was riveted by the wall décor and I could hear him effing and blinding softly to himself, as he stood in the middle of the room and slowly turned a full circle. You'd have thought, with a roomful of people, the effect of the paintings would be diminished, but in fact the power of them was such, they became even more overpowering. Cornwall had seen a thing or two in his time, but this little lot was shaking even his years of experience. He pulled himself together with an effort, looked at me and shook his head,

"Thought you were just supposed to be keeping an ear open, not jumping into the bleeding middle of everything." He said. "What happened?"

254

"Don't talk to her like that, she needs a doctor, not a telling off." David said.

"And who might you be?" Cornwall, eyed him with disfavour. Boris, stepped in smoothly, "He's engaged to Stella," he said. Cornwall knocked a cigarette out of a battered pack, lit it, coughed and muttered,

"Blimey, well you've got your hands full then, haven't you Sir? We'll need to take your statement too." I was tempted to make him drop his cigarette again, but Boris shook his head sharply. I pursed my lips and was about to launch into my pre-prepared story, courtesy of Rachael, when I felt my knees giving out. Cornwall showed an astonishing turn of speed and caught me round the waist as I went down, yelling across the room,

"Stretcher over here. Move your arse!' I read his instant and genuine concern, which was a further surprise. He didn't trust, like or fully believe in anything he understood I could do, but he had a daughter of Isabelle's age and his anger at the perverted little sod who'd taken her was immense. Never mind all that woo woo stuff, he was thinking, my being there and diverting attention had probably saved her life. For that, he was prepared to cut me a lot of slack.

We'd arrived at the hospital in a rather dramatic fleet of three ambulances. Kitty and Isabelle in one, Jamie in another and David and I sharing the third, which I wasn't that keen on, until I realised he was still processing stuff and didn't think this was the time or place for us to talk. That was just fine, I was still doing a bit of processing myself.

There'd been a bit of a stand-off when it came to Kat. A burly officer had been delegated to put her in the back of a police car, but having discovered, in the last frantic hours, an unexpected level of autonomy, Kat was having none of it. She jumped into the ambulance after me, planted herself firmly on the floor and did the howling thing, refusing to budge, no matter how much collar-tugging was applied. There was a swift consultation and general consensus, that for everyone's sake, a couple of fingers would have to be put up to rules and regulations and she could travel with us.

As we arrived at the hospital, things for the umpteenth time that evening, descended into chaos. A cavalcade of fraught family members arrived, just as our ambulances pulled in. Mrs de Freyt stumbled out of a police car, accompanied by a large, shambling bear of a man who, I gathered, was Isabelle's father. They were both crying, and despite the paramedics' attempts to maintain some kind of order, Isabelle hurtled out the back of her ambulance and straight into their arms. She flat out refused to get back on the stretcher, so they were all taken inside, in a sort of ungainly huddle. I'm not sure who was holding who upright.

My parents had brought Aunt Edna and Brenda and none of them knew who to be more frantic about first, Kitty or me, although I think Kitty won by a margin, because she was old and still unconscious – luckily they didn't know quite how unconscious she'd been.

And then, of course, there were the Golds who, I gathered from a quick scan, had been blissfully unaware of the whole unfolding drama, until they received a frantic late-night call from my mother, heavy on panic but light on detail, informing them their son had been involved in a kidnap, people had been hurt and no she didn't know whether or not that included David, but this was the hospital everyone was being taken to.

Understandably, they were not a little disturbed and set off in a high state of alarm, with no clear idea as to what had gone on, nor what they could expect to find when they got there. On the way, they'd got lost several times and reversing rapidly, out of a dead end road taken by mistake, Melvyn had a negative experience with a concrete bollard, something that had never before happened to him, in forty years of careful driving. Naturally, under the circumstances, at some point Laura had recourse to the pill bag. As David and I were helped out of our ambulance, she leapt forward to embrace him, with a shriek that didn't do much for his sore head, already re-assaulted by Kat's caterwauling. She was firmly detached by the staff and set to one side, where I could hear her thinking balefully, nothing remotely like this had ever happened to David, before he got involved with me. She wasn't wrong.

What with the shock of the situation and the bollard, poor Melvyn had gone to pieces completely and was probably in a worse state than anyone. Unfortunately, by the time David and I had been seen by a doctor and were re-united with the nearest and dearest, Laura had persuaded him that one of her migraine pills might relax him a little, pointing out, the last thing needed right now, God forbid, was for him to drop dead with a heart attack. I understood he'd consented to take half a pill. However, not as inured as she, this had the effect not only of relaxing him, but rendering him so totally out of it, that my father flatly refused to let him drive anywhere.

Much later that evening, they all eventually departed, Kat included, crammed into one car. From my hospital window, it looked as if they were attempting to make it into the Guinness Book of Records – how many agitated people can you get in a Ford Escort? I was worried about Melvyn, but didn't seem to have much emotion left to get too worked up, after all he wasn't my father-in-law yet and, quite frankly, the way things were going, the chances that he ever would be, were looking slimmer by the minute.

Isabelle, was discharged too, and whisked swiftly away by her still traumatised parents. I hadn't tried to see or speak to her, what was the point? She and her parents had no real idea who I was, nor what I had to do with anything. I was certain, from scanning her before she left in the ambulance, that Isabelle's memory had been gently wiped, she'd no recollection of the others being in the room at all and at the same time I saw, Glory and Sam had also eliminated a lot of the horror. She'd never be able to recall in detail what was on those walls, within which she'd spent such a terrified time. Wiping, the way they had, seemed to make sense, although I'm not sure I'd have been prepared to stand and debate the ethics. But they'd made a swift decision to do it and who was I to argue? Sometimes there just wasn't a lot of thinking time and choices had to be made and stood by.

Kitty was, despite her vociferous protests, being kept in a bit longer. I went to see her before we left. She was surprisingly perky, although the stitched cut, running all the way down one side of her face and under her chin, confirmed she'd been in one hell of a fight. She'd have a scar, but didn't seem that bothered.

"Listen, dolly, my time of life, what difference is it going to make?" The abdominal wound was giving her quite a lot of pain, but a nice nurse was apparently coming along with a regular morphine injection, that worked wonders said Kitty. She couldn't remember much of what had happened after she'd been stabbed, which wasn't a bad thing, so I gave her the abbreviated version, which skipped the advent of the others, and moved straight on to the police arriving. I was guilt-wracked at having inadvertently involved her. I said I'd absolutely understand if, after this, she didn't want to come back to work.

"Not bloody likely," she said, "I'm back like a shot, soon as they let me out of here. If you get into this much trouble when I've got my eye on you, what'll you get up to, if I'm not there? You always were a bit of a liability, even when you were little. And I'm not leaving it all to Brenda." She shifted a little in the bed and winced, "Who'd have thought," she commented, with a touch of pride, "I'd be getting stabbed at my age?" As I kissed her and made to leave, she reached for my hand again.

"Who was he?" she asked.

"Who?"

"That kid."

"You mean Isabelle?"

"Don't be stupid, the young boy. I'm not so old, I can't tell the difference."

"Kitty, there was no boy." I told her. "You were unconscious for a quite a while, you must've been dreaming." She frowned,

"Funny damn dream, he was there, clear as you are now. Never mind." She pulled me back one more time, "That David of yours." She said, "He's a mensch, although not so sure about that mother of his – she's right away with the fairies. But look how he came after you, got to love that. You hang on to him, you hear me?" I nodded, God she'd go mad, along with everyone else in the family, if I mucked things up, but I could see there were substantial hurdles ahead to be cleared, before anybody did any walking up any aisles.

CHAPTER FIFTY-SIX

"Are you scared of me?" I said, He gave my question the thought it deserved, and then grinned.

"Oddly enough, no." he said. "Should I be?"

"No. Well, not unless I lose my temper, but I'm careful about hanging on to it."

"Good to know." He said.

Heading home from the hospital, was as good an opportunity as any, to get things out in the open particularly as I didn't have to look directly at him while we did. The other advantage was that prior to discharge, I'd been given some hefty pain-killers, these had gone straight to my head and left me feeling slightly distanced from reality.

As with many an event you've been dreading, the big reveal was slightly anticlimactic. After all, as he pointed out reasonably, he had been there and seen and heard things. And when there's no possible logical explanation for something that's happening right under your nose, the only thing left is an illogical one, and what I was telling him, certainly fell into that category.

My story was coming out a little garbled, hard to know quite where to start with something like this and I wandered a bit all over the place, until he stopped the car outside a convenient coffee bar along the way, and insisted we go in, sit down and take things a bit slower. He thought it might be a good idea if I started from the beginning and worked my way along from there, which I suppose was fair enough. I won't say he wasn't surprised at everything that came out, including the couple of cautious demonstrations with some condiments and cutlery, but he didn't fall over, frothing at the mouth, which I took to be a promising sign. In fact, by the time I got to the Newcombe Foundation, he was ahead of me.

He'd done work experience, about ten years ago, on a national newspaper. He'd been shadowing Roger Simstridd, an award-winning, investigative reporter of the old school, known for sticking his – by that time – extremely florid nose into places where it was neither wanted nor welcomed. Welcomed it may not have been, but he was known for getting some uniquely angled stories on the back of his intransigence. By the time David was entrusted to his not so tender care, he was a man, somewhat diminished by whisky, regrets, 60 daily Rothmans and past glory days, but he was still a news-hound, through and through.

He'd spent years, accumulating files on cold-war spurred, government funded, psi experiments, not just in this country but in the US, Russia and China as well. They didn't come, said David, much more cynical or hard-boiled than Simstridd and he'd certainly started researching, with the straightforward intention of holding up for ridicule, the cash poured by governments into crazy projects. But he was nobody's fool and over a period of time, what he dug up, turned his views – 'arse over tit' – as he used to say to David and he became convinced, there were things out there, that simply didn't fit the rational parameters they should. To his gasket-blowing frustration, he was never able to put together enough to persuade his editor, they could run with impunity and not be tarred with the red-top brush. However, the number of notes, grainy photos, and speculative conclusions David had pored over in their stifling, smoky little office, had left him with a far more open mind than most.

"But you never told me any of that." I was highly indignant.

"Pot and kettle." He snorted, "And why would I have thought you were interested anyway?" I conceded the point. Strangely enough, of all the oddities I poured into his ear that day, the one he seemed to find the most contentious, was why I hadn't told him sooner.

"Never seemed to find quite the right moment." I said defensively. By this time, we'd vacated the coffee bar, we'd been there a couple of hours and they were starting to look sideways at us. He re-started the car.

"Weak excuse." He said.

"So," I said, "What happens now?"

"Well, we could do with a bath and a change of clothes. I'll drop you home and…"

"I meant with the engagement and everything." He thought about it for a moment, I was glad, I didn't want him to answer out of politeness. He shook his head.

"Nope, doesn't change anything from my end." He said, "Yours?" I shook my head too, I was relieved, but wasn't going to get gushy,

"Probably not." I said.

Luckily, after things have been a bit hectic, they tend to settle down for a while, so you have a brief chance to catch a breath and gather yourself together. And so it was after the whole Jamie thing and my shamefully, long-postponed, 'something I should mention', conversation, which I was hugely relieved to have out of the way. Whilst still firmly of the belief I'd been brought up with, that some things are best kept to yourself, I did feel if he was going to marry me, it was only fair the poor chap knew what he was taking on.

The Jamie incident didn't get the same news exposure as had the encounter with the Lowbells, maybe because the body count was lower. I gave the police a brief statement, and not too many more questions were asked. David gave his account which held water, and Kitty didn't remember much about anything after she was hurt, acerbically informing the young constable, sent to talk to her, neither would he if he'd been stabbed in the stomach. I did ask about Isabelle and her family and was told she was well, but the family had decided to move. I wasn't surprised. Even painted over, those eyes would still be watching from the walls.

Jamie was lying in a hospital bed somewhere. Was there anything else I could have done? Should I have tried harder, to get past the other in his head? I replayed things over and over, but each time came to the same conclusion, there'd been no chance of getting through to him. By the time that he'd been more or less taken over by something even more violent than himself, it was a straight choice – him or us. He was though a tortured soul, had been all his life, and I was painfully aware, there for the grace of God, had I not had the luck to be born into a family where hysteria was balanced by pragmatism. My feelings were in no way as ambivalent when it came to his exploiter. I'd touched that mind with mine and felt the cold, blended with the white heat of excitement, generated by violence. I hated and feared the fact that I now knew it was a continued threat.

But the Peacock gang had clammed up on that score too. It was frustrating, when they wanted something from me, any one of them was prepared to push as hard as necessary to get it. But when I wanted to find out more, I was told the less I knew, the less risk there was. Half of me resented that intensely, the other half was relieved because I just wanted normal and was making a determined effort to get back there. I had a business to run, which was going in the right direction. I also had a wedding to plan, although to be honest, once I'd put forward a couple of thoughts and suggestions and had them soundly trampled by my mother and Aunt Edna I thought, best leave them to it, after all what did I know?

Kitty had returned to work, against the strenuous advice of the doctors and indeed, everyone else. But as she pointed out, what did she have to lose. She wouldn't be talked round from this rather cavalier attitude insisting she wasn't ready to sit at home all day, dunking biscuits and staring out the window. Brenda, Trudie and Ruby were delighted to see her back, and I think she rather enjoyed being feted as a bit of a hero. As indeed did Kat who, if anything, had adopted even more of an aristocratic air, although still shivering delicately every time the phone rang.

CHAPTER FIFTY-SIX

Your wedding day is supposed to be the happiest of your life – mine may have been happy, it certainly wasn't the most comfortable, for various reasons.

In those days, we had our hair 'set' for big occasions. This was a tortuous procedure which entailed wedging both you and a large number of fat rollers, under a hairdryer where you got hotter and more flushed by the moment. When you were sufficiently sweat-drenched, you'd be taken out from under and the resulting, sausage-like wedges of hair, styled, before being iron-clad by chokingly copious blasts of hair spray. Tiara and veil were then riveted onto the structure with strategically placed hair grips, rendering you virtually immobile from the neck up.

There were a lot of people crying, as they always do at weddings. My mother and Auntie Edna were sobbing, because they'd thought they'd never live to see the day. Laura Gold was crying equally hard, because she'd feared she might. Now, don't get me wrong, I was happy, excited and nervous – all the sorts of things you're supposed to be.

There were just a few niggles. At first I thought it was because I was worrying I might accidentally knock someone unconscious, with my rigid hair. Then I thought it might be because of the tussle, getting my bottom into the wedding dress. Luckily, my sister, mother and aunt weren't women easily defeated, and with some pushing, shoving and a whole lot of breathing in, I was finally zipped up. The result, even I had to admit, was a rather fetching hour-glass figure, the only problem being it wasn't remotely mine and I was apprehensive that irresistible force and the natural laws of physics would come into their own and the zip might give up the ghost. To avoid this, I kept my breathing shallow although panting my way up the aisle, caused my father to cast anxious glances and mutter under his breath,

"Not too late to change your mind." But beneath everything, the natural nerves, the hair helmet, the zip and the hyperventilating – which was actually starting to make me feel a little dizzy – there was something else. It was something different, something I didn't recognise and I do so dislike the unexpected, especially when there's a lot of other stuff going on.

I didn't want the day spoiled, which was why I didn't mention anything to David, but, whilst he wasn't in the least bit psychic, he was observant.

"Out with it." He said. We were heading to the hotel, where we were going to spend the first night of our honeymoon. I'd changed out of my wedding dress, enabling me to breathe again and, divested of tiara and veil, had movement restored to my head and neck.

"What?" I said, trying and failing to run my hands through my hair, I'd taken out what seemed like hundreds of hair clips, but the hair spray was there to stay.

"Whatever it is you're mulling over."

"Not mulling over anything."

"You're a lousy liar." He said.

"I'm not."

"You are, your mouth goes lop-sided when you fib. Anyway, thought we were sticking to a straight-forward policy from now on. Isn't that what we agreed?" I nodded,

"We did but..."

"Go on then." He said. I sighed,

"Honestly, I'm not sure." Then I paused, because that wasn't true. I was sure. "This is going to sound really daft." I said. He laughed,

"It'll fit in nicely with everything else then, won't it?"

"It hasn't happened." I said.

"What hasn't happened?"

"This thing. What I've been feeling all day. It hasn't happened yet." Saying it out loud, immediately gave it substance, although no more sense. Whatever this was, it was different from normal – at least my kind of normal.

"So, what is it then, some kind of premonition? That's not something you do, is it?" David, glanced sideways at me, then back at the road.

"No." I said, "Of course not. How crazy do you think I am?" There was a brief pause, while we both considered that from all angles.

"Well," he said reasonably, "What makes you think something's going to happen?"

"It's in my stomach," I put a hand to where the twisting sensation was continuing to twist, "It's apprehension." I said, identifying it properly. "That's what it is. And it's Ruth."

"What's Ruth?"

"Something's going to happen to Ruth." I said. "I think." He stopped the car in a layby, put on the hazard lights, I liked it that he was always so sensible, and turned to face me.

"Think or know?" he asked. I shrugged,

"Not sure."

"Well, if you know something," he said, "Even if you just think you know something, you can't ignore it, can you?"

"Well, what can I do?"

"Shouldn't you at least, tell her? Maybe she can take steps to avoid whatever it is."

"Look, forget it." I said, "Forget I said anything, this isn't something that's ever happened before, it can't mean anything, it's just my imagination and wedding nerves. Now I think about it, I'm really not sure it's even what I feel at all."

"Your mouth's going to one side." He pointed out.

"It is not." I snapped, "I'm sorry you made me say anything. Just drop it. Look we're heading off on honeymoon, we're supposed to be enjoying ourselves, aren't we?"

"Your call." He said equably and started the car, pulling onto the road again. At the same time, he leaned forward, switched on the cassette player and Karen Carpenter let us know that Rainy Days and Mondays Always Let You Down, she wasn't wrong. We drove on a little way, it was late, past 11.00 and traffic was light. I felt sick, probably all the excitement of the day, or maybe the twisting in my stomach.

"Oh, for goodness sake," I said. "If it will stop you going on and on about it, just stop at the next phone box, I'll call and tell them. But that's all I'm doing. I'm not getting involved."